The Revolt of Gunner Asch

The Revolt
of Gunner Asch

TRANSLATED FROM THE GERMAN BY ROBERT KEE

by **Hans Hellmut Kirst**

LITTLE, BROWN AND COMPANY

BOSTON • TORONTO

LIBRARY OF CONGRESS CATALOG CARD NO. 56–5044

Published February 1956
Reprinted February 1956

Published simultaneously in Canada
by Little, Brown & Company (Canada) Limited

PRINTED IN THE UNITED STATES OF AMERICA

The Revolt of Gunner Asch

THOSE already detailed — fall out to the left!" shouted Sergeant Major Schulz, better known simply as "the Chief." His voice boomed out across the parade ground and went ricocheting around the barracks. It was a rich, powerful, self-satisfied sort of voice, rough with the smoke of many cigars and well lubricated with beer. Schulz liked the sound of it.

The men who had already had jobs allotted them trotted happily off to the left. Those who had not yet been detailed closed in mechanically to the right. Gunner Vierbein, who was one of those, found himself being squeezed out of his place in the ranks. He tried using his elbows to get back into line but soon had to give this up, and stood at attention just as he was.

"Wait for it!" shouted the Chief happily. "Not a movement anywhere! Still as statues!" And he looked across for a moment to the windows of his own private quarters in the barrack block. They were wide open. He could just make out his wife Lore standing behind the curtains and he felt sure that she was admiring him. The N.C.O.s in charge of the details had gathered round their Chief and tried hard not to grin. On the whole they succeeded, for they'd had a lot of practice at this sort of thing.

Gunner Vierbein stared straight ahead of him. He picked on a point where the wooden slats of a window in the building opposite intersected and glued his eyes to the spot. Lore Schulz's head appeared at the window, but the gunner forced

3

himself to see nothing but wood. The sergeant major went by in front of him as if he were being wound past on a piece of tape. He appeared in the gunner's field of vision like something caught for a moment in the headlights of a car, then drifted out again into other equally rigid fields of vision.

The sergeant major stood with legs apart surveying the men drawn up in ranks before him. He was shaped like a cupboard mounted on two columns. His red, round, shining face stretched suddenly lengthways and an enormous hole appeared in it at the place where his mouth had been.

"Right then, let's get moving."

Standing Orders laid down "billet-cleaning" for Saturdays. The period prescribed for this was three hours, but Schulz could always extend it to five without any difficulty if he felt so inclined. He usually felt so inclined.

Every Saturday he was left in sole charge of the barracks. Captain Derna, the troop commander, who had recently been generously placed at the disposal of the Greater German Wehrmacht as a result of the Austrian *Anschluss,* devoted himself to his growing family. Lieutenant Wedelmann, the second in command, spent his time looking for a girl. Even Major "Lumpface" Luschke, commanding officer of the battery, treated his week ends as sacred. The Chief was thus left free to celebrate the week end in his own fashion. This gave him the opportunity, which he never failed to take, of making quite clear to the troop "who was the real boss hereabouts."

"Stand at — ease!" shouted the sergeant major. The men, who were wearing fatigue uniforms, pushed their left feet forward mechanically. The Chief waited to see if anyone would dare to speak. When he gave the order "Stand at ease" it was by no means synonymous with "Stand easy!" This always had to be given separately. No one said a word.

"Stand easy!" he barked condescendingly.

The men still preferred to say nothing. Some of them just

4

grinned broadly. Others looked at the Chief, waiting for orders. Only Gunner Asch, who was standing among those already detailed for a job, gave Gunner Wagner — Christian name: Richard — a powerful nudge in the ribs and said: "Make a bit of room there for God's sake."

"Don't bellow like that, Asch!" shouted the Chief at once. "There's only one person here does any bellowing, see, and that's me!"

"Yes, Sergeant Major," Asch bellowed back.

In a sudden fit of generosity Sergeant Major Schulz decided not to treat this as a piece of insubordination. He called the N.C.O.s across to him and handed over the men already detailed. These immediately took themselves off to huts and barrack rooms, to waste their time in quite a variety of different ways. Asch proceeded at a leisurely pace to his post in the clothing store, where he usually spent his time playing *vingt-et-un* with Sergeant Werktreu, the N.C.O. in charge there, taking very good care not to win too often.

The large body of men who formed the remainder and had not been detailed were due to start cleaning out the billets from top to bottom. Gunner Vierbein found himself among the group now detailed to the ground-floor latrines. He didn't really mind this. It was what he had expected. Cleaning the latrines was one of his specialties. He had been detailed to it consistently ever since he had been with the troop. The honest Vierbein seemed hardly to be part of the scene at all as he stood there ready to bring his heels smartly together the moment the order "Attention!" should be given. This would be followed immediately by the word "Dismiss!" Whereupon the cleaning detail would rush to their rooms, seize brooms, buckets and mops and present themselves without delay in the immediate vicinity of whatever it was that they had to clean. There one of the younger N.C.O.s, or perhaps a gunner first class who was considered reliable, would be waiting for them.

5

As Vierbein stood there waiting for things to run their usual course he noticed the sergeant major's eyes resting on him thoughtfully. And Vierbein trembled, for although he sensed something almost like goodwill in the sergeant major's glance, he knew from experience that it was a bad sign when N.C.O.s began to show any unusual interest in their men. Various possibilities passed before him like a sequence from some well-worn film: cleaning operations would be prolonged into the late afternoon; the natural resentment of men suffering under an injustice would be met by the withdrawal of Saturday night passes; his name would find its way into the Chief's notebook, underlined, and that meant automatically the cancellation of his Saturday night pass. And it all added up to one thing: that he wouldn't be able to see Ingrid.

"Vierbein — fall out on the extreme left," shouted the Chief. And Vierbein ran down to the end of the line, and stood away forlornly to one side.

Sergeant Major Schulz swept the parade ground clear with a single word of command. A hundred pairs of hobnailed boots clattered across the square. The next minute they could be heard rushing up the stairs and along the corridors of the barrack block. Vierbein alone remained in the middle of the parade ground.

Schulz turned slowly round and looked towards him.

"Vierbein," he said, and his powerful voice was fruity with goodwill, "I wonder if you'd care to do me a favor?"

Vierbein felt himself turning pale.

"Certainly, Sergeant Major," he called out bravely.

"You don't need to if you don't want to. This isn't an order, Vierbein. I can't order you to do this. If you don't feel like doing it, don't hesitate to tell me. You can just go straight off and clean out the latrines if you prefer. Well, what about it?"

"Certainly, Sergeant Major."

"What? You'd rather clean out the latrines?"

6

"Whatever you say, Sergeant Major."

"Good," said the Chief contentedly. "That was the answer I expected from you. Go and report to my wife for carpet-beating."

⚑ ⚑ ⚑

Sergeant Major Schulz strolled down the corridors of the barrack block and his appearance was everywhere followed by a noticeable increase in working tempo. This gave him a certain quiet satisfaction, although deep down in his barrack-square soul he took it for granted that people should react to his presence like this. It would have been remarkable if they had not done so.

The sergeant major was an expert in detecting dirt in any form. He could tell at a distance of ten yards whether the cracks between tiles were free from dust. If they were not he would run his thumbnail along them and then rub the little heap of dirt he had collected under the nose of the unfortunate soldier who was responsible. This would naturally lead to a bad mark against the man's name in his little black notebook, which was popularly known as the coalbox. And so he would stride complacently through his troop's billets, spreading disquiet wherever he went.

On this occasion, however, he got little pleasure from his tour of inspection although he had no difficulty at all in establishing at least a dozen cases of what he called "the grossest negligence." A dozen was enough for one day. He was a clever fellow and it had taken him only seven years of service to discover that too many punishments had a blunting effect in the end. Subtle doses were the secret of success.

He stood by the notice board for a while admiring his own signature which adorned an order there — SIGNED: *Derna, Captain.* COUNTERSIGNED: *Schulz* (very bold, very energetic, florid yet very masterly), *Troop Sergeant Major*. With only the barest perceptible effort he tore his eyes away, pulled out his notebook, opened it and, just to make sure once again, counted up the number of men whose names he had taken. It turned out to be only eleven — one less than he had thought. Very carefully, painfully carefully in fact, as the situation demanded of a man in his position, he counted all over again. But, of course, he had made no mistake.

Slightly annoyed, he shut up his notebook and wondered where he could go, without having to put himself out too much, to find the twelfth man to complete the list. He decided to combine business with pleasure and go to the latrines.

He was a man who knew that he commanded respect, but he was by no means entirely happy at that moment. His service life left nothing to be desired; it was his private life which was giving him trouble.

Nor was it the abnormally large bill he was running up with the contractor who ran the canteen that worried him. The fellow could consider himself lucky to have the Chief of No. 3 Troop as one of his customers at all. His personal presence there raised the prestige of both canteen and contractor — a fact which could be seen clearly enough from the increase in turnover.

It was his wife's behavior that was interfering with his happiness, and interfering with it to a very considerable degree.

Lore had once been an assistant in a florist's, at the entrance to the cemetery, and he had raised her to his own level. That had been nearly two years ago, when he had been no more than an ordinary sergeant. Everything had gone splendidly at first: they had been like two little lovebirds. But ever since he had been promoted to sergeant major and allotted the married quarters in the troop's barrack block, things had gone from bad to worse. The question he had to ask himself was: Why was this so?

8

"Be so good as to bring those two bow legs of yours to attention when an N.C.O. passes you," he shouted to a soldier who was on his knees mopping up the water in the corridor.

He couldn't make out what had got into Lore. She had become positively frigid recently, as cold as the ice which cooled the canteen beer. Things used to be very different, he remembered, very different indeed. But there had been a sad falling off lately. And with some anxiety he had to ask himself how it was that he, who enjoyed the universal esteem of others, was unable to command even the smallest respect from his wife.

Schulz pushed open the door of the latrine and looked around him critically. Gunner Hermann was scrubbing away at one of the seats. The Chief knew at once that this was his man. It was nearly three weeks since Hermann had had his name taken. It was now his turn.

"Well, you lazy swine!" shouted the Chief with sinister heartiness. We'll get him in a minute, he thought. And he put out the forefinger of his right hand and ran it along the rim of one of the light green tiles. He smiled. The test was conclusive. Hermann knew that his hour had come.

"Have you been granted a Saturday night pass?"

"Yes, Sergeant Major."

"But you haven't been issued it yet?"

"No, Sergeant Major."

"I thought as much," said the Chief. He snapped open his notebook, wrote the man's name down and walked away again.

At any other time he would have derived a genuine pleasure from this, but now he was merely doing his duty, fulfilling his quota as it were. His thoughts kept going back to his wife all the time, to the fact that she didn't understand him. She was obviously not even prepared to give him a child — a fine strapping boy as he knew it would be. He even sometimes suspected her of being unfaithful to him — unfaithful to *him!*

Nor was that the worst of it. If such was the case — and both

9

the circumstances and his own experience of human nature led him to believe that it was — then she could only be betraying him with members of his own troop. And not only with the N.C.O.s, which at least had a certain fitness about it, but possibly even with private soldiers as well. And that, thought Schulz, trembling with indignation, was enough to upset any man.

He hadn't been able to prove anything against her so far, but he was absolutely certain that he was right. In the first place there was the outrageous indifference she showed towards the fulfillment of her most elementary marital obligations. There was something more than suspicious about that. That sort of attitude might be good enough for an ordinary common laborer, but it wouldn't do for him, a sergeant major serving in the German Wehrmacht.

Two weeks ago, returning early from an evening of bowling, he had caught his wife — the wife who had pledged herself to him, "to love, honor and obey him" — with Sergeant Werktreu, a man who was not only a brother N.C.O., but supposed to be his friend. It was eleven o'clock at night and they were sitting together on the sofa. Werktreu had stammered out some excuse or other. If he hadn't been badly in need of three new suits of underclothes from Werktreu's clothing store at the time he wouldn't have hesitated to make mincemeat of him — yes, to give him the treatment he handed out to the lowest of the low, the rawest of raw recruits.

These, then, were some of his problems. And this had to happen to him of all people, a man who in his prime had had four girls one after the other in quick succession and made them all happy, as they had duly confirmed in writing. When he eventually did marry, wet handkerchiefs had fluttered on all sides and there was even some talk of an attempt at suicide. Lore ought to consider herself lucky to have got him. He was somebody who counted! What the hell did the woman think

10

she was up to? She had married a keen and efficient soldier in whom even Major Luschke, old "Lumpface" himself, could find nothing to complain of. Why then was she not the happy and contented wife she ought to be? She had no sense of the finer things of life!

Sergeant Platzek, "Bully" Platzek as he was called, for he was the most successful trainer of recruits in the whole regiment, came striding springily down the corridor. He was all dressed up in his dress uniform. He was wearing white gloves and had even put on a clean collar. He saluted the sergeant major amiably.

"Well?" said the Chief. "Where are you off to today?"

Platzek grinned in anticipation of the pleasures ahead of him.

"Coming to Bismarckshöh this evening? There's a dance on there, you know. Why not? It's at least two weeks since you've been out on the town."

"I'd like to," said the Chief.

"All work and no play, you know, Chiefie . . ." said Platzek, who fancied himself as a wag. He saluted and marched off again with long powerful strides.

Schulz watched him go. That's life all over, he thought bitterly. Just because he's not married he can do as he likes. But I am married and I can do as I like too. I don't care what anyone says, there's nothing dull about me.

He decided with a certain amount of relief that for the moment at any rate his personal honor stood in no danger. He had diagnosed the cause of the trouble and that meant that he was halfway towards curing it. Vierbein was with Lore at the moment and Vierbein was a complete halfwit, a milksop who was scared stiff of everyone. A typical mother's darling. He'd rather have his great ears torn off than risk being caught making eyes at Lore.

And so, continued Schulz's reasoning, now that he had col-

11

lected his daily quota of victims, he could allow himself a few hands of cards with Sergeant Werktreu in the clothing store. If he won, a few hands more.

☙ ☙ ☙

Gunner First Class Herbert Asch was no longer capable of being put out by anything, or so he thought. He never did any more work than he could possibly help; he was not fond of work and he had learned the secret of getting himself a relatively easy job wherever he happened to be. The underlying principle of his barrack-room philosophy was this: Never take risks. Or, in more popular terminology: Don't stick your neck out.

It could even be said that there was no need for him to do so. For Asch had a remarkable father who was proprietor of a café much frequented by the N.C.O.s of No. 1 Battery of the artillery regiment. Asch Senior was known as a generous-hearted fellow and his son appeared to want to follow in his footsteps. On busy evenings in the café he would exchange his field-gray tunic for the white coat of a waiter and draw the beer, and his superiors would turn a blind eye. He could be relied on to see that the glasses belonging to the N.C.O.s of his troop were filled to the brim and this had a thoroughly beneficial effect all round. What was more, Asch would make no fuss about dispensing additional schnapps every now and again, would allow credit and even lend money — though only with extreme discretion and that strict regard for the discipline and dignity of the service which was to be expected from other ranks at all times.

One of his most favored customers was Sergeant Werktreu, "the king of the clothing store." Werktreu rewarded Asch for his consistent generosity towards him by consistently picking him for work in the clothing store. On weekdays the two of

12

them would shut themselves away in the store for hours at a time. There they would pass their official working day performing one or two light duties and recovering from them in a good deal of heavy sleep. On Saturdays they usually spent their time, at Werktreu's insistence, playing *vingt-et-un*.

At this Gunner Asch cheated shamelessly. He declared incorrect totals, added up hurriedly and wrong, pushed high cards to the bottom of the pack for himself and could, if he wanted to, soon have brought Werktreu to the verge of ruin. But he didn't want to. It even quite often happened that he actually cheated in the sergeant's favor, thus cunningly keeping him well disposed towards him. Before they began playing Gunner Asch would calculate how much he could afford to let the sergeant win. The sum varied between two and five marks according to the extent to which Werktreu had left Asch in peace during the week.

It would never in his life have occurred to Sergeant Werktreu that anyone, let alone a subordinate, would try to cheat him at cards. For in the first place he imagined himself to be an unrivaled master of the game, the best proof of this proficiency being, he thought, the fact that he so consistently won. But secondly he was absolutely convinced that he had been born lucky, and it must be admitted that his military career, which had been one almost unbroken run of progress to his present position as king of the clothing store, had indeed been extraordinarily successful. Thirdly, he himself cheated. Quite shamelessly and not even particularly skillfully. Gunner Asch tolerated the fact indulgently.

He handed Werktreu another card, knowing perfectly well which one it was. According to his calculations the sergeant must now have more than twenty-one: twenty-five to be precise. Which meant that he had lost.

Sergeant Werktreu's eyes narrowed. He cleared his throat noisily and sent a great arc of spit with fair accuracy into the

13

box of sand which stood about three yards away. He tried hard to decide whether he should simply throw in his hand or try to get rid of a card in some way.

Gunner Asch took a pull at his cigarette and looked intently at one of the regulation NO SMOKING notices that hung round the store. He let the sergeant take his time. And when he saw that he was trying to get rid of a card he said to him innocently: "Does the sergeant want more than four cards?"

Werktreu realized at once that the gunner had counted his cards. This caused him a great deal of annoyance, though he couldn't allow himself to show it. Desperately he tried to think of some other way of cheating, but found himself stumped. However, he had no intention of admitting defeat so easily.

There was a loud knocking on the door.

Werktreu seized the opportunity to muddle all the cards up in a heap in the center of the table.

"Who's that?" he called. "I haven't any time just now, I'm in the middle of some work.

"Come on, open up!"

Gunner Asch recognized the sergeant major's voice at once, but didn't tell the sergeant who it was.

"Whose deal?" said Asch in a businesslike way.

"Open up, man, for God's sake," roared the Chief.

Sergeant Werktreu recognized the voice mainly by its volume. He jumped up quickly to put an end to the din.

"Come in," he said, opening the door like a good comrade. "We're just busy sorting out a few socks here."

Schulz, the Chief, nodded understandingly. He looked down patronizingly at Gunner Asch, who had pushed the cards and all the money into his pocket and was indeed now apparently engaged in sorting socks.

"Well," he asked, "who's winning?"

"I am of course," said Werktreu proudly, without a moment's hesitation.

14

"I wouldn't mind a little game myself," said the Chief condescendingly. And he sat down on a pile of overcoats close to Gunner Asch, rubbing his hands in anticipation.

The sergeant locked the door again. The gunner pulled the cards out of his pocket and the sergeant major began to play.

"If you do the dirty on me, Asch," he said, genially enough, "it'll be the end of our beautiful friendship."

"No need to worry about that, Sergeant Major!" said the gunner. He was very much put out by the visit. He had to face up to the fact that this suspiciously loudmouthed goodwill of the sergeant major was going to cost him at least another two marks.

The sergeant major won the first hand, and the second. After the fifth hand he was already five marks up. His goodwill began to assume alarming proportions. He lost three marks at one go in the sixth hand after Asch, who had a natural gift for sleight-of-hand, had changed two of the cards round.

"My dear Asch," he said with a note of menace in his voice. "Have you been issued your Saturday night pass yet?"

"No, Sergeant Major," replied the gunner very politely and immediately let Schulz win two marks.

"What's your wife doing?" Sergeant Werktreu asked the Chief. He was cross because he didn't seem to be having any luck. Schulz won hand after hand. Werktreu was determined to break in on this run somehow and was inexperienced enough to think that he could do so by turning the conversation to the subject of the sergeant major's wife.

The Chief didn't lose the hand but neither did he miss the hint which Sergeant Werktreu had dropped about his wife. My very good friend, he thought, half angrily, half contemptuously, my wife is absolutely no business of yours. I know perfectly well that you're keen on her, but you're not coming poaching on my territory, I'll simply keep her away from you. Even if I have to lock the bitch up. I'm not going to have

15

anyone making a cuckold out of me. Certainly not someone from my own troop and least of all someone lower in rank.

He cursed himself, for he had just lost two marks. He decided that a short break would be a good idea, but he still held on to the pack.

"Tell me, Asch," he said. "This little chap Vierbein, he's in your section, isn't he?"

"Yes, Sergeant Major."

The gunner looked at him curiously. He didn't quite see how this question followed on from what had gone before. How on earth, he wanted to know, did a game of cards lead to the sergeant major's wife, and the sergeant major's wife to Gunner Vierbein?

"He's just a mother's darling, isn't he? A wretched little milksop, eh? Do you think he knows anything about sex?" And speaking with absolute confidence from the depths of his vast experience, the Chief went on: "What do you bet that he doesn't even know the difference between the sexes, eh? Probably he still believes in storks!"

Sergeant Werktreu whinnied appreciatively. It was as if he had made the joke himself. Gunner Asch thought it wise to laugh too. The Chief fancied himself as a wit.

"Suppose I were to put a naked girl down beside him," he went on, thoroughly enjoying himself. "What would he do with her, eh? Cover her up with a blanket, I suppose!"

"I don't know," said Gunner Asch warily. "I think he's quite normal." He decided to do what he could for Gunner Vierbein. He felt sorry for him. He was just a poor little swine who knew well enough that he was being fattened for the slaughter later on. And Gunner Asch knew his Schulzes. He knew just the sort of thing that would impress them, and what their idea of manliness was. So he let himself go a little:

"Oh there's more to this Vierbein than meets the eye, you

16

know. Still waters run deep. He's a smart chap. He has his own way of doing things."

The Chief slowly put down the cards. At first he was merely astonished, but then he began to draw certain conclusions, conclusions which he didn't altogether like.

"You're lying, Asch," he said uncertainly and with less than his usual volume. "That's just the sort of drivel I'd expect from you, you dirty-minded bastard."

The gunner automatically ignored the "drivel" and the "dirty-minded bastard." It was impossible for anyone to insult him because it was one of his fundamental principles never to feel insulted. He was therefore thoughtless enough to let his imagination run away with him. In short, he invented a typical piece of ordinary barrack-room gossip.

He said: "I can tell you this: Gunner Vierbein pulled off in four hours dead what it took our pure Nordic Aryan hero, Gunner Wagner, three weeks to manage. He simply took the girl by storm. It's a fact. We were watching through the key-hole. We had a bet on it."

Sergeant Werktreu nodded. He couldn't quite make out what was going on. But Schulz was remarkably put out about something. The gunner was staggered by the effect which this completely fictitious story of his had on the sergeant major. But he was given no chance to probe into the matter further.

The sergeant major rose to his feet with a very determined expression on his face.

"I must get back home at once," he said.

☙ ☙ ☙

Gunner Vierbein was neither a halfwit nor a poor little swine. He was just a normal human being without any particularly remarkable qualities. He even had a certain amount of

17

what is usually known as healthy common sense, and his physique was quite up to the demands made upon it by army life. It was in his soul that he suffered.

His father, a simple decent sort of fellow, a very reliable police official, had seen the trouble coming. There was something different about his son Johannes. It was nothing much, but what there was was unmistakable. The truth of the matter was, he read books! And Father Vierbein never remembered once having seen a book in his own or his wife's family in his life. If he had, it had been a Bible or a songbook or an illustrated calendar.

In every other way Johannes Vierbein had been a thoroughly promising child: very industrious and almost always well disciplined; he helped his mother with the washing, was fond of his German teacher and carried his briefcase home for him after school. He always behaved courteously towards women, whatever their age. He fought with his school friends, was bad at mathematics and fair at religion. Singing was torture to him, sport an unadulterated pleasure, and in German he was far and away ahead of all the others in his class. And here lay the cause of his present distress. For Vierbein, Johannes, allowed himself the luxury of a mind of his own.

Within the first twenty-four hours of his military career he was made to realize that everything he had learned up to that point was just "so much crap." Now at last they would "make a man of him." He was sensible enough to see the funny side of such a primitive theory of adult education and his physique was sufficiently good to enable him to accept it. But it was not long before he had succumbed completely to the steamroller methods of the barrack square. He went under with his eyes open, knowing quite well what he was doing.

For he soon learned that there were advantages in letting oneself become an automaton. He also recognized that there had to be some sort of discipline where a large body of men

18

were herded together into a small space. What he couldn't stand was the endless saluting, the wearing of identical uniforms, the marching in step, the obligation to sing at a given word of command, the unnatural barking form of speech. He, who knew pages of Schiller by heart, was a passionate idealist. But he wanted to be able to express his idealism in his own way and not to have it forced out of him as if he were a complete moron.

Thus, though Johannes Vierbein was once at any rate a willing soldier, he had never been a happy one. He obeyed orders. He did what he was told, neither more nor less. He took care not to attract attention to himself in any way. He had plenty of acquaintances among his fellow soldiers, but no friend; and there was in fact only one man whose friend he wanted to be, and this was Gunner Asch. For Gunner Asch had a sister whom Vierbein found very attractive. Her name was Ingrid.

He beat away industriously at Frau Schulz's carpet, that is to say at the carpet belonging to the sergeant major's wife. He beat it very systematically. He was carrying out an order. His fatigue tunic, which was too big for him, flapped about him. His trousers, which were too small, were stretched tight across his bottom. He was sweating and his young, red, very serious face shone in the sun.

Lore Schulz sat on a window seat inside the apartment and watched him. She was wearing a light summer dress with nothing to speak of underneath, for she was feeling hot. It was the fault of the summer's day or the amount of work she had to do or her hot blood or something. Perhaps it was just that she wanted to save on her underclothes.

"All right!" she called out to Gunner Vierbein. "You can bring the carpet in now."

"Very good," said Vierbein. Orders were orders. He pulled the carpet down from the line and rolled it up. He didn't pause

19

for a moment in his work, doing everything very thoroughly, methodically, unostentatiously, always bearing in mind his motto: Never draw attention to yourself. Especially here, on the grass in front of the troop barrack block, in full view of about a hundred windows. One of his superiors might be standing behind any of them. Any of his superiors. Perhaps even Lumpface the major himself. He was well known for his love of catching people unawares.

Johannes Vierbein shouldered the carpet and marched off, not too quickly, not too slowly, towards the entrance of the block. At the bottom of the steps he decided to allow himself a little breather. But Lore Schulz was standing in the open doorway of her apartment, waiting for him.

He crossed the short stretch of corridor, went into the living room and let the carpet slide smartly to the floor.

"Help me unroll it, will you?" said Lore Schulz.

She knelt down at his feet and he could see right down her dress.

"Very good," he said and knelt down beside her.

His peep down her dress hadn't escaped her notice. She knew very well that there was plenty for him to see, so she didn't mind at all. She was quite used to being stared at by men. It gave her pleasure; a strange exciting pleasure all her own. She quite often went out of her way to bring it about. She would dress carefully, wait for the troop to fall in outside and then leave the block and walk out past the ranks, swaying very slightly as she went. Lately, however, her husband the sergeant major had forbidden this. Once he had been proud of her but now he seemed to want to hide her away.

Lore was really very different from the person she seemed to be. At heart she was just a silly little girl with romantic ideas. She had been one of a family of eight and had slept in the same bed with two of her sisters for ten years. Then she started working as an assistant in a flower shop near the ceme-

20

tery. She adored films and the Führer's speeches. And always she was full of romantic longings. She longed to travel to Italy, to have a husband with an automobile, to have a home of her own. She even read the women's columns in the newspapers and borrowed fashion magazines.

Schulz, who was then still a sergeant, won her heart the very first evening she saw him. He was simply irresistible. He pressed her so close to him when they danced that she forgot about Italy and the automobile. Certainly he wasn't the first man in her life, but she had never fallen so hopelessly in love with anyone before. Schulz realized that he was a lucky man. He loved her very much, particularly when they slept together. He married her and became a sergeant major. And she got a home of her own.

But he didn't succeed in either satisfying her romantic longings or making her forget them. He himself soon began to take her for granted. It seemed to him that she was just one more gun which he had got to know by heart. Since he was an ambitious man he didn't want, as he put it, to remain in charge of only one gun for the rest of his life. He had a vigorous constitution and was used to training people and then packing them off. . . . So he almost automatically started looking around for "new material to practice on." All in all, as he was constantly saying, he was quite a fellow!

But Lore's secret longings started to blossom again. Italy and the automobile were synonymous with love and self-fulfillment. She looked for these things in novels but didn't find them. Then, with considerable discretion, she tried being unfaithful to her husband with one or two of the N.C.O.s from his troop, but she found them all greedy and hurried and lacking in tenderness. In their uniforms there seemed to be about as much difference between them as between guns of the same caliber.

But she found young men like Gunner Vierbein very touching, for she was a sentimental girl. I too was young once, she thought. Two or three years ago I was just as young as he. Now I'm a married woman, almost worn out. I've lost all my freshness. The tension has gone from my body. My lips are no longer soft and full. My skin is getting flabby. And this is happening to me already. Already!

"What's your name?" she asked softly, edging up to the young man in the fatigue uniform.

"Vierbein," he said wearily. "Gunner Vierbein."

They were now kneeling beside each other on the carpet. He could see her various curves very clearly. She noticed that his fatigue uniform smelled of soap.

"There's something different about you," she said with the sort of surprise a child might show. "Your hair is different, it's much softer. Your hands are finer too, more delicate. Let me see your hands."

Vierbein hesitated. He looked into her eyes. They were soft and small and sad. He gave her his hand and said cautiously: "You're keeping me from my work, you know."

She smiled slowly and said: "Does that matter?"

"Well, no," he said. And almost automatically he added: "That is, if you'll take the responsibility."

She couldn't think what to answer. She wanted to say, "Responsibility? Whatever for? Responsibility to whom?" But she said nothing. She looked at his fresh pink face and his straightforward honest eyes, his unlined forehead, and his chin which showed no trace of arrogance or brutality.

Lore let go of his hand, stretched her legs out in front of her and lay down full length on the carpet.

"Have you got a girl?" she asked.

Johannes Vierbein found himself confused by the question. He blushed a little, thinking of Gunner Asch's sister Ingrid. And he realized at once that he had no right to think of her as his girl. "No," he said decisively.

22

Lore seemed pleased by his answer. Her lips parted slightly. Her teeth were very good, if a little large. Her tongue appeared curiously between them. She wanted to laugh. But she didn't laugh. For at that moment the door opened to reveal Sergeant Major Schulz standing on the threshold.

"Vierbein," said the Chief. And there was a sinister softness about his voice. "Vierbein, you will get out of here at once and report immediately to Corporal Lindenberg for latrine cleaning."

"Very good, Sergeant Major," said Vierbein. He rose obediently.

"Double up!" roared the sergeant major. "I'll be seeing you later."

¥ ¥ ¥

Corporal Lindenberg, who was in charge of No. 2 Section, of which both Gunner Asch and Gunner Vierbein were members, was a man with a great deal of energy and ambition. There was no doubt that he had a future. His ambition was rather a strange one. It had nothing in common with the usual ways in which men wish to distinguish themselves in life. There was something almost unique about it: it consisted solely of a desire to produce men for the defense of the Fatherland. He was quite open about it. Even his superiors shook their heads slowly in amazement.

Lindenberg was twenty-four. He had soft black wavy hair, was neither particularly tall nor particularly well built, but was wiry and very energetic. He never made his men do anything that he was not prepared to do himself. That is to say, he was always the first on parade in the mornings and the last off duty at nights; his uniform was always spotless; he knew all the regulations by heart; he cleaned his own boots — openly in the corridor, so that everybody could see him; and he had a keen

23

look in his eye and a smartness of bearing that was quite inimitable.

But Lindenberg was not merely a strict disciplinarian. He was also a stanch comrade. It was his aim always to be scrupulously correct. He only really felt properly alive when he was on duty. He would volunteer for anything. And he expected and demanded that "his" men should follow his example. He was even quite prepared to yield second place to anyone with a good grace, although this of course was never necessary, for he could do a five-foot-high jump or march twenty miles with full pack at any time without the slightest difficulty. He was also breast-stroke champion of the battery and the second best shot in the regiment. And at the local tavern in the evenings he would stand on a chair and sing "The Volga Boat Song" in the manner of Richard Tauber in a way which would not have disgraced any small-town light opera company.

It went without saying that Lindenberg would become an officer one day. His remarkable qualities simply could not be overlooked. And his inexhaustible capacity for duty was always being taken advantage of, generally by appeals to his sense of comradeship. As he neither drank nor was particularly interested in women, and only went to films when some saga of heroism and endurance with a suitably victorious ending was being shown, he was always available to take over the duties of his fellow N.C.O.s at week ends.

He made the sort of orderly corporal who would have satisfied the strictest of martinets. For him orders really were sacred. He carried them out to the utmost of his ability and in strict accordance with his conscience. His ability was prodigious, his conscience always on the alert. It was his one determination to turn the mediocre material he received into fine upstanding soldiers with no other thought in their heads but *Ein Reich, Ein Volk, Ein Führer*. But he also made a point of behaving in what he considered an honorable manner.

24

Gunner Vierbein reported to Corporal Lindenberg for latrine cleaning as he had been told to. Lindenberg, himself a model soldier, looked him slowly up and down. He couldn't find much wrong with him. He was on the point of reprimanding him for untidy hair, but changed his mind when, with his meticulous sense of justice, he remembered that the gunner had just come off another fatigue.

"What have you done so far, Gunner?"

"Carpet-beating, Corporal. For the sergeant major."

Correct as ever, the corporal did not allow the shadow of disapproval which crossed his mind to show on his face. He told himself that it was none of his business to criticize his superiors. To have expressed such criticism, however justified, in front of the rank and file would have been tantamount to an undermining of discipline, an indirect incitement to mutiny. And that was an idea which should never be allowed to enter a soldier's wildest dreams for one moment.

He went ahead into the latrine and looked round the place, which was much used, and now positively shone with cleanliness. No one was allowed in during cleaning operations, with the exception, of course, of N.C.O.s and those defined by Battery Routine Order No. 104/38 as "acting in compliance with the most urgent demands of Nature."

Corporal Lindenberg noted the state of the room with satisfaction. He ran his hand expertly over the windows, along the pipes, and around the lavatory seats and the taps in the basins. The taps were a little dull so he ordered Vierbein to polish them up at once.

He himself returned to the orderly corporal's room, where he found Gunner Asch waiting for him. The gunner saluted in an exemplary fashion, which won the corporal's full approval. He returned the salute in the same style.

Asch knew just how to handle the corporal. He barked out: "Might I have the corporal's permission to speak?"

25

"You have my permission," answered the corporal correctly.

Gunner Asch's crisp, clipped words rang out loud and clear: "Might I ask the corporal for my Saturday night pass?"

"Have you finished your work, Gunner Asch?"

"Yes, Corporal. Sergeant Werktreu has given me permission to go."

The corporal noted the fact.

"And your equipment, Gunner Asch? Is everything in order? Your locker? Your rifle? Your bayonet?"

"I beg to inform the corporal that everything is in order."

Gunner Asch had no hesitation in lying to the corporal. He knew perfectly well that everything was not in order, or at least not in that apple-pie order which alone would have satisfied Lindenberg. But he also knew that it was impossible for the orderly corporal to leave his post for more than a few minutes at a time and that he simply couldn't examine the lockers of all those applying for Saturday night passes with the thoroughness which he would have liked.

The corporal seemed to hesitate for a second. Gunner Asch remained quite unperturbed. He decided to follow up his advantage.

"Might I beg to inform the corporal," he said with apparent enthusiasm, "that the regimental handball team is playing the Hansa Sports Club today!"

This was quite untrue. The match was not for another two weeks. But he reckoned that Lindenberg, who had no particular interest in handball, would be unaware of this. If by any chance he should be aware of it, Asch had committed no offense by getting his dates muddled up.

Lindenberg knew nothing about the match. Curtly he nodded his approval.

"Excellent, Gunner Asch. I'm glad to see you taking an interest in sport. Sport is a healthy way of preparing oneself for active service. It fosters the aggressive spirit. Let us hope we manage to beat the civilians."

"Of course we will, Corporal!"

Lindenberg sat down and opened the Saturday night pass book. He took out the pass forms and began looking through them. At that moment the telephone rang and without in any way altering his soldierly bearing, which was as always exemplary, he picked up the receiver.

"No. 3 Troop. Orderly Corporal, Corporal Lindenberg speaking!"

Gunner Asch looked down at the corporal's rigid form with a touch of contempt. He let his knees give very slightly and stood there perfectly comfortably with every appearance of still standing rigidly at attention. Gunner Asch could stand like this for hours on end without getting tired. It was one of the many tricks that he had learned and perfected.

"Very good, Sergeant Major!" the corporal said into the telephone. "The sergeant major is in the canteen. Very good. Coming with the pass book to the canteen at once, Sergeant Major."

He hung up and began quickly searching through the pile of passes.

Gunner Asch had a sudden hunch.

"Might I beg to ask the corporal for Gunner Vierbein's pass at the same time?"

Seeing Lindenberg hesitate, he added: "Might I beg to inform the corporal that it was Gunner Vierbein who drew my attention to the handball match this afternoon?"

"Vierbein?" said the corporal in astonishment. "Gunner Vierbein drew your attention to it? I'm delighted to hear that. I never credited Gunner Vierbein with an interest in sport. Good. I'll give you his pass while I'm about it."

"Thank you, Corporal," rapped out Asch without thinking.

27

He had hardly spoken before he realized his mistake. He had acted impulsively and foolishly. It was a mistake that might well prove dangerous.

As he had expected, Lindenberg gave him a look of intense disapproval.

"Gunner Asch!" he said, and his voice was level and impersonal as always. "You have nothing to thank me for. I am merely doing my duty. You ought to know that."

Contrary to Gunner Asch's expectations, he then handed over the passes, took receipt of the regulation twenty pfennigs, and concluded coldly: "You may dismiss now. And I expect your bearing in uniform to be an example to any civilians you may meet."

※ ※ ※

The canteen was leased to a man called Bandurski. He had served in the Reichswehr and, knowing what N.C.O.s were like, had no particular love for them, though he had worn a corporal's stripes himself in his time. But now he was a businessman and he knew that unless he was on good terms with them, his business could never prosper, though in strict terms of cash it depended on the men in the proportion of five to one. The N.C.O.s therefore were privileged guests in his canteen. He had a special extra room for them, and saw to it that they always had a particularly pretty girl to wait on them. By far his best customer — so far as ordering if not paying was concerned — was Sergeant Major Schulz.

Bandurski gave him preferential treatment and supplied him with free beer and flattery in generous quantities. Even Elizabeth, the waitress for the N.C.O.s' canteen, had special instructions to look after him well, and she carried these out faithfully if without any particular enthusiasm.

"What will you have, Sergeant Major?" she asked in a

28

matter-of-fact voice. "Herr Bandurski would like you to have a drink with him."

Not bad, thought Schulz. He wondered if she was very passionate. Obviously she was. She was fair-skinned and this type was always ready for anything. Or so he had read in a novel which had been confiscated from one of the men in the course of the last locker inspection. The filthy beast! Pornography in his locker indeed! The C.O. should have had him punished for it.

"Bring me a lager," he said, "Danish — a large one. And then some beer, strong beer — also a large one."

Elizabeth brought the drink over to him and he stared with pleasure at her well-built shoulders, her wide hips and her long shapely legs. Lore, he thought, my wife Lore is smaller and skinnier. This afternoon, for instance, as she lay on the carpet — his carpet — with hardly anything on at all, and this gunner beside her . . .

He got up quickly.

"I must go and telephone," he said. "I'll be back in a minute."

And he went and put a call through to the orderly corporal.

In the meantime Elizabeth Freitag went on filling up the glasses. She had her own views about men and these views were neither favorable nor unfavorable. She knew that there were many different sorts of men, even in a place like this where a not altogether unsuccessful effort was made to reduce them all to a uniform mental and physical pattern.

She knew this because she knew Gunner Asch. Herbert Asch had made an impression on her, or rather he had taken good care to see that he should make an impression on her. He was very different from the average run of them, not just a mere cipher. Even under his army cap his face stood out as that of an individual. Moreover, his intelligence was by no means despicable and he knew how to use it. She had often admired the way in which he hardly ever said what he really thought and yet nearly always got what he wanted.

Sergeant Major Schulz had finished his telephone conversation. He came and sat down at the table again. He looked at the well-filled glasses with satisfaction. Then he looked at Elizabeth with something of the same feeling.

"What are you doing this evening?" he asked her.

"Why? Do you want to take me out?"

"Why not?" Schulz could see nothing odd in this. "Well, what about it?"

"What about your wife?"

Schulz brushed the question aside. "She's badly in need of a rest. She'll be staying at home."

Elizabeth kept a straight face, although it looked very much as if she wanted to laugh. But she managed not to. She merely said: "I'm already going out with someone this evening. We're going to the dance at Bismarckshöh."

Sergeant Major Schulz wanted to tell her that there was a good chance that he would see her there. Bismarckshöh was the chief rallying place of No. 1 Battery of the artillery regiment. Admittedly there was always a preponderance of other ranks there, but it was not at all unusual to find quite a number of N.C.O.s as well after midnight and even one or two officers in civilian clothes. For Bismarckshöh was close to the barracks, and those on their way home often dropped in there for one last drink.

Sergeant Major Schulz wanted to say, "Perhaps we'll meet there, then." But he never got round to it. For at that moment Corporal Lindenberg appeared before him, clicked his heels and said:

"Corporal Lindenberg reporting, Sergeant Major."

The Chief knew Lindenberg well enough and had no particular love for him. He found his exaggerated correctness nauseating. But he couldn't help respecting him. He knew that any human conversation with this iceberg in uniform was quite impossible so he came straight to the point.

"Have you given out the passes yet?"

"Yes, Sergeant Major, seventeen of them."

"Have you given one to that swine Vierbein?"

Lindenberg maintained a strict impartiality.

"Gunner Vierbein," he said, and he managed to substitute the word gunner for swine without any positive suggestion of reproach — positive, mark you, for the reproach was there all right and even Schulz sensed it, renowned as he was for the thickness of his skin. "I gave Gunner Vierbein's pass to Gunner Asch to give to him."

The sergeant major restrained himself only with difficulty. But he knew that there was no use in shouting at Corporal Lindenberg. You had to get at him in some other way.

"Gunner Vierbein," said Schulz, "is at this moment cleaning out the ground-floor latrine, if I'm not mistaken."

"He's finished his work there, Sergeant Major," replied the corporal unperturbed. "As I had received no further orders or instructions I saw no reason to withhold a pass from Gunner Vierbein. Especially as Gunner Vierbein wished to watch the handball match between the regimental team and the Hansa Sports Club."

"But that's not for another two weeks!" yelled Schulz. He knew all about it for he had read about it in regimental orders only that morning. "You've let him make a fool of you, Lindenberg! The fellow's simply put a fast one over on you as if you were the rawest recruit in the regiment! You of all people, Lindenberg!"

The corporal stood there rooted to the spot. He didn't move a muscle. He just flushed the color of a ripe tomato.

"What are the sergeant major's orders?" he asked, keeping perfect control of himself.

The Chief felt an overwhelming sense of superiority. He

found it very satisfactory that the prize boy Lindenberg, "the eternal soldier" as he was called by the other N.C.O.s, should have got himself into such a mess. He brought his fist down heavily on the table and seemed, as far as it was possible to tell with him, to be in an excellent mood.

"When did you give out the passes?" he asked.

"Just now, Sergeant Major. . . . About five minutes ago."

"Were they in their dress uniforms?"

"No, Sergeant Major. In their fatigues. Gunner Vierbein can only have been gone from his work in the latrines about three minutes."

"Well, Lindenberg." The Chief rose to his feet with a grin of pleasure. "You've certainly made an appalling mess of things, but I'll clean it up for you. Just leave everything to me. And don't do anything else idiotic. I'll merely hold one of my little inspections."

Sergeant Major Schulz went off without delay to his "inspection point." This was a bench immediately opposite the barrack block's only entrance and exit. Anyone who wished to leave the building had to pass in front of him. There was no other way — no other orthodox way, that is — out to the main gate.

The Chief sat down with his notebook open beside him keeping a sharp lookout for Gunner Vierbein. Meanwhile he passed the time inspecting the turnout of those soldiers who were about to leave the barracks. He checked the state of their fingernails, of their socks, of their shirts, of their ears and feet, as only he knew how to.

But though he derived a considerable amount of pleasure from all this, he saw no sign of Gunners Asch and Vierbein. Gradually Schulz grew impatient. Finally he became openly agitated. He sent someone to look for Gunners Asch and Vierbein. But they were nowhere to be found. Both of them, he was finally informed, had already left the barracks. White with

32

fury and frustration, he asked himself what on earth could have happened. For it was absolutely impossible that they could have taken the normal way out of the camp.

¥ ¥ ¥

What in fact they had done was to leave, in broad daylight, by the route which people usually only dared to use at night. They had climbed out of the camp. It had been Asch's suggestion. He was always up to every sort of trick. They had climbed out of a cellar window at the back of the barrack block into a little garden and had scaled the wall from there.

They were just on the top of this wall and in full view of the street when to their horror they saw a corporal from another battery making his way along the pavement towards the town. He saw them at once. But he had no wish to see them. He quickly looked the other way and pretended to find something fascinating about the flat dreary landscape in which the barracks were situated. A gunner who was coming along the pavement at the same time ran up to the wall and helped them down.

They thanked him and invited him to have a drink with them later, which he promptly accepted. Then the corporal who had turned a blind eye came past and they saluted him — particularly smartly. He gave them a broad grin, which made them feel much better.

They made straight for Asch's house, where at the express wish of Gunner Vierbein they had been invited for coffee. Vierbein thought it very friendly of Asch to have arranged the invitation for him. But Asch was secretly convinced that he was doing his friend a disservice. He had no special regard for his family; and his sister Ingrid, who was the cause of Vierbein's visit, was very much a member of the family.

"I can't make out what you see in my sister," said Gunner

33

Asch, shaking his head. "She's just a little Nazi bitch. You can't fall in love with, or admire, a girl like that; the most she's any good for is pushing the birth rate up a bit."

"You're going too far," said Vierbein passionately, though he knew well enough that there was something in what Asch said. "What have your sister's political ideas got to do with it? Or rather, what's wrong with them? In these times in which we live . . ."

"*Heil Hitler!*" cried Gunner Asch, saluting with a flourish a tree which they happened to be passing.

This made Vierbein laugh. It showed that his friend Asch was in excellent form and augured well for a pleasant afternoon with his friend, Ingrid and their father. He would be quite one of the family.

Vierbein was determined not to say a word against Ingrid.

"Your sister has the same upright way of looking at things as your father has. I find that admirable."

"I find it ridiculous," said Asch, in a friendly enough tone. "God preserve us from our fathers' ways of looking at things. I'm very fond of my old man of course, but only in a sentimental sort of way. If you look into him closely you'll soon find out that he's nothing but a businessman at heart and any so-called political convictions he may have at any given moment are simply part of his business technique."

Vierbein felt himself obliged to give his friend Asch a gentle reprimand. "You really shouldn't talk like that about your father," he said.

Herbert Asch brushed the remark aside.

"You misunderstand me," he said calmly. "You're out of touch with the spirit of the times. What I said just now was an indirect form of praise. The old man's realized what's going on all right. He sees there's a lot of good business being done under cover of a high political morale and he doesn't see why he shouldn't take his cut."

"Your sister doesn't think like that."

"Of course not." Asch nodded. "She's much more dangerous. She really believes in all this nonsense. She's identified herself completely with this pseudo idealism and alas all too genuine lunacy. She thinks it makes her heroic. She's too short-sighted to see what's really happening."

An infantry sergeant was coming towards them. Vierbein saluted smartly. Gunner Asch, carried away by enthusiasm for his theme, only saw him at the last moment. He gave him a very perfunctory salute when it was already almost too late. And he brought his hand down again as if he wanted to brush the sergeant out of his mind.

The sergeant, who had a girl with him, didn't take this in at first. In fact it was about six to eight seconds before he realized that he had been saluted in a manner which, if you could call it saluting at all, was by no means the regulation one. He wasn't a bad sport on the whole. He was sure his recruits would be the first to admit that; but lack of respect, particularly in public, was something which he couldn't afford to tolerate. He had to ask himself what his superiors would say to such a thing, what the civilians would think, and above all what his girl would think who, not without good reason, considered him a man of some consequence. He himself always saluted in exemplary fashion, and he demanded, and had a right to demand, that he should be saluted in exemplary fashion back.

He stopped in the middle of the busy Goethestrasse with a look of determination on his face and called out: "Hey!"

One or two passers-by stopped and turned around. The two soldiers continued on their way. Certainly Gunner Vierbein tried to get Asch to stop, but Asch saw no reason to. His name was not Hey, he told himself, and he therefore didn't see why he should assume that a parade-ground roar behind him was necessarily meant for him. He knew from experience that very few N.C.O.s were prepared to keep up their parade-ground

35

manner for long on such occasions. Their first reaction in public was usually quite instinctive. They automatically got excited and it was just a question of giving them time to cool off. Only the very toughest would ever try to persist with a matter of this sort.

The infantry sergeant in question was one of the very toughest. He told his girl to wait and hurried off after the two soldiers. He quickly overtook them and planted himself in front of them.

Gunner Vierbein was terrified. But Gunner Asch was incapable of being surprised by anything. There was nothing new to him even in the present situation. And he knew exactly what technique to use to get himself out of trouble.

"Why didn't you salute?" said the sergeant, pointing at Asch.

Gunner Asch played up brilliantly. He stood stiffly at attention as if he had been on the barrack square. His voice sounded both firm and submissive at the same time. He looked his superior straight in the eye — a proud, honorable and loyal soldier.

"I beg to inform the sergeant that I did salute!" he said firmly.

And he snapped his right hand smartly up to the peak of his cap, palm outward, fingers extended. The salute would have drawn a smile of acknowledgment from the strictest of N.C.O.s, from a Corporal Lindenberg himself.

The sergeant in the present case was more than just astonished. He was completely taken aback. He didn't know what to do next. His considerable experience told him that without any doubt the soldier he was dealing with was a quite exceptional man, a model of all that a soldier should be. And yet he had seen with his own eyes that one of these two had saluted him in a far from regulation manner. And he could have sworn that it was the one he was now addressing.

Asch saw that his technique had been successful. Things

36

were turning out just as he had expected. He found it a comparatively simple matter to defeat the system of regimentation into which the state had pushed him by taking it on with its own weapons. But though he had reckoned with the sergeant's stupidity he had not reckoned with his meanness. This the sergeant called his conscientiousness.

For the sergeant now reasoned to himself as follows: It can't have been this man, for he is obviously in every way a first-class soldier, but it was one of these two, and since it can't have been this man it must have been the other. Whereupon he turned to Vierbein and said curtly and with a certain impatience:

"Why didn't you salute properly? What the hell do you think you're doing? What's your name?"

"Gunner Vierbein," said Vierbein promptly. He was taken completely by surprise. He was so surprised that he was quite unable to think. He didn't even have time to think, as he usually did, how ridiculous it was that some absurd regulation should have changed his name to "Gunner."

Of course Gunner Asch hadn't meant this to happen. Not even he could have seen it coming.

It wasn't that he felt particularly sorry for Vierbein, or particularly contemptuous of the sergeant, it was just that the whole business suddenly seemed to him too stupid and idiotic. And, much less smartly than before, he said: "The gunner saluted before I did. I can witness that — I was the one who was rather slow."

The civilians who had collected round them were now beginning to grow restless. The majority of them seemed to be on the sergeant's side. Most of these looked as if they had either already served with distinction in the army or at least were destined to do so at some time or other. The rest, the minority, began to protest. A woman said angrily: "What a way to treat the poor boys! Why don't you let them go?"

37

Even the sergeant's girl came timidly up to him and said: "Oh, do come on!"

The sergeant sensed that it was time to bring the business to a close. He had no wish to start giving a bunch of miserable civilians a lesson in discipline. And yet he knew that he couldn't afford to go without at least registering a nominal victory. So he said to Asch: "What's your name?"

Asch saw at once that the sergeant wanted to extricate himself from the situation as quickly as possible. Without a moment's hesitation he answered: "Gunner Kasprowitz, No. 6 Battery, the Regiment of Artillery."

The sergeant nodded grimly, and wrote the name down. He saw no reason to ask for the soldier's paybook. He hadn't got time anyway.

"You'll be hearing more of this!" he said and turned on his heel.

"That's what you think," said Asch under his breath, grinning after him.

☙ ☙ ☙

Asch Senior was a restaurant proprietor, and as such, a tolerant sort of man. He poured his customers' drinks out; it was a matter of indifference to him why they drank them. Those who were happily in love and those who were miserable, those who talked politics or pedantry, those who drank from habit and those who drank because they regarded it as a sort of social obligation — they were all one to him.

Asch Senior was in favor of the Wehrmacht on principle, for it automatically increased his turnover. He had nothing against the party, for it left him in peace. He was even openly friendly towards the party, for it was thanks to the initiative of the local *Kreisleiter* that a garrison town had been created here in the first place. And that had meant, first of all, that the barracks had had to be built. The architects came and drank in his

38

café, and he provided beer for the workmen on the site. Then came the infantry and the artillery. The existence of canteens in the barracks was a thorn in his side, but he made up for this by getting the vast majority of N.C.O.s as his regular customers.

He was tolerant of anything that didn't happen to be forbidden by the laws prevailing at the time. He didn't care whether people sang "The International," "The Horst Wessel Song" or "The Lorelei" in his café. He even knew that the text of "The Lorelei" had been written by a Jew called Heinrich Heine. But he didn't know it officially. It was all the same to him. The only thing that mattered was that his turnover shouldn't drop.

But Asch Senior always took pains to keep his business separate from his private life. In his rooms above the café the atmosphere was thoroughly bourgeois and respectable. The furniture was solid and always looked slightly dusty, although the place was kept scrupulously clean. A portrait in oils of his wife, who had been dead for many years, hung on one of the walls of the sitting room, and whenever Asch Senior saw it he was moved by feelings of kindliness towards her and even a little sadness. But most of the time he sat with his back towards it.

"Herbert," he said to his son, "why have you taken your uniform off?"

They were sitting at the table drinking coffee. Asch Senior's sister was waiting on them. It was she who kept house for her brother, and she did so with grim determination, for regularly once a month he threatened to turn her out into the street. He never really meant this but the threat always had an excellent effect. Asch Senior sat with Ingrid opposite him, Gunner Vierbein on his right and his son on his left. And his son had taken off his tunic and was sitting there in his shirt sleeves, obviously feeling very much at ease.

39

"My dear Father," said Asch amiably, "have you ever been in uniform?"

"Of course," said his father. "I'm a good German, aren't I? Before 1914 I was a member of the Kaiser Wilhelm youth. Then I became a soldier. As you know my service record hangs on the wall downstairs."

Herbert Asch confirmed this.

"Yes," he said. "You hung it up in 1933."

Asch Senior ignored this mild little piece of irony.

"In 1920," he said, "I became a member of the Kyffhäuser League, and my restaurant was the meeting place of the local branch. Then I joined the Stahlhelm, the League of German Front-line Soldiers."

"I thought you were a mess orderly during the war."

This insult made Father Asch very indignant.

"Of course I was a mess orderly as well, but only after I'd been wounded. Wounded twice, too. Before that I was on the Western front, you know: Verdun and all that."

"You're a real hero, Father," said Herbert Asch. And it almost sounded as if he meant it. "A real hero of a father."

Asch Senor didn't quite know what to make of this. He decided to take it as a genuine tribute. And he went on telling about his uniforms:

"So that was the Stahlhelm. Well, then I was going to join the S.A."

Herbert Asch nodded.

"I know," he said. "Only it wasn't necessary because the S.A. had started coming to your café anyway."

"Quite so," said Asch Senior with a certain pride, and he winked at his son. "I know what I'm doing all right."

"And I am your son," said Herbert.

"You both ought to be ashamed of yourselves," said Ingrid furiously. She had been listening to the conversation with growing indignation, entirely neglecting her guest, or rather, the guest whom her brother had invited. This guest sat wrapped in admiration of her. He found her astonishingly beautiful.

"You ought to be ashamed of yourselves," she repeated. "You forget the times in which you live."

"Not at all," said Asch, friendly as ever.

"If it wasn't for the Führer," said Ingrid with conviction, "we would never have liberated the Saar, or Austria. We would still be a small nation."

"Quite, quite," said old man Asch. "You're right there. I can see the difference in my turnover. Profits have increased steadily ever since 1933. I'm making about four times as much now as I did then."

Ingrid became more and more enthusiastic.

"And look at the youth!" she said. "We're being taken seriously at last. We have an important place in society now. And the workers! They travel about on Strength Through Joy trips to places like Norway and Italy!"

"I don't really see that that's necessary," said the old man thoughtfully. "They might just as well spend their money on drink in here."

"And if it wasn't for the Führer," went on Ingrid with no less enthusiasm, "we wouldn't have a Wehrmacht. Isn't that true, Herr Vierbein?"

"Yes," said Vierbein, "that's quite true."

He too was enthusiastic, but about the girl rather than her political ideals. She could have said what she liked as far as he was concerned. He would have found no fault with her. He wasn't in fact at all clear what she was saying. He simply wasn't listening to her. He was only looking at her.

"Idiot," said Herbert Asch forcibly, and threw his napkin on the table.

Father Asch withdrew from the discussion.

"I must go down to the café," he said. "There are a lot of customers today. The Women's Institute are meeting here this

41

afternoon, and the N.C.O.s will be coming this evening. Saturday's my busiest day."

He said good-by to Vierbein.

"Come and see us again if you've enjoyed yourself," he said.

And he looked round at his two children for a moment with a troubled expression on his face; they had so little understanding for his business interests. Then he left the room.

Gunner Vierbein remained behind with the two Aschs. He felt uncomfortable there, almost as if he weren't wanted. It was very hot in the room; he felt he would suffocate. Ingrid sat motionless on her chair. She was very annoyed, and she showed the fact quite plainly. Herbert Asch wasn't in the least bit interested. He requisitioned one of his father's best cigars and took his time about lighting it.

"Come on," said Ingrid to Johannes Vierbein. "I'll show you some of my photos. Would you like to see them?"

"I'd love to," said Johannes Vierbein eagerly. "I really would."

"Look out!" said Herbert Asch. "She'll show you nothing but pictures of German girls in Youth Camps. Those tigresses play at preparing themselves for war in the same sort of way little boys play at cowboys and Indians."

Ingrid didn't even deign to look at her brother. She led Vierbein over to the sofa which stood in one corner of the sitting room and reached out for an album which lay there. She opened it. It was full of pictures of girls, "Hitler Maidens," doing physical training, walking through woods, peeling potatoes, sitting round campfires, singing, and dancing folk dances.

"The camp motto," said Ingrid, "was 'A Healthy Mind in a Healthy Body!'"

Johannes Vierbein stared at the groups with growing admiration. A lot of the girls were pretty, even very pretty, but Ingrid was the prettiest of them all. There was one picture in particular which showed how pretty she was. It was one in which she was climbing out of the water in a bathing suit.

"Well," said Ingrid, "what do you think of my album?"

"Tell me, Fräulein Ingrid," he said, "did you enjoy it? I mean, were you happy there?"

"Happy?" she replied in astonishment, and she didn't notice her brother leaning over to catch what she said. "But happiness isn't the point. This is a communal business, an experience that we all share together."

"Yes, I see," said Vierbein enthusiastically. "An experience you share together. Yes, that sounds wonderful."

Herbert Asch burst out laughing.

"My dear old friend, I know what you're thinking of. Don't blush! That's one thing we do agree about. That sort of experience shared between two people can be very pleasant indeed. Even friends can share experiences, or a family. But I'm afraid my pious little sister means something rather different. It's the regimentation of women she's talking about."

"How dare you say that?" said Ingrid, furiously. "You've no right to say a thing like that."

"Who's going to stop me?" said her brother stoutly. "I want my girl to be someone quite special, someone who belongs to me. I don't just want a girl off the peg, like a suit of ready-made clothes. Women in uniform! My God! All with the same swinging stride, the same hair-dos, the same strained faces without any make-up on, the same jackets, the same blouses and the same thoughts running round the same-shaped heads! God preserve us from the mass production of German women if that's what they're going to be like!"

Ingrid's pretty eyes opened wide in astonishment. They were full of tears. Two large drops rolled slowly down over her scarlet cheeks. She said nothing. She just wept in silence.

Herbert Asch looked at his sister quite unmoved. He was very fond of her, but he saw no reason why he should show

43

her that he was. I'll knock all that romantic campfire nonsense out of her, he said to himself. What she needed was a man — not just any sort of good-natured weakling, but a real man who would take her in his arms and crush her to him until she felt at last that there were only two people who mattered in the whole world. And this man must have the strength to hold her for the rest of his life.

"Please don't cry," said Johannes Vierbein tenderly. He was at a loss what to do next.

Herbert Asch slowly shook his head. No, he thought sadly, this fellow Vierbein won't do. He isn't a real man, he's just a little boy whom they're trying to bully into being a man. He's too soft. Quite soon they'll be able to do just what they like with him. He's like wax in their hands. They'll have molded him into a little toy soldier before he's had time to realize what's happening to him.

"Please don't cry," said Johannes softly. And more softly still, so that it was almost impossible to hear him, he added: "There *is* something special about you. Really. Something very special!"

☙ ☙ ☙

Second Lieutenant Wedelmann, second in command of No. 3 Troop, was on the point of being promoted to full lieutenant. He was a professional soldier who came from Southern Germany, and had already spent six years in the army.

Wedelmann had originally wanted to be a lawyer, but he had became a soldier to please his father, who stressed the financial advantages of the shorter training period involved. Moreover, Wedelmann Senior had a secret hope that his home town might one day be graced by a bronze statue of his son in a general's uniform.

The second lieutenant had never really expected very much from soldiering as a way of life, and therefore was hardly disappointed by it. The Wehrmacht noted his excellent physique, and raised no particular objections to his intelligence. On his first day he was full of enthusiasm. But it wasn't a week before that romantic life of honor and glory which is supposed to be the birthright of every nation's heroes, and of which the immature always dream so longingly, had collapsed about his ears. Six years later he was a man who could be described as a mild, almost harmless sort of cynic, whose cynicism was sometimes taken for shrewdness.

Wedelmann soon discovered what might be described as the system of vertical responsibility. That is to say, for every seven soldiers, one N.C.O.; for every seven N.C.O.s, one officer; for every seven officers, one commanding officer; for every seven commanding officers, one general. The figures weren't always the same. There was a certain elasticity about them, but that was the general principle: pyramids of discipline. To be someone in authority merely meant seeing that seven people under one were under constant pressure from above. Then the machine would run smoothly enough. The rank and file provided the main cog in the machine. It was the N.C.O.s who kept it moving. A general could afford to be on friendly terms with all except his commanding officers. It was advisable for officers to observe a certain curtness with the N.C.O.s, but to make themselves popular with the men. And that was easy enough to do. This well-tried system proved extraordinarily effective, though it was the N.C.O.s who bore the brunt of the work. But in any case, reasoned the second lieutenant, it was always the stupidest people who became N.C.O.s; it was only right that they should be kept hard at it all the time. And there was no doubt they worked wonders. Hence the higher ranks referred to them as the backbone of the army, while the rank and file situated them anatomically somewhat lower down.

45

The second lieutenant had learned that the most important part of his duty consisted in dropping oil into the machine now and again to keep it running smoothly. So he came to the following conclusion: he would do nothing to slow down the main cogwheel and occasionally even do something to hurry it up. That was what being in authority meant.

It didn't take him long to realize that for anyone who wasn't altogether halfwitted activity of this sort provided certain opportunities for relaxation. He was fully prepared to make the most of such opportunities, but the relatively small garrison town was hardly an ideal place in which to enjoy one's leisure to the full. He saw the same faces over and over again in the officers' mess — most of them those of his superior officers. In the town itself there were at the most a dozen families whom he was able to meet, and even in their houses he was only welcome as "the lieutenant," an object of bourgeois snobbery, a gigolo for ladies of a certain age or a candidate for the hands of boring little girls without a thought in their heads.

The lieutenant found none of this very congenial. To say that there was absolutely nothing else for him to do would have been a slight exaggeration. There were always a number of alternatives: for instance, he could spend his week ends in the nearest big town or the provincial capital. But to do either would have cost him almost his entire month's pay. He could spend his time playing billiards or poker in the mess with equally bored brother officers, and gradually drink himself into a state of oblivion, but he didn't find that particularly amusing. He could try and combat boredom by a fanatical officiousness in his duty, by holding snap inspections of the guard, locker inspections, and improvising other similar refinements in military routine. But he himself had once been an ordinary soldier and in the whole of his six years of service had never been unable to forget what that was like. It didn't occur to him that such a sympathetic attitude to the men was rather phenomenal in an officer. To him it just seemed the normal human reaction.

On this particular Saturday afternoon he did exactly what he always did on Saturday afternoons: that is to say, he slept for a bit first and then put on his none too smart civilian suit and went out to wander about the town. He was looking for a girl as usual, but as usual he didn't find one. It had been going on like this for three years now. The odd thing was that he was perfectly good-looking. He might have been some top sales-man in a well-known store, a salesman who was very keen on exercise too. But there was something wrong with him, and most girls could tell it straight away. They could smell the uniform. Those who didn't like uniforms immediately disliked him; while the others, who admired uniforms, despised him for not wearing his. But he couldn't bring himself to wear a uniform when it wasn't absolutely necessary.

So he dropped into a coffeehouse for a cup of coffee and then went off to the movies, where he saw a film called *In the Saddle for Germany*. He found himself irritated by the actor who played the part of the officer. He stank of scent and powder instead of sweat and leather as he should have. And the girl was far too perfect; it would have been impossible to pull off one's boots and walk about in front of her with one's socks full of holes. And yet when the lights went up at the end of the film he could see that the audience had been delighted by the idea of such an officer. If he had had his uniform on at that moment, he couldn't have failed to have a success.

He wandered off to a restaurant where he ordered himself a large meal and a bottle of hock. He took his time over this, looked through a number of newspapers, all containing iden-tical items couched in identical jargon, stared in boredom at the decorations on the wall and pondered the wisdom of a slogan which proclaimed: *German food and German wine — only in the land that's yours and mine!* Nothing wrong with

47

that, thought the lieutenant, yawning. Then he sent for the bill and signed it, saying that he'd settle up as soon as he possibly could. The waiter found this quite in order; he would have been surprised only if the lieutenant had paid in cash.

Not that the lieutenant was broke. He just didn't want to spend too much cash too soon, for the whole of the week end still lay before him, and he wasn't yet quite certain how he was going to spend it. Besides, he'd decided to go on to a dive called the Excelsior. And he couldn't get credit there, in spite of the fact that not so long ago he had been on the most intimate of terms with the girl called Inge who worked behind the bar. But Inge was angry with him now and insisted on payment on the spot.

The Excelsior was the only real bar in the place. The two barmaids were called Erika and Inge and there was a man called Paul who was the owner and looked after the till. Paul was suspected of being a homosexual but that didn't prejudice the takings in any way. Most of the men who came there came to see Erika and Inge, and they found it pleasant not to have to be afraid of Paul's jealousy, for they nearly always got what they wanted.

Wedelmann found the man repellent and went and sat down on a bar stool opposite Inge.

"Well, my sweet little Lieutenant," she said. "You're quite a stranger."

"Give me a *nikolaschka,*" said the lieutenant.

"On the house, please, my dear Lieutenant," said Paul fawningly. "I can't tell you what a pleasure it is for us to see you."

Wedelmann gave Paul a dirty look but Paul continued to leer at him. Inge had a sneer on her face. The lieutenant stirred uncomfortably. He really found this pansy nauseating.

He leaned over the bar and said to Inge, loud enough for Paul to hear: "Well, what about tonight?"

Inge looked him up and down resentfully.

48

"What the hell's the matter with you?" she asked. "Have you got barrack fever or something? Why don't you get a girl of your own so that she's always there for you when you want her? Anyway I'm busy tonight. Besides I don't like being treated as if I were just a common tart. You're not the only man in this town you know — nor the only one in the Wehrmacht."

Wedelmann drank up his *nikolaschka* and ordered another.

"What is it you are after?" he asked. "Marriage?"

"Not to a lieutenant! Nothing less than a major for me, thanks!"

Wedelmann turned away in disgust.

"All right! All right!" he said.

His head ached and he wanted to get out into the fresh air. He paid and left.

He wandered out into the cool night air without any idea of where he was going. He felt exhausted. He didn't care what happened to him. He had no real friends, only comrades, and they were divided up into superiors and subordinates. He had no girl. The girls he did know were either dull and wanted to get married, or temperamental and expensive. As for love! Who would ever love a lieutenant! Either they loved him for the uniform, and he didn't want that, or else they loathed him for the uniform, which meant that they could never love him.

Slowly he made his way back to the barracks. He stopped in a little bar and drank a beer laced with whisky. He put some money down on the bar and went out again. He thought of buying himself a bottle of schnapps and drinking himself into a coma with it. He also thought of taking a look in the mess. But neither of these alternatives really appealed to him because on the one hand he didn't want to be alone and on the other he didn't want to be with his superior officers, who would tell him exactly what he was to drink, how much and how often.

The beer parlor called Bismarckshöh was brightly lit as he

49

passed it. Dance music floated out into the night and there was the raucous sound of people enjoying themselves. A girl laughed. Somebody cried: "Cheers!" The music stopped and there was a burst of applause. The band started up again at once, playing the tune about the swallow that flies off to Heligoland with a last message for the loved one.

Lieutenant Wedelmann suddenly decided to go in. The proprietor, who had his table in a corner near the door, welcomed him effusively, in spite of the fact that he wasn't in uniform. He invited the lieutenant to join him at his table, where a number of senior N.C.O.s — Troop Sergeant Major Schulz among them — were drinking as his guests.

Wedelmann politely declined the invitation. He went through the front room to the dance hall at the back. He watched the rhythmical swaying of the dancers and began to feel better. He looked round for a place for himself. And he saw Gunner Asch sitting alone at a table staring at the dance floor.

He went up to him.

"Is there any room here, Asch?" he asked. And he tried as hard as he could to sound friendly, which in fact wasn't very difficult for him.

Asch looked up and saw his civilian clothes. He seemed to be wondering for a moment whether he ought to stand up or not. Then he decided that the best thing for him to do was to treat the man in front of him as if he were an ordinary civilian. So he remained seated.

"Yes, there's plenty of room," said the gunner, taking a great swig from his beer mug.

‡ ‡ ‡

The combined restaurant, café and dance hall known as Bismarckshöh was the recognized haunt of No. 1 Battery of the Regiment of Artillery. It had several advantages, mainly topographical: that is to say, it was situated on the edge of the town, right at the end of the main street, and about four hundred yards from the barrack gates. Anyone on his way back to barracks from the town automatically found himself passing it.

Bismarckshöh was the special haunt of lance corporals and gunners first class. Ordinary gunners were tolerated amicably enough, N.C.O.s were allowed to sit there undisturbed: but both groups remained there only on condition that they respected the special rights to the place of the lance corporals and gunners first class. If they failed to show such respect, they were immediately ejected without mercy. In these cases the ordinary gunners were dealt with by the lance corporals and gunners first class, while it was the landlord who was made responsible for the ejection of the N.C.O.s. This he carried out with the minimum of delay. He handed them straight on to Emil, his chucker-out, and Emil never had any difficulty in dealing with anyone, for he had been a professional prize fighter in his time and was always glad of a chance to keep his hand in.

Incidents of this sort were relatively rare. There were hardly more than two or three an evening. It was only on Saturdays, when the place was fuller than usual, that the tension was correspondingly greater, for on Saturdays there was also a dance. Girls arrived from all parts of the town, and men came after them. The knowledge that a long night lay ahead, and that one didn't have to be on duty the next day, added to the fun. On Saturdays therefore the lance corporals and gunners first class were hard put to it to hold their own. They not only had the ordinary gunners and the N.C.O.s to contend with, but also civilians, though admittedly these provided no very great problem. It was the soldiers from other units whom they had to look out for, particularly members of the infantry.

The attitude of the lance corporals and gunners first class

seemed reasonable enough in their own eyes. After all, the officers had their mess, the N.C.O.s frequented the Café Asch, and Bismarckshöh belonged to them.

On this particular Saturday the atmosphere was tenser than ever, for there had been a considerable invasion of infantry. Lance Corporal Kowalski, the handiest man with his fists in the whole battery, was wandering about the rooms, collecting his forces. He had left his girl behind under escort at his table.

"Come on, Asch," he said. "Action stations. There are some people in here in need of a little fresh air."

Asch merely nodded. He was sitting with Elizabeth Freitag and Johannes Vierbein at a side table. Elizabeth was the girl who served in the N.C.O.s' canteen and this was her evening off. Vierbein had come along with his friend Asch, and whenever Asch went off to dance with Elizabeth he looked after their beer for them. He was perfectly happy doing this. He had no interest in any of the girls who had come there in the hope of being picked up. He hardly noticed them. He was thinking of Ingrid all the time. And whenever Elizabeth and Asch went off to dance, and were far enough away from him, he looked to see that no one was watching from the next table and then pulled out the photograph which he had got Ingrid to lend him. It showed a girl in a bathing suit stretching herself as she climbed out of the water and putting one hand elegantly behind her head.

When Kowalski, the powerful lance corporal, had gone again, Johannes Vierbein said to Asch curiously: "What did he want?"

Elizabeth, a little flushed from dancing, looked at Asch out of her big bright eyes and laughed.

"I can guess," she said. "He wants to take him off to the bar."

"Never mind," replied Asch with a smile. "My friend Vierbein will dance with you while I'm away."

52

Vierbein obediently asked her to dance. And Asch sat there alone watching them for a moment. He thought Elizabeth was quite wonderful; far more wonderful than any girl he had ever met before. Fortified by one last glance from her, he braced himself to go and assist his comrade-in-arms Lance Corporal Kowalski.

It was at this moment that Lieutenant Wedelmann appeared before him in civilian clothes and asked him if there was a spare place at the table. After a moment's hesitation Asch said "Yes" and stayed where he was.

The lieutenant ran his finger round the collar of his blue sports shirt. It was a little too tight for him.

"By the way, Asch," he said, "I just wanted to say I'm here entirely in a private capacity, you know. Entirely private. Don't let me disturb you in any way."

"I wasn't going to, Lieutenant," said Asch calmly.

"Good," said Wedelmann. Somehow or other he found the situation embarrassing. Here he was, a lieutenant, trying to get a gunner to understand his position. Or of course one could put it another way and say that here he was, a lieutenant in civilian clothes, wanting to make contact with the men, wanting to show his sense of comradeship with them — and trying to find understanding for the fact. But that was all nonsense. The truth was simply that he had felt lonely and wanted to be among his fellow men. What he had to try to do now was to forget that he was technically their superior officer.

"Lieutenant," said Gunner Asch, after nodding to Lance Corporal Kowalski, who was waiting for him at the entrance to the dance hall, "as you are wearing civilian clothes I'd advise you to behave accordingly."

"What do you mean, Asch?" The lieutenant did his very best to ignore Asch's slightly impertinent manner but he couldn't help just noticing it.

"What I mean, Lieutenant, is that when one's in civilian

53

clothes it's a bad thing to get oneself too involved in anything. One ought to be thankful to be out of uniform, and should keep out of things as if they were nothing to do with one."

The lieutenant still didn't understand what the gunner was driving at. But he thought he sensed that he was well disposed towards him. And this pleased him. He too was well disposed towards the gunner. He's a good chap, thought Wedelmann, rather different from the others. He's not just a robot, a mere number, a Comrade Spit-and-Polish. He's got a personality of his own. He'd probably make a good officer. Can one really tell? In any case, he said to himself, I'll watch out for him in future. There was an increasing tendency these days to promote officers from the ranks and from among the N.C.O.s.

The lieutenant didn't have to sit alone for long after Gunner Asch had gone. The dance came to an end and Vierbein brought Elizabeth back to the table. The gunner was overcome with embarrassment when he saw the lieutenant sitting there.

"I beg your pardon, Lieutenant . . ." he began.

But Elizabeth saw nothing embarrassing in the situation.

"This is our table," she said. "We were sitting here with Gunner Asch."

The lieutenant had risen. He behaved almost as if he were in the officers' mess. He bowed to Elizabeth and said:

"Of course. But it was Gunner Asch who gave me permission to sit here. I trust you have no objection."

"No," said Elizabeth, haughtily.

Wedelmann tried to make conversation, but before he could get very far, a deafening uproar broke out in the room where the bar was. The battle was on! The band immediately started playing louder than ever, and the remaining lance corporals and gunners first class hurried from the room.

At the first sign of trouble the N.C.O.s had taken themselves off to the dance floor or the lavatory according to their inclinations of the moment. The unwritten law of the place forbade

54

any intervention on their part and from a disciplinary point of view too it was advisable to turn a blind eye. The landlord quickly brought his most valuable bottles to safety. The chucker-out opened wide the two doors of the exit and made them fast. The cloakroom woman collected everything that belonged to the infantry into one huge pile.

The lieutenant's first reaction to the uproar was to spring to his feet. But then he remembered his conversation with Gunner Asch. He wondered what to do for a moment. He stood there with a look of determination on his face. But he didn't move off in the direction of the battlefield. He bowed to Elizabeth and asked her if he might have the pleasure of the next dance. Elizabeth said he might. And he took her out on the dance floor.

In the meantime the lance corporal's forces were gaining the upper hand. And his auxiliaries, consisting of the landlord, the chucker-out and the cloakroom woman, were doing all they could to bring the struggle to a successful conclusion as quickly as possible.

The whole affair took only about ten minutes from start to finish. By the end of that time the place was cleared of infantry. The lance corporals and gunners first class felt a certain manly pride in their achievement. They managed to overlook the fact that they had heavily outnumbered their opponents or, if they did remember this, they dismissed the thought at once. Nor were the N.C.O.s grudging in their admiration on their return.

Only Troop Sergeant Major Schulz looked grimly ahead of him and seemed to take no pleasure in the victory of the artillery. Something had made him very angry and he made no attempt to conceal the fact. He had left the landlord's table just before the fight broke out, meaning to do some dancing. He knew whom he wanted to dance with too. But before he could manage to ask Elizabeth, she was already on the floor with someone else and this someone else, he saw, was Gunner Vierbein. Vierbein again!

Suddenly he remembered that Corporal Lindenberg had told him that, according to Gunner Asch, it was Gunner Vierbein who had said that the handball match was being played today. It wasn't in fact due for another fortnight. This was a clear case of misleading an N.C.O. He rose to his feet and sent Gunner Vierbein back to barracks at once. On the spot. Off the dance floor and back to barracks.

Only it was annoying that Elizabeth refused to dance with him. It was even more annoying that Lieutenant Wedelmann was sitting at their table in civilian clothes and fixing him with a remarkably cold gaze.

To hell with it. None of these people had any sense of discipline.

⚑ ⚑ ⚑

Elizabeth Freitag was a bright girl, endowed with her full share of healthy skepticism. She was twenty-two and she had learned that men could be divided into many more different categories than women usually realize, particularly when they are in uniform. Elizabeth looked at a man's hands and at the way he walked and at his handwriting. The picture she built up of a man was composed of a great variety of details of this sort. And yet her collection of such pictures was a small and exclusive one.

Her father was a foreman on the railway, a little man with a sharp foxy face. He was a specialist of many years' experience, a socialist by instinct and a passionately conscientious craftsman. Her mother was a midwife, a large robust woman full of kindness and loyalty towards her husband. By dint of much strength of character and not a little hardship they had saved enough to buy themselves a small house. Many an engine in the repair sheds owed its long life to the skill of Father Freitag;

56

almost the whole of the younger generation of the flourishing little provincial town had been assisted into the world by his wife.

Elizabeth's elder sister had been married two years earlier to a steady-going cabinetmaker who was not merely a master of his craft, but also an ideal husband. Her younger brother was doing his second year of military service in the tank corps at Königsberg. Thus it came about that Elizabeth was able to have a room of her own. Her mother and father let her have it empty, to furnish as she liked. "For," said her father, "you must learn to lead your own life as early as possible. No one stays a child forever."

They made no objection when Elizabeth told them one day that she intended to get a job in one of the artillery canteens. The pay was good and the work not too hard, the hours were reasonable and the place was not very far from where the Freitags lived. "Why not?" said the old railwayman. "You can take care of yourself by now."

She took care of herself by not letting herself get involved with any of the men. Bandurski, the civilian who rented the canteen, found this very satisfactory. He knew from experience that there were only two possibilities for a girl in a job of this sort: either go to bed with everyone or with no one. The thing to be avoided was favoritism for one or two at the expense of the others.

Elizabeth worked with the same sort of steady imperturbable rhythm with which others wash clothes or work on production belts. She let nothing escape her and kept herself very much to herself. And when she looked twice at anyone it was the man she saw and not the uniform. This was what had happened in the case of Gunner Asch. He reminded her partly of her father and partly of her mother. He had the shrewd intelligence of the one and the healthy robustness of the other.

She had fallen in love with him; it was as simple and uncomplicated as that. When he asked her if she would go out with him she answered "Yes" without further ado. They had gone for a walk and then had had supper together. Later they had taken a boat out on the lake for an hour or so, talking of the weather and of their childhood and love in general.

Then they met Johannes Vierbein. He had been to see a film called *The Muzzle*. They all went off to Bismarckshöh together. And there they danced and drank beer, and Herbert Asch and Elizabeth Freitag talked a great deal of nonsense in order to hide the serious thoughts about each other which were running through their heads. They were both in excellent spirits.

Asch treated Elizabeth with a rough sort of tenderness. He was gauche and clumsy. But this didn't worry her. The important thing was that it came from him. She made no attempt to conceal her fondness for him. She held tightly on to his arm, and looked at him without a trace of shyness.

She danced again with Johannes Vierbein while Asch was away answering Kowalski's summons in the next room. Asch had told her that Vierbein was obviously hopelessly in love with his sister Ingrid, and Elizabeth had heard little good of her. She felt she had to be kind to Vierbein for Asch's sake.

The lieutenant in civilian clothes who was sitting at their table didn't worry her. She knew him slightly from the barracks and found him not unsympathetic. As he made no attempt to spoil their evening by talking shop, she didn't mind his staying there in the least.

Her attitude to Schulz was very different. Up to this moment she had had nothing particular against him. She had in fact had absolutely no feelings about him one way or the other. But now as he came up and stopped her and Vierbein in the middle of a dance, she turned strongly against him. And when he sent Vierbein back to barracks and on top of that actually dared to ask her to dance with him, she grew livid with rage. She flashed

58

her eyes furiously at him and left him standing in the middle of the floor.

She went back to the table where Wedelmann and Asch were sitting.

"What have you done with Vierbein?" Herbert asked her.

"He's been sent back to barracks," she said indignantly. "Just like that. By Sergeant Major Schulz. It's absolutely monstrous."

Lieutenant Wedelmann did his best to calm her down.

"There's nothing so terrible about that," he said. "Things like that happen every day."

"Unfortunately," said Asch.

"Oh, it's nothing to get worked up about." The lieutenant tried to brush the whole matter aside.

But Gunner Asch wouldn't let him do so.

"We can't dismiss it quite so easily," he said.

"It's a question of discipline," said the lieutenant.

"Of decency, rather."

Wedelmann looked up involuntarily. This, he thought, was going a bit too far. He remembered his rank, though it required an unpleasant effort to do so.

"Are you accusing the sergeant major of behaving in an underhand manner?"

"No, Lieutenant."

The answer came back promptly with the crispness of the parade ground. Asch decided not to discuss service matters with the lieutenant in civilian clothes any further. It just showed once again how completely pointless this sort of thing was bound to be. They could never forget their official positions. One always had to be on the lookout with them.

Gunner Asch rose to his feet, made Elizabeth a little bow, and asked her to dance. She got up immediately. They left the lieutenant sitting there alone.

Wedelmann felt slightly annoyed, but it was himself he was

59

annoyed with. And the more he thought about it all, the more annoyed he became. He felt that he had been in the wrong. Not so much in what he had said but in the manner in which he had said it. He should have avoided talking to the gunner in that almost domineering tone. After all he was not on duty. He was not even in uniform. And he was sitting at the same table with the man, had in fact been welcomed to it by him. In the circumstances there was an obligation on him to show a certain spirit of generosity.

Quite apart from this, he found that this time the sergeant major had taken the law into his own hands in a manner he could not possibly approve of, though he had to defend it for the sake of good discipline. Whatever grounds he might have had for acting as he had, the barracks rather than the dance floor was the proper place for dealing with the matter.

Undoubtedly Gunner Asch had a certain amount of right on his side. It wouldn't do him any harm, though, to give a little more thought to discipline. The sergeant major was his superior and it was no business of his to criticize him, whatever grounds he might have for doing so. That, Wedelmann told himself, was the business of an officer.

The lieutenant suddenly rose to his feet, and pushed his way through the throng of dancers into the large anteroom where the bar was. There he saw Sergeant Major Schulz installed at the landlord's table, obviously not in the best of moods. He beckoned him over to him.

The sergeant major came to attention in front of him and looked at him inquiringly.

"Listen," said the lieutenant, "it seems to me you've had rather too much to drink. It's about time you went home."

"Very good, sir," said the sergeant major, completely taken aback. His eyes blazed with fury. "Very good, Lieutenant."

Wedelmann turned on his heel and went back into the dance hall. He didn't feel at all satisfied with himself. He felt he had

60

acted in an almost cowardly manner. Certainly he had beaten the sergeant major at his own game, but it was just this that he found so painful. And, quite apart from that, he had to ask himself if it might not turn out to be rather dangerous.

He returned dejectedly to the table where Elizabeth Freitag and Herbert Asch had sat down again. He took several long pulls at his beer. Then he began to try and justify himself.

"You see, my dear Asch," he began, "the Werhmacht can only function properly if all orders, whatever they may be, are going to be obeyed promptly and unquestioningly."

"Even senseless orders?" asked Asch.

"Of course," said the lieutenant. But he was by no means convinced himself by what he said. To try to overcome his own doubts he went on emphatically: "There's no such thing as a senseless order. There are orders which may appear to be senseless to the person who receives them, but he can never be in a position to judge. You see, the whole principle of the thing is that superior officers should be able to give orders without having to explain them. Really, my dear Asch, wherever should we be if we had to give our reasons for issuing an order every time? Unquestioning obedience must be the first rule of all. Every order has got to be carried out!"

"And what if the order is merely a way of putting over a dirty trick on someone?"

"It must be carried out just the same." Wedelmann was now in his element. He felt as if he were giving a lecture on the subject and therefore simply had to be convincing in order not to appear ridiculous. "Orders are orders! And if there really is some dirty trick at the back of them — which may indeed be the case from time to time — the ordinary soldier always has the right to lodge a complaint — *after* carrying out the order, my dear Asch!"

"Have you ever known anyone to lodge a complaint, Lieutenant? Or even heard of anyone doing so?"

61

"No," admitted Wedelmann. But he added enthusiastically: "Why is that, though? It's not our fault. There are no complaints. Therefore, obviously, there is nothing to complain of."

Asch shook his head. "I see it rather differently, Lieutenant. But I don't want to create any more misunderstanding just at the moment."

Elizabeth thought it was high time this delicate conversation was brought to an end.

"Goodness me!" she said. "Whatever do we come here for? A dance hall doesn't seem to me the right place to talk shop. Or aren't any of you capable of talking about anything else?"

"Of course we are!" said the lieutenant with a smile.

"Thank God we are," said Asch. "Would you like to dance?"

"I'd love to."

"And I won't disturb you any further," said the lieutenant, rising to his feet. "I must get back to barracks." He turned to Elizabeth. His voice was resigned and sad: "It seems to me that you have realized instinctively something that we all forget too easily. And sometimes even have to forget. Have a good time."

⚑ ⚑ ⚑

The barracks never slept. At night it was like some huge restless animal which might open its eyes and spring out on people at any moment. There it lay: six blocks of stone with windows let into them, some of which were still illuminated. The lights shone not only in the barrack rooms where the soldiers who had come home — home? — were undressing, devouring last-minute snacks, swapping experiences and pouring what drink they had left into themselves. They also shone in the long corridors, in the rooms of the orderly N.C.O.s and in the guardroom. And over the main gate there hung a lamp beneath which a sentry inspected passes.

Gunner Vierbein made his way slowly up to the barracks. He

62

wondered whether he ought to be angry, angry because this lout of a sergeant major had turned him off the dance floor in the middle of a dance and sent him back to barracks. Then he wondered if he ought to be frightened, frightened just because the sergeant major had taken it into his head to do such a thing. But he found it impossible to reach a conclusion on either point. Today is Saturday, he thought, tomorrow is Sunday, and I don't have to be on duty again until the day after tomorrow. Who could tell what Monday might bring? It surprised him to find himself thinking in this way. He might have been Asch himself.

He saluted everyone he met, everyone he overtook, and everyone whom he saw just standing in the shadows. He didn't want to risk being pulled up again or having his name taken for "showing insufficient respect to a superior." A corporal whose stripes were only just discernible in the darkness was standing by a tree. Vierbein saluted smartly. The corporal did not return the salute. Probably he had never seen it, and even if he had he was in no position to return it. For he was wedged up against a girl and his hands were otherwise engaged.

Vierbein tried to pretend that he had seen nothing. He didn't want to let his thoughts wander in that direction. He forced himself to think of Ingrid, Ingrid whose photograph lay in the pocket of his tunic. Everything to do with her seemed pure and bright and clean. She was like the water and the sunshine, like the lake from which she was stepping in the picture, like the woods by which she was surrounded. Above her was the bright blue sky, and he found himself wishing that beneath this sky there were no one in the world but him and her.

"Come on, hurry up!" shouted the sentry at the gate. "You wretches keep on trickling up. You don't seem to care how late you are."

"Here's my pass," said Vierbein. "It's a Saturday night pass."

"All right, all right," said the sentry. "I can see it's a Satur-

63

day night pass. What do you want me to do about it? Be off with you."

Vierbein felt embarrassed.

"I want the corporal of the guard to put on it the time at which I came in," he said.

"Why?"

"I've been ordered back to barracks."

The sentry, a gunner first class, looked at him with pity. "Oh, bad luck," he said simply. "All right, come along."

The corporal of the guard was asleep in his chair. The sentry woke him up and Gunner Vierbein repeated his request. The corporal nodded, looked at the time, wrote it down on the pass, added his name and rank, then laid his head on the table and went off to sleep again almost at once.

Johannes Vierbein made his way towards No. 3 Troop's barrack block. He walked even more slowly than before. What sort of life is this, he thought; a superior gives you an order and you have to obey it. It doesn't matter what the order is. If you don't carry it out, you've refused to obey an order. And refusal to obey an order means a court-martial. Good, he had obeyed the order and, for the time being at least, had avoided a court-martial — for one could never tell what the future held in store. And here he was back in barracks.

Besides, he told himself, it was a good thing that he had left the dance. He should never have been there in the first place. He should have shown more respect to Ingrid. He should have gone straight back to barracks after leaving her at home. Ingrid was sleeping now: he had no right to be hanging around cafés and dance halls at such a time. And what was it his father had always said? "You never know what all that sort of thing's going to lead to." And he had been quite right. It was an excellent thing that Sergeant Major Schulz had turned him out of the dance hall.

What a night it was! The sky shone with stars. It was like

some softly illuminated canopy made of dark blue silk. The air too was soft and came gently towards him like the breath of a young girl. The main gate creaked on its hinges. He could hear the roaring of a couple of drunks. Some water rushed away down a nearby drain.

"Is that you, Herr Vierbein?" The voice spoke uncertainly. It came from an open window in the sergeant major's quarters.

Johannes was now standing in front of the entrance to the barrack block. He looked up. He could just make out the shape of a woman leaning out of a window. It was Lore Schulz, the sergeant major's wife.

"Good evening," said Johannes Vierbein.

He didn't know whether to go on or not. The woman's voice had sounded very friendly, and not only that, but cautious and rather anxious, as if all were not well with her.

"It's a lovely night," he said.

"Come a bit closer, if you've a moment to spare; a moment to spare for me, that is."

Vierbein, lost in thoughts of the night and a girl, of the touch of a young girl's breath, of girls in general in fact, found it impossible to refuse. He left the cement path which led up to the entrance to the block and stepped onto the strip of turf which ran round the building. He looked up to the window on the ground floor out of which Lore was leaning.

Lore was trembling. She longed for a little tenderness. On a night such as this tenderness meant a voice she liked the sound of, someone who would look up at her, a physical presence which she could take in with every breath. And she was breathing in deeply all the time.

"Have you been to the dance?" she asked. "Have you been out with your girl?"

"Oh no," said Johannes.

"I believe you," said Lore. She was glad to have found someone to talk to. "Otherwise you wouldn't have come back so soon. Or haven't you got a girl at all?"

Lore Schulz was not offended when Vierbein didn't answer her question. She even found his silence a good answer. She gave a little laugh. And she was astonished to hear herself laugh. I can still laugh, she said to herself, though I've got no reason to. I haven't the slightest reason to be happy.

Schulz, her husband, had simply locked her up. She had tried drinking but it had been no good. Then she had listened to the radio but it was a boring program and every station was broadcasting the same one. Then she tried to write the letter home which she should have written weeks ago. But she could get no further than: *My dearest Mother and Father — Everything here is fine, as always. . . .* She had scrunched up the letter and thrown it into the waste-paper basket. Then she had burned it. She had stood by the open window for a long time, with the light out. Her eyes had gradually become accustomed to the darkness.

She waited. She could not have said what she was waiting for. Soldiers whom she didn't know made their way into the barrack block. Some of them were drunk, most of them were only very tired. About midnight she saw Corporal Lindenberg walking very smartly across the square in the direction of the guardroom, presumably with the Saturday night pass book. Shortly afterwards he came back again, carrying himself erect as ever. The next person she saw was Gunner Vierbein and she recognized him at once.

"Give me your hand," she said. And it was as if she were drowning in a sea of sorrow and reaching out desperately for some support to cling to. Besides, she was in a sentimental mood. The sound of violins would have been enough to bring tears to her eyes; the touch of a living person would have sent a shudder of joy through her. If she looked too long at the moon, her eyes tended to grow misty.

66

"Give me your hand," she said.

Without hesitation, without considering for a moment what he was doing, Johannes Vierbein stretched up his hand and felt her take it.

Lore Schulz leaned out towards him. She held on to him with both hands. And it was as if she were indeed clinging to a life belt. Tenderly she ran her hands over the young man's fingers. Then she said: "How young you are!" And her voice sounded shy, almost frightened. It was full of regret and underlying the regret was a sense of helplessness.

Vierbein sensed at once that the creature who was holding his hand was in a desperate state. It seemed to him that emotional patterns of sadness and longing, of misunderstanding and loneliness and self-pity were being woven in the air before him and he hadn't the strength to put his fist through them all and destroy the lot. He felt a sudden tenderness for Lore as if she had been a sister. He had always wanted a sister. But he had always been alone. Always alone.

These two creatures, lost now with their desires in the soft darkness of the night, were quite oblivious of the large stocky figure who was approaching them. The figure let out a great roar:

"What the hell's going on here! This is something quite new!"

It was Sergeant Major Schulz.

His powerful voice rang out into the night, echoed back from the walls of the barrack block and seemed to strike the stars. It was a voice which seemed able to fill the whole world without the slightest difficulty. It was thick with beer and harsh with anger.

"You little worm!" yelled the sergeant major at Vierbein. "Get out of here. I'll deal with you later."

Vierbein saluted as best he could and disappeared at full speed into the barrack block. In the sinister silence that followed he could be heard scurrying up the stairs as if the devil himself were after him.

Sergeant Major Schulz listened to the sound of the retreating footsteps. It was impossible to see his face. He was leaning forward and his powerful shoulders were slightly hunched. He pulled himself up smartly at the sound of someone behind him.

It was Lieutenant Wedelmann.

"Don't make a noise like that at this time of the night, Sergeant Major," he said as he went by.

"Sorry, sir," roared the sergeant major, saluting much against his will. He could hardly contain himself. He was boiling with rage. He was fit to burst. The dirty . . . the . . . But he preferred to keep his resentment to himself and not to give expression to that thought which was never very far from the surface of his mind: These bloody officers! They didn't understand a thing about army life and were always sticking their filthy noses into things that didn't concern them. This one particularly.

Even now the sergeant major found himself reluctant to face up to the full implications of his feelings. But it was not the first time his thoughts had wandered in this direction. They were always doing so though he took good care to hide the fact. He was convinced that his reactions were entirely justified. It was made clearer and clearer to him every day. He and his N.C.O.s did all the work. The officers merely supervised their efforts. And they nearly always had to admit that there was no need for such supervision because everything was in order. Everything was in order because he, the sergeant major, and his fellow N.C.O.s had seen to it that it was. Then why, he asked himself, were these lazy good-for-nothing officers always poking their noses into things? Merely to try to justify their own existence.

The sergeant major had never properly realized what this Lieutenant Wedelmann was up to before. God knows why!

But it was clear enough after this evening. He was sucking up to the rank and file behind the backs of the N.C.O.s! He put on civilian clothes and went and sat about with them in bars and cafés, making up to their girls and showing in an unmistakable manner his contempt for the whole principle of authority. It was a shameless assault on the whole structure of military discipline. That was the type of officer they were getting these days! Sergeant Major Schulz stared contemptuously into the darkness after the lieutenant. When I become an officer, he said to himself, there won't be any of that sort of thing!

But he was a man who was too full of his own self-importance to be put out by such a thing for long. He looked up to the windows of his quarters. The light was still on there. He was overwhelmed by a deep sense of personal bitterness. Lore was a real burden to him. She had not proved worthy of him. He had picked her up literally out of the gutter, made her his wife, given her a home of her own — and this was how she paid him back. He had made her the wife of a troop sergeant major. A troop sergeant major's wife! Wife of a man with twenty-two N.C.O.s and a hundred and thirty men directly under him, prepared to obey his slightest whim. Wife of a man whom several hundred thousand men all over Germany had to salute.

But none of this meant anything to Lore. He had often explained to her in great detail just how important her position was, but she had never seemed to appreciate it properly or else had simply forgotten about it. Yes, she was unworthy of him. And it was therefore his duty to treat her accordingly. It was regrettable but there was no alternative.

Slowly he fumbled for the keys in his trousers pocket. Carefully he selected the key which fitted the door of his lodgings. He busied himself first with the main lock and then with the special security lock. All this took up a certain amount of time and gave him a chance to pursue his thoughts a little further.

The root of the whole trouble, he said to himself, was that his wife Lore had absolutely no respect for his rank. She ought to have been proud of him. And her pride in him would have given her a certain self-respect. And if you had self-respect you had everything. But she was mean and miserable and under-hand, and not only that — she was shameless. Utterly shame-less!

There was, it might be said, something almost fitting about her attempt to betray him with Sergeant Werktreu. Werktreu was at least close to him in rank. The whole incident had some-thing in common with the anecdote about the commanding officer's wife and the lieutenant of No. 2 Troop being caught together behind a hedge after an officers' mess party. Some-thing to wink and snigger about.

But what he had just caught Lore at was quite unpardon-able. Unpardonable! She was giving herself to a man who held the lowest possible rank in the Wehrmacht. To a simple gun-ner! And what was more, a gunner of his own troop, and a particularly sloppy, weedy, unsoldierly specimen of a gunner at that.

By God, it made him furious.

And he determined to give his wife a thorough hiding. That would knock a bit of sense into her. For a day or two at least.

🏴 🏴 🏴

The mornings seemed to hover over the barracks as if on the alert for signs of activity. They never looked in vain. Only on Sundays were the everyday noises more subdued, and they started up a couple of hours later than usual.

Lindenberg, orderly N.C.O. of No. 3 Troop, was the first to rise. His alarm clock went off at five to seven. Reveille was at eight. Lindenberg knew how slack the other N.C.O.s were. He disapproved of the way they went on; it was prejudicial to discipline. About eight o'clock on Sundays they would begin shouting round the block, and that would pass as reveille. Then they would immediately get back to bed again. Their motto for Sundays was: Leave well alone! About ten o'clock they would instigate a hasty clean-up of the billets. And that was all.

Not so Corporal Lindenberg. He kept rigidly to the time-table as laid down in the routine schedule. And everyone knew that he did. Indeed he would anticipate the schedule by beginning to get people up twenty minutes before the official hour, so that he could always be certain of having the whole operation completed on time. And this habit of his also was well known. The troops took Corporal Lindenberg for granted as a natural phenomenon like rain or wind. The corporal knew this and the knowledge filled him with secret pride, though he took good care not to betray the fact.

Lindenberg made a point of considering himself on parade at all times. Those who were ill-disposed towards him maintained that he even slept at attention, and that even his bearing in the lavatory was always strictly military. Certainly he only required a very few seconds in which to be ready for duty. His alarm clock had not stopped ringing before he was out of bed and doing his morning exercises in the middle of the room. As he completed them he remembered his decision to pay special attention to Gunner Vierbein. It had been Vierbein who had been responsible for Asch giving him certain wrong information. And it had been this wrong information which in turn had led to a reprimand for himself from Sergeant Major Schulz, an otherwise almost unheard-of event.

Lindenberg put on shorts, a running vest, and running shoes and trotted off down the deserted corridor into the open air. He set off in a determined jog trot for the sports ground. Once there he increased his pace and completed three circuits of the track, which as he knew worked out at approximately six kilo-

71

meters. He pulled his shirt off as he ran and noted with satisfaction that his torso was glistening with sweat. He was in excellent shape, and glad to know it.

He then went off and had a cold shower. The water poured down over him and his flesh seemed to steam a little. He then shaved very carefully, brushed his teeth, and measured out exactly seven drops of hair oil on his hair, which immediately took on a glossy finish. He reached out for his boots, which he had polished the night before. Punctually, by twenty minutes to eight, he was ready.

Before he set out on his round of duty he cast one last glance in the large mirror fitted up near the door. He smoothed out a crease which his belt had made in his uniform. Then he gave his cap a very slight tilt to the right. The figure before him in the glass was superior to any of the illustrations in *Reibert,* the service handbook.

The first room he went into was that of his own section. It included Gunner Vierbein. He pushed the door open, gave a short shrill blast on his whistle and rapped out sharply: "Rise and shine!" The men leaped out of bed. They were headed by Gunner Vierbein. Lindenberg made a mental note of the fact. It gave him a certain satisfaction. He stood in the doorway, fresh and alert, looking the exhausted figures up and down for a moment as they turned out cursing beneath their breath. Then he shouted: "See to your bedding!" and slammed the door behind him.

He repeated this procedure eighteen times — eighteen times! — with faultless precision. Punctually by eight o'clock every man in the troop was out of bed.

At ten past eight he began his second round, after spending approximately nine minutes of no particular interest in the lavatory.

He again visited all the rooms and made certain that everyone was up and busy making his bed. The next stage for the men was a thorough wash to obliterate all traces of the previous night.

He detailed one man for cleaning in each room, except in his own section's room where he detailed two. Not just any two. He named them individually: Gunner Asch and Gunner Vierbein. Regretfully, but without any outward show of annoyance to mar the correctness of his attitude, he noted that Gunner Asch, being in possession of a Saturday night pass and having relatives in the town, to wit his parents, had not returned to barracks for the night. "In that case, just Vierbein," said the corporal firmly.

Lindenberg was an extremely industrious man. He loved those Sundays on which he took the early turn as orderly N.C.O. There was no one to interfere with him. The entire block was his for him to do what he liked with. He had a free hand to exploit the regulations to the full.

He planted himself with legs astride in the middle of the corridor, blew his whistle and snapped out the orders: "Coffee carriers forward! Those detailed for billet-cleaning forward!"

Gunner Vierbein could clean out the ground-floor latrine all by himself.

Lindenberg worked strictly according to the plan which he had drawn up in his mind the evening before. It went something like this: Ground floor: one man for the latrine, one for the orderly N.C.O.'s room, one for the washroom, one for the shower room, two for the corridor, including the windows. The same thing on the first and second floors. In addition there were the staircase, the basement, the attic and the outbuildings to be seen to.

When Corporal Lindenberg was on duty, the men's work on Sundays and holidays usually lasted until ten o'clock. On this Sunday it was almost eleven before Vierbein was finished. However hard he worked, the corporal always seemed able to find something which needed further attention.

In the meantime it turned out that a man had gone sick. There could be no question of his shamming, although it certainly looked suspicious on the face of it, for he was a gunner who had been detailed for guard duty that evening. But Corporal Lindenberg gave him a thorough going over before he was eventually sent off to sick quarters. There at first they gave him an aspirin. It was not until late that afternoon that he was removed to the local hospital with acute appendicitis.

However that might be, it now became necessary to bring the guard up to strength for the evening. At about ten o'clock therefore Corporal Lindenberg rang the bell of the troop sergeant major's quarters. The sergeant major, still tired from his exertions of the night before — for he had first given his wife a severe thrashing and had then felt obliged to show her that he had no intention of allowing their conjugal bond to lapse — the sergeant major now looked yawning out of the window.

"I beg to report to the sergeant major," called out Corporal Lindenberg, correct as ever, "that one of the men detailed for guard duty this evening has gone sick. We need a replacement."

The sergeant major's eyes were puffy with sleep. He yawned again and looked the corporal up and down unpleasantly. But Lindenberg stood there, rigidly correct, without moving a muscle.

"Take Gunner Vierbein," said Sergeant Major Schulz.

"Gunner Vierbein. Very good, Sergeant Major."

And he didn't for one moment let it be seen how much he approved of the sergeant major's choice.

☙ ☙ ☙

Johannes Vierbein received the order to go on guard that evening with a certain feeling of relief. He had known that some sort of punishment was coming to him. He wasn't exactly

74

clear what the punishment was for, but he had known that it was coming.

Guard duty, he told himself, was by no means the worst thing that could have happened to him. Two hours on sentry duty, two hours in the guardroom, two hours' sleep. For twenty-four hours at a stretch. The most rigid regulations governed guard duty; it was almost impossible for an N.C.O. to push the guard around in any way. It was the best protected form of duty there was.

The only drawback was that he wouldn't be able to see Ingrid. He had a date with her for five o'clock. But the guard had to parade in front of the barrack block at half-past five. The old guard had to be relieved punctually at six. He decided to ask Asch to apologize to his sister for him the next day. He couldn't help it. He had his duty to do. Ingrid, he felt sure, would understand.

He made up three hours' worth of sleep in advance in the course of the afternoon. At about four o'clock he began to get himself ready. Carefully he brushed his best uniform, polished up his belt, ammunition pouches and boots, and cleaned his rifle. By five o'clock he was ready.

The N.C.O. in charge of the guard that evening was Corporal Schwitzke, generally known as "Slacker" Schwitzke, on account of his marked tendency to take his time about everything the army wanted him to do. No one could ever think how he had managed to become a corporal. Everyone was certain that he would never become a sergeant. His motto was: A quiet life and a long one.

However, Schwitzke was only in favor of a quiet life for himself. What made such a quiet life possible was the systematic and if necessary ceaseless activity of others. Schwitzke was not a shouter. He gave his orders calmly. He had a thorough understanding of how to comply with regulations with the minimum amount of fuss. He sized up a situation and took all the

75

necessary steps to deal with it. He never did more than he absolutely had to. At the same time he was a past master of the art of seeming to be busy. When reading one of his favorite detective stories — yellow paperbacked editions which appeared in serial form at thirty pfennigs a time — he always took good care to place them inside the covers of the guard book, and to hold a fountain pen ready poised in one hand.

In addition Schwitzke possessed an almost miraculous intuition about human beings. He knew at once how to pick out the one man under his command who would make the least fuss about doing anything. It goes without saying that in the present case this man's name was Vierbein.

Gunner Johannes Vierbein performed all the tasks that were demanded of him without a murmur. He fetched fruit juice for the corporal from the canteen, swept out the guardroom, and always had a match ready when Schwitzke needed a light for his cigarette. The astonishing thing about life in the guardroom under Schwitzke was that there was no bullying, no shouting, no swearing. The place was practically a convalescent home.

The best time for Vierbein was when he was out on sentry duty. Quietly he made his rounds: along the barrack wall, past the gun sheds, and across the sports ground. He tested the padlocks on the ammunition dumps and the seals on the water hydrants. There was no need to fear a snap inspection. For some weeks now the duty officer had been making a habit of giving warning of his approach. Lance Corporal Kowalski was the man they all had to thank for this. One night he had fired at the officer on his rounds before he could manage to stammer out the password.

Vierbein, alone with his thoughts and his rifle on his shoulder — a bullet up the spout, safety catch on — felt himself to be a real soldier. He was on guard while the others slept. His comrades were in their beds, the guns were in their sheds, the

76

ammunition was safely stored — and he stood on guard over the lot. And if a spy or a saboteur should come, he would shoot on sight, with live ammunition, to preserve the great secret with which he had been entrusted. He had got five rounds in his rifle altogether and fifteen more in his ammunition pouches. He would do his duty. The Fatherland could sleep in peace.

And as he marched up and down in the bright moonlight, calm, sure of himself, making a good deal of noise, with his boots scrunching on the concrete and the barrel of his rifle clanging in warlike manner against the side of his steel helmet, he found his thoughts beginning to wander. Why, he asked himself, why was it always he — who was so conscientious — who became the butt of the N.C.O.s? He put all he knew into his work. He did everything that was required of him, and even more. He was always keen and ready for anything, always volunteering. He never grumbled. But he got no credit for this at all. On the contrary unpleasantness pursued him wherever he went. If anyone was picked on it was always he. Others might shirk duty for hours on end and get away with it, but he had only to slack off for a few seconds and every N.C.O. within a hundred yards spotted him.

However, as there was nothing he could do about any of this, he decided that it was useless to worry about it. He went over to the rear gate and tested the lock. He wandered along the fence. Barbed wire which had only recently been renewed there shone brightly in the moonlight. He thought of his parents and how proud they would be if they could see him. And then he started thinking about Ingrid and wondered what she would be doing at this moment. It seemed almost certain that she would be in bed. He began to form a picture of her there, but preferred not to pursue the matter too closely.

Some hours later he was on duty at the main gate. He spent his time walking backwards and forwards between it and the guardroom — twelve yards in each direction — whenever any-

77

one appeared asking for admittance. He collected Sunday passes from the men and saluted the N.C.O.s. And sometimes he would pause at the open gate in the lamplight, take two or three steps out into the street and look down towards Bismarckshöh, from which the last of the stragglers were making their way back to barracks.

Gradually, very gradually day began to dawn. A dull leaden light appeared on the horizon. Ground mist seemed to be forming.

Sergeant Platzek, Bully Platzek, came staggering up to the gate. He was drunk and therefore in excellent spirits.

"Open the gate there, you little swine!" he yelled. "If I don't manage to get through, it's your fault, see?"

"Very good, Sergeant," answered Gunner Vierbein mechanically.

Bully Platzek held on to the gate.

"One of us two is tight!" he said. "See? Well, which one of us is it?"

Vierbein saluted again and avoided giving an answer.

"One of us two is stinking," persisted Platzek. "Now, come on, man, worm, louse — tell me. Am I stinking?"

Verbein knew perfecty well he couldn't say: "Yes, Sergeant, you're absolutely stinking!" He knew what Platzek wanted him to say. And so he said: "No, Sergeant."

Bully Platzek fixed Gunner Vierbein with his beady little eyes and leaned against the gatepost panting for breath.

"Good," he said thickly. "I'm not drunk. But one of us is. So it must be you, see?"

"Yes, Sergeant!"

"You ought to be ashamed of yourself!" said Platzek. "Drunk on guard!" He staggered on a few yards, stopped and looked round. "I shall report the matter," he announced with difficulty. Then he lurched off in a series of great curves in the direction of the barrack buildings.

It never occurred to Vierbein to laugh. He watched the sergeant go and shrugged his shoulders. Obviously this was some sort of barrack joke, and he must admit he didn't quite see it. He was about to shut the gate and return to the guard-room when he heard a voice that he recognized.

"Vierbein!" it called softly. "Is the coast clear?"

Vierbein recognized Gunner Asch's voice at once. He stepped out of the gate, screwed up his eyes and stared into the darkness on the other side of the road where the voice seemed to be coming from.

"What's the matter?" he asked. "Where are you?"

"Is there anyone about?" asked Asch.

"No," said Vierbein, who had no idea what was going on.

"Good," said Asch. "Then open the gate. I'm coming across."

And the figure of Gunner Asch appeared out of the darkness and came towards him. Vierbein saw with horror that Asch was wearing nothing but a shirt.

There could be no doubt about it. Gunner Asch walked in at the main gate, past the astonished Vierbein, clad only in his shirt. And as if it were the most natural thing in the world.

To Vierbein it seemed the end of everything. He imagined the most appalling complications.

"But you can't do that," he stammered. "I'll have to report you. You'll get me court-martialed."

"Hold your trap!" said Asch, stepping briskly past him. "Look the other way. Leave everything to me. I'll tell you how it happened in the morning."

Gunner Vierbein shut the gate with trembling hands. If only it all passed off all right. This was all he could think of. He listened anxiously, peering into the darkness which had swallowed up the figure of Gunner Asch in his shirttails.

At first all was quiet, ominously quiet. Then a great shout of triumph rang out.

"Now then, what's this!" cried Platzek with all the excitement of a drunken man. Presumably he had felt bad, had leaned against a wall to be sick and was just pulling himself together again when he caught sight of a man in his shirttails. "I don't believe it! The man's in nothing but his shirt! Where have you been, Asch? Where the hell have you been?"

As Vierbein heard the words he went hot and cold all over. He clenched the key of the main gate in his right hand and his palm was wet with sweat. He already saw himself being court-martialed, sentenced, lying in prison. For what had just happened could only be construed as negligence at his post.

Then he heard the calm self-confident voice of Gunner Asch in the darkness, that reassuring voice which always sounded as if it were thinking of some tremendous secret joke of its own.

Asch said: "I beg to inform the sergeant that I've been sleepwalking."

Bully Platzek seemed bowled over by this answer.

"You don't say!" he cried. "You must tell me about that, Asch."

"Certainly, Sergeant," said Gunner Asch.

And the two of them disappeared together. Verbein could hear no more. Only once there was a great roar of laughter which obviously came from Platzek. Then all was still.

Gunner Vierbein found himself paralyzed with fear. If only he gets away with it, he thought. If only nothing comes of this!

☛ ☛ ☛

Gunner Asch had been fully determined to behave honorably with Elizabeth. He loved her more than he did himself, and he wanted his love to last. He wanted to save it up for better, happier, freer times. The extent of his love for her almost frightened him. He wanted there to be room for it to blossom fully.

On this gentle summer evening they had held hands as they lay together on the grass and looked up at the sky. He imagined the two of them taking over the Café Asch. His father, freed of the responsibility of it all, would merely wander through the rooms occasionally, greeting the bigwigs of whatever political party happened to be in power at the time. Somewhere a couple of children would be playing happily. And if he, Herbert, were feeling in a particularly good mood he would tell stories of his two years' service with the Wehrmacht and of the extraordinarily funny things that had happened in it.

"What are you thinking about?" asked Elizabeth, looking at him. "What are you so happy about?"

"I'm thinking," he said, "about the children who won't ever have to wear uniform."

Elizabeth looked at him doubtfully.

"Do you really believe that?"

Herbert Asch pulled up a blade of grass and stuck it between his lips.

"I'm certain of it," he answered. "Either we'll have conquered the world, in which case we won't need an army any more, or else the world will have conquered us, in which case we still won't need an army."

Elizabeth stretched herself full length and shook her head.

"I'm not so sure," she said thoughtfully. "That's probably just what my father was saying in 1913 when he was a young man."

"But that," said Herbert, turning over onto his stomach, "that was before the great catastrophe. We're cleverer now, we've learned from experience. We wage cold wars these days."

Elizabeth laughed in spite of herself.

"Well, that certainly ought to suit you," she said. "You're not exactly the most ardent soldier I ever met."

Herbert Asch bit his lip.

81

"I'll soon show you whether I'm ardent or not," he said and he kissed her on the lips.

Elizabeth stopped laughing. Her hands felt for his shoulders. She felt the warmth of his body. She lost all will of her own. She lay quite still and calm, as if she had given herself to him.

"Elizabeth," said Herbert, and his hand slipped down to her hips.

She tore herself away from him, and jumped to her feet.

"I'm sorry," said Herbert, and got to his feet as well.

She laughed again.

"Come on," she said. "I must be getting home."

And she took hold of his arm as if it were a perfectly natural thing to do.

"We mustn't do anything foolish," she said.

"No, Elizabeth."

"There'll be time enough for that," she said, "later on."

"Yes, Elizabeth."

As they walked along together he gently took his arm from hers and put it round her shoulders. She not only didn't object to this but leaned in towards him. It made walking uncomfortable and they looked terribly silly, but it was what they wanted to do. For they loved each other.

Asch took a circuitous route so as to avoid meeting N.C.O.s and officers. He was on the lookout for them all the time as his hand stole round under her arm and began to feel for her firm little breast.

For a long time they wandered on through the night, pressed close up against each other. They hardly spoke but it was as if they were saying all manner of things to each other without having to speak. There was only one thought in both their heads: yesterday had been Saturday, they had been to the dance together, and they had kissed on the way home and called each other *du* and it had all seemed completely natural. And today had been Sunday and they had spent it together as

82

if they had known each other for years; the whole day had passed so quickly, this wonderful Sunday so full of talk and aimless little walks and passionate kisses from which they drew back in alarm — even though it did all seem completely natural.

"You must go now," she said.

"Yes, Elizabeth."

They were standing under a lime tree about forty yards from the Freitags' house, and they were locked in each other's arms.

"I can't go yet." His voice sounded almost desperate.

Her hands wandered over the coarse stuff of his uniform. Her body seemed to be on fire, but she didn't let go of him.

"Elizabeth," he said, and his lips brushed the side of her neck. "Elizabeth."

"Come on," she said. She took his hand and led him into the house. They walked through the darkness as if in a dream.

Elizabeth led the way. She unlocked the door and took him into her room. Softly the door closed behind them. They were together in her room.

"Elizabeth," he said, "I love you."

"Take off your uniform," she said softly.

They were lost in each other's arms and the moon looked down upon them. The moon fell placidly on the light-colored furniture of the room. It seemed to be holding its breath with excitement.

They lay side by side, exhausted, smiling happily. Tenderly they ran the tips of their fingers over each other's bodies. They were glutted with happiness, at peace with themselves and the world. Even soldiers have time for this moment in their love affairs, the moment in which the world stands still. A soldier's world, however, turns more quickly than other people's.

She slept and he lay there awake, thinking first of her and then of the fact that he must be back in barracks on time.

Just at present, though, he had a more urgent need.

Carefully Herbert Asch got out of bed, pulled on his shirt, and whispered to Elizabeth, who had stirred in her sleep:

"I'm coming back, darling."

"All right," she answered automatically. She was so tired that she hardly realized what he had said.

Barefoot and wearing nothing but his shirt, Asch tiptoed out into the front room. He found himself in a quandary. He thought he couldn't very well go round trying all the doors. There was no knowing who he might run into. He thought it better to go outside the front door.

He opened this with the greatest care and stepped outside. And the door fell to quietly behind him.

He didn't notice this until he was ready to go in again. He saw to his dismay that the door had an automatic lock on it and couldn't be opened from the outside without a key. A sound piece of craftsmanship on the part of old Freitag, who was not a first-rate mechanic for nothing.

It was some seconds before the full significance of this dawned on him.

He examined the situation with typical military thoroughness. He couldn't get back into the house without having to ring or knock. Elizabeth was obviously still asleep, and it might be some time before she missed him and came to look for him. He must avoid making a noise at all costs. He must do nothing which would compromise Elizabeth — his Elizabeth.

There was only one thing for it — to get back to barracks just as he was. For Elizabeth's sake. And who could tell? Perhaps he would be lucky enough to get in without meeting any trouble at all. If he were really lucky he would find Vierbein on guard.

A number of subsidiary considerations prompted his decision to return at once in this state. In the first place it was beginning to get rather cold. Then, the first signs of the new day were already beginning to appear as a streak of silver on the horizon. Finally, he could hear a voice in the Freitag house. So off he went.

The voice he had heard was that of Foreman Freitag himself. He had been waked up by the sound of the door shutting. It seemed to him that he had already heard the door shut once before that night, about an hour ago. He knocked on the door of Elizabeth's room.

"Are you there?" he called.

"Yes," said Elizabeth. She was terrified.

"Have you only just come in?"

"No. Some time ago. I was asleep."

"Then sleep on, dear child," said Freitag in a fatherly tone. But he said to himself: "It's funny, I could have sworn . . ." And he went upstairs to his room and lay down again. But it was quite a time before he could get to sleep again, for he had an uneasy feeling that something had occurred to give him something to think about.

All this time Elizabeth sat on the bed, listening to the sound of her own heartbeats. She couldn't quite make out what was happening and had no idea what was going to happen next. She felt exhausted and anxious. Then she saw various articles of Gunner Asch's clothing and equipment scattered about the floor of her room: underpants, socks, trousers, tunic, boots, belt and cap. Only his shirt was missing. And her father had heard the door shut.

Finally she put her mind to the problem. She thought of everything that could have happened. She thought of Herbert waiting outside in the cold without any clothes on. She imagined her father coming back again and finding his uniform in the room. That couldn't be allowed to happen under any circumstances. So she piled all the things together into a bundle and carried them outside. She quickly put them down just beside the front door.

And here, by the front door, they were found the next morning by Foreman Freitag as he left the house on his way to work. He stood there staring in astonishment at his extraordinary find. He seemed to spend a long time thinking the matter over. Then he collected all the things together, carried them back into the house and put them on the kitchen table, where his wife and daughter were at that moment having breakfast.

He didn't look at either of them. He merely said:

"One of the soldiers must have lost these. It's rather peculiar but it's the sort of thing that happens. I think we'd better not make too much fuss about it. We'll just return them."

¥ ¥ ¥

Singing puts heart into a man, develops his lungs and gives him a thirst. In the army singing also serves to make marching more tolerable and prevent the men from talking.

"Let us thankful be!" sang twenty powerful voices on the first floor of the No. 3 Troop barrack block.

It was just after five o'clock on Monday morning, and Troop Sergeant Bully Platzek's birthday was being celebrated by his brother N.C.O.s in suitable fashion. Sergeant Werktreu stood on a stool conducting. The N.C.O.s, with the Chief himself in the center, stood in a semicircle round the king of the clothing store and sang with him.

They had quickly thrown on any old clothes. Several of them were still wearing their nightshirts stuffed into a pair of shorts. Tufts of hair stuck up on end. Enormous feet had been pushed hurriedly into slippers and gym shoes. Only Corporal Lindenberg was properly dressed in regulation sports kit. They all stared at the birthday boy's door, and sang at the top of their voices with unmistakable emotion.

Slowly the door opened, and Sergeant Platzek, who could hardly see out of his eyes after the excesses of the night before, beamed at them in manly pleasure. He opened the door still further and there for all to see on the table in the middle of the little room stood two crates of beer and four bottles of schnapps.

"Let us thankful be!" sang the N.C.O.s.

And as they brought the chorus to a close with a joyful flourish, Schulz went up to Sergeant Platzek and said:

"My dear Platzek, many happy returns of the day. And now tell us, what is your favorite song?"

" 'On the Lüneburger Heide,' " answered Platzek without a moment's hesitation. He had known he would be asked this question and had got the answer ready. He wasn't very fond of singing himself and was always out of tune. But he knew that "On the Lüneburger Heide" was Sergeant Major Schulz's own favorite.

"One, two, three," roared Schulz and burst into song. The other voices immediately joined in. And while they sang their way through verse after verse of this merry anthem, each N.C.O. came up in turn, in order of precedence, to shake the birthday boy by the hand and receive a bottle of beer.

The little room was absolutely packed. Schulz, Platzek and Werktreu sat on the bed; other sergeants had taken their places on the desk or on the two chairs. The junior N.C.O.s had thoughtfully brought stools with them. Soon they were all smoking and drinking to their hearts' content. There was an overpowering smell of beer, schnapps, smoke and sweat.

The Chief, as always, felt himself to be the central figure. The idea of greeting people on their birthdays like this had been his in the first place. One of his clerks kept a special list for the purpose. Three days before the actual event both the man whose birthday it was and those who were to celebrate it with him were warned so that the necessary preparations might be made. The ceremony began long before reveille with a birthday chorale — always the same one. Then the Chief took advantage of the atmosphere of solidarity and good-fellowship produced by so much alcohol on empty stomachs to deliver a sort of pep talk.

"As far as artillery drill goes," he told his listeners, "we're the best troop in the whole regiment. It's largely Platzek we've got to thank for that. Spit and polish! Ah, that's the stuff! No, no one can touch us for drill. Major Luschke, Lumpface himself, was saying that to me only the other day. And if Major Luschke says a thing like that, then it really means something. We can feel proud of ourselves. But general discipline is another matter. It's lousy. There are one or two people in the troop who are mucking everything up for us. Mucking everything up. Vierbein for example."

A number of the N.C.O.s heartily agreed. Others, centered round Werktreu, seemed to be more interested in singing, probably in order not to have to make conversation. Schulz was determined to rally the N.C.O.s round him.

"This man Vierbein," he said, "is a little runt. Isn't he in your section, Lindenberg?"

"Yes, Sergeant Major," said the corporal, smart and keen as ever.

"Well, Lindenberg?"

"Yes, Sergeant Major, Gunner Vierbein is a little runt. My whole section consists of little runts."

Before Sergeant Major Schulz could manage to neutralize the effect of this last sentence, which rather spoiled his thesis, Sergeant Platzek joined in with a loud "Hear, hear!"

"Nothing but rotten little runts in Lindenberg's section," he went on. "It really is a section and a half. Why, only last night I ran into one of them wandering about dressed in nothing but his shirt. A sleepwalker!"

Several people pretended to find this very amusing and roared with laughter. Others just went on drinking.

"Who'd have thought it?" someone said.

88

Corporal Lindenberg sat very erect on the stool which he had brought with him.

"Might I ask the troop sergeant which of the members of my section it was?"

"It was that oaf Gunner Asch.

"Is the sergeant quite sure he didn't make a mistake?" asked Lindenberg in astonishment. He simply couldn't believe it. He knew Asch. He was a thoroughly normal, healthy soldier. Surely it was impossible that Asch of all people . . .

"Just a minute!" Platzek was getting angry. He drew himself up and looked at the corporal from behind lowered lids. "What exactly are you getting at? Are you trying to make out that I was tight?"

"Of course he isn't," said Werktreu, trying to patch things up. "I was pretty surprised myself when you said it was Asch. You must see it is rather astonishing. This fellow Asch has never sleepwalked in his life."

"Oh yes, he has," said Platzek stubbornly.

The sergeant major was anxious to avoid any unpleasantness, in addition to which he wanted to get back to his point. "Well, let's not argue about that," he said. "Let's get back to that little squirt Vierbein. On Saturday he procured a late pass for himself under false pretenses. The bastard said he wanted to go to the handball match, but there wasn't a handball match being played that day. Isn't that so, Lindenberg?"

"That is so, Sergeant Major."

"What is more," went on the sergeant major like some public prosecutor, "the little worm must have left the barracks on Saturday afternoon by an unauthorized means."

"He went over the fence?"

"No! In broad daylight?"

"But how did he manage it?"

"For some time now," went on the sergeant major, and he sounded very convincing, "I have been of the opinion that this

89

fellow Vierbein constituted a threat to discipline. There's only one thing for it. We must give him the treatment."

"Up to now," remarked Corporal Lindenberg boldly, "there's been nothing against him. He hasn't been a good soldier, but he hasn't been a bad one. He's always done his best and shown himself keen."

"And just what do you mean by that?" asked the sergeant major, drawing himself up with an air of great astonishment. "Are you doubting my word, Lindenberg?"

"No, Sergeant Major."

"I should hope not," said Schulz, looking for support to the sycophantic faces all around him. "And in order, Lindenberg, that you may have plenty of time in which to consider just why you allowed a lousy little gunner to make a fool of you on Saturday afternoon, you can take over early P.T. this morning."

"Very good, Sergeant Major."

"And after that you can supervise billet-cleaning."

"Very good, Sergeant Major."

It had been necessary to do that, Schulz told himself. It was always necessary to put a subordinate in his place when he showed signs of getting above himself. There must be discipline at all times even when a party was in progress. Particularly when a party was in progress. It was all too easy for people to take advantage of the atmosphere of good-fellowship created by a few bottles of beer and go too far. But Schulz wasn't having any of that.

The sergeant major watched his N.C.O.s carefully for their reactions, and he saw that once again he had scored a bull's-eye. Wherever he looked he found approval. It was because he had a sense of tactics. He had picked on the right man. He could always deal with someone like this easily enough, for Lindenberg was not particularly popular and was thought to be too full of himself. An unsympathetic fellow! If he were to have his way, life for the Chief and the other N.C.O.s would be twice as tough as for the recruits themselves. They weren't having any of that!

"We must put on the pressure a bit," said Schulz. "This isn't a rest cure. A little runt like Vierbein needs a kick in the pants from time to time. He must be made to realize that he can't make a fool of an N.C.O. and get away with it."

"Leave him to me," said Platzek with relish. "I'll settle him all right."

"And now," cried the Chief cheerfully, "one more song, eh? 'On the Lüneburger Heide.' One, two, three . . ."

✠ ✠ ✠

It was discipline which was the soul of the military colossus; its heart was known as the "routine schedule." It was discipline which kept the mechanism, the "routine schedule," going. The commander in chief wanted a Wehrmacht that would be invincible. The generals wanted competent divisions to juggle with. Commanding officers of units devised training schemes. And the N.C.O.s saw to it that these schemes were carried out.

The indispensable factor, occasionally known as the backbone of the system, was discipline. The "routine schedule" set the pattern of life. The battery commander got his adjutants to draw this up in its broad outline; the commanding officer of each troop got his sergeant major to work it out in detail. Schulz could have done this in his sleep, he knew all the material so well.

The toughest drill period of the whole week he placed traditionally on Monday morning. It lasted for a good two hours. Every member of the troop had to take part in it, even the clerks and other administrative personnel. Officially, according to the routine schedule, the whole operation was supervised by the C.O., Captain Derna himself, but in fact he always dele-

91

gated this duty to his second in command, Lieutenant Wedelmann, and didn't appear on the parade ground until it was almost over.

All in all, it was the most unpleasant two hours of the week for the troop as a whole; and the quietest for the sergeant major. He would make an inspection of them as they stood there on parade, taking at least three names and sometimes as many as seven for his little black book. Then he would report to Lieutenant Wedelmann, hand over command to the senior sergeant present, and have the men marched off singing to the drilling area.

The sergeant major stood and watched the troop disappear. Then he went in and had breakfast. On this particular Monday morning he was not in the best of moods. Certainly the parade had gone off all right, and no one had had any difficulty in hearing his orders. He was recognized as having the best word of command in the whole regiment. But what had upset him was the absence of Gunner Vierbein. He, the troop sergeant major, had specially worked up the N.C.O.s against this man Vierbein, and he had escaped scot-free by being on guard duty. What's more, he would be on until six o'clock that evening. And during the day at least, guard duty was a coveted job.

As Schulz made his way to his quarters he considered for a moment whether the methodical thoroughness with which he was picking on Vierbein might not spring from personal motives. He answered the question with a decisive negative. His conscience was clear. He was, in his own opinion, and in that of his officers, an outstanding soldier. He had worked his way up from the ranks in eight years of continuous good conduct. Never in all that time had he done anything which was out of line with the regulations or at least which could not be brought into line with them. This fellow Vierbein was, in his view, simply not a soldier at all — and this was the only reason he couldn't stand him.

92

He settled himself at the kitchen table and shouted out: "Coffee!"

His wife Lore set the coffee jug down in front of him. She made it plain that she was cross with him and not prepared to talk to him.

Schulz didn't mind. He was quite untroubled by the silence. In fact it made it easier for him to pursue his thoughts, which never, even in his most intimate moments, were entirely dissociated from service matters.

"Pour it out!" he ordered.

Lore poured him out a cup, sat down beside him at the table and looked straight at him.

"Don't talk to me now!" warned Schulz. "You know nothing about the service. You can't even make a cup of coffee properly. This is worse than dishwater. It tastes of soap." And he pushed the cup away so roughly that the coffee slopped over onto the cloth. "The tablecloth is absolutely filthy," he said.

Then he got up and went out. He whistled a tune that bore some resemblance to "The Three Lilies." He looked in the large looking-glass that hung in the ground-floor passage, straightened his uniform and smiled at himself. He liked what he saw.

When he arrived at his office, he sat down at his desk. He lit one of the C.O.s cigars, stretched his legs out in front of him and gave himself up to thought. A few words of command could be heard in the distance and there was the sound of marching men on the road outside, but otherwise all was silence.

Suddenly the telephone rang. He took his time about picking up the receiver. He put his cigar down in the ash tray and said: "No. 3 Troop. Sergeant Major Schulz speaking."

And although he was practically on the point of yawning he managed to make himself sound extremely busy.

A fraction of a second later he was sitting bolt upright in his chair. Lumpface, Major Luschke, the battery commander himself, was on the other end. And Luschke was a time bomb of a man. He might go off at any moment.

"Yes, Herr Major," barked Schulz.

Lumpface's tantalizingly soft voice hissed in his ear like the burning of a fuse.

"No, Herr Major," barked Schulz.

Then there was a crackling in the telephone. Lumpface had hung up. Schulz found himself wondering what the real object of the call had been. Major Luschke had merely made a few routine inquiries: whether the soldiers on guard carried muzzle caps in empty ammunition pouches; whether the different clocks in the barracks showed different times.

What could old Lumpface have been up to with such questions? Perhaps he had done it out of mischief? Or perhaps there was some cunningly contrived trap with quite unforeseeable consequences behind it all? Anything was possible with Luschke. You never knew where you were with Lumpface.

After much thought Schulz came to the following conclusion: Lumpface had been checking up on him. He had wanted to see if Schulz was at his post. If he was at his post indeed! As if he had ever not been!

This train of thought delighted Schulz and restored him to his usual Monday morning humor. He reached for his cigar and took a long pull at it. Then the telephone rang again.

This time Schulz hurried to answer it, for it was quite possible that it was the major again. But after he had been listening for a few seconds he assumed the usual look of bored superiority with which he dealt with all routine matters.

"No," he said, "there's no Gunner Kasprowitz here. And there never has been."

It was an infantry sergeant major at the other end. This alone was sufficient reason to keep his voice from sounding too welcoming, though he remained civil. Suddenly he pricked up

94

his ears. "Yes," he said, plainly interested, "we've got a Gunner Vierbein. What's he been up to?"

He was almost disappointed when he heard that it was only a question of improper saluting in public and that it was not Gunner Vierbein himself who was the guilty party, as he had hoped and supposed, but some man who had given his name as Kasprowitz.

"You're sure it wasn't Vierbein? It's just what I'd expect from him."

He listened carefully to the suggestion which his infantry colleague had to make. Then he said: "Yes, of course, you're quite right. We'll confront him with the man. Get your battalion people to send the sergeant over here. Vierbein's on guard at the moment. I'll tackle him there."

Schulz rubbed his hands. Not without a certain relish he said: "Vierbein again! Wherever one turns it's Vierbein. It's really time the little wretch was taught a lesson he won't forget."

He picked up his cigar again, but it had gone out. Carefully he lit a match, and began to puff away. Thick clouds of smoke rose to the ceiling. There was a certain class about a cigar, he thought. In fact no one but the C.O. and himself ever smoked cigars in this office. And that was how things should be.

He opened the cupboard and pulled out a number of personnel files. Two recommendations for promotion had to be sent in to the battery today. Lance Corporal Kowalski and Gunner Asch were to be put up for their corporal's stripes. He had gone into it all thoroughly with the C.O. and his process of reasoning had been something like this: Neither Kowalski nor Asch were exactly angels, one was handy with his fists and the other was as smart as they make them, but both stood out from the rest of the rank and file, and had shown what could only be called qualities of leadership. In other words, promising N.C.O. material, when one took into consideration the fact that both would settle down a good deal after getting their stripes.

The sergeant major filled in the promotion form and the personal report. By tradition the remarks which appeared on this were as fulsome as possible. It was only right that this should be so where a question of rank was involved. Under Asch, Herbert, Gunner First Class, Schulz wrote as follows:

1. *Character:* Reliable and co-operative. Marked qualities of leadership, not yet fully developed. Respect for his superior officers. Great potentialities.
2. *Physique:* Tough. Natural aptitude for sport. A good man in a tight corner. Swimmer.
3. *Military knowledge:* 98b and k guns; '08 pistol; '08/'15 light machine gun; '08 heavy machine gun; 8.8 cm. (mobile).
4. *Remarks:* A pleasant fellow to have under one; should be effective in a position of command himself.
5. *Recommended for:* Corporal.

Schulz looked over his morning's work and found it good. He lit another cigar, tucked the papers under his arm, and after opening the padded door which separated his office from that of the troop commander he took them through and put them down on Captain Derna's desk. Then he sat a little longer at his own desk, watching the smoke from his cigar curling out of the window.

Shortly before ten o'clock he heard the troop returning. Lieutenant Wedelmann was giving the orders, which was a sure sign that the C.O. himself was present. He had presumably gone straight out to the drill ground and had been watching the work there for the last quarter of an hour or so. The boots rang in step over the cement roadway. The Chief went over to the window, and the sight of the men sweating in their field-gray as they marched filled him with joy. It's only a pity, he thought with real regret, that that miserable louse Vierbein isn't among them. Two hours under Sergeant Platzek would have done him a power of good. But his turn would come all right. Words of command rang out across the parade ground. (This Lieutenant Wedelmann's voice is much too high, thought Schulz, it almost goes up into a squeak.) Then the troop was allowed to dismiss and a hundred and thirty pairs of boots went clattering up the stairs and along the corridors of the barrack block. The sergeant major, back at his desk again, listened contentedly to the sound and a smile spread over his smooth square face. He opened a couple of files and spread them out and a few other papers over his desk so that it looked as if he had been working very hard.

Captain Derna, the commanding officer of No. 3 Troop, came into the room. The sergeant major came to attention in his usual exemplary fashion: "Nothing to report, sir!" The captain thanked him. He disappeared into his office and closed the padded door behind him. The Chief knew from experience that the captain had to be left in peace for the next fifteen minutes. It was his habit to take off his boots and change his riding breeches for ordinary long trousers.

The next person to come into the room was Lieutenant Wedelmann. The sergeant major merely saluted and waited a few seconds for orders which did not seem to be forthcoming.

Wedelmann pushed open the swing gate in the barrier which made a sort of artificial anteroom on the front part of the office. He went up to the sergeant major, who appeared to be concentrating very hard on his work.

"What I wanted to say . . ." began Wedelmann uncertainly. "On the night of Saturday-Sunday you turned a gunner off the dance floor and sent him back to barracks."

"Yes, sir," said the sergeant major without getting up. He felt very safe and sure of himself. That "What I wanted to say . . ." of the lieutenant's showed clearly enough that there was no need to get worried. "Gunner Vierbein procured a Saturday night pass for himself by false pretenses."

"Really?" The lieutenant seemed skeptical.

"Corporal Lindenberg is a witness," said the sergeant major.

Wedelmann knew that if Corporal Lindenberg really was a witness, his evidence could be regarded as incontrovertible. Lindenberg would rather be shot than give false witness even against a subordinate.

"All the same," said Wedelmann with a cautious note of criticism in his voice, "what you did wasn't right. That sort of thing's simply not done, Sergeant Major. Duty is duty and spare time is something else."

He had put this relatively politely, but it was none the less a smack in the eye for the sergeant major. He took it as best he could. And all because of Vierbein, he thought. Always this wretched Vierbein! Then he thought: It's a good thing there's no one about to hear a troop sergeant major being reprimanded like this.

"Yes, sir!" he said, visibly annoyed. "But I beg to be allowed to explain . . ."

"There's no need for any explanation, Sergeant Major," said the lieutenant and turned on his heel.

Fuming, the sergeant major watched him go. And because the lieutenant did not look round he was able to avoid saluting him. He felt furious, "But, Lieutenant," he had wanted to say, "this Vierbein, this Gunner Vierbein, procured himself a Saturday night pass by false pretenses; he presumably left the barracks by an unauthorized route; he is involved in a matter, at present under investigation, of failing to salute properly. Nor, Lieutenant, is that all. But we won't speak about the rest just now, Lieutenant."

But Lieutenant Wedelmann wouldn't listen to him. He cut him short as if he had been some impudent schoolboy. And all because of this wretched Vierbein.

There were people who said that Lance Corporal Kowalski was a complete ass. But he only behaved like one. He was really as cunning as a fox. He didn't give a damn for the Wehrmacht. He did almost everything he was told to, and nothing more. He was considered a sound, reliable sort of fellow. He worked for Corporal Wunderlich, the N.C.O. in charge of the armory, and as the corporal had no use for anyone who might in any way ruffle the smoothness of his existence, the two of them got on very well together.

Kowalski's father was a small farmer. He had a farm in Pomerania right in the middle of the area which the Wehrmacht wanted for artillery ranges. He was given generous compensation for his land and moved into the town, where he got a good job as a gardener in a large market-garden. Kowalski Junior, however, went off to the Wehrmacht. He didn't originally go as a volunteer, but he had decided to stay on for the time being. Never in his life had he been paid so much for doing so little.

The lance corporal didn't have much idea of what went on inside people. Nor quite honestly did he really care. But on this particular Monday morning he saw clearly enough that all was not well with his friend Gunner Asch. He didn't ask him what was the matter at first, he merely kept him under observation. And it struck him that Asch wasn't nearly so talkative as usual. There were not even any of the usual half-muttered comments about the people taking drill parade. Asch concentrated on his work, and this need to concentrate on something which he should have been able to do in his sleep made Kowalski suspicious.

"What's the matter with you?" he asked.

"Nothing," said Asch.

"Oh yes there is! It sticks out a mile."

Foot drill was followed by artillery drill, as laid down in the routine schedule — ten-fifteen to twelve noon. Gunner Asch was stationed in one of the gun sheds during this period. He carried out his duties with his own particular brand of conscientiousness, that is to say, he sat down on an ammunition basket in a corner, arranged a dummy shell and an oily rag carefully beside him and stared into space. He was thinking of Elizabeth and what they had done together. Kowalski, who was busy carrying an oilcan which nobody had asked for from the armory to the shed, would have found it beyond his comprehension that a fully grown man should let himself get into a state over a girl.

"Do you want me to beat anyone up for you?" asked Kowalski in a friendly way.

"Yes," said Gunner Asch. "Me. I've behaved like an absolute swine."

"Well, and what's odd about that?"

Herbert Asch didn't answer at once. He tore the lid off an ammunition basket, of which the leather hinges were already damaged. He then hoisted the basket, which was of course empty and weighed only about four pounds, but which looked as if it were full, to his right shoulder and prepared to leave his post.

"Idiot!" called out Kowalski. "That won't do."

He knew the trick well enough. All that was necessary was to find some object — as light as possible — which on close inspection looked as if it needed to be taken to be repaired. One could then spend the rest of one's time moving backwards and forwards across the barracks without anybody asking awkward questions.

What annoyed Kowalski was the clumsy way in which Asch was going about it. This was one more proof that there was something wrong with his friend. One had to be prepared for every sort of surprise check by the authorities. Only the most plausible excuses were good enough in such circumstances. So Kowalski took the basket from Asch for a moment, moistened the two broken ends of the strap, which looked suspiciously clean, and wiped them over with an oily rag.

"There you are," he said. "Now anyone will believe that it's a regular repair job."

"Oh, well," said Asch. "If it makes you feel better."

"No good doing things by halves," said Kowalski. "And now I think I'll just take a little nap."

Herbert Asch shouldered his basket and wandered off across the barracks. From the gun shed he went via the gym to the canteen. There he suddenly dived into the other ranks' bar and ordered himself a beer.

Bandurski, the canteen contractor, who had been an N.C.O. himself in his time, thought it pretty good cheek coming in like this in the middle of morning drill to knock off a pint of beer. Such a thing would never have been possible in the Reichswehr. Not for gunners at any rate; one would have needed to be a sergeant at least. But the canteen contractor in him told him that business was business. He poured Asch out a large beer without batting an eyelid.

"Is Miss Elizabeth about?" asked Asch.

"No," said Bandurski. "She hasn't come today."

"She's not ill?"

Bandurski laughed.

"It depends what you mean by ill," he said with a leer.

Gunner Asch paid and left without another word. He walked out of the canteen with the empty basket on his shoulder and was about to go back to the gun shed when he caught sight of Sergeant Major Schulz walking along with the infantry sergeant whom he had failed to salute properly on Saturday and to whom he had given a false name. He nipped smartly off in the opposite direction.

At the corner of one of the buildings he stopped and peered round a buttress. He saw that Schulz and this bully who didn't know the difference between the main street of a town and a

101

barrack square were making for the guardroom. The very place where Vierbein was. Asch didn't like the look of things at all.

In spite of the heat, he completed the last stretch of the journey to the gun shed at the double. Sergeant Platzek, who was putting his four gun teams through their paces with his usual thoroughness, smiled at him in approval.

No sooner was Asch inside the gun shed than he flung his basket away into a corner and shouted to Lance Corporal Kowalski:

"Quick, man! Go to the guardroom at once. See that Vierbein doesn't make a fool of himself. Hurry up, you lazy beast. I can't let myself be seen there."

"Right," said Lance Corporal Kowalski. "Right."

He suppressed a yawn, snatched up his oilcan and trotted off at once. He was sweating slightly as he arrived at the guardroom. His practiced eye told him that nothing serious had happened so far. People were standing around waiting and there was as yet no sign of Gunner Vierbein.

"Lance Corporal Kowalski reporting for duty," he called out, and came smartly to attention in the doorway with his oilcan. In order to forestall any awkward questions he added: "Come to oil the hinges on the doors and windows."

"Less talk and more work, Kowalski," said the sergeant major. And he and the infantry sergeant went on waiting for Gunner Vierbein, whom Corporal Schwitzke had just sent out for some cigarettes.

In the meantime Kowalski had carefully taken the windows off their hinges. He wiped off the old oil with a rag, poured new oil onto the shining surface in its place, and then wiped it off again.

Gunner Vierbein appeared in the doorway and saluted.

"That's the man," said the infantry sergeant.

"Yes," said the sergeant major, "that's him."

Gunner Vierbein stood by the door and looked helplessly round the room. Everyone was staring at him, taking good care to dissociate themselves from him. Only Kowalski, who was standing right at the back, waved at him in friendly encouragement.

"Right now!" said the sergeant major, taking up an imposing stance. He was like a judge who was determined to get at the truth. "On Saturday afternoon, Vierbein, you were walking along the Goethestrasse in the company of another gunner. Isn't that so?"

"Yes, Sergeant Major."

"What was this gunner's name?"

Vierbein avoided the question.

"But I saluted the sergeant properly," he said.

The sergeant confirmed this.

"Yes, he did! But the other one didn't, the one who gave me the false name. He said his name was Kasprowitz, but there isn't a Kasprowitz in the regiment."

By now Lance Corporal Kowalski had fully grasped the situation. He saw clearly enough what had happened. Asch had given a slovenly salute as usual and then when he had been pulled up for it had given a false name. Right.

"Well now," said the sergeant major, anxious to get on with the business, "what was this gunner's name?"

Gunner Vierbein could feel the sweat pouring down his face. God, what was he to do? He looked desperately past the sergeant major for help and caught sight of Lance Corporal Kowalski shrugging his shoulders in an exaggerated manner which quite clearly meant: I don't know.

"I don't know, Sergeant Major," said Gunner Vierbein automatically. And he was appalled to realize that he was now guilty of lying to a superior. Admittedly he had only done it to protect his friend, but that didn't make it any less of a lie.

103

"Aha!" said the sergeant major with an unmistakable note of menace in his voice. "So you don't remember, eh?"

Vierbein was bathed in sweat. He did what he could to save himself. He said quickly:

"I didn't know the gunner. He wasn't one of our troop. I met him by accident and we just happened to be going along the street together."

Lance Corporal Kowalski nodded approval. He raised his arms and turned the palms of his hands outward as if to say: There you are, you see!

The Chief smelled a rat.

"If that's a deliberate piece of false evidence, you'll be up before a court-martial, you know, Vierbein. I'm warning you. You've got a lot on your plate as it is, you know. My patience is becoming exhausted. If I catch you out in anything from now on, God have mercy on you."

"Would you recognize the gunner if you were confronted with him?" inquired the sergeant. "Or the next time you met him about the barracks?"

"I don't know," stammered Vierbein. "I think so."

"I'll know what to think of you all right in future," said the sergeant major.

"Shall I oil the door now?" asked Lance Corporal Kowalski loudly.

"Don't interrupt, damn you!" shouted the sergeant major furiously. "Nobody asked your opinion. Mind your own business."

� ✘ ✘

Freitag, the railway foreman, Elizabeth's father, was a man of fifty, but he had not forgotten his own youth. And now when he saw others sowing their wild oats he tried to have some understanding. He was a respectable citizen and yet sensitive

104

enough to see that not everything which transgressed the laws of so-called respectability should be condemned outright.

He was a man who was never in too much of a hurry about anything. He knew that a piece of good craftsmanship always required a certain amount of time. He himself gave a lot of thought to a job of work before he set about it. But when he did start, he worked swiftly and surely, knowing just how he wanted things to be.

On this particular Monday, Foreman Freitag left his work two hours earlier than usual. The manager was pleased to be able to do his best worker a favor and gladly gave him permission to go.

Freitag gave himself a thorough wash as if he were going out to a party and then changed his clothes by his locker. He took out the suitcase which he had left in the locker, put it on the table and opened it. He looked thoughtfully at the clothing inside, the property of a certain Gunner Herbert Asch of No. 3 Troop, No. 1 Battery of the Regiment of Artillery. All this information, together with much else, such as his date and place of birth, height, color of hair, color of eyes, and other characteristics, was to be found conveniently enough in the blue service paybook which he had put in the top left-hand pocket of his tunic. In addition his name, rank and unit were to be found on almost every item of his clothing. Even a photograph of the said Herbert Asch was available. It showed a man in uniform who looked as if he were incapable of counting up to more than three staring halfwittedly at the camera — a typical photograph of a recruit in fact.

Freitag shut the suitcase up again. He wasn't a man of great imagination. But it wasn't difficult for him to put two and two together and see that the disturbance he had heard during the night was in some way connected with the uniform he had found. He hadn't pressed Elizabeth for an explanation. He didn't want to, and in any case it wasn't necessary. If she had come to him of her own free will he would have been glad to listen to her. But he felt he understood her silence and he respected it.

Foreman Freitag left the repair shop, climbed on his bicycle and rode off to the artillery barracks. He wasn't particularly worried by the fact that this man who had upset Elizabeth turned out to be a soldier. He had a dislike of uniforms, admittedly, and he could never really understand how any normal healthy hard-working man could bring himself to waste his time in an activity of which the ultimate aim was to kill and destroy. But in times like these when no one had any choice in the matter, a uniform could conceal all sorts of different people: idealists, sadists, those who were indifferent to their fate and those who fought against it, fanatics, opponents of the regime, clever men, fools, and even halfwits. Gunner Asch might belong to any one of these categories. It was well worth finding out which.

The foreman went up to the gate and the sentry directed him to the guardroom. Freitag propped his bicycle up against the wall, unstrapped the suitcase, and went in to see the guard commander.

To Corporal Schwitzke, Slacker Schwitzke, the friendly little old man's arrival merely represented an interruption of his afternoon nap. He was due to be relieved in three hours' time, when he intended to make up for the Sunday he had missed in no uncertain fashion. His girl Thusnelda — he called all his girls Thusnelda — had promised to meet him in the park.

"Where do you want to go?" he asked sullenly.

"No. 3 Troop," said the foreman, who had had some experience of the insides of barracks in his time. He was quite prepared for more questions.

"What's your name?"

"Freitag."

Schwitzke filled in a pass and handed it to him.

"A sentry will go with you," he said. He immediately forgot all about the visitor and returned to thoughts of his Thusnelda and the evening he was going to spend with her on the very comfortable bench hidden behind the syringa in the park. He had often, even in winter, enjoyed his Thusnelda there — not always the same Thusnelda of course.

Freitag followed the sentry, who took him to No. 3 Troop's block and left him at the desk in the orderly room. Sergeant Major Schulz was very busy as always but interrupted his work to devote a little patronizing attention to the newcomer. Civilians in the orderly room always made a change.

"Let me see your pass. Yes — that's in order. You've come to the right place. No. 3 Troop — that's me."

He looked challengingly at his visitor.

Freitag smiled wanly.

"It wasn't actually you I wanted to see. I wanted to see a gunner called Asch. Herbert Asch."

"And what do you want with him?"

"I want to have a word with him."

The sergeant major began to show some interest. He looked first at the man behind the barrier and then at the suitcase, which he had put down on the floor. A suitcase, he reasoned instinctively, with enough room in it for a uniform and full equipment. Then an idea occurred to him and he looked more closely at the pass.

"Your name is Freitag? Are you any relation of the Fräulein Elizabeth Freitag who works in the N.C.O.s' canteen?"

"She's my daughter."

The sergeant major became a little more affable. He did his best, though without any success, to create a warm, friendly sort of atmosphere. "I'm delighted to meet you," he said. And he stretched out a large hand which the foreman took with some hesitation.

"So it's all right to see Gunner Asch?"

107

"Of course," said the sergeant major, like a king graciously granting a subject his dearest wish. "But of course you can. One of my men will take you to him. And, as I say, it's been a great pleasure." He put out his hand again, and again the foreman took it after some hesitation. Then he left the room. The clerk of No. 3 Troop led the way.

But the Chief sat down at his desk again. He lit himself another of the C.O.'s cigars and reached for a pad on which was written in large letters the one word: VIERBEIN. He began to put two and two together. So that, he thought, was old Freitag, the father of that stunning-looking girl Elizabeth. He had brought a suitcase with him and he wanted to see Gunner Asch, who had been found wandering about the barracks clad in nothing but his shirt at three o'clock that morning. Now supposing . . .

At first he rejected the idea. But his imagination wouldn't leave him alone. It was certainly not beyond the bounds of possibility . . .

He gave a little shudder, although whether of pleasure or horror, he couldn't quite say. He smoked away continuously. Certainly this girl Elizabeth was high up on his own list. She was a splendid girl; worth taking risks for, worth putting up with a lot for. As for Asch himself, well, it was almost impossible to get at him now. He himself had put him up for promotion to corporal, and the troop commander had already given his approval in the form of his signature. To hell with it, he wasn't going to be petty about a thing like that. Besides, he had other worries. Vierbein, for example!

And Schulz's train of thought, aided by one of the troop commander's best cigars, went something like this: Elizabeth — Asch in his shirttails at three o'clock in the morning — Father Freitag with a suitcase — Vierbein on guard!

He seized the telephone and asked to be put through to the guardroom.

"Schwitzke," he rapped out sharply. "Who was on guard at the main gate between two and four this morning?" He sat there with his ear glued to the receiver. Suddenly a broad smile appeared on his fat potato face. "Aha, Vierbein! Good," he said and hung up.

He reached for the pad which had nothing but the single word VIERBEIN written on it in large letters. To this he now added, clearly, the words: *on guard between two and four*. He underlined this. And he continued to puff away contentedly at his cigar.

In the meantime Foreman Freitag was waiting in the reading room for Gunner Asch. He was aware of a certain feeling of tension. He sat on a chair with the suitcase beside him. He looked at the door and his eyes narrowed to pinpoints.

Gunner Asch came into the room. He was wearing his fatigue uniform and holding his cap in his hand. He had been told there was someone to see him. He had no idea who it was going to be.

Asch stared at his visitor and his visitor stared back at him. They both seemed to feel better after looking each other over for a time like this, particularly Asch.

"Good day," said the gunner.

"Good day," said the foreman. "I've brought your clothes back. I found them in the street."

And he didn't let his eyes drop from the face of the man opposite him for a moment.

Herbert Asch was visibly embarrassed.

"Oh," he said. "Yes, that's fine."

His visitor made a gesture towards the suitcase and Asch picked it up, opened it and examined the contents. "Yes," he said, "it's all there." He became more and more embarrassed. "Thank you very much, Herr — er . . ."

"My name is Freitag," said his visitor, helping him out. He watched Asch carefully as he did so.

109

Asch, who had just taken his boots out of the suitcase, dropped them on the table with a clatter. He sat down.

"I don't know how far you . . ." he began.

Then he brought himself up short and said firmly:

"I think I owe you an explanation, Herr Freitag."

Freitag smiled.

"That's not necessary," he said. "I was young myself once. I was even a soldier once. It's easy enough to imagine what happened. It was a wonderful night, and the girl was attractive. Circumstances were favorable, and you took advantage of them; or better still, you abandoned yourself to them. My God, there's nothing so very strange about that! Who do you want to blame for it? The moon? The fever in your blood? The favorable circumstances? I found your clothes lying about the street somewhere and you can thank your lucky stars it was I who found them and not the girl's father."

Asch winced. It was obvious that this man was anything but a fool. He was Elizabeth's father and Asch liked him. Asch definitely had the feeling that he knew or suspected a good deal more than he was letting on. He was just making absolutely sure, first. He wanted to avoid any possible mistake. He, Elizabeth's father, was giving him every possible chance.

"There's something more I must tell you," said Asch grimly. "You ought to know . . ."

"No, that's enough," said the foreman, getting to his feet. "I haven't very much time just now. But if you like you can come and see me tomorrow evening. Come to supper with us — if you'd like to, that is."

"I'd like to very much," said Asch, feeling utterly confused.

"Then if you like you can get to know my family."

"Certainly I'll come."

"I'd be very pleased if you would," said the foreman simply and made ready to leave.

The door was flung open. The sergeant major stood there.

110

He ignored the gunner's salute and looked straight at the table where the suitcase lay open with the uniform in it.

"Carry on," he said condescendingly and shut the door again.

"Right," said Foreman Freitag. "Till tomorrow, then. That is, if you'd care to come."

꿔 꿔 꿔

The guard was dismissed. The men executed a smart right turn, pushed their rifles under their arms and moved off in the direction of the barrack block. Gunner Vierbein looked up and saw Corporal Lindenberg standing by an open window on the second floor. He stood there as if carved from stone.

Vierbein quickened his pace. He felt certain that Lindenberg was waiting for him. He found the thought depressing. For the eternal soldier to manifest such a sudden interest in him could only mean that trouble was on the way. And this was just what he wanted to avoid at the moment for he had determined to go and see Ingrid and himself explain why he had not been able to keep his date of the day before.

As he hurried up the steps he looked at the clock that hung over the swing doors. There was another two hours before he was due to meet Ingrid — but what were two hours to Corporal Lindenberg? If he wanted to — and all the signs seemed to point that way — he was perfectly capable of keeping him at it until lights-out. Vierbein looked worried. He prepared himself for the worst.

Gunner Asch was waiting for him by the door.

"Nice work," he called out. "You carried off that business with the infantry sergeant splendidly."

"Lindenberg seems to be waiting for me," said Vierbein as he came up.

"Don't worry," said the gunner, "we're on to that. It's what

111

you might call a chain reaction. The Chief is putting his best men into the field. The thing for you to do is to clear out as quick as you can."

"Lindenberg may be here any minute."

"No," said Asch, who was more experienced in these things than Vierbein. "Lindenberg knows the regulations. He'll take good care to stick by them. You've been on guard, and he'll give you time to put your equipment and rifle in order. Then he'll turn up and before you know where you are he'll have shown you that they're not in order at all."

"I know," said Vierbein. "Then I'm in for it."

Asch was quite unperturbed. He laughed.

"We won't let it get as far as that. You've just done me a good turn. Now I'll do you one. I'll take over your equipment and guarantee to see that it's in perfect order. You go straight off to the lavatory and then disappear as fast as you can."

"But Lindenberg'll go mad with rage," said Vierbein doubtfully.

"No he won't, not that one. He's got far too much self-control. He'll be mad enough but he won't show it. And by to-morrow morning he'll have calmed down again."

"Do you really think so?"

"No doubt about it. Off you go then! Into the lavatory. I'll go and fetch your dress uniform."

Gunner Asch pushed Vierbein towards the other end of the corridor, where the lavatory was. Vierbein locked himself in and quickly began to undress. He banged his steel helmet against the door and his rifle slipped out of his hand and clattered on the tiles. He was terrified for a moment that he might have damaged his rifle in some way and quickly inspected it in the half light, but to his relief found that there was nothing wrong with it. He leaned against the wooden partition and felt the sweat breaking out all over him. Soon after that Asch came and hammered on the door.

"Here are your things," he said. "Dress uniform. Peaked cap, shoes, ceremonial belt. Anything else?"

"Thanks very much," said Vierbein.

"You've nothing to thank me for."

Vierbein quickly began to get dressed.

"If you hadn't helped me," he said, "I would never have got out of camp today."

"You're not out yet. And you're just wasting time talking."

"I'm going to see your sister this evening," said Vierbein through the lavatory door. "I hope you don't mind."

Asch didn't answer at once. Then he said slowly: "If I'd known that . . ."

"Wouldn't you have done it?"

"No," said Asch with a certain hostility. "No. I would rather have seen you fall into Lindenberg's clutches. He's far more harmless than my sister."

"I don't see what you mean," said Vierbein.

"That's because you're a fool," said Asch in a more friendly tone. "But you will one day. Let's just hope it won't then be too late."

Vierbein had finished changing by now and he stepped out of the cubicle. He felt rather bewildered. He knew he had to hurry. He handed over the clothing and equipment he had worn on guard.

Asch looked him up and down. As far as he could see there was nothing wrong with his turnout.

"Have you got everything?" he asked. "Paybook? Money? Handkerchief?"

Vierbein said he had.

"Then we'll just see how the land lies."

Asch went out into the almost empty corridor, strolled up to the swing doors and took a look down the stairs. He immediately drew his head back, and called softly to Vierbein, who was peering out of the lavatory door:

113

"Look out! Lindenberg's coming."

Then, apparently overcome by keenness, he pulled open the doors and gave the corporal a faultless salute.

Lindenberg, whose own bearing was of course always faultless, strode past him, returning the salute in a splendidly correct manner. His hobnailed boots clattered across the stone floor. There was a look of determination about him and yet he in no way betrayed his haste as he made for the barrack-room door, behind which he imagined he would find Vierbein.

Lindenberg was hardly out of the corridor — there was a loud shout of "Attention!" from the barrack room — before Asch was piloting his friend out of the lavatory.

"Quick, man! Run for it! This is your chance."

And without another thought Vierbein scuttled off past the gunner. He ran down the stairs without once looking back. He felt enough trepidation as it was about seeing Ingrid.

The swing doors were well oiled and Asch gave them a great push so that they banged noisily backwards and forwards. Then he slowly made his way back along the corridor towards the barrack room.

Corporal Lindenberg was standing motionless in the center of the room. For the first time in his life he seemed to be in danger of losing his composure. He was absolutely flabbergasted. He had asked each member of the room in turn if they had seen Vierbein, and all had insisted that they hadn't. But they could only be telling him a whopping lie, for he himself had seen Vierbein go into the block when he came off guard only a quarter of an hour before. He simply must be there somewhere. He couldn't have just disappeared through a hole in the floor.

So Lindenberg was certain he was being lied to. This didn't anger him so much as completely mystify him. He simply could not take in the fact that someone should have dared to lie to him.

114

"And you," he said to Gunner Asch as he came into the room. "I suppose you don't know anything about it either?"

"No, Corporal," answered Gunner Asch promptly.

"What don't you know anything about?"

"Anything, Corporal."

"To hell with it!" roared Lindenberg.

He was astonished to hear himself roaring like this and he saw the men of his section rooted to the spot in terror. The sight restored his equilibrium a little.

"You, Asch, dare to maintain that Gunner Vierbein didn't enter this room after coming off guard duty? Do you dare to maintain that?"

"Yes, Corporal," said Asch quite truthfully.

Corporal Lindenberg left the room, slamming the door with a mighty crash behind him. When he got into the corridor he stopped, panting for breath. He simply couldn't understand what was going on here. And he set about combing the barracks for Vierbein.

"That's really got him worried!" said Gunner Asch to his companions. "It's made him quite human!"

☙ ☙ ☙

Corporal Lindenberg regarded all orders as sacred. Regulations and official instructions constituted his Bible. With him there could be no question of compromise, only implicit obedience. And he never demanded anything of others that he was not prepared to demand of himself.

Lindenberg had received a categorical order from Troop Sergeant Major Schulz "to make a thorough inspection of the clothing and equipment worn and used by Gunner Vierbein during his tour of guard duty and see that it is properly clean." Or in simpler, more graphic language: "Give him the works!"

There could be no doubting the meaning of this order. And

115

since, to his own utter astonishment, it had proved impossible to carry it out as soon as Vierbein came off guard, it represented an order that had still to be carried out. There were only two alternatives. Either the order had to be rescinded — and this could only be done by the person who had given it — or it had to be carried out at the first available opportunity.

So Corporal Lindenberg walked around with his order as if it were some sort of pregnancy. First of all he searched the entire barrack block from top to bottom. Of course without success. He roared for Vierbein like a cow roaring for its calf. But Vierbein didn't answer. He returned to the section barrack room several times, repeating his urgent request. Had anyone there seen Vierbein? But the men always gave him the same answer, and it began to dawn on him that they were getting rather fed up with him.

Fair-minded as always, he found himself able to see their point of view. Free time was free time and the good soldier was not only entitled to it, but ought to be allowed to enjoy it. There was even a special decree of the High Command to this effect though it was phrased in very woolly language.

No, he had received the order. It was up to him to carry it out. Not the least of his duties was to set an example to others. Nothing on earth, he was convinced, would ever prevent him from doing his duty. It so happened that he had intended to go to the military baths that evening to train for his lifesaving badge. If he didn't succeed in getting hold of Gunner Vierbein soon, his training would have to go by the board.

For a long time he fought against the idea of going to see the sergeant major. Eventually he gave in to it. Not, of course, that there was any question of telling the sergeant major that the order had not been carried out. Such an idea was quite inconceivable. The only possibility was to tell him that it had not being carried out *yet*. There was always a hope that the sergeant major might then rescind it.

Lindenberg put on cap, belt and gloves — the dress prescribed by regulations to be worn when reporting to superiors
— and presented himself at the sergeant major's private quarters on the ground floor of the barrack block. He rang in the
approved manner for corporals. Then he waited outside, standing smartly at attention.

After a few minutes Schulz opened the door. His stocky
figure was clothed in a bright red dressing gown. When he saw
Lindenberg his beery features settled in a contented grin.

"Well?" he roared. "Have you put him through it?"

In clipped well-chosen phrases Lindenberg gave an account
of his troubles. He saw the sergeant major's mouth open and
shut again. And it was as if the Chief were doing his level best
to turn the same color as his dressing gown.

"What the hell do you mean?" asked Schulz after a short
sinister silence. "This man didn't return to his barrack room
after coming off guard? He simply made straight off?"

"Yes, Sergeant Major."

"Balderdash!"

"Yes, Sergeant Major."

"And you're a fool!"

Corporal Lindenberg didn't feel it necessary to answer "Yes,
Sergeant Major" to this. Of course he didn't feel in any way
insulted. This was all part of the normal language of the barracks — it was in no way contrary to regulations to call a man
a fool — that was clearly laid down somewhere.

Sergeant Major Schulz slammed the door in a fury. Lindenberg noted the fact without emotion. He found the sergeant
major's behavior thoroughly understandable, although he
couldn't help regretting his lack of self-control. But presumably
this was simply a question of loss of temper, a common enough
phenomenon in life.

At any rate Lindenberg saw no alternative after this conversation but to consider the previous order as still in force.

117

It remained his task to inspect "as soon as possible" the clothing and equipment used by Gunner Vierbein on guard duty.

For the fifth time Lindenberg returned to the section barrack room. Vierbein was of course still not there. Lindenberg stood thoughtfully in front of the gunner's locker, which was fastened by a large padlock. He regretted the fact that he didn't have the right to force it open. But there were bound to be flaws in even the best regulations.

So there was nothing else for him to do but give up his evening's lifesaving training and wait. He, a corporal, had to wait for an ordinary gunner! And he waited: one hour, two hours, three hours, four hours. He sat uneasily in his room, with a routine manual open in front of him on the table, but quite unable to summon the concentration to learn the range tables properly by heart.

He went over to the window and looked out onto the parade ground. Then he sat down again. Then he got up and went out into the corridor. He did a few pull-ups on the horizontal bar that stood outside the washroom. Later he cleaned his boots, his belt and his teeth. Later still he went and brushed his best uniform, although it was in fact spotlessly clean already.

He thought he detected a certain nervousness in his movements. This was something quite new for him and he found it disturbing. Rather gloomily he came to the conclusion that Gunner Vierbein was upsetting him. And he told himself that such a thing was all wrong. Of course, he told himself, he had to remain strictly impartial in this matter, and set an example of fairness at all times. But he didn't find it easy.

Just before lights-out he went to the barrack room once again. This was his ninth visit of the evening. Three men were playing *skat,* two were having their third supper, another was in the washroom, and the rest were already in bed. Vierbein was still not there. Corporal Lindenberg looked at his watch and nodded portentously. "Twenty minutes to go," he said.

Lindenberg did not go back to his room. He remained outside in the corridor. As he walked up and down he became aware of a tremendous feeling of rage building up inside him. But he told himself he mustn't allow such a thing to happen. He made himself take several deep breaths. Ten more long minutes went by.

Then Gunner Vierbein appeared, panting.

His evening with Ingrid had not gone well. In the course of it he had given vent to a good deal of indignation about the Wehrmacht's interference with a man's private life. She had been pained and shocked by his attitude. It had reminded her too much of her brother's lack of patriotism for her liking.

Now Vierbein's face was shiny with sweat and it was obvious that he had been running. He hurried towards the barrack room and practically ran into Corporal Lindenberg.

"Vierbein," said the corporal in an absolutely correct, official tone of voice — it cost him a great deal of effort to control himself, but he succeeded — "you were on guard duty today, I think?"

"Yes, Corporal."

"You know, Verbein, that there is an order, a written order, to the effect that every man coming off guard duty must see that his uniform and equipment are to be put into spotless condition forthwith, that is to say that they must be fit to pass inspection?"

"Yes, Corporal."

"Then you will kindly show me," said the corporal, bringing himself back to the case in point, "belt, ammunition pouches, and bayonet frog?" He said this in a curt matter-of-fact tone of voice. He was not going to waste words, or indulge in accusations. He wanted to let the facts speak for themselves. And he had no doubt that they would speak clearly enough.

119

Vierbein, still breathing heavily, hurried over to his locker. He pulled the key, which Gunner Asch had just slipped him, out of his trousers pocket, and opened the padlock. He swung the locker door open. Lindenberg looked in impatiently. At a first glance the general condition didn't look too bad.

The ammunition pouches were hanging up on hooks. They positively shone. The belt was wound round the special semi-circular rest. It too positively shone. The bayonet frog and bayonet had been carefully laid on a special piece of cloth. Everything positively shone.

It took Corporal Lindenberg several seconds to take this all in. Gunner Vierbein felt greatly relieved. His roommates had obviously done him proud. Gunner Asch grinned from his bed.

"Boots," said Corporal Lindenberg.

They were held up before him, and lo and behold, they too shone like new. Lindenberg turned them over and inspected the soles. They had been carefully washed. He looked for dirt clinging to the studs. He looked in vain. He felt his control beginning to go.

"Rifle," said the corporal, just managing to contain himself.

Vierbein hurried to the rack and took down his rifle. He held it in his left hand in the regulation manner, with the breach open for inspection. Lindenberg's glance passed cursorily over it from butt to muzzle. He couldn't find anything to object to at first sight.

"Muzzle cap off! Bolt out! Magazine out!" he ordered.

Now he thought his inspection would really begin. He was determined to find something wrong. And he knew from experience that there wasn't a rifle in the world with which he couldn't find something wrong if he wanted to.

Then Gunner Asch spoke up from his bed in a friendly voice: "I beg to inform the corporal that it's time for lights-out." Lindenberg didn't take in the full significance of this at first. "What's that?" he said in alarm.

120

"Lights-out," said Gunner Asch politely enough, raising his blankets a little.

And Lance Corporal Kowalski, whose bed was in the farthest corner, acted as if he were already half asleep and didn't quite realize what was going on in the room.

"Quiet there!" he called out with a loud yawn.

Lindenberg understood. He knew it was forbidden to disturb the men between lights-out and Reveille; and he knew that the men knew this. But he had never thought the day would come when anyone would be in a position to draw his attention to the fact. This was a threat to his whole equilibrium. He felt the anger rising up in him once again and it cost him all his strength to keep it down.

"We'll see about this tomorrow," he said, turning on his heel.

"Good night, Corporal," Gunner Asch called after him amiably.

🚩 🚩 🚩

It was seven-fifteen in the morning. The three members of the Freitag family were having breakfast together. Elizabeth poured out the coffee.

"This evening," said Father Freitag to his wife, "you must cook rather more supper than usual. I'm expecting a guest, a rather special guest. But I want him to get to know us as we are. So don't do anything elaborate."

"Who is it?" asked his wife curiously. "Someone from the factory?"

"No," he said, looking quizzically towards his daughter. "It's someone from Elizabeth's factory."

Elizabeth put down the cup she was about to drink from. She sat up in astonishment.

"Who is it, Father?"

"A very interesting young man. I met him for the first time yesterday. I think you might like him, Mother. I'm certain

121

Elizabeth will. He's a gunner in the artillery. His name is Asch, Herbert Asch."

Elizabeth leaned back in her chair and looked at her father out of big round eyes. She wasn't particularly surprised. She knew that her father was capable of jumping to some pretty bold conclusions.

"Did you tell him he'd got to come?" she asked. "Did you force him somehow?"

Frau Freitag couldn't understand what was going on at all. She was extremely curious.

"But do you know him, then, Elizabeth?"

"Why shouldn't she?" Freitag said as if there were nothing strange about it at all. "He's a soldier in the barracks where Elizabeth works. There are only about eight hundred soldiers there altogether. Why shouldn't she know him?"

"Father," said Elizabeth very firmly and seriously, "I see now I made a great mistake in not telling you."

The old man shook his head energetically.

"You mustn't tell me everything that goes on in your life," he said.

Frau Freitag stared in astonishment.

"What on earth are you two talking about?"

"Nothing very extraordinary, Mother." Freitag cut himself a fresh slice of bread. "This is the young man whose clothes we found in the street yesterday morning."

"And Elizabeth knows a man like that?" asked Frau Freitag sharply.

Elizabeth nodded.

"Yes, Mother, I know him."

"And I've nothing against it," said Freitag.

"But I don't want to have anything more to do with him," cried Elizabeth. And she meant what she said.

She felt that Herbert Asch had betrayed her. He had simply gone off and left her. He hadn't made the slightest attempt to

122

see her all yesterday. He had just forgotten all about her. He had got her into the most awkward situation and then abandoned her. And here was her father trying to bring him to heel by force. She didn't want that. It made her feel ashamed of herself. She hadn't expected that; it mustn't be allowed to happen.

"I'm beginning to wonder," said her father, "whether you really know him properly."

"I know him all right."

"I'm afraid you only know one side of him, and that is the side in which all men most resemble each other. You probably think this Asch is just an irresponsible fellow who makes the most of his opportunities. But he isn't. If you'll come some of the way with me now — for it's high time I was off to work — I'll tell you my reasons for thinking that he's got all the makings of a thoroughly decent fellow."

Frau Freitag rose to her feet. She felt irritated.

"Come on, out of here the two of you," she said firmly. "I've had just about enough of your mysteries."

And she pushed her husband out through the door. She watched him as he went along the street talking animatedly to his daughter beside him. Frau Freitag shook her head.

"He talks an awful lot of nonsense," she said. "But he's a good man."

🦋 🦋 🦋

It didn't take Sergeant Major Schulz long to decide that so far as he was concerned, this Corporal Lindenberg was little better than useless. He was like a piece of clockwork that has been overwound. He was more than "the eternal soldier"; he was a military monstrosity. In short, in Sergeant Major Schulz's eyes, Corporal Lindenberg was right out of touch with reality. He didn't possess the basic qualification for training men; he was incapable of putting them through it!

123

The eternal soldier's disastrous Monday evening, in the course of which he had allowed himself to be made a fool of by the scruffiest soldier in the whole garrison, if not in the entire Wehrmacht, could be ignored. It could be regarded merely as a technical hitch and dismissed as such. But what was inexcusable was that he should waste the whole of Tuesday morning just keeping an eye on Vierbein instead of getting on with the job of knocking the stuffing out of him.

Corporal Lindenberg's greatest defect was, still according to Sergeant Major Schulz, his lack of imagination. He stuck to the regulations far too rigidly. He was trying to be "correct," but he only succeeded in making a fool of himself. He knew nothing of the art of improvisation. He couldn't even see the possibilities inherent in the concept "inculcation of discipline."

It was therefore with some reluctance that the Chief had to admit that Corporal Lindenberg was unfortunately not the man to put his section through it in suitable fashion. This caused him considerable anxiety. He sent for the corporal to make a last desperate appeal to him.

"Yesterday evening, Lindenberg, you let the lousiest recruit in the whole regiment make a laughingstock of you."

"I beg to inform the sergeant major that my attitude was completely correct throughout. Gunner Vierbein's uniform and equipment were in order. There was no cause to reprimand him or to report him."

"You've let them make a fool of you, Lindenberg. You know that perfectly well yourself. This oaf Vierbein was out having a good time — playing around with women again probably — and he got the others to clean his things for him."

"That, Sergeant Major, could be described as being in the best traditions of comradeship."

"You're just an ass, Lindenberg," said the sergeant major forcibly. "You simply haven't realized what's been going on here. The men only acted in 'the best traditions of comrade-

124

ship' in order to make an idiot out of you. You must be off your head to describe that as 'comradeship.' Personally I call it precious close to mutiny."

Lindenberg remained silent. As was often the case he found himself in disagreement with the sergeant major, but he kept a firm enough grip on himself as a soldier not to contradict him. He was merely concerned to put his point of view, in which, in any case, he was beginning to lose confidence.

"Up to the present I haven't seen the faintest sign of anything that could be described as a refusal to obey an order."

"That's because these fellows are too smart for you!" said the sergeant major, incensed at the thought of the man's stupidity. "Why do you think Lance Corporal Kowalski and Gunner Asch have gone sick this morning?"

"One has diarrhea and the other is suffering from fainting fits, Sergeant Major."

"They both want to get off rifle drill, you ass! They can both make rings round you, Lindenberg. They're a pretty slick pair, those two. They've got what it takes to be an N.C.O. As for you, you're just an old regulation cart horse."

Lindenberg didn't answer. He felt very strongly that he hadn't deserved this. He was one of the best N.C.O.s in the whole regiment, certainly one of the most correct. He knew that perfectly well. He was absolutely incorruptible and always did his duty. He felt deeply offended.

The sergeant major dismissed him with a gesture. He had found this conversation very satisfactory. He had high hopes of it. Lindenberg, he felt, would be much more on the alert as a result of it, not only in a routine way but in more subtle ways too. In the two hours of rifle drill which was to follow, Lindenberg's section must be driven to the utmost limit of endurance. The entire section! They must all be made to feel that they were being put through it because of Vierbein, that it was entirely Vierbein's fault that things were being made so hot for

125

them. That was the only way in which they could be brought to co-operate in dealing with him as he deserved to be dealt with, and give themselves a bit of peace.

Lindenberg had been worked up to the right pitch. But even so there was always the possibility that he would prove incapable of treating his section and this Vierbein in particular with the necessary harshness. It was therefore very fortunate that the overall supervision of rifle drill that day happened to be in the experienced hands of Sergeant Platzek. It was not for nothing that Platzek had been nicknamed Bully Platzek, and not for nothing that he was a close friend of Schulz's. Schulz told himself that Platzek would see to it that the men were given something they wouldn't forget in a hurry — particularly Vierbein.

The sergeant major simply couldn't stand this creature Vierbein. He was the very antithesis of a soldier, the very negation of discipline and military bearing: in short, he was a typical civilian. And it wasn't because this creature Vierbein had dared to lay his filthy paws on the sergeant major's wife that he detested the man so much, or at least not solely because of that, although that itself was clear enough evidence of Vierbein's complete lack of respect for his superiors.

Such reflections brought Schulz back to his wife. He remembered his new determination to seize every opportunity of showing who was the real master in the house. He went to his quarters and called for a cup of coffee. Lore hastened to provide it.

"You're in a hurry to get rid of me, eh?" asked Schulz.

She didn't answer. She knew that if she had been slow about getting the coffee he would have attacked her for that. But to try and please him she took things more easily.

"Can't you be quicker than that?" he asked at once. "I haven't got all day, you know."

He quickly drank up his coffee and left, not, however, with-

126

out first having run his finger along one of the shelves of the kitchen dresser and found some dust there which delighted him.

"That's just what happens," he said, "when you don't keep your mind on your work."

Then he walked through the barrack block and looked out of one of the back windows to the drill ground. He found some satisfaction in what he saw. Lindenberg's section had been separated from the rest and was employed on an extremely complicated and very strenuous form of rifle drill. Corporal Lindenberg, determined as ever to set an example to his men, was drilling with them. The section consisted of ten men altogether.

This reminded the sergeant major that Kowalski and Asch had been smart enough to go sick. He grinned. He knew their tricks. The two of them thought they were just getting out of rifle drill. But they hadn't reckoned with him. He hurried off to his office and put a call through to the sergeant in charge of sick quarters.

In the meantime Lindenberg was putting his section through his own notorious version of rifle drill. And in order to avoid being classed as a bully, he not only demonstrated the drill but carried it out himself with them. His movements were faultless. And thanks to his magnificent physique they cost him no effort at all.

His specialty was "knees bend" in eight separate movements with rifle — the 98k rifle — held at arm's length. A splendid exercise which made the arms and legs tremble with the strain. He delivered his criticisms in a loud but even tone. He noted that Gunner Vierbein, among others, was sweating profusely and slowly turning red in the face. He noted this, not in triumph, but with a certain amount of concern. He was appalled at the lack of resistance possessed by the men under his command. And he was determined to toughen them up.

127

Sergeant Platzek, Bully Platzek, approached the section with interest. He watched them for a time, with obvious disapproval. Then he said:

"They're not even getting their bottoms off the ground, Lindenberg."

There could be no doubt what he meant by this. It was a favorite phrase of his. The corporal at once made an effort to quicken the pace of the exercises and to increase the volume of his word of command. He succeeded. The men exerted their last ounce of effort, for they knew from experience that it was unwise to annoy Sergeant Platzek. They were panting as they drilled.

But they knew quite well that however hard they tried it was no use. Platzek's determination to break them was something they could almost feel physically.

"Rotten," he shouted. "Rotten, Vierbein. What a sight Vierbein is! Wonder what he was doing last night. All because of him — over to the fence; double march!"

And that was the beginning of one of Platzek's "little bits of fun." He made Corporal Lindenberg stay where he was and sent his section chasing backwards and forwards across the parade ground. The men flung themselves about the place, trying to save as much of their strength as possible. Vierbein alone exerted his last drop of effort to carry out each order with the utmost speed and accuracy. He shot across the parade ground like a rocket, and buried himself in the ground like a shell. But in vain. Over and over again Platzek's nagging voice rang out across the parade ground: "Vierbein again . . . !"

The first man to faint went down fifteen minutes later. The world swam before Vierbein's eyes. Platzek's voice gradually grew hoarse. Lindenberg stood in the background rigid and aloof. This, he felt, was going too far. He disapproved profoundly.

Platzek was now quite hoarse and began to be worried about

128

losing his voice altogether. He changed over to his whistle. A blast on the whistle took the place of an order. It went something like this: One blast, flat on the ground! A second blast, on the feet up! Another blast, kneeling position, move! Another blast, on the feet up! Another blast, squatting position, move! Another blast, on the feet up! Two blasts, about turn! Three blasts, attention! One long-drawn-out blast — but this was very rare — stand at ease! It wasn't until this had been going on for ten minutes that Vierbein collapsed and was dragged off into a corner.

"Milksop!" said Platzek contemptuously, and it was easy to see that he felt very pleased with himself.

☙ ☙ ☙

Captain Derna, commanding officer of No. 3 Troop, could be described as one of German Austria's contributions in kind towards the development of the Greater German defensive system. He had at one time been a member of the Imperial Austrian Army, and had subsequently occupied positions as a traveling salesman, a surveyor, and an insurance representative. After the *Anschluss* the German Wehrmacht welcomed him with open arms. He became an officer again and found himself among the Prussians.

Derna, Joseph, had Viennese charm, a soft voice and a pleasant manner. The true Prussians among the officers found him somewhat ludicrous, but they tolerated him and even found him a not altogether unsympathetic companion in the mess.

Joseph Derna, captain, moved about the Prussian barracks like a man walking about a minefield. He half expected to be blown up at any moment. He took good care to step as quietly as possible. He modeled himself at all times and in everything

129

he did on the other officers of the regiment, and he was glad when they found nothing to object to about him.

Everything was quite new to him. In the last few months of the Great War he had been in command of an Austrian howitzer battery at half strength. Then he had received a pension and started fighting for jobs. He knew nothing of the rules of the barrack square, and the finer points of the Prussian way of life were entirely lost on him. In public he was in the hands of Lieutenant Wedelmann, in administrative matters he was at the mercy of Sergeant Major Schulz. Wedelmann accepted him as he was; Schulz, however, tried to treat him as if he didn't exist.

The sergeant major had seen at once what sort of soldier this Austrian captain, now back on the active list, was going to make. He realized that, being a Viennese among so many Prussians, he needed someone to lean on. Schulz knew just what had to be done in the way of administration and had quickly made this clear to the captain. He did all the paper work himself. He devised training schedules, prepared judgments, answered applications for leave — and Derna signed everything which the sergeant major put in front of him.

But Schulz was clever enough never to let Derna see how much better he was at all this than his troop commander. And Derna put himself to some trouble to show the sergeant major how indebted the captain was to him. They lived through a sort of honeymoon period together. They went out of their way to be polite to one another and took every opportunity to reassure each other of the extent of their mutual respect.

"Good morning, Captain!" Schulz bawled out cheerfully. He flung open the door which led to the inner office and produced a salute which Derna felt with some satisfaction lent a thoroughly Prussian atmosphere to the place. The captain seized the hand which came towards him and beamed his confidence in the sergeant major.

130

Then Derna shut himself up alone in his office for ten minutes or so. He sat down at his desk and read the sergeant major's daily report, which lay in front of him. He signed it before reading it through. He knew he could rely on Schulz. He tried to get some of the figures into his head: theoretical strength, actual strength, numbers seconded for special duty, numbers on leave, numbers gone sick. It was always possible that Major Luschke, the battery commander, would find an opportunity to question him about them. And Schulz had made it clear to him that the Prussians expected such figures to be known by heart.

The comforting sound of the telephone interrupted his sincere attempts to acquire something of the Prussian military spirit. His voice sounded extremely amiable as he picked up the receiver and said "Hullo!"

The sharp nasal hiss of the C.O.'s voice came clearly and penetratingly over the wire. Every soldier in the barracks with the exception of Derna referred to Major Luschke as Lumpface. Now his first question was whether Captain Derna imagined he was sitting in a café.

"No, Herr Major," said Derna genially, but a little surprised.

Luschke then explained that this unfortunate impression had been given him by Derna's answering the telephone in a manner which sounded as if he were ordering a package of cigarettes from a waiter. Derna might have grasped by now, continued the major, that such was not a suitable tone of voice in which to conduct the business of a barracks.

"Very good, Herr Major," said Derna submissively.

Lumpface then wanted to know if Derna was aware of the fact that most of the men in his troop who went sick went sick on Mondays, that is to say on the day before rifle drill. Had this struck him at all by any chance?

"No, Herr Major," said Derna, feeling crushed. "But I'll look into it. . . ."

131

The major interrupted the troop commander to say that he should indeed look into the situation thoroughly but *before* his battery commander got on to it in future and not afterwards. Sitting back and lettings things take care of themselves might be all very well in Vienna, but Prussians had a somewhat different way of doing things. And what did Derna mean by "I'll look into it" exactly? Did he doubt the major's statement?

"Of course not, Herr Major."

Or did he accept it as correct?

"Yes, Herr Major."

As always when dealing with Major Luschke, Derna felt himself sweating blood. You never knew where you were with the C.O. He was like a permanent thundercloud over the barracks. No one knew when and where it was going to burst. He was greatly relieved when Major Luschke briskly brought the conversation to a close.

Derna brought out a spotless white handkerchief and mopped his brow. He sat there recovering for a few minutes. Just his luck to have fallen on a C.O. like Luschke. . . . But he hurriedly dismissed such thoughts and tried to concentrate on the papers which his good friend Sergeant Major Schulz had set before him.

And among them he eventually found a recommendation to the following effect: Gunner Vierbein — disciplinary punishment — various offenses. This was something quite new for him. He had never encountered anything like it before. He tried to see what Schulz could have meant by it. He made little headway. He only knew that the words "disciplinary punishment" made him feel uncomfortable. Only a short time ago Major Luschke, the battery commander, had said: "Disciplinary punishment should only be used as a last resort when all other methods have failed. Any officer of mine who resorts to it will automatically be assumed incapable of establishing his authority in the normal way."

Derna rang for the sergeant major. He was prepared to do almost anything to avoid bringing Major Luschke's attention down on himself.

The sergeant major planted himself in front of the captain and did his best to look him loyally and truly in the eye.

"Now, then, Schulz, what's all this about this man Vierbein?"

"He needs to be punished, sir," said the sergeant major, with disarming simplicity.

Derna's voice took on a fatherly tone.

"My dear Schulz," he said, "I don't mind telling you I'm not very fond of disciplinary punishments. They ought only to be used as a last resort when all other methods have failed. We don't want people to think that we're incapable of maintaining our authority in the normal way."

Without for one moment giving away the fact, Schulz found himself wallowing in a sense of his own superiority. He knew quite well that this was one of the battery commander's favorite expressions. You're nothing but a parrot, my fine-feathered friend, he thought.

"Punishment cannot be avoided in this case," he said. "I recommend three days' bread and water. I have taken the liberty of preparing a list of the man's offenses."

He tore a page out of his fat black notebook and put it on the table in front of the captain.

"Very sensible," said the captain, feeling rather cornered.

He didn't feel at all comfortable. Everything about him protested at the thought of awarding this punishment, which would also be his first. That Major Luschke should be a sworn enemy of disciplinary punishments on principle was an additional consideration. He managed to avoid looking at the sergeant major's piece of paper, or even taking it from him.

"Well," he said, "what's the fellow done?"

"A number of things," said Schulz, and he began to let his

133

impatience show a little. "Gunner Vierbein obtained a Saturday night pass last week end by false pretenses. He left the barracks by an unauthorized route. He was guilty of negligence while on guard duty. After completion of guard duty he left the barracks without putting his uniform and equipment in order as prescribed by regulations. In addition to which Vierbein is altogether an impossible soldier. It's high time he was punished, sir."

Derna leaned back in his chair.

"I see," he said thoughtfully, and began tapping out the Rakoczy March with his fingers on the top of the desk. "Yes, I see." He opened the little wooden box which lay in front of him and helped himself to one of the cigarettes which he rolled himself. Schulz gave him a light.

"Yes," said the captain again, blowing out a cloud of smoke. And he saw clearly enough that the Chief was determined to have his pound of flesh. He was a hard man, very hard. It was going to be difficult to talk him out of it. And it was going to be even more difficult to justify a disciplinary punishment to Major Luschke, who was sometimes also known as "old Fritz."

The captain felt the strain beginning to tell on him. Even his charm of manner was affected. He was on the point of becoming positively unfriendly, but he just pulled himself up in time, remembering that it would be madness, virtual suicide, to fall out with the all-powerful indispensable Schulz for the sake of a mere trifle.

"Bring the fellow in," he said.

Schultz thought, Well and why on earth didn't he say that in the first place? He executed one of his smartest salutes and left the room. He was in the best of moods as he gave the order for Gunner Vierbein to be brought in. He'd show him!

Meanwhile Captain Derna was turning over the pages of the punishment regulations. He found them complicated, vague and difficult to grasp. He rang up the battery commander's

134

adjutant and after a pleasant preliminary conversation learned that there had been only one disciplinary punishment awarded in the last six months. "The old man's all for discipline," said the adjutant, "but all against disciplinary punishment."

Derna found this a somewhat remarkable statement, but comforting in the circumstances. He would have been glad to do Schulz this little favor, always assuming that he was justified in doing so. But he couldn't possibly act contrary to one of his battery commander's basic principles. It would have been plain suicide to snap his fingers at Luschke like that. He would need all the skill he could muster. He would have to call in Austrian flexibility to counter Prussian rigidity, and bring about a subtle blend of the two.

He looked Gunner Vierbein up and down with all the coolness at his disposal. This wasn't a great deal but it was enough to have some effect. He said nothing at first, for he had learned that silence was more significant, more sinister and more disturbing than speech. He let his eyes wander over the pale face of the gunner. It looked small and ill beneath the enormous steel helmet. Sergeant Major Schulz took up his position behind him.

"Unhealthy complexion," said the captain.

"Comes from the sort of life he's been living," said the sergeant major.

"You ought to be ashamed of yourself," said Derna, meaning the gunner. "You have the honor to be a soldier and wear a uniform, but you behave like a . . . like a . . ."

"Like a bitch in heat," suggested the sergeant major helpfully.

Derna nodded. He felt that the sergeant major had in fact gone a little too far but he preferred not to reprimand him, at least not in the presence of a subordinate. He looked the gray-faced gunner up and down again. He certainly didn't look like a mutineer, but he had all the appearance of being a shocking

135

soldier. And in the presence of this heap of misery, he himself felt powerful and strong. Once more he was aware of his pride in finding himself, an Austrian, an officer of the Greater German Wehrmacht, on Prussian soil after years of squalid privation. He felt himself immeasurably superior, and this put him in a good mood.

"What's your father's profession?" he asked.

The sergeant major was painfully shocked. What the hell's going on? he asked himself. Does he want to start a conversation with the man or give him his punishment? Here he was talking about the man's family when all he had to do was to rap out the sentence.

"Police official, sir!" said Vierbein.

Derna looked up in astonishment.

"I can hardly believe it," he said, shaking his head. "Your father is an honest reliable official, a guardian of law and order, a public example, so to speak. And you, what are you? You're just a rotten soldier, an unusually rotten soldier, so the sergeant major reluctantly informs me. Your father would be very sad to see you here. Aren't you ashamed of yourself?"

"Is there something wrong with your hearing, Vierbein?" shouted the sergeant major angrily. "The captain asked you if you were ashamed of yourself."

"Yes, sir, I am," said Vierbein.

Derna tried to sound as strict as possible.

"And if your father knew what a rotten soldier you were," he said, "he would be ashamed too. Remind me that I am considering writing to Herr Vierbein, Sergeant Major."

"Very good, sir," said Schulz grudgingly. He was also beginning to feel ashamed, but for the captain's sake. Here he was supposed to be doling out punishment to a man and talking about writing letters instead. He was no sort of commanding officer, he was more like a clergyman. But what else could one expect of an Austrian?

136

"Our sergeant major," said Derna, glancing affably at Schulz, "has been compelled to report your various offenses to me, Vierbein. He has been reluctant to do so, but he has to do his duty."

Schulz, standing behind Vierbein, lost all control of himself. He even went so far as to shake his head. He was sure that his hearing, which had otherwise always been impeccable, must be letting him down. He simply couldn't believe his ears. This couldn't be true. They were in a barracks, not a children's home.

"I have considered giving you severe disciplinary punishment," went on Derna. "You were booked for a long spell of close arrest, but I will once more temper justice with mercy, not least because it is the sergeant major's wish that I should do so."

"But, sir!" protested the sergeant major.

"Of course," said the captain hurriedly, "you don't get away with it as easily as that. You will be deprived of Saturday night passes for the next two weeks. And if I hear any more complaints against you" — Derna tried to shout but his voice merely shot up into a squeaky descant — "then I shall put you in jail at once without more ado. You have my word on that."

Sergeant Major Schulz couldn't help growling to himself. What a circus! But at any rate the old man had committed himself. He had given his word. If there were any more complaints about Vierbein, he'd put him in jail. All right, jail it would be. He won't have to wait long before he's able to keep his word, he thought.

Vierbein was allowed to dismiss. His knees seemed to have turned to water as he left the room. He had the feeling that someone had been at him with a stomach pump. He tottered off in the direction of the lavatory.

Captain Derna smiled at his sergeant major.

"That'll be a lesson to him," he said very firmly.

137

The sergeant major didn't condescend to reply.

Each was dissatisfied with the other and felt a hidden resentment towards him. The captain was afraid he might be losing the invaluable co-operation and support of his subordinate; the sergeant major was afraid he might be losing his influence over his superior. Both of them thought angrily: And all because of this wretched gunner called Vierbein.

☙ ☙ ☙

Lindenberg's section got their "evening treat" early that day, and had soon had enough of it. Sergeant Major Schulz had thought out something special for them, something particularly ingenious. He felt quite proud of himself.

It was actually his wife Lore who had given him the idea. After helping him off with his boots she said she thought it was really high time he washed his feet again. The "high time" was naturally an exaggeration but the word "wash" set him thinking. Washing — bathing — swimming: that was how his train of thought went.

Schulz immediately went off to see Captain Derna and suggested to him that it was about time they made a really determined effort to improve the standard of swimming in the troop. Swimming had been sadly neglected of late. It should be their aim to have everyone in the troop able to swim. "Major Luschke has said several times how important he thinks this is."

Captain Derna was delighted by his sergeant major's keenness. He was particularly anxious to demonstrate his confidence in him after their little difference of opinion that morning. So he said:

"That's an excellent idea, my dear Schulz. A particularly apt one for the time of year. Start on it right away." But he added with a note of caution: "Don't overdo things, though."

138

"I'll just begin with one or two small groups," Schulz reassured him.

The first of these small groups turned out of course to be Lindenberg's section. They had had an absolutely hellish day but had come through it with credit. They were all tired. Vierbein, who had had a particularly bad time, was on the point of dropping. They slumped over their rifles, cleaning them as if in a trance. Corporal Lindenberg disapproved of this. He understood what they felt though it couldn't be said that he had any understanding for it. He stood by the window and stared keenly out of it.

He was a man who believed strongly in discipline, but he was no bully. He had given his men a hard time — it was what they expected of him — but he hadn't strained them beyond the limits of endurance. He had squeezed them almost dry, but not quite. He had extracted the very last ounce of effort from them, in rifle drill, in artillery drill, and on the sports field (with a cross-country run to finish up with) but his aim behind it all had been to develop them physically, to steel them for the future. He was not just systematically "giving them the treatment."

Now that it was late afternoon and time for rifle-cleaning, he had a profound sense of having done his duty and of having made the men under him do theirs. He was filled with a sense of pride: his work that day had been quite first class. He took an unsympathetic view of Sergeant Platzek's brutal intervention, for it could be interpreted as an expression of lack of confidence in himself.

They hadn't finished cleaning their rifles when Sergeant Major Schulz walked into the barrack room. He beamed cheerfully and everyone knew that this was a very bad sign.

"Anyone here not passed his swimming test?" he asked cheerfully.

Of the eleven men in the room, seven, including Vierbein,

139

put up their hands. Gunner Asch, who had made the mistake of leaving the clothing store for a few moments and who had just come into the room, pressed himself into a corner and tried to remain invisible. He could see what was up.

"Only seven of you?" asked the Chief, still in the best of tempers. He knew very well that there had been very little swimming in the troop that year and that he had constructed a trap in which he could catch anyone he wanted to. "And what about the rest? What about you, Asch?"

"I passed my swimming test last year, Sergeant Major," said Asch.

The Chief grinned.

"That doesn't count, of course," he said. "What guarantee have I that you're still able to swim? The swimming test must of course be passed each year. Every soldier who's worth his salt must be able to swim. Isn't that so, Corporal Lindenberg? You've passed your swimming test, haven't you?"

"I've also passed my first lifesaving test," said Lindenberg stiffly.

"There you are, you see. I must congratulate the section. Now, are there any of your people who can't swim at all?"

"No, Sergeant Major," Lindenberg assured him. He had always made the most of the few swimming periods that had been allotted to the section. He himself had passed his first lifesaving test, and all his men were at least able to keep themselves afloat.

"Splendid! Splendid!" cried Schulz. "Then we won't delay any longer. Your section will begin swimming at once."

"At once?" asked the corporal in astonishment.

"Is your hearing defective by any chance?" asked the sergeant major brutally. "It is now shortly after six, it won't be dark until half past eight. You can get in plenty of swimming in that time."

Lindenberg didn't approve of this at all. So strongly did his

140

point of view differ from the sergeant major's, in fact, that he actually went so far as to put forward an objection.

"I think a certain amount of swimming drill is necessary beforehand, Sergeant Major," he had the audacity to say.

With the exception of Vierbein, who was all in, and who merely stared vacantly in front of him, the members of the section followed this unusual form of argument with the keenest interest. Gunner Asch even edged forward to try to get a better view of what was going on.

"So you want to do a little drill, first?" said the sergeant major, and he gave not the slightest sign of being ruffled. "Well then, you shall. An excellent idea. You can arrange half an hour's swimming drill first, say from six-thirty to seven. Then you can have a short cross-country run to the baths, and start swimming at seven-fifteen. Sergeant Platzek will be in charge. I shall also be there. All quite clear?"

"Yes, Sergeant Major," gasped Corporal Lindenberg.

Schulz left the room in the best of spirits, not without first staring pointedly at Gunner Vierbein. He immediately went to find Sergeant Platzek, Bully Platzek, to discuss the practical details with him.

The members of Lindenberg's section were left alone with their thoughts. Several of them expected the corporal to make some sort of pronouncement. But he said nothing. For him orders were orders. It was not his place to criticize. The idea of making any comment on a senior N.C.O.'s behavior in front of the rank and file would have been abhorrent to him.

"Put your rifles away," he ordered. "Get ready for swimming drill. Bring your swimming things with you."

The members of his section reluctantly obeyed. The exhausted Vierbein closed his eyes for a moment and took a deep breath. He moved almost like a robot.

"Hell's bells!" muttered Asch.

"Did you say anything, Asch?" asked the corporal sternly.

141

"Yes, Corporal. I said, I hope the water's not too cold."

Lindenberg accepted the explanation. He looked anxiously at Vierbein. He didn't like the look of things there. The fellow didn't seem to have any powers of resistance.

"Now then, Vierbein, pull yourself together! Don't let me down."

The gunner could hardly feel his exhausted limbs any more. He seemed to see everything through a veil of mist and his feet skated about the floor. All his movements were mechanical and lifeless. He changed his clothes, fetched himself a stool and a pillow and stood ready, leaning against his locker.

Gunner Asch saw the state he was in. He went up to Vierbein, took him by the arm and said: "Grit your teeth and stick by me."

Vierbein nodded mechanically. He was hardly able to think any more. The day had been too much for him. Bully Platzek had concentrated almost entirely on him. Captain Derna's reprimand that morning had put the fear of God into him; now when he was pulled up for something he knew he could expect to be jailed as well. At lunchtime Sergeant Major Schulz had sent him to work in the cookhouse. During the physical training period he had had to do endless pull-ups on the horizontal bar. This had been followed by jumping over the horse, rope-climbing, push-ups, a wrestling bout and finally a cross-country run. Now he was ready to drop. And when he managed to snatch a second or two for his own thoughts, he thought of Ingrid and of their quarrel of the night before.

Corporal Lindenberg blew a shrill blast on his whistle. The men picked up their stools and pillows, pushed their way through the door into the corridor and then ran out onto the barrack square, where they fell in. Gunner Veirbein let himself be carried along with the crowd. He stumbled on the stairs and would have fallen if Gunner Asch hadn't caught him.

Sergeant Platzek was there waiting for them. He grinned

with pleasure, got the men into open order, glanced proudly up at the faces poking curiously out of upper windows, and set to work.

The men laid their pillows down on the stools in front of them and at a blast on the whistle flung themselves across them. The words of command rang out monotonously — One! Two! One! Two! The men went through the motions of the breast stroke in the regulation manner. They went on doing this in time for some minutes. It was no easy matter to keep the body properly balanced on the stool. It was even less easy to make the correct movements of arms and legs. It was agony for the stomach muscles.

"Vierbein!" roared Platzek, beaming with joy. "You're moving like a drunken crab. It's all Vierbein's fault that we've got to keep at it so long."

Johannes Vierbein was on the verge of collapse. He tried to make the correct movements, but his arms and legs hung almost helplessly from the stool. Vierbein saw the gray cement of the barrack square beneath him. It seemed to be coming up in waves to meet him.

"Head up, Vierbein!" yelled Platzek. "If you think you're here for a nap you've got another think coming."

By a great effort of will Vierbein raised his head. The muscles of his neck tried to force it down again. Vierbein stuck out his chin. The cement disappeared from his field of vision; he saw clipped grass, the long wall, the tall fence with its iron poles, and beyond it the road leading into the town. He saw soldiers walking along it. He saw Lieutenant Wedelmann walking with a girl. And his eyes suddenly opened wide and a searing stabbing pain went through him, and it was as if the mists which swam before him had suddenly cleared. For he saw that the girl with whom Lieutenant Wedelmann was walking was Ingrid Asch. He seemed unable to move for a moment; then he collapsed over the stool.

143

"I didn't say anything about diving!" yelled Platzek menacingly. "Kindly pull yourself together, you wretched little mess!"

Vierbein managed to survive even this crisis. His limbs moved like the parts of some badly oiled machine working at half speed. Asch, who was vaguely going through the motions of swimming on his stool just behind him, was all ready to come to his rescue, but it didn't seem necessary.

At seven o'clock sharp the stools were all piled up together. Corporal Lindenberg put himself at the head of his section and led them off at a comfortable jog trot to the military baths. Sergeant Platzek followed on his bicycle, blowing his whistle.

Sergeant Major Schulz had gone on ahead in his own time and was already waiting for them. Lindenberg had been keeping his eye on Vierbein. He could see that he was exhausted and moving about in a trance. Much to the sergeant major's annoyance he insisted on his men first cooling off and having a shower. Only then was he prepared to start on the swimming.

The sergeant major looked at his watch. "Right, off you go," he said. "Twenty minutes' breast stroke, beginning with a dive from the three-foot board, and ending with a dive from the nine-foot board. Everyone in on the word Go."

The men dived in one after the other. They had to swim round and round the pool in a great circle. Schulz stood with Lindenberg on one of the two little bridges that spanned the water. For very different reasons each kept his eyes glued on one man: Gunner Vierbein.

After the men had been swimming for ten minutes Schulz looked at his watch and cried out cheerfully: "You've had five minutes of it!"

Almost all of them were now in difficulties. They had had a strenuous day and it had left its mark on them. One man tried to give up altogether, but Schulz just burst out laughing.

"Oh no! You go on swimming till you sink. Don't worry! We'll come and pull you out."

144

Gunner Asch completed two circuits of the pool without much difficulty. He was a good swimmer, but he didn't see why he should put himself out at all. Besides, he was keeping an eye on Vierbein. He looked over to the bridge on which the sergeant major and the corporal were standing. As soon as he saw a favorable opportunity, he dived out of the circle, swam under the bridge and hung on to one of the beams beneath the two men's feet.

Johannes Vierbein was only just afloat. He could hardly see where he was going. A typhoon was roaring in his ears. A red watery mist swam before his eyes. A great weight seemed to be dragging him slowly under. He felt as if he were disintegrating altogether and being washed away. Suddenly he sank like a stone.

Lindenberg, who had seen this coming, swung himself over the railing of the bridge. Schulz tried to stop him.

"The fellow's only shamming. He'll come up again."

But the corporal took no notice. He jumped into the water and swam quickly over to Vierbein. Asch had also darted from his beam below the bridge. The two of them brought Vierbein to the side of the bath.

"Typical of the fellow," said Schulz grimly. "No strength, no energy, an utter milksop, a dirty shirker. Just spends his time pawing women who don't belong to him. But we'll soon put an end to all that."

☙ ☙ ☙

The Freitags' supper was on the table punctually, but there was no sign of their guest of the evening, Gunner Asch. The old man looked up from the newspaper which he had been vainly trying to read and glanced up at the clock. Then he pretended to go on reading again.

"There you are," said Elizabeth querulously. "You see what sort of man he is. He doesn't keep his appointments."

145

"It can't be his fault," said her father. "A soldier can't come and go as he pleases, you know."

Frau Freitag was standing by the stove, getting impatient. "It's all ready," she said. "If we wait any longer everything'll be spoiled."

"Well, let's begin, then," said Herr Freitag.

"But what if he's been kept late?" asked Elizabeth anxiously.

Freitag smiled. His daughter wasn't finding it easy to hide her nervousness. And he thought this was as it should be. She had first of all attacked Asch and then defended him. Her behavior was erratic but thoroughly understandable. Such behavior was — as Freitag remembered very well — one of the inevitable accompaniments of being in love. He was glad to see it. He wouldn't have liked it if she had simply been indifferent.

"What about waiting just another quarter of an hour?" suggested Elizabeth tentatively.

"We'll start," said the foreman. "I don't think he'll expect us to change our habits to suit the demands of barrack life. Or can't you eat without him, Elizabeth?"

"Don't let's wait another minute," she said.

The meal was brought in. It smelled delicious. Father Freitag had the plates put down in front of him. He filled them to the brim.

"Let us work hard and eat well," he said. "Let us sleep peacefully and leave the future to take care of itself."

They began eating. They spooned up the delicious thick stew almost without a word. The two older Freitags were hungry. Only Elizabeth ate little and kept on looking towards the empty chair.

But before Father Freitag could fill the plates a second time, Gunner Asch arrived. He was a little out of breath. Freitag made things easy for him. He showed him to his place and treated him as if he had already been with them some time and had often been a guest in the house.

146

Frau Freitag found him by no means unsympathetic. Perhaps he talked a little too loudly and rather too uninhibitedly, but not unpleasantly. Elizabeth avoided looking at him. Father Freitag asked quietly:

"Well, did you have to work late today then?"

"I had to do a spot of swimming before I could get away."

Freitag nodded understandingly. "At the double I suppose?"

"Exactly," said Asch.

The stew tasted excellent and he said so. He even gave his reasons for saying so and Mother Freitag was astonished how much he seemed to know about cooking.

Elizabeth kept herself very much to herself. She didn't say a word to Herbert, and he thought it best not to speak to her directly either. Neither knew whether it would be right for them to address each other as *du* in front of her parents. Moreover, they knew that in the circumstances they would never be able to say any of the things they wanted to say to each other. So they just said nothing.

Much to Mother Freitag's delight, Asch ate three platefuls of stew. When he had finished, the foreman asked him to come out into the garden with him and smoke a cigar. They wandered down the flowerbeds while the women washed the dishes in the kitchen.

"Was life in the army always like this?" asked Asch. "I imagine you were in it in your time?"

"Yes, before the Great War," said the old man. "And what do you mean, was it always like this? My dear boy, I don't mind telling you sometimes I get the impression that you're living in a sanatorium compared with what it used to be like."

"You mean it was even worse?"

"It was all taken more for granted. I might almost say it all seemed more natural. There was a sort of stag-party atmosphere about the whole thing. A lot of people didn't mind it at all. They were physically fit and completely uncultured. Very

147

few people absolutely hated it. Things are much more complicated today. What could once be regarded as a crude but virile sort of pleasure is now regarded as an assault on a man's finer feelings. People have become much more sensitive and things are therefore more difficult for the N.C.O.s. They have to be more brutal to get what they want. It's all a vicious circle."

"But didn't anyone in those days see that what the N.C.O.s wanted was senseless in any case?"

"It isn't as simple as that," said Freitag. "There was something to be said for drill even in those days, or at least it wasn't entirely useless. I myself remember an instance once, in 1914. We were making a counterattack and the section of troops I was with panicked. Those in front threw their rifles away and tried to turn and run. And what happened? Up sprang one of your barrack-square bullies, roared at the fleeing men and began drilling them there and then in the middle of the battlefield. After a bit they calmed down again, which is to say they were once again ready to face the enemy."

"Well," asked Asch, "and what does that prove? Merely that in the old days the troops on the battlefield behaved in the same way as they did on the barrack square. But time doesn't stand still, you know."

"The men who held junior ranks in the Great War are brass hats today. The barrack-square bully of yesterday, a lieutenant I think he was, is probably a colonel today. And all these people want to conduct the next war on the basis of their experience in the last. People like that don't think ahead; they think backwards. They don't adapt themselves to new techniques; they spend their time extolling the old ones. Look at it another way and you could say that though they've all been made bankrupt once, they can still find people who are foolish enough to give them credit."

"And we're the ones who have to foot the bill," said Asch bitterly.

148

"Drill is a way of getting quite a lot done in the easiest possible way," said the old man thoughtfully. "It's always been like that. The barrack square is a paradise for the small mind. It's the place where more subtle, more complex natures can be steamrollered into submission. That's the whole secret of it."

"And isn't there anything one can do about it?"

Freitag seemed to find the idea amusing.

"If a revolutionary could ever become a general, then something might be done. But I can't believe he'd really have any success. I'll tell you what happened to us once in the days before the Great War. A certain private told a certain sergeant to go to bloody hell. The result was a court-martial. But at the court-martial the private stubbornly maintained that he had never said anything of the sort. And the court-marital took him at his word. There were no witnesses. The private was known to be a good soldier, and they were simply incapable of believing that any man in his senses could have thought such a thing, let alone said it."

"I suppose this private's name was Freitag?"

"Let's go in again," said Foreman Freitag, just managing to suppress a smile. "It's getting chilly. Besides, the women will be waiting for us."

They went indoors and sat down at the large table in the sitting room.

"What about a bottle of red currant wine?" said the old man. "It's not particularly good, but I made it myself from my own red currants."

They tested the wine and Herbert Asch found that it wasn't at all bad. His only criticism was that perhaps it had been kept a little too long in the barrel, about two weeks too long.

"I can see you're trying to deprive me of the remains of my authority in this house," said Freitag with a wink. "You're backing up my wife, who, I must admit, was of a different opinion from me and wanted to put the wine into bottles two weeks earlier."

"Your wife was completely right," said the gunner emphatically.

Mother Freitag beamed with pleasure. She not only found this young Herbert Asch sympathetic but positively charming as well. A well-mannered young man, not too full of himself, but not fawning either. He behaved as if he felt at home in the house. And she liked that. It was clear that not every soldier was as cheeky and loudmouthed and full of himself as she had imagined.

They drank up the bottle of red currant wine and opened another. There was a very friendly atmosphere. The two young people still didn't speak to each other. Shortly after half-past ten Asch took his leave. "I must get back to barracks," he said.

"I would have walked back with you with pleasure," said the old man, "only I have to be up early tomorrow morning. I'm sure Elizabeth would be glad to go, though."

Elizabeth pretended to hesitate.

"All right, if you insist, Father," she said.

Father Freitag smiled at her.

"Well, I don't want to force you, you know!"

Mother Freitag laughed, and Asch felt embarrassed. But he was pleased to see that Elizabeth was even more embarrassed than he was. He said good-by, was told to come again any time he felt like it, and promised he would.

He walked off slowly in the direction of the barracks. In the darkness it looked like some mighty ship plowing its way across the ocean. Elizabeth walked beside him. She kept her distance from him.

Asch stopped.

"Elizabeth," he said. "Have I annoyed you in any way?"

"No, you haven't annoyed me," she said. "You simply

haven't bothered about me at all and I've adjusted my feelings accordingly."

"But I didn't have time to come and see you," said the gunner. "I simply didn't have time."

"You didn't have more than a few hundred yards to come. Of course you could have come and seen me if you'd wanted to."

"Yesterday — Monday," said Herbert Asch. "You weren't there. I tried to find you several times. It wasn't until the evening that I heard you hadn't been to work all day."

"I was only at home. That isn't as far off as all that. It's only ten minutes from our house to the barracks."

"I couldn't come to your home," said Asch defensively. "Not after what had happened. I simply couldn't."

"And what had happened?" asked Elizabeth coolly. And to prevent him from answering she added hurriedly: "But I've been in the canteen all day today and you never even tried to see me."

"I've been busy all today. I was either being pushed around by N. C. O.s all the time or else hard at work trying to keep out of their way. I've been in a most terrible state all day. Honestly I have."

Elizabeth leaned forward a little.

"Was it my fault?" she asked, and she sounded worried. "Did you have trouble because, last Monday, you . . . I mean, was it because you had to leave your clothes behind?"

"Oh no, that was just funny," said Asch. He had to laugh in spite of himself. And to his astonishment he heard her laugh too, softly but unmistakably. They laughed together.

He took her arm and she didn't resist. He could feel her firm warm body through the thinness of her dress. "That was a nice business, wasn't it?"

She nodded. Already they had shared too much for her to be able to be angry with him forever. He didn't seem to have the

151

sort of tenderness for her that she had always dreamed of in a lover, but she loved him just the same.

"Do you think your father noticed anything?" he asked. "I mean . . . Does he know what happened?"

She withdrew her arm.

"Is it for your own sake that you're worried?" she said mistrustfully. "Is that all you mind about? Don't worry. You can just carry on as if nothing had happened. My father knows nothing and I have forgotten all about it."

"There's been a misunderstanding," said Asch hastily, looking at his watch. It was high time for him to be back in barracks.

"Oh, don't bother about me," said Elizabeth angrily. "It wasn't even a misunderstanding. Nothing has happened at all. I've never even seen you, if that makes you feel better. And if anyone asks me if I know the man I slept with I shall say no."

"But Elizabeth . . . I . . . I . . . Look, I'll explain everything to you tomorrow. I must fly now."

"Yes, go off to your barracks," she said. "That's just where you belong."

"Good God, you can be maddening!" he cried furiously, and he left her standing there and ran on.

☙ ☙ ☙

A rosy dawn crawled exhaustedly up the sky. It stared at the barracks, which lay like some huge stone animal in its path. Sounds of life could be heard inside but the animal itself didn't move.

Gunner Vierbein lay like a corpse in his bed. The orderly corporal's whistle made him sit bolt upright. He stared round the room. His limbs were like lead and there seemed to be a metal band round his head. The air seemed to be going past him in thick stale waves. The men slowly dragged themselves out of bed. They felt that they had made enormous advances since a few months ago, when as recruits they had leaped out of bed like jack-in-a-boxes. Now they were "old sweats" and took their time about it, especially as it was only Corporal Schwitzke, Slacker Schwitzke, who was on duty. Schwitzke never swore at anyone unless there were specific grounds for it or he had received explicit orders to do so.

The conversation proceeded in a desultory fashion. There was a lot of yawning. Two men were quarreling about how far a locker door could be opened without disturbing the owner of the next locker. Another flung open the windows with some hearty remarks which drew applause from those whose beds were in the corner and abuse from those by the window. Lance Corporal Kowalski and Gunner Asch slept on for another quarter of an hour or so. This didn't involve them in much risk, for their beds were well screened by lockers and couldn't be seen on a first glance into the room.

"I showed her a thing or two yesterday," said Wagner, who was renowned for his virility. "She loved it. I never fail to give them a good time — they all know that by now."

Some of the men wanted more details. A boot came flying over in Wagner's direction from the corner of the room.

"Quiet!" roared Kowalski from his hideout. "Or do you want me to come and give you something to make you quiet?"

Vierbein still lay on his bed apparently unable to move. He simply hadn't the strength to get up. The morning noises of the room floated round him like heavy waves of tobacco smoke. He had a splitting headache. The world seemed to spin round him.

Corporal Schwitzke flung open the door to make sure that everything was going according to plan. He was just about to shut it again when he caught sight of Vierbein sitting up on his bed like a stuffed dummy.

153

"Vierbein again!" roared Schwitzke triumphantly.

Slacker Schwitzke was a lazy creature who seemed to have been specially selected by Providence for a nice cushy job in the Wehrmacht. But he was also an extremely sharp fellow. There was nothing he didn't miss. He had a sort of sixth sense for what would please his immediate superiors. And although he never did anything much, everything that he did do was always well thought out and very much to the point. No other man had such a gift for currying the maximum amount of favor with his superiors with the minimum amount of effort. And he knew very well that this Vierbein was the sergeant major's weak spot at the moment, his Achilles heel, if one might make use of such a bold analogy.

Gunner Vierbein leaped out of bed and tried to stand at attention in his nightshirt. But he swayed and had to steady himself. He looked exhausted. He stared vacantly across the airless room.

"He can't even see out of his eyes," cried Schwitzke delightedly. "Been dreaming of women again, eh, Vierbein?" He looked around him expecting a roar of laughter, but no one moved. "We'll soon knock that sort of nonsense out of you. You'll report to me for fatigues, see?"

"Yes, Corporal," said Vierbein obediently.

Schwitzke looked him grimly up and down again, shouted "Little runt!" at him and left the room feeling very pleased with himself. He determined to allot Vierbein to some job where the sergeant major or Sergeant Platzek at least couldn't help noticing him. The sight would be bound to please them and put them in a good temper.

Gunner Vierbein climbed into his trousers, threw his nightshirt on the bed and hurried into the washroom. He made his way to a basin, filled it with cold water, and pushed his head deep into it. This made him feel much better, though it didn't remove the leaden weight from his limbs.

154

In the meantime Kowalski and Asch had got up. The cheerful shouting of the corporal had eventually awakened them. They blinked at each other and began to dress.

"Vierbein's meant to be on barrack-room duty today," said Asch.

"All right," said Kowalski. "I'll detail someone else. Of course." He looked round the room. The virile Wagner was busy telling a dwindling audience how he intended to spend the coming evening.

"I'll show her a few tricks," he said. "I'll make her see how lucky she is to have found a man like me."

"You're just the man for me too," cried Kowalski. "You can be barrack-room orderly for the day."

The virile Wagner became indignant.

"Me? Why me? It's that lame duck Vierbein's turn for barrack-room orderly. Not mine."

"If you don't shut up," said Kowalski, "I'll break every bone in your body. You'll be a good deal worse than a lame duck by the time I've finished with you."

The virile Wagner knew from experience that Kowalski wasn't a man to be trifled with. He cursed and muttered to himself, but he did what the head of the room told him. Kowalski laughed.

"Anyone as strong and virile as you ought to be able to cope with a miserable little room like this in no time."

Vierbein had no time to dress properly. There was a blast on a whistle and he snatched up broom, shovel and bucket and ran down to the parade ground. He tried to do up the buttons of his fatigue tunic as he ran.

Schwitzke looked at Vierbein exactly as if he were late on parade. But he was too lazy a man to tick him off properly. He merely shouted out: "Ground-floor latrine!" The latrine wasn't far from the orderly room. Thus he could keep an eye on it in comfort. Besides, it was a place which he imagined the

155

sergeant major would be likely to visit early on his tour of inspection. It goes without saying that the sergeant major had such a place in his own quarters but it was well known that he liked to display his sense of duty on every possible occasion and that, in this particular case, he made a point of killing two birds with one stone.

But Schwitzke left Vierbein alone for a time, partly to give himself a bit of peace and partly from a certain feeling of sympathy for him. If the sergeant major had appeared, Schwitzke would have put up a performance of some sort for him at once. But as things were he could let things rest for a bit and give that poor little swine Vierbein a chance to recover.

Vierbein, however, was prepared for the worst and had worked as hard as he knew how. He panted as he scrubbed away on all fours at the tiles, slopping wet rags and buckets of water all over the place. When he had finished and there was still, rather surprisingly, no sign of Schwitzke, he hurried off to the barrack room.

The men were eating their breakfast, which they washed down with tepid coffee. The virile Wagner was making a nuisance of himself by trying to start cleaning the room, but Kowalski threatened to crown him with a coffeepot. A few desultory conversations were in progress.

"The best thing," said Asch to Kowalski, "would be for Vierbein to report sick."

"Not a bad idea," replied the other. "They'll tear him to pieces otherwise. But what can we say is the matter with him?"

"We'll think of something," said Asch. "After all, he did collapse twice yesterday."

"H'm," said Kowalski. He spoke from long experience. "This sort of illness can only really be classified as fainting fits or exhaustion. Neither sound too good."

"What about heart trouble?" suggested Asch. "After all, it's not so wide of the mark. Besides, it isn't so easy to prove. You

156

need a thorough examination. It'll give time for the storm to blow over."

"Fine," said Kowalski, and he turned to Vierbein, who was just about to begin his breakfast. "Listen, my boy," he said, "you're going sick today. We've decided that for you."

"But I'm not sick," said Vierbein.

"Your answer alone is sufficient proof that you are."

Kowalski was a man who would not allow himself to be contradicted when he knew himself to be in the right. "Off you go at once and report sick. Pains in your heart. Or do you want to take your punishment? Just try and think what today's going to be like! It's shooting on the range today, out at Wilhelmsruh. Not much doing, in fact; plenty of time for them to concentrate on you. And on the way there and back they'll load you up like a mule. I don't mind betting we'll be made to carry full pack (in this section at least) and if you're with us you'll have to carry more than anybody. That's certain. Now hop it."

Gunner Vierbein left his breakfast and ran off downstairs. He reported sick to the orderly corporal. Schwitzke, who had been taking a little snooze, looked up at his visitor. He called him *du*, which was always a sure sign that he was in a bad temper. "What the hell do you think you're playing at?" he said. "Don't you know that if you want to report sick you must do it first thing in the morning when the orderly corporal comes round for the second time?"

"Yes, Corporal, but . . ."

"Oh, you know, do you, you little rat! Just listen to that. You know that perfectly well. And what do you think you're doing coming here like this, then? Well, louse? You want to make a fool of me, do you? Well, you'd better go and find someone else, see?"

Vierbein tried to speak but he didn't get any further than opening his mouth. Schwitzke picked up the orderly book. "Now listen here, you ape! What do you see written down

157

here? 'Reported sick: none.' Is that clear? You didn't report sick at the right time so you're not sick, see? You must wait until tomorrow, you miserable little worm."

Vierbein tried to leave the room. But Schwitzke, who was really indignant at the thought of someone not only daring to disturb him, but on top of that actually imagining that he was going to alter his morning report, had been stirred into action.

"So you've cleaned out the ground-floor latrine, eh?" he said. "Well, we'll just go and see how you've done it."

He went off with Vierbein to the ground-floor latrine, made a thorough inspection and found it in a totally unsatisfactory condition. He ordered it to be cleaned out again immediately, and this time he decided to stay and watch. His temper gradually improved. A brilliant idea had occurred to him. He would tell the sergeant major the story of how a gunner had come to him to report sick, obviously shamming, and how he had seen through it and sent him off to creep about on all fours in the latrines for his pains. It would make the Chief double up with laughter!

This idea put Schwitzke into such a good mood that he actually dismissed Vierbein a little earlier than he had intended to. Vierbein shot off like an arrow from a bow.

On the way back the gunner looked at the clock and saw that he wouldn't have time to finish his breakfast. He didn't feel hungry anyway. He went over to Kowalski and Asch and told them what had happened. They merely looked at each other. There was nothing to say. Vierbein began to get ready for the range.

He went up to Asch. "I wanted to have a word with you yesterday evening," he said.

"Sorry," said Asch, "I had an important engagement."

He pretended to be very busy with something in his locker and buried his head inside. He simply couldn't bear to look into

158

the pale, worried, exhausted face of his friend. Moreover, he felt rather guilty.

"I saw your sister yesterday evening," said Vierbein in a low voice as if it were causing him pain to speak.

Asch stopped what he was doing but still didn't look up.

"Oh," he said. "You saw her?"

"Yes. With Lieutenant Wedelmann."

Asch slowly straightened up. You poor wretch, he thought, you poor miserable little bastard. So you saw. And he said:

"You don't want to worry about that, Johannes. Women are like that. Ingrid's no exception."

"I see," said Vierbein weakly.

But Asch wasn't going to let him get off so easily. He had no wish to spare Vierbein's feelings. He wanted to make him tough. He didn't want to see him just wallowing in self-pity. He wanted to get him out of the state of sickly sentimentality he was in. So he said as brutally as he could:

"She's not worth wasting a single tear on. She's just a cold vain egotistical little bitch. A typical Greater German hothouse plant. The higher the rank the greater her love. If you were to become a general she'd be mad about you."

Vierbein couldn't find any answer to this. He did his best to think of one but failed entirely. Asch left him standing there. Just at that moment a runner came in with the mail. And just at that moment Corporal Schwitzke's whistle blew in the corridor outside.

"Get ready to fall in!" he shouted.

Vierbein put on his belt and ammunition pouches. He tightened his belt by one hole. Someone handed him a letter. It was from his mother. He shut his locker and fastened the padlock. He ran his eyes quickly over the first few lines:

My dear darling boy:
I wanted to spare you this, but I can't go on any longer. I have decided to leave your father . . .

159

The orderly corporal's voice could be heard outside shouting: "Fall in!"

Vierbein folded the letter up and put it in his coat pocket. He was white in the face and his hands were trembling. He let himself be hustled out by the others.

※ ※ ※

The sun beat down remorselessly on the shooting range. The air was like molten glass. The earth was cracked and parched.

Shooting proceeded according to plan. The troop was divided up into three large groups and each was allotted to a separate set of targets. Those who had already fired lay about on the grass at the bottom of the range. A day like this was regarded as a day of rest, though of course it was anything but that for those who hadn't earned it. Such people were kept busy marking targets, putting up new targets, bringing up ammunition, sweeping the stands, cleaning the N.C.O.s' rifles and even doing rifle drill if they had shot particularly badly.

Apart from this no one bothered about anybody. The main thing was that the shooting should proceed without a pause. It didn't much matter when a man shot. He wasn't needed for long in any case. This of course didn't apply to Vierbein, who was needed both before and after shooting. The Chief had seen to it that this particular friend of his should not be bored for a single moment.

Schulz was in his element on the range, for he was an excellent shot. He didn't appear much on the barrack square and only rarely at the baths, but on the range he was always in evidence. And since today was the day of the individual championship, which it was a point of honor for him to win, he was in a particularly good mood. He was everywhere at once, radiating self-confidence. In fact he was so full of energy that there were whole quarters of an hour in which he forgot about Vierbein altogether, and left him with almost nothing to do.

Lance Corporal Kowalski and Gunner Asch intended to spend most of their time sleeping in the bushes, but for appearances' sake they got hold of two nice cushy jobs for themselves for a while. One entered up the scores on the score sheets and the other distributed the ammunition. Sergeant Platzek was in charge of operations. Everyone had a pretty easy time, for the first rule of the range is that strict silence must be observed.

Bully Platzek, who, with his ten years in the service, knew every trick there was, got Vierbein to fetch him a bucket of cold water. This served a double purpose, being used both for refreshment and as a means of cooling off those who were in too nervous a state to shoot well. Anyone who trembled, hesitated, or so much as flickered an eyelid was made to dip his head into the bucket, and this gave Platzek a great deal of amusement.

The men marched up in bunches of five, showed their empty pouches to Gunner Asch, who carefully counted them out six cartridges. Then one after the other they went over and gave their names to Kowalski so that he could enter up the amount of ammunition they had drawn and their eventual score in the score book. After that they reported to Sergeant Platzek and began to shoot. And Platzek did all he could to see that the best possible results were achieved.

It all worked as smoothly as a well-oiled machine. The fact that there were three groups, each under separate supervision, rather took the edge off the supervision generally. In individual shoots like this, the responsibility was felt to be shared between the supervisors. Section shoots were a different matter altogether. In them, each N.C.O. was responsible for the men under his command. It was the average of the whole section which counted. Each individual's score was a reflection of the standard of training he had received, that is to say on the ability

161

of the N.C.O. who had trained him. In the individual shoot, however, there could be but one victor, so that only those who were likely to come out near the top could be interested in the result. The others didn't care.

So marked was this tendency that those N.C.O.s who fancied themselves as good shots and regularly occupied one of the top places were rather pleased when their men did badly, as they didn't want to have to face too much competition. A man fired off six rounds and trotted off again; it was the next man's turn. It didn't matter at all if the scores weren't very good. Even misses which at other times made the N.C.O.s furious were no more than a cause for ribald laughter on such a day.

Sergeant Platzek yawned loudly. The sultry atmosphere of the summer's day made him sleepy and he took little interest in what was going on behind his back. He knew he could rely on men like Asch and Kowalski. They had had plenty of experience. He could leave them to look after things all right. From time to time he cracked a good-natured joke with the men who were firing, and if he managed to put one of them off his shot so much the better — he got a good laugh out of it.

One of the men in the group whose turn it was to shoot next was Gunner Vierbein. Asch gave him a searching look, but Vierbein avoided his gaze. Asch saw that he looked absolutely miserable but didn't pay much attention to the fact. He gave him six rounds of ammunition like everyone else. Then he went over to have a chat with Kowalski.

The shots rattled out continuously. The markers' boards were raised and lowered with monotonous regularity. Somewhere in the background the Chief could be heard roaring away.

After a time Asch turned round to say an encouraging word to Vierbein. But Vierbein was no longer there. He had slipped away unnoticed.

It took Gunner Asch a few seconds to realize what had happened. It took Lance Corporal Kowalski, who was suddenly struck by the look of strain on his friend's face, a few seconds longer. Then he too understood.

"I don't like the look of this," he said quietly.

Asch nodded. He went over to Sergeant Platzek.

"May I be excused a moment, Sergeant?"

"All right by me," said the sergeant. "But don't stay away too long. Lance Corporal Kowalski can take over your job in the meantime."

Gunner Asch ran down to the bottom of the range.

"Looks like you've been caught rather short," called Sergeant Platzek after him, with a hearty laugh.

But Asch didn't hear. He was looking for Vierbein.

He pushed his way through the crowd of waiting soldiers, almost knocking over Lieutenant Wedelmann as he did so. Wedelmann was about to pull him up, but when he saw who it was he gave him a warm smile. Asch ran on. Then he saw Vierbein standing among the trees behind an ammunition dump.

"Vierbein!" shouted Asch.

Vierbein jumped and turned round. There was a feverish light in his eyes and his face was very pale. He looked as if he might turn and run at any moment.

Gunner Asch went slowly up to him. He tried to slow down his breathing. He could feel his heart beating against his ribs. He walked on as if in a dream.

"Vierbein!" he said. "Give me that ammunition."

Vierbein didn't answer. He stood there listlessly, slightly hunched. His rifle hung in his left hand.

"Give me that ammunition, Vierbein!"

"No," said Vierbein.

Asch stopped. The pale face of his friend was wet with sweat and tears. His lips had lost almost all their color. His mouth hung open.

Asch was appalled by the sight of him. He felt a wave of pity

163

go through him. There was a catch in his throat and he had to fight back his own tears. But he said:

"You ought to be ashamed of yourself. You rotten, miserable contemptible little coward!"

"Leave me alone," said Vierbein. "I can't go on."

"I'll give you a punch in the jaw if you don't let me have that ammunition at once."

"I've had enough!" shouted Vierbein in an agonized voice.

Asch leaped on Vierbein and flung him to the ground. The rifle clattered down with him. Asch held his writhing body with his left hand, and hit him in the face with his right.

Vierbein yelled. Asch hit him again and again.

Vierbein continued to yell.

Asch pressed his knee into Vierbein's heaving chest, tore the ammunition pouches off him, found the six rounds and stuffed them into his own pocket. "You swine!" he shouted. "You miserable little swine! So you want to put a bullet through your skull, do you? But you don't get out of it as easily as that. Not while I'm around anyway."

And he looked into the huge eyes staring up at him. He saw the blood running over the grayish-white skin. He got to his feet.

He was breathing heavily, and when he looked up he saw that a number of soldiers were standing round watching. Someone at the back called out: "He's killing him!"

Asch smiled bitterly.

Sergeant Major Schulz came rushing up and pushed the soldiers aside. "What's going on here?" he cried.

"Just a little difference of opinion," said Asch. He knelt down beside Vierbein, bent over him and began to pull him to his feet. Vierbein could only just stand up. He swayed for a moment and then righted himself.

"Vierbein again!" cried the sergeant major.

"I've been polishing up his jaw for him a bit," said Asch. "It

164

was a purely personal quarrel. Between man and man. Wasn't it, Vierbein?"

"Yes," said Vierbein.

The Chief nodded, satisfied. He wasn't, as a rule, the person to let this sort of thing pass. Normally he would have reported the matter to the C.O. or at least would have made a scene about it. But this was a special case. He thoroughly approved.

"Well, you've got hold of the right man, anyway, Asch," he said.

Schulz looked the battered bloodstained Vierbein up and down and scarcely attempted to hide his pleasure. He clapped Asch on the back. He did this with such an overwhelming feeling of self-satisfaction that he never noticed how the gunner winced.

"Bravo, Asch," he said gratefully. "Well done."

And he walked away.

The man whom he had praised so generously stared after him.

"And you're the next," he said softly.

And so began the remarkable revolt of Gunner Asch.

⚑ ⚑ ⚑

The No. 3 Troop shooting championship was slowly drawing to a close. It seemed certain who the winner would be. It wasn't likely that there would be any surprises. People were already congratulating the Chief on his victory.

A field kitchen came up at midday, with pork stew. Gunner Vierbein was detailed to serve it round, wash the dishes and scrub the copper out afterwards. All this he did relatively calmly. His face now wore a thoughtful rather than an agonized expression. It was as if the fight with Asch had brought him back to his senses at a moment when he had been about to take leave of them altogether.

165

"I made a nice mess of you," said Asch, looking at him affectionately.

"You treated me as if I was a punching bag."

"I did my best, Vierbein."

Vierbein's face was battered and swollen and it hurt him to speak. He smiled wryly. He couldn't bring himself to answer Asch in the same affectionate tone, but he didn't hold anything against him.

"You simply lost control of yourself. You just went on hitting and hitting, even after I'd stopped defending myself. You were like a man in a trance."

"Alas," said Asch, mocking him gently, "not everyone is gifted with as much self-control and good sense as yourself."

"I'm sorry, Asch," said Vierbein at once, and his voice sounded husky.

"That's all right. Don't let's say another word about it."

Herbert Asch turned away, but Vierbein came after him and caught him by the sleeve.

"I suppose you think," he began, "that I . . . that I was going to commit suicide?"

"I don't think anything," said Asch, refusing to commit himself. "I don't even believe the evidence of my own eyes. Anyway in this particular case I didn't see anything. If you prefer it that way I was just taking precautions. Or if you like I wanted to let off steam! What could be nearer the truth? But one always uses one's friends to let off steam. That's what they're for."

"Herbert," said Vierbein softly, but felt no shame in saying it, "it *was* what you thought. I did want to do it. I couldn't go on."

"Forget it!"

"I can't ever forget it, Herbert. But I don't think I'll ever try to do it again."

"Good, Johannes. It's not worth it. What's the point? Who's

166

it going to benefit? If anyone ever tries to persuade you that there's any sense in doing such a thing, knock him down."

"I felt," said Vierbein, "as if I was being driven to it, brutally, quite intentionally. I hadn't any will of my own left. It was too much for me all of a sudden."

"You let them drive you to it. You were as weak as water. And who are these people? A bunch of professional megalomaniacs and halfwitted bullies!"

Johannes Vierbein wanted to say that there had been a bit more to it than that, that there were other things that had made him feel so desperately lost and rejected. He wanted to say that he had felt quite numbed, as if he had no will or feeling left at all, as if he hardly existed, and that he had had only one wish: to obliterate himself altogether, to bring everything to an end. He looked about him and said:

"I've done my best, I've tried as hard as I could, but I'll never make anything of this life — I'm not a soldier at all really."

Asch burst out laughing.

"But this isn't the only life," he said, "even though there are a lot of people who try to make out that it's the only one that counts. But you must — somehow or other — manage to come to terms with it. If you don't it will be the end of you."

"It's all very well to say that," answered Johannes Vierbein bitterly.

"Perhaps someone," said Asch with apparent indifference, "someone will succeed in showing you that you're wrong, and just how wrong you are. It's high time someone made it clear once and for all that there's nothing sacred about a barrack square."

Gunner Asch left his friend and went back to the range. Lance Corporal Kowalski seemed to want to speak to him about something.

"Did you get the ammunition back from Vierbein?" he asked.

Asch stared at him blankly.

"What ammunition?" he said.

The lance corporal let out a low whistle.

"I see," he said, "but if there are six rounds missing at the end, there's going to be some trouble coming for someone, isn't there?"

"Let there be," said Asch cheerfully. "The main thing is, they won't be able to pin anything on us!"

"That's true," said the lance corporal, grinning. "I handed the ammuntion over to someone else just after Vierbein made off. He was one of the usual halfwits, he took my word for the amount. That's to say he was either too lazy or too stupid to check. That was at eleven o'clock. Someone else came along at one, and someone else at three. No one's noticed anything so far."

"This'll make them sit up, eh?"

Kowalski nodded and chuckled with delight.

"There'll be hell to pay for someone," he said.

There were now only a few more soldiers left to shoot. The rest began to gather in little groups. Even Captain Derna appeared on the scene, although he had taken no active part in the competition for he was not a particularly good shot.

Captain Derna, who was taken round by Sergeant Major Schulz, made a great show of being interested in all that was going on. He inspected the score sheets and saw with satisfaction that the sergeant major, his good friend Schulz, was well in the lead.

"Congratulations," he said with evident pleasure and in a voice which could be heard for some distance around. "There's no better way of telling a really good soldier."

Schulz modestly reminded the captain that the competition was not yet over.

168

But in fact he knew that he had little to fear. The best shots in the troop had already tried their luck and he was still unbeaten. He had scored sixty-four with his six rounds, out of a possible seventy-two. It was a very respectable score. Corporal Lindenberg followed with sixty-two and Sergeant Platzek with sixty-one. It was the sort of result that people had expected.

When the shoot was finally complete, a number of men were detailed to dismantle the range, carry away the used targets, collect the odd scraps of paper that were lying about, and generally clean the place up. Vierbein of course was among them. The N.C.O.s in charge checked through the score sheets and the ammunition registers. The rest of the men fell in and prepared to return to barracks. They had had a quiet day. All they had had to do was to fire off six rounds into the blue, after which they had been able to let things slide. They had dozed and chatted, played cards and generally devoted their energies to avoiding any extra duty that might be going. Now they were about to march back. There would be an hour's rifle-cleaning and then: off they could go! There seemed no reason to expect complications. The Chief's victory had put him in a good mood, and besides, this was the evening which the N.C.O.s always set aside for a party in honor of the champion.

But there seemed to be some delay. Nos. 1 and 3 ranges reported all correct, but No. 2 was not yet ready. Sergeant Platzek counted through the ammunition over and over again and was quite unable to make it come right. There seemed to be six rounds missing.

The sergeant major cursed when this was reported to him. He counted the ammunition through himself. But even he couldn't get it right. There were six rounds missing.

The Chief made no bones about it: this was something quite unheard of. Ammunition simply couldn't be missing. It was distributed with the utmost care and an exact account had to be kept of every round used. The sergeant major saw appalling complications ahead.

"This is a nice mess, Platzek," he said.

Platzek turned towards him in embarrassment. This disaster which had befallen him, of all people, was more than painful; it was full of dangerous possibilities, it might have quite unforseeable consequences. He saw himself being court-martialed, imprisoned, reduced to the ranks. The Chief looked at him coldly.

Platzek instituted a preliminary inquiry. He had everyone who had assisted on his range brought before him, and among these were Asch and Kowalski. He put a number of very pointed questions to them. He made no attempt to conceal his suspicions.

"That's stupid, Platzek," said the sergeant major angrily. "You're being idiotic." He nodded towards Asch and Kowalski with special confidence. "I'm not going to have aspersions cast on some of my best men like that. We'll go back now and you, Platzek, will take the score sheets and go through everything once more when you get back to barracks. In addition, compare the entries in the score sheets with the number of holes in the targets."

"Very good, Sergeant Major," said Platzek, looking crushed.

The sergeant major nodded grimly. "And everything had better be in order by tomorrow morning at the latest. How you manage to do this is your own affair. But in order it shall be. Or you'll have the shock of your life coming to you."

¥ ¥ ¥

Lieutenant Wedelmann was feeling very dissatisfied with himself and the world in general. It seemed to him that this profound dissatisfaction of his was fast developing into a permanent state of mind. Nothing he did gave him pleasure any more.

When his day's work was over he went and sat in the officers' mess. He sat in a corner at the back of the reading room, turning over the pages of an illustrated magazine for a while, staring at the pattern on the tablecloth, counting the fringes on the tapestry that hung on the wall.

Then he saw Major Luschke coming towards him, obviously looking for someone to play chess with for the rest of the evening, and he fled into another room. It was not an easy thing to run away from Luschke like that, but it would have been torture to have to play chess with him, on this of all days. For Luschke always played very methodically and with maddening slowness. He also made it clear from time to time that as the senior and thus the better officer it was only logical that he should win. He usually did win in fact, because he really was the better player, and took a fiendish delight in defeating his opponent.

What troubled Wedelmann most was the fact that though he was surrounded by comrades, there wasn't one of them he could call his friend. There were three other lieutenants of his age group in the battery, and all three had their own ways of spending their time. One had a liking for tarts; the second's idea of pleasure was to be permanently on duty; the third was practically engaged. Thus it came about that Wedelmann very often sat about the mess in a state of unutterable loneliness, having to rely for comfort on the occasional remarks that came his way from senior officers.

The lieutenant lay sprawled in an armchair, with his legs stretched out in front of him. He hadn't got a girl, that was the trouble! He didn't just want a girl he could take out for coffee or play tennis with or go for a walk with, what he wanted was a real girl who would let him take her in his arms with pleasure and be in love with love itself. Not any cheap little girl off

171

the streets, but a real woman with good hands and a big heart. But apparently they were not so easy to find. They mostly seemed to exist only in the pages of novels and magazines.

One of his chief reasons, in fact, for disliking novels was that they aroused all sorts of uncontrollable passions within him. And he found that however hard he looked in this Godforsaken hole he could find no remedy for his condition. Every woman he came across here seemed either too young, too promiscuous, too old or too closely attached to someone else. He didn't yet know which of these categories Ingrid Asch came into.

This Ingrid Asch was a remarkable girl, he thought. She had the face of someone in a painting, an excellent figure, and was by no means stupid. He didn't even mind being seen in uniform with her. He found himself getting mildly excited whenever he thought of her.

"Like a game of chess?" asked Major Luschke, who had come up on him unawares. Lumpface gave a particularly sinister smile, which was usually enough to throw even senior captains off their balance.

Lieutenant Wedelmann leaped to his feet. He was feeling slightly confused in any case. Luschke confused him still further. He could never make out whether he liked this inscrutable man or was afraid of him.

"Stay where you are, Lieutenant," said the major in a soft voice that seemed to cut through the air like a razor blade. "I have no intention of drilling you, I merely wanted to know if you would like a game of chess."

"Of course, sir," said Wedelmann hurriedly. And he looked up submissively into Lumpface's lumpy face.

"No, my dear boy," said the major dryly, "you don't seem quite in the right mood for a game. I expect what you need is some fresh air.

172

And he stalked away with short sharp strides, snapping the fingers of his right hand contentedly.

The lieutenant stared after his commanding officer in admiration. There was a man who had his ear to the ground all right.

Wedelmann went to the telephone booth, looked through the pages of the directory and dialed the number of the Café Asch. One of the employees answered. He asked to speak to Fräulein Asch and was put through to her at once. Ingrid's voice sounded pleasantly welcoming, and he was ready to believe that there was something almost sensual about it. He felt excited.

"I just wanted to ask if you would care to come out with me this evening. I'd suggest the Café Liedke, but say if there's anywhere else you'd rather go. I'll come in uniform if that's all right with you."

Ingrid hesitated for a moment. That wasn't a bad sign, he told himself — just coquettishness. Then she accepted. It was quite all right if he came in uniform, and she thought the Café Liedke a good idea too; she understood the food there was excellent. There was only one thing: could he possibly let her brother, Gunner Asch, know that she was going to be in the Café Liedke, for it was possible that he might want to see her.

"But of course. I'll see to that at once. I'll look forward to seeing you there then. In half an hour's time? Right, in an hour, at the Café Liedke."

Wedelmann put down the receiver, nodded to his reflection in the glass, left the telephone booth and went over to his room to get ready. He told the orderly N.C.O. to let Asch know that his sister was to be found in the Café Liedke.

He gave himself a shower and sang "O sole mio" to himself as he stood under it. Then he shaved, although he had shaved once that day already and didn't have a particularly strong

173

beard. He rubbed his smooth face with Eau de Cologne, looked at himself in the glass and found himself a thoroughly presentable young man.

He met Ingrid in the upper part of the Café Liedke, where there were a number of armchairs, and where the officers' wives were usually to be found. He recognized the wife of a captain on the battery staff and saluted courteously. The captain's wife nodded haughtily and looked Ingrid Asch critically up and down.

Ingrid was wearing a gay low-cut sleeveless summer dress of some striped pattern. Wedelmann thought she looked splendid. He bowed graciously, obviously very much taken with her.

"Just in case there should be any misunderstanding," said Ingrid Asch warily, "I've only come to have a bit of a chat with you, you know."

"But of course," said Wedelmann.

"I hope you don't think that there are any strings attached to my coming like this."

"How on earth could I think so?" said Wedelmann reassuringly, and he thought, rather disappointedly: She doesn't seem to be very forthcoming, but perhaps that's just all part of the act.

"I'm as good as engaged, as a matter of fact," said Ingrid Asch spontaneously; and hardly had she said it than she was astonished by what she had said.

"Aha!" said Wedelmann. And he added: "And that's just as it should be; men would have to be quite blind not to propose to you." And he thought: This charming girl doesn't seem so easy after all; she's probably one of the old-fashioned sort who don't want to go to bed with anyone until they're married. "But anyway," he concluded, "you're not actually engaged yet?"

"Of course not," said Ingrid Asch.

"Quite right too," said Wedelmann approvingly. "You're

174

still very young. You don't want to get tied up with anyone in too much of a hurry, do you? You've plenty of time."

Ingrid didn't answer. It was as if she simply weren't there. She was staring across the room to the tables over by the window. He followed her gaze. A soldier was just sitting down. He knew him. He was a man from his troop called Vierbein. Gunner Johannes Vierbein.

"Excuse me a minute," said Ingrid Asch. "I think my brother has sent a message for me." She got up without waiting for him to give permission. She went over to Johannes Vierbein. He stared at her.

Wedelmann began to feel rather uncomfortable, for the captain's wife who was sitting two tables away was becoming more and more interested in him. And he thought he could detect a mixture of astonishment, curiosity and disapproval in her look. He drank up his coffee at one gulp and ordered a large brandy from the waiter.

With ill-concealed misgiving, and soon with open displeasure, he looked across to where Ingrid Asch and Gunner Vierbein were sitting together. They were now sitting side by side, talking animatedly. That is to say, Ingrid was doing most of the talking. Vierbein listened impassively and only spoke a word now and again as if he had to stick up for himself. But, thought the lieutenant, they could hardly be said to look like lovers.

He sipped his brandy. He found it disgusting — there was no life in it, it had no bouquet. He drank it up and ordered another.

This fellow Vierbein, thought the lieutenant, looked a wretched sight! He had got a strip of sticking plaster down the left side of his face; his dress uniform was too large and hung in folds across his chest. No, there was no competition to fear there. And then he saw Ingrid take hold of the man's arm, the man who he thought represented no competition for him, and

175

take hold of it almost tenderly. She put her hand on his and left it there.

The lieutenant decided that this was going too far.

"Waiter!" he cried. "The bill, please!"

But Ingrid Asch heard nothing. She went on talking to the gunner, who was moving closer and closer to her.

Wedelmann paid and left. He went straight past Ingrid Asch and Johannes Vierbein, but neither of them noticed him. This didn't worry him, it merely made him more determined than ever.

He went out into the street and looked about him. It was now quite dark. One or two people were wandering about the pavements. There was hardly a vehicle in sight. The electric light from the street lamps and the shop windows fell flatly onto the Tarmac. He found himself moving towards the bright red neon sign of the Excelsior bar.

Paul, the owner, known to regular customers of the bar as "dear cozy little Paul," was delighted by the arrival of his visitor and came forward to welcome him. Wedelmann pushed him away. He went over to Erika at the bar and quickly knocked off four gins one after the other. Erika let him understand that when she had finished work she might possibly be prepared to have "quite a long chat" with him. He slowly shook his head. He didn't feel altogether against the idea at first, but the price she was asking plus the brazen materialism with which she did so put him off.

He left the Excelsior in disgust, stood about helplessly for a while in the lonely street and then decided to go off to Bismarckshöh, the regular haunt of the lance corporals and gunners first class and there drink himself into a state of oblivion. But just as he was about to plunge into the whirl of dancers — "Every Wednesday: 'Excuse Me' Dance" — the landlord tactfully drew his attention to the fact that he was in uniform.

176

"Oh, all right," said the lieutenant crossly. "Then I'll just drink myself silly at home. Wrap me up a bottle of cognac."

Wedelmann went into the landlord's office, where the bottle of cognac was discreetly packed up for him. He had it put down on his account and walked out rather hesitantly into the darkness.

The night, so it seemed to him, was full of desire. It was a warm, sultry, suffocating sort of night. He made his way past several couples who were locked in each other's arms.

"Damn it," he said, "it's about time, it really is about time that something happened to me. If I don't get married soon, I'll end up in a madhouse."

The sentry pulled open the gate. Wedelmann saluted mechanically and walked past him. I'll drink myself into a coma, he thought. It'll do me good. I'll be able to forget that I'm capable of being cut out by a miserable little gunner like Vierbein.

He walked rather unsteadily across the roadway to No. 3 Troop barrack block. His quarters were on the top floor, above the sergeant major's. The corkscrew would be on his bedside table.

"Good evening, Lieutenant," said a woman's voice huskily, close beside him.

Wedelmann looked up in surprise. It was Lore Schulz, the sergeant major's wife. She was reclining on a window seat, staring out into the night.

"Good evening, Frau Schulz. Not gone to bed yet?"

"I can't sleep. My husband's at the N.C.O.s' party. It's bound to go on until very late."

"I can't sleep either," said Wedelmann. "I'm going to drink myself into a coma."

"Good idea," said Lore Schulz. She laughed to herself. "I wouldn't mind doing the same."

"What about getting drunk together then?" asked Wedelmann.

"Why not?" said Lore Schulz. "Come in."

☙ ☙ ☙

Lore Schulz regretted asking Lieutenant Wedelmann in almost as soon as she had done so. She was frightened — of herself as much as anything else. But it wasn't so easy to undo things this time.

Lieutenant Wedelmann entered the sergeant major's apartment rather diffidently. He was shown into the best room, where he sat down on one of the four dining-room chairs. He looked about him. He felt slightly embarrassed.

"Don't you think it's rather late really?"

"Do you want to go away again then?"

"If you really don't mind, perhaps I'll stay a quarter of an hour or so," said Wedelmann. He had brought the brandy bottle in with him and now put it down on the table. "Have you got some glasses and a corkscrew?"

"Of course," said Lore Schulz. She was glad to have an excuse to leave the room for a moment. She stared critically at herself in the looking glass which hung in the kitchen. Her hair was rather untidy, but there was something almost romantic about that, something rather daring in fact. Her face was shiny; cold water would soon put that right. Her dress was certainly crumpled, but it was a dress she was very fond of because it made the most of her figure. She would have to turn out the overhead light in the sitting room. These little flaws in her appearance wouldn't be so noticeable then.

In the meantime Wedelmann was taking a look round the room. It was a room in which everything had been bought on installments. The imitation oak furniture was crudely made. A print of Boecklin's "Island of the Dead" hung on the wall

178

in a pompous plaster frame. Sporting and shooting trophies, some rather arch little ornaments, and a few clumsy pieces of cut glass stood about on the sideboard. There were a lot of gaily embroidered cushions on the sofa. These were covered in gnomes, four-leaf clovers, roses and water mills.

Lore Schulz came back into the room and Wedelmann noticed that she smelled strongly of some scent made of violets.

"The light's rather bright in here, don't you think?"

"If you do."

She switched off the central light. A lamp threw a soft kind light on the two of them. The grandfather clock ticked loudly.

Wedelmann opened the bottle of brandy.

"You've got a nice place here," he said.

"Oh, we just bought everything on installment," said Lore. "My husband and I had a few savings — not much, but they were enough for the deposit. We're paying out fifty marks a month at the moment. It goes on like that until August, 1939. And we're pretty short of money. You know yourself: a sergeant major doesn't earn as much as a lieutenant, and a lieutenant has only got himself to look after."

"Some lieutenants are married."

"But not many. You're not, for instance. Why not, actually?" Wedelmann carefully filled their glasses up to the brim.

"Well, you know, it's not my fault. It's just that I can't find the right woman."

Wedelmann raised his glass to hers, and they both drank deeply.

"And whenever I do find a woman I like," went on Wedelmann, "she nearly always seems to be married already. Like you, Frau Schulz."

"Oh, I'd never do for a lieutenant," said Lore Schulz modestly. She felt flattered and embarrassed at the same time.

"Don't say that," said Wedelmann. He filled their glasses again.

179

Lore Schulz tossed off her brandy. She had lain down among the embroidered cushions on the creaking sofa. She spread herself out comfortably. She thrust out her breasts which were full and round, and abandoned herself to daydreams.

She always liked doing this. Her powers of imagination were not very great but they were quick and impulsive. She had a vast unsatisfied appetite for life. She was ambitious but lacked the energy to translate her ambition into action. She was very passionate, but all she had learned in her meager life so far was how to be a housewife. Even her emotions were part of the household economy.

"When I was young," she said and her eyes rested on the brandy bottle, "I lived with my parents and my sisters in two third-floor rooms. For years I shared a bed with my two younger sisters. Father was a good man but he was stupid, and he didn't even earn enough money to keep himself in drink each month. He used to beat us when he was in a bad temper. And the whole world seemed to conspire to put him in a bad temper."

"My father was a post office official," said Wedelmann. "That's to say, to be honest, he was a postman. I'm his only son. He used to say that there were quite enough children in the world as it was. Several times a week we had herrings and potatoes in their jackets for supper. And every morning there was bread and jam. He never beat me. He was an emaciated-looking little man. He used to talk a great deal, often until long after midnight."

They drained their glasses and stared at each other. They found the situation a strange one. The room was hot and the brandy made them sleepy. The atmosphere was less seductive than it had been. They both felt the need to explain themselves to each other. It was a way of arriving at a better understanding of why they were there.

"When I was fourteen," said Lore Schulz, "I had to go out

to work for my living. I worked in a market garden for two years for fifty pfennigs an hour. Then I started actually selling the flowers at the entrance to the cemetery. I was even allowed to sleep in the back room and I had a bed all to myself and when I looked out of the window I could see the graves. But it wasn't gruesome at all, it was just lonely. I used to go out dancing on Saturdays. And that was how I met Schulz. He was a sergeant then. I married him because I wanted to improve my position."

"I lived at home all the time," said Wedelmann. "I knew only two rooms: our living room, which was also my bedroom, and the classroom at school. I matriculated when I was eighteen and became a soldier because my father hadn't got enough money to send me to a university. That's all."

"And here we are," said Lore Schulz.

"Let's drink to ourselves."

He drank up his brandy but didn't put the glass back on the table. He held it between his two hands, playing with it.

"Neither of us are exactly what you'd call happy," he said.

"What are you talking about?" said Lore Schulz. She seized the bottle and filled their glasses up again. She did this very suddenly so that the brandy overflowed and spilled onto the tablecloth. "Don't let's think about that. Let's try and forget it."

"But can you forget that I'm a lieutenant?" asked Wedelmann. "And what's more a lieutenant in the same troop as the one in which your husband is a sergeant major?"

"I'm the sergeant major's wife."

"I know. And I'm his superior officer."

"And of course it's all wrong that a sergeant major's wife should be sitting together with the sergeant major's superior officer at midnight, particularly in the sergeant major's own quarters. I've got to forget all that too, haven't I?"

"Can't you?"

"I want to. Don't you see that?"

181

She looked at him anxiously. At the same time she seemed to be demanding something of him.

"Come on," she said. "Come over and sit by me. Or are you afraid to?"

He shook his head. He got up and walked round the table which stood between them. He sat down beside her.

"Come closer," she said. Her voice was husky again. "Closer still. I won't bite."

He moved up beside her. He put his arm around her. Her body was firm. He could feel her trembling. She collapsed on him with a sort of helpless gesture. She shut her eyes and threw her head back. He kissed her.

Her lips were dry and yielded reluctantly. She lay lifelessly in his arms. His own eyes were open and they saw the green pattern on the wallpaper opposite and a photograph that hung there of the sergeant major looking proud and virile on a motorcycle.

Her arms were clasped tightly round him. Slowly he sat up and pushed her away.

"Let's have a drink," he said.

Obediently she filled up the glasses. As she did so she lowered her head and said:

"I'm not always like this, you know."

And almost inaudibly she added:

"I've never done this before."

Then she laughed softly and said: "Unfortunately."

Wedelmann emptied his glass with a flourish. He took off his tunic and threw it over the back of a chair.

"You don't mind, I hope," he said.

"Of course not," she answered. "Please do. My husband always does that. I mean, you'll be more comforable without your tunic."

"Yes, I feel more at home like this," said Wedelmann, but in fact it was so hot in the room that he felt he was going to

182

suffocate. He seized the bottle but it was empty. "We've finished it already," he said.

"There's some more under the sideboard," said Lore. "There's nothing specially good there, but choose something. I'm terribly hot. Do you mind if I put on something cooler?"

"But of course not," said Wedelmann calmly. "Please do."

She left him and went into her bedroom. She quickly pulled her dress over her head. She took off her stockings and girdle. She looked at herself in the wardrobe looking glass. She thought she looked worn-out, dull and listless. I'm not meant for this sort of thing, she thought; I'm always wanting to do it and then at the last moment I can't. My courage always fails me. It's always been like that.

She slipped into her dressing gown, which she hardly ever wore. It was dark blue and had a dull sheen on it. When she tied it up in front and straightened her shoulders and let her arms hang loose, it looked very smart. But it wasn't made of particularly good material, it crumpled too easily. She hoped Wedelmann would like it. She wanted him to find her beautiful, or, if not that, attractive or at least desirable — for this one evening at least. She felt drawn towards him, for she sensed that he was lonely and disillusioned too.

Lore Schulz went back into the sitting room. She looked into his eyes to try to see what he was thinking and it seemed to her that she could see desire there or at least some liking for her. She sat down beside him and felt for his hands.

"All right?" she asked.

"Fine."

"What is there to drink?"

"Wine," he said. "Some wine or other. It doesn't matter what we drink."

He opened the front of her dressing gown. His left hand felt its way tenderly, almost shyly, over her breast. She lay down. They kissed for a long time. They closed their eyes.

Suddenly she sat up and pushed him away from her. "Not that!" she said. She seemed to be listening for something.

"What's the matter?"

"No," she said very definitely. She shook her head. "No! We mustn't, I can't."

"But why not?" he said reassuringly.

"I can't," she repeated. "Don't you see?" She seized her glass and drank it up. "You've got the same sort of hands as he has. All men have hands like that."

"It's not true," he said. "Please don't talk like that." He felt confused. "But I love you," he said.

"You love me?"

"Yes."

She closed her eyes. For a moment or two she felt happy.

"Then I don't mind," she said.

He sat up a little.

"What don't you mind about?"

"Anything, anything that happens. Anything that can happen. Anything this may lead to. Anything at all."

He drank up two glasses one after the other. But the alcohol seemed to have no effect on him. He didn't notice that Lore Schulz was crying quietly to herself. She had an overwhelming sense of melancholy. And when she laid her hand gently on his arm, he pushed her away.

Then they both suddenly sat stockstill staring at the light. The clock ticked on remorselessly, seeming to hack up the silence. The wine tasted rough.

The sound of the front door shutting came quite clearly through the silence. Steps were heard crossing the hall towards them and suddenly Sergeant Major Schulz was standing there in the doorway. He swayed and leaned against the side of the door. His face was distorted. He couldn't believe his eyes.

The lieutenant got to his feet.

"Good evening," he said.

184

Schulz said nothing. Lore stayed just where she was.

The lieutenant said: "I've been keeping your wife company, Sergeant Major."

Schulz still said nothing. His brain was befuddled with drink and he simply couldn't take in what he saw.

The lieutenant put on his tunic and started to button it up. "I hope you won't misunderstand this," he said.

Wedelmann waited for an answer for several seconds. He waited in vain. He didn't know what to do next.

"I'll say good-by then," he said to Lore. He took her hand and bent low over it. Then he walked past the motionless sergeant major out of the room.

The front door fell to behind him.

Schulz rushed at his wife and hit her in the face.

※ ※ ※

The first man to fall a victim to the revolt of Gunner Asch was the N.C.O. in charge of the cookhouse. The fight wasn't a particularly stiff one, nor was the victory particularly resounding. In fact it hardly amounted to more than a preliminary reconnaissance of the enemy line.

The day began with a little diversion. When reveille sounded both Lance Corporal Kowalski and Gunner Asch refused to get up. Only when the orderly N.C.O. told them for the second time in an unmistakably menacing tone of voice to "get themselves out of bed and be quick about it" did they both mumble out some excuse about the sergeant major having given them permission to stay in bed longer that morning because they had been acting as orderlies at the N.C.O.'s shooting championship party the night before. He had practically ordered them to do so, they said.

Of course there wasn't the slightest bit of truth in this. The most that could be said was that they had misunderstood the

185

sergeant major's expressions of gratitude and goodwill. But the orderly N.C.O. didn't want to be suspected of not knowing his immediate superior's orders. So he withdrew, muttering, and left them both lying there. They slept on undisturbed long into the morning and in fact, through an oversight, it was nearly twelve o'clock before they were eventually roused again.

The orderly N.C.O. was so annoyed at forgetting about them like this that he immediately put them to work in the cookhouse to make up for it.

"But by all means," said Gunner Asch obligingly.

They were allotted to No. 2 cookhouse, where they arrived extremely late. The N.C.O. in charge of the cookhouse, a man called Rumpler, who was normally one of the mildest N.C.O.s in the entire battery, but who for the few hours round midday did his best, though all in vain, to turn the cookhouse into a barrack square, received them with undisguised hostility.

He planted himself firmly in front of them, pulled out his watch and said: "It's already twenty past twelve."

Wherupon Asch pulled out his own watch, stared at it seriously and said: "Correct."

The corporal started. His fruity voice rose an octave.

"What I meant by that was that you're late!"

"Also correct," said Asch. "We weren't able to come any sooner. We were busy sleeping ourselves out."

Lance Corporal Kowalski, who began to think that Asch was going a little too far, thought it necessary to put in an explanation at this point: "We acted as orderlies at the N.C.O.s' party after the shooting championship last night," he said. "It went on into the early hours of this morning. We had to get some sleep, Corporal."

The relatively smart way in which the lance corporal gave this information had a certain pacifying effect on Rumpler. He was after all an N.C.O. himself, and he was able to understand what had happened; but he was very sensitive to anything that

186

sounded like disrespect. It was his secret ambition to enjoy exactly the same amount of respect in the cookhouse as his colleagues enjoyed at rifle drill on the barrack square.

"All right," said Corporal Rumpler. "Then we'll get down to it. You, Kowalski, will take charge of the orderlies working in the cookhouse, and you, Asch, of those in the dining hall."

This, in Rumpler's eyes, involved a certain drop in status for Asch. For everyone knew that it was possible to obtain extra rations if you were working in the cookhouse itself, whereas in the dining hall you got nothing but the dirty work.

Somewhat to the astonishment of Corporal Rumpler, Asch didn't in the least seem to mind the prospect of the dirty work in the dining hall. It was only later that the corporal realized just what a viper he had taken to his bosom.

At first Asch and his four orderlies did their work tolerably enough, though one could hardly have said that they worked well. It was their job to bring in the soup and give out the plates, and then, when one shift had eaten and the other was still waiting outside, to clean the tables and wash up the plates.

But during the first break, Asch set about drawing up a sort of chart. He then went and borrowed a freshly tested pair of scales from the canteen. And now something happened which at first left the corporal speechless, but then sent the blood rushing to his cheeks. Asch began checking the weights of the individual meat rations which were being issued. He entered the results carefully on his chart.

Rumpler approached him like a panther ready to spring.

"What the hell do you think you're doing?" he roared.

"Weighing," said Gunner Asch simply.

"Who told you to do that?"

"No one. I have the right to see that the actual rations issued are correct."

"That's none of your damn business. Or are you trying to make out that we're cheating on the rations?"

187

"I'm not saying anything just at the moment," explained Asch amiably. "My comparative figures aren't complete yet. At any rate it seems clear that there's some considerable percentage short."

"That's none of your damn business!" roared Rumpler again.

"You said that once."

For a moment it seemed that Rumpler was going to go through the ceiling with rage. The men who had collected round the two of them grinned cheerfully. They had little sympathy for the corporal in his ordeal. Everyone knew that the rations issued were less than they were supposed to be, but so far it had never occurred to anyone to try to prove it in cold blood like this.

Rumpler took a deep breath. Asch entered a new figure on his chart. Rumpler had just opened his mouth wide as if to speak, but he clapped it shut again. He didn't like the look of that chart. If the gunner really did succeed in bringing the results of his investigations to the notice of the authorities — and it was not altogether beyond the bounds of possibility that he would — a great deal of unpleasantness might result.

The corporal at first tried to put on a superior air.

"Have you never heard of such a thing as wastage?" he said.

"Certainly," said Asch amiably. "Of course I've heard of wastage. But according to the regulations the percentage of wastage should never exceed ten per cent. What's more, each ration of meat is supposed to weigh a hundred and fifty grams; some weigh more and some less."

Rumpler gasped.

"Well, you little runt! What do you think you're doing then?"

"Only when I have sufficient figures to arrive at a statistically valid average," said Asch, "will I be in a position to say what the exact percentage of wastage is. I've weighed thirty-eight

188

rations so far; I'll stop when I get to fifty. But even the early figures seem conclusive enough. Ten rations ought to weigh one thousand five hundred grams, but in fact they weigh just one thousand two hundred. The wastage in that is three hundred grams, that is to say not ten per cent, which would be permissible, but twenty per cent, which might almost be called criminal."

"I'll report you!" shouted the corporal, suddenly exploding with rage. He hurried away. He stormed into his office and immediately rang up the quartermaster and told him what was going on.

The quartermaster said nothing for a long time. Then he asked cautiously:

"Isn't everything as it should be with you?"

"But, Quartermaster," bellowed Rumpler, "of course everything is as it should be."

"I hope so for your sake," said the other noncommittally. "And if it really is then you've no need to let a mere gunner upset you."

"Of course not, Quartermaster. But I'm not going to have my rations checked up on like that."

"If everything is as it should be then you've nothing to worry about."

"But it's a question of discipline!"

"That's none of my business," said the quartermaster and hung up.

The corporal derived little satisfaction from this telephone conversation. None of his business indeed! But the cookhouse was his business; it was just that he didn't want to get involved in anything. Gunner Asch was Sergeant Major Schulz's business, then, but unfortunately the sergeant major was an old enemy of Corporal Rumpler's. He had once tried in vain to fill the post of N.C.O. in charge of the cookhouse with one of the N.C.O.s from his own troop. Rumpler had to face up to the

189

fact that he must deal with Asch alone. Not that there was anything so very difficult about that! After all, he knew how to put a man through it as well as any drill sergeant on the barrack square.

Rumpler knew the technique that usually proved infallible: keep them busy, wear them down, work them to the bone! Damn well make them see that they couldn't get away with things. Give a man plenty of work and he'd respect you all right. In any case it was about time the cookhouse orderlies understood that there were to be no more handouts or special favors of any sort. Charts, like this one that Asch had started, were a real threat to a nice cushy job like his.

The N.C.O. in charge of the cookhouse left his office again and returned to the cookhouse. He had a look through the hatch into the dining hall. Gunner Asch had given up his work on the chart or at least had given it up for the time being. He was supervising the scraping of the leftovers into the buckets. Hot water was also being brought in for the dishwashing. In other words he was working, and a man who is working has no time for idle thoughts. All that seemed necessary was to think of further work for him to do.

With this in mind, Rumpler dismissed Kowalski and the rest of the cookhouse staff.

"All right, you can go now," he said. "Gunner Asch can see to everything in here."

Then he went off down to the storeroom to get himself a delicious ham sandwich.

As he sat on a sack of sugar chewing away, a crateful of canned peaches caught his eye. He decided to open it and test the quality of the fruit. But before he could do so there came a heavy knocking on the door.

"What is it?" he asked surlily.

"Come quickly," called out a shrill voice. It was Lisbeth, the kitchenmaid, a fine strapping girl who always cleaned his

190

room and also ministered to his more personal wants whenever required.

Rumpler opened the door.

"Don't shout like that," he said crossly. "No one's doing you any harm."

"Come quickly," said Lisbeth. "The gunner's making trouble again."

The corporal shot upstairs like a streak of lightning.

Gunner Asch was sitting in the dining room with his assistants quietly consuming his midday meal. The cookhouse women were standing round him in a state of great excitement.

Corporal Rumpler looked the scene over. At first glance there didn't seem anything odd about it.

"What's the fellow up to now?" he asked.

Asch chose not to regard this as being addressed to him and went on quietly with his meal. One of the women said excitedly:

"He refuses to clean up the dining room."

Rumpler planted himself firmly in front of Asch.

"You refuse to?" he asked.

"Of course," said the gunner calmly. "I've heard nothing to the effect that the cookhouse women are now in a position to order soldiers about."

"I'm giving you the order," roared Corporal Rumpler.

"May I draw your attention to the fact that you're giving me an order outside the range of my military duties?" said Asch. "I've just been looking at the cookhouse regulations hanging up over there. According to them the orderlies are required only to clean the tables, wash the dishes, collect the leftovers and place them in the bins provided. It is the cookhouse women who are responsible for cleaning up the dining hall, that is to say principally the floor."

"But the soldiers have always helped us up till now," cried one of the women, who was as round as a barrel.

191

"If the soldiers have been so stupid as to do that, that's their lookout," said Asch. "But you don't get away with it in our case."

Rumpler looked as if he were going to burst. Hitherto he had been undisputed master of the cookhouse, a sort of demigod for these women, someone who was thoroughly conscious of his position, a stickler for discipline.

"Louse!" he yelled. "What the hell do you think you're doing, you — you swine! Just what do you imagine you're playing at, eh? Do you realize who you're talking to?"

"Yes," said Asch, regarding him curiously.

"Then kindly get to your feet. Stand at attention when an N.C.O. speaks to you. Wash your filthy ears out and listen to me. I'm giving you an order to clean out the dining hall. This instant. If you don't I shall report you for disobeying an order."

Asch was determined not to let himself be browbeaten. But it wasn't easy all the same. He felt himself going weak at the knees. By God, it wasn't easy! But he made a supreme effort and forced himself to look indifferent.

"Do you refuse to carry out my order?"

"If you insist on it," said Asch, "I shall carry out this order, even though my military duties do not oblige me to do the thing you order. But I must tell you that I shall lodge a complaint afterwards."

"I'll make you pay for it if you do," roared Rumpler.

"Am I to take that as a threat?"

"I'll report you!" shouted the corporal, and his voice shot up into a squeak. "I'll report you to the sergeant major!"

He whipped round and strode from the room.

Asch sat down again.

"Well, let's have something to eat," he said to the other soldiers. "When we've finished, we'll call it a day."

"And what about the dining hall?" whined one of the cleaning women, who looked exactly like a tub.

192

"That's your affair," said Asch. "That's what you're paid for."

Rumpler ran across to the sergeant major, who was very busy trying to sort out the ammunition muddle of the day before. He simply couldn't get the figures right; it made him furious.

He didn't pay much attention to Rumpler's report. He couldn't stand the cookhouse corporal. He regarded him as an upstart who had deprived his troop of a most valuable post. He looked up from the score sheets, which seemed impossible to straighten out, and gave Rumpler a frigid scathing smile.

"Just say that again, will you?" he said to his visitor.

Rumpler once more spluttered out his — as he thought — hair-raising story. But the sergeant major interrupted him crossly even before he had got to the end of it.

"You must be mad, Rumpler," he said. "Gunner Asch is one of the finest and most reliable men I've got."

"But he's been weighing up the rations, and has refused to clean the floor."

"I'll look into that," said the sergeant major. "If you insist, I'll look into it. But God have mercy on you, Rumpler, if it turns out that you've been trying to swindle my men. And what's more, if the rations prove to be incorrect and it turns out that you've been trying to get my men to do the work that's supposed to be done by the cleaning women, then I shall put in a report to the battery and you'll be in for it. So think it over well. Do you really insist that I look into the matter?"

"But, Sergeant Major, this Gunner Asch . . ."

"Yes or no?"

Rumpler was sweating. His head moved slightly as if he were about to shake it. Then he suddenly became like a wax dummy. And with a catch in his voice he declared:

"I withdraw my report."

193

Elizabeth Freitag found herself experiencing the strangest sensations. At one moment she seemed to be on the crest of a wave, and the next she was sunk in deepest melancholy. She had never known anything like it before, and now looked upon it all with mingled delight and astonishment. A more sentimental girl might have said: I'm in love. Elizabeth only said: Something seems to be happening to me!

Her work in the canteen, which had previously always seemed so monotonous, now became extraordinarily interesting, almost rather exciting. While she was drying the glasses she knew that at any moment the door might open and she would find herself taken by surprise, caught up in a mysterious thrill. In other words, Herbert Asch might walk in.

Herbert Asch walked in just before the end of the morning break. Elizabeth thought she must be blushing, which of course was not the case, but she did her best to look as calm and collected as possible.

"You're quite a stranger," she said.

Asch gave her his hand.

"I must be off again at once," he said. "I just wanted to tell you that I'm coming round to your place this evening."

"What an honor for us," said Elizabeth, who didn't much like his brusque hurried manner. "Shall we put a garland of flowers over the doorway for you?"

"Now then," said Asch, trying to pacify her. "Don't play the injured innocent with me. I really haven't got a moment. You've no idea how complicated life is just now."

"So I gather," said Elizabeth acidly. "You must be very busy. I'm really quite touched that you can spare the time to come and say good morning to me."

"I'll try and come in again a bit later. If I don't I'll see you

194

this evening. And please tell your father I want to have a word with him."

"Anything else you'd like me to do? No? And what do you want to have a word with my father about? Nothing to do with me, I hope!"

Gunner Asch was already at the door. He smiled at her, but Elizabeth had quite lost all her former carefree gaiety.

"No, nothing to do with you," he said. "I don't think that's really necessary, is it?"

"Have you written me off so soon, then, or are you counting your chickens before they're hatched?"

"I'm in a hurry," said Asch. "We'll go into the matter carefully when I've got a little more time."

"And when will that be?"

"Soon, I hope, Elizabeth. As soon as all this business is over."

"What business?"

"I must go now. Good-by, Betty."

Gunner Asch opened the door. He was on the point of leaving.

"I'm not a horse," Elizabeth called after him. "Betty is a horse's name. Will you be looking in again?"

"If I can, Betty, yes, of course."

Asch shut the door behind him.

She listened to his hobnailed boots clattering up the stone stairs. She shook her head. She didn't know what to think of him. And she realized at once that she couldn't be cross with him. The fact annoyed her.

Elizabeth collected together the canteen vouchers which she had taken during the midday break. Trade had been brisker than usual. The N.C.O.s of No. 3 Troop in particular had eaten and drunk much more than usual. They had been particularly keen on long drinks. It seemed that they had had quite a party the night before.

The canteen contractor came walking through the empty N.C.O.s' canteen. He seemed in good spirits, which was rather disturbing. He smiled genially at his assistant and said:

"Well, Fräulein Freitag, and how was business this morning?"

"We took in eighty-three marks, forty pfennigs," she replied, handing him the full statement.

"That's not bad," said Bandurski in a satisfied tone of voice. "In fact that's really quite good. You're my best asset, you know, Fräulein Freitag. I don't mind admitting it. And I should hate to lose you."

"You won't lose me unless you fire me," said Elizabeth. She always liked to stand up to her boss. She got on best with him that way.

"My dear Fräulein Freitag," said Bandurski cheerfully, and he pushed both hands out in front of him as if trying to ward off the very idea of such a thing. "If I were to do that, it would be a real loss to me. I don't mind admitting it, I have no wish whatsoever to give you the sack. I am not contemplating any such thing. But you mustn't force me to."

"And what do you mean by that, Herr Bandurski?"

The canteen contractor seemed to be very interested in the vouchers which Elizabeth had just handed to him. He looked at them and said: "What's going on between you and this gunner in No. 3 Troop exactly? I've seen him with you a good deal lately."

"That, Herr Bandurski," said Elizabeth, "is nothing to do with you."

"Oh, don't misunderstand me," said the contractor. "I have no wish to interfere in your private affairs. But I just don't like complications very much."

"I know what I'm doing all right, Herr Bandurski."

"Of course, of course," he said. "But this part of the canteen is for N.C.O.s, and when you're on duty up here it's the

196

N.C.O.s you're supposed to serve. Business comes first, you know."

"Have I been neglecting my work in any way?"

"No, no, of course not. Your work is admirable. And I want it to stay that way. But if you're going to go on showing an interest in this gunner from No. 3 Troop, then I'm afraid we're going to have trouble."

"Why, Herr Bandurski?"

"Listen to me, my dear Fräulein Freitag. I'm an old army man myself. I know just what life in barracks is like. No one can put anything over on me. And this is a nice little business I've got here. . . ."

"But what's all this got to do with Gunner Asch?"

"A very great deal, my dear Fräulein Freitag. This Gunner Asch did something today I've never heard of in my whole life before, either as canteen contractor or when I was in the army myself. He borrowed a pair of scales from me downstairs in the canteen and started weighing up the rations. And then he had a row with the N.C.O. in charge of the cookhouse which came precious close to mutiny. I tell you I've never known anything like it in the whole of my life."

Elizabeth looked at Bandurski incredulously.

"But why did he do that?"

The contractor shrugged his shoulders.

"Don't ask me! But that's what he did. And do you think he's going to be allowed to get away with that? And even if he does get away with it, where's it all going to lead? Why on earth you should have had to go and pick on this one fellow Asch out of all the hundreds of men here, God alone knows! It's just my bad luck, and yours, and heaven knows who else's!"

"I really think you're taking rather too gloomy a view of things, Herr Bandurski."

Bandurski stood up.

"I hope you're right. But I can't do more than warn you.

197

And do me a favor, Fräulein Freitag: just think of my business a little. And if you can't bring yourself to give up this fellow Asch, then try and talk a little sense into him at least. I'd really hate to lose you."

The canteen contractor looked honestly worried. He gave his assistant a parting nod as if somehow trying to put courage into her. Then he left the room.

Elizabeth sat down in the first chair she could find. She stared thoughtfully at the well-scrubbed counter. She felt partly frightened, partly astonished and partly delighted. She would never have thought Herbert capable of such a thing. He obviously possessed qualities which she hadn't yet suspected in him. She felt her curiosity aroused.

She finished making up the accounts and checked over the stores. Then she looked at the time. It was just before three. Her day's work in the canteen began at twelve. She was kept relatively busy for the first couple of hours or so. Then she had peace for three hours, during which only the occasional N.C.O. on duty put in an appearance. It wasn't until five that things started getting lively again. It continued like that until eight. At eight she normally packed up for the day and the canteen contractor himself took over from her.

Elizabeth thought about Herbert Asch as she again washed a lot of glasses that were perfectly clean. She knew a good deal about him in one way, but in another nothing at all. She had known him as intimately as it was possible to know anyone and yet he remained a mystery to her. And she smiled. This, she thought, was as it should be. He would always be able to keep her guessing. She would never be bored so long as she was with him. She remembered her mother had said something rather like this about her father not so long ago.

Just after three Sergeant Major Schulz came into the canteen. He seemed to be in a terrible mood. He threw his cap down on a bench over by the window and collapsed into a chair.

198

"I've got an appalling head!" he roared at the top of his voice. "What can I take for it?"

Elizabeth told herself that it might be wise to treat this snarling customer as gently as possible, for Herbert's sake at least.

"Well," she said, "the old ladies' cure is aspirin, but knowing you I'd recommend a large glass of beer."

"Admirable!" said the sergeant major, looking at Elizabeth in a by no means unfriendly fashion. He liked the look of her more and more. She was attractive and yet a decent respectable sort of girl at the same time. And that was rare. He ought to have married a girl like this instead of the little bitch he had got.

Elizabeth brought up a large glass of beer, set it down, said "All the best" and, contrary to her usual practice, stayed where she was by the customer's table. He was the only customer in the room at the moment. She gave him a friendly smile.

Schulz took a great swig of beer. He started swallowing it with a deadly serious expression on his face as if he were somehow doing his duty, but this changed to a look of obvious pleasure.

"Ah!" he said, beginning to recover. "That's more like it!" He put down his glass. He looked noticeably better. "Won't you sit down with me? I don't bite, you know."

"And I don't let myself get bitten," said Elizabeth. She tried to say it as gaily as possible. "Besides, it's a pleasure to sit with you. I don't think anyone will mind as long as the canteen's empty."

Schulz laughed — a brisk manly laugh.

"As far as I'm concerned you can hang a card outside the door saying 'Closed till further notice'!"

Elizabeth sat down beside him. She put her elbow on the table and leaned over towards him.

"Worried about something?" she said.

199

Schulz nodded.

"We all have our worries," he said. "It's the way things are. Not all the N.C.O.s are of the sterling quality they ought to be. Some of them I'm afraid have feet of clay."

"But you can deal with them, can't you?"

Schulz swallowed this flattery without the slightest effort.

"And how!" he said. He felt better already for the interest and admiration of this charming girl beside him. It was possible to talk to her. He could tell at once that she was a woman who understood him.

"Bring me another beer," he said.

He took the glass, drank from it, put it down carefully and wiped his mouth with his sleeve.

"Yes," he said, "it's not an easy life. Sometimes the best of people go wrong. There are these six rounds of ammunition that are missing, for instance. Just imagine that: six rounds! It's simply impossible to trace them."

"They must have got lost."

Schulz couldn't help laughing at such naïveté. He felt immensely superior and the sensation did him a lot of good.

"Lost? There's no such a word as lost in a case like this. It simply doesn't exist. Oh, don't worry, they'll be found all right. And if the worst comes to the worst, I'll take a hand in the matter myself."

"Oh, but it won't be as bad as that!"

"Let's hope not," said Schulz, pouring the beer down his throat. Yes, he thought, one can really talk to her. He put one of his great hands on Elizabeth's forearm and noted with satisfaction that she didn't seem to object. He took this as a good sign. It made him feel much better.

"By the way," he asked suddenly, "do you find me sympathetic or not?"

Elizabeth started a little in surprise, but she tried not to let him see this.

"That's a funny question," she said. "Of course I do; I even like you very much."

"I just wanted to know," said Schulz. He squeezed her arm affectionately with his huge hand. She still raised no objections, and he was delighted.

"Does it seem possible to you," he asked, "that anyone should deceive me? I mean, that a woman should deceive me?"

"Your wife, you mean?"

"I'm only speaking generally. Only theoretically, so to speak. But I mean does it seem possible to you?"

"No," said Elizabeth quickly. "No, certainly not. You know, women are much more faithful than men usually think."

"Do you really think so?"

"I'm sure of it. Women like to flirt. They delight in making the man they love feel jealous. It's a way of proving to themselves that they're loved in return."

"I see," said Schulz, kneading her forearm thoughtfully. "So it's like that, is it?"

He looked up as the door opened. A gunner was standing there. He was looking round the room.

"Looking for me, Asch?" asked the sergeant major.

Elizabeth quickly took her arm away. She seemed extremely embarrassed. Schulz smiled to himself.

"I'm looking for Lieutenant Wedelmann," said Asch vaguely.

"But you won't find him here!" cried Schulz. "That really would be the last straw!"

And as the gunner had already shut the door behind him, Schulz turned once more to Elizabeth Freitag.

"There's no need to be worried," he said. "This fellow Asch is all right. He's a first-class man."

"I'm sure you're right," said Elizabeth, perking up. "You're a good judge of men, aren't you?"

"I certainly am," said the sergeant major modestly. "It's only

201

with women that I'm not so sure of myself. They're such complicated creatures. But perhaps not really. Perhaps they're just silly."

"When in love, often," said Elizabeth charmingly. It no longer worried her that Herbert should have seen her with Schulz. She hoped it might make him a little jealous, and that wouldn't do him any harm. She was positively delighted to find out that Schulz not only had nothing against Asch but actually had something to say in his favor.

Schulz was unable to tear his thoughts away from the subject that dominated his mind.

"Look here," he said. "I'm somebody. I count for something. I may be an officer one day; if there's a war, for example. I know a good deal more than many captains, and am a good deal more efficient too. People just don't deceive me. I simply am not the sort of man whom people deceive."

"Of course not."

"You would never deceive me, would you?"

"Of course not, if I were in love with you."

Schulz nodded smugly. And once again he looked up as the door opened.

There stood Lieutenant Wedelmann. The sergeant major sat up stiffly. Lieutenant Wedelmann hesitated. He seemed uncertain whether to go on or not.

"This is the N.C.O.s' canteen here," said Schulz coldly.

Wedelmann was plainly embarrassed.

"I wanted to have a word with Fräulein Freitag."

"A lot of people," said Schulz quietly to Elizabeth but without bothering to make the remark inaudible to Wedelmann, "seem to be sticking their noses into places where they're not wanted."

Wedelmann ignored this offensive remark and the sergeant major's entirely undisciplined attitude towards him.

He bowed pointedly to Elizabeth and left the room.

"But Herr Schulz," said Elizabeth, horrified. "You can't treat the lieutenant like that."

"Oh yes I can," said Schulz. "I can treat him far worse than that if I want to, and what's more I damn well will."

🏷 🏷 🏷

Sergeant Platzek, Bully Platzek, was in a frightful state. He was tortured by the affair of the six missing rounds of ammunition. They seemed to have vanished into thin air. However hard he looked, he could find no trace of them.

The score sheets were official documents and as such couldn't be touched. They showed the number of rounds issued and the number fired. From these figures it was possible to deduce how many rounds were left over for return to the armory. And it was this final figure which wouldn't work out right. There were always six rounds missing.

Platzek already saw himself scrubbing out latrines in a military prison. His notoriously brisk and hearty manner, which was so much resented by the men under him, gave way to a deep depression. He went about with a long face, roared bad-temperedly at everyone who crossed his path, and seemed to have become thoroughly irritable and nervous.

It particularly annoyed him that he couldn't find anyone to take even part of the load off him, and he ascribed this to lack of comradely spirit. On this Thursday the whole of his primitively constructed little soldier's world threatened to tumble about his ears. For what shook him was the discovery that though he had so much experience as a drill sergeant and served as a model to the other N.C.O.s, who however never succeeded in equaling him, he was immediately left in the lurch the moment he got into any sort of trouble. He had proved his worth a hundred times, nay, a thousand times over — times beyond number, in fact. And now he had made one single mistake — and he was in trouble at once.

"Listen, Schulz," he said in a private and confidential tone to his old comrade the sergeant major, "this business with the ammunition is a terrible mixup — I'll admit that. But couldn't we just lose the score sheets or something like that? Or what about forgetting about them until the next time we're out on the range and making up the missing rounds then. Now what about it?"

"Platzek," replied the sergeant major in an equally private and confidential tone, "I simply haven't heard what you've just said, see? I'm waiting for the score sheets to be sent in. I have to show them to Captain Derna. But I'm not going to go on waiting much longer. And they've all got to be in order, or there's going to be trouble. If any ammunition's missing a summary of evidence has to be taken, and I don't want to let you in for that."

"Good God, Schulz, man, just for six lousy rounds of ammunition?"

"I'm not a man, Platzek, I'm a sergeant major. And as for the six lousy rounds; they're capable of blowing up six N.C.O.s."

Platzek went over to see Corporal Wunderlich, the N.C.O. in charge of the armory, whose assistant was Lance Corporal Kowalski. The sergeant was quite unable to conceal the state of nerves he was in. It hardly came as a surprise to him to find that his visit to the armory, far from being welcome, was regarded almost as a nuisance.

Wunderlich and Kowalski were squatting on the floor among a pile of rifles, machine guns and unprimed hand grenades. The spare parts for the guns lay well greased on racks all round the room. There was a strong smell of oil and a slight smell of tobacco smoke. It was of course strictly forbidden to

204

smoke in the armory; but it didn't occur to Platzek to draw attention to this infringement of the regulations just at the moment.

"Now listen, gentlemen," he said, and he said it in a blustering sort of way to try to cover up the state he was in, "I'm in a nasty fix about this ammunition. You'll probably have heard about it?"

"A very nasty business indeed, Sergeant," said Kowalski, putting on a show of sympathy.

Corporal Wunderlich looked as if he were thinking the matter over. He was no particular friend of Sergeant Platzek's. Before becoming a corporal he had several times had a very bad time from Platzek on the barrack square. And the corporal was not one of those naturally generous creatures who are able to treat this sort of bullying as a personal compliment and to look back on it afterwards with something like nostalgia. But above all Wunderlich was a devout believer in a quiet life at all costs, which was one of the reasons he had made such strenuous efforts to get himself the job of corporal in charge of the armory.

"What's your view, Wunderlich? Do you think we'll be able to straighten the matter out?"

"What matter?" asked Wunderlich, putting on a stupid expression. This came naturally to him.

"It's quite simple," said Platzek. "I need six rounds of ammunition. You must have a few spare."

"It's strictly forbidden to keep any extra ammunition," said Wunderlich blandly, winking at Kowalski. Of course he had supplies of his own, but they weren't for a man like Platzek.

"And what about your colleagues in the other troops? Or the fellow in charge of the battery depot? You don't mean to tell me that one of them hasn't slipped a cartridge or two away from time to time!"

Wunderlich looked over at his bosom friend Kowalski again

205

for a moment and grinned. Of course everyone had private supplies. But not for Platzek!

"They don't want to run any risks either."

Platzek didn't much like his role as a suppliant. He felt humiliated. His vanity was hurt.

"So you won't help, eh, Wunderlich?" he said angrily.

Wunderlich saw at once that a powerful threat was being leveled at him. He considered how he ought to react to it. And he couldn't help wondering what would happen if he were to replace Platzek's six missing rounds for him. It wouldn't be much trouble for him and in the long run it could only lead to the sergeant's feeling under an obligation to him. Who could tell what good might not come of that?

But before Wunderlich could say the word which would have released Platzek from all his misery, Lance Corporal Kowalski broke in.

"It's not really so much of a problem as all that, Sergeant," he said. "You've simply got to alter the entries in the score sheets."

"You can't do that," said Platzek. "The entries are all made in indelible ink."

"Still, there's such a thing as corrections," persisted Kowalski. "The scorer can make them and the N.C.O. in charge of the range has to confirm the alteration with his signature."

"That's an idea," said Platzek, pricking up his ears. It seemed to him that he could see a ray of hope at last.

Wunderlich shook his head knowledgeably.

"If it ever gets out," he said, "it's tantamount to a falsification of the records."

"Who said it would ever get out?"

"If it were done skillfully," said Kowalski helpfully, "such an idea would never occur to anyone. For instance, let's suppose that one of the men fired off his six rounds in the wrong order, that is to say, not two lying, two kneeling, two upright, but

206

the other way round if you like. It's the sort of thing that happens. Well, and what happens then? He has to fire off six more rounds. And the first six are struck out on the score sheet. And there you have your six missing rounds."

"Not so bad," said Platzek.

"It's quite simple," went on Kowalski. "You merely have to take the score sheets to whoever first had charge of them and get him to make this — er — slight alteration. And if I know anything about him he'll do it. Gunner Asch isn't petty-minded about this sort of thing if you put it to him in the right way."

"I'll do it," said Platzek, suddenly full of hope. "What do you think about this, Wunderlich?"

"I don't know anything about it," he said cautiously. "I haven't heard a thing."

"Neither have I," said Kowalski.

"And I'll be glad when I've forgotten all about it too," said Platzek. He had now recovered almost all his old self-confidence. He could see land at last. He felt all his old energy returning. He left the armory and went to look for Asch. In fact it turned out to be not at all easy to find him, but Platzek showed no sign of impatience.

He searched for Asch as intently and persistently as if he were searching for his own salvation.

Gunner Asch could after all have been found without much difficulty. As always when in need of relaxation and a slight diversion from the dreary round of duty, he had made his way to Sergeant Werktreu's clothing store, the entrance to which lay just opposite the armory.

Asch had procured an assistant for himself in the shape of Gunner Vierbein, and had put him onto the job of sorting out some sets of long underpants. He was determined to give Vierbein a little private tuition in how to deal with N.C.O.s. But however hard Asch tried, it proved quite impossible to rouse Sergeant Werktreu out of his lethargy.

"This work here in the clothing store is just about as boring as it could be," he said provocatively. And he was delighted to see that Vierbein had pricked up his ears. "A miserable job. It's only really fit for halfwits."

"That's why we have you here, Asch," said Sergeant Werktreu, refusing to take offense. It never occurred to him that Asch might be getting at him. He was thinking of the girl he had a date with that evening. A nice plump girl, plenty of fun in her and dumb as they made them.

But Gunner Asch wouldn't let him alone.

"You're not really a proper soldier at all," he said offensively to Werktreu, sitting down on a pile of trousers. "You're more of an old-clothes merchant really, a sort of superior rag-and-bone man."

"You will have your little joke, Asch," said the sergeant, quite unperturbed.

Asch looked across to Vierbein, who was staring at him in amazement. He had never heard anyone talk like that to an N.C.O. all the time he had been in uniform. He found it strangely exciting. He was on tenterhooks to see what would happen next. He was worried for Asch's sake.

But there wasn't the slightest need to be worried on Asch's account. Werktreu's mind was so full of delightful anticipation at the thought of the evening ahead of him that it never occurred to him to feel annoyed. Besides, he needed some money to finance his plan of campaign.

"Well, Asch, what about a little game?"

"I suppose you just want to cheat one of your wretched subordinates, eh?"

"You're quite a wag today, Asch."

"Or do you want to borrow from me again?"

"Perhaps," said Werktreu. "But we'll just have a few hands of *vingt-et-un* first. And then, if I lose, you can always reach down into that long purse of yours. And by the way, what

208

about a bottle of wine at a special price for me, if I bring my popsy along to your café this evening?"

"So you want to do a bit of cadging too, do you?"

"Let's have a little game first, Asch. Here are the cards. I'll take the bank to start with. Come on now."

Asch shook his head like a stubborn horse. It was simply impossible to get a rise out of Werktreu. Whatever one did he remained quite unperturbed. The only thing he seemed interested in was a game of cards! He wasn't like an N.C.O. at all, he was more like a companion one went out on a party with.

The gunner determined to make one last effort before giving Werktreu up as a bad job. He sat down opposite him, tapped the pack of cards and said: "I'm not playing with these. They're marked."

Even this enormity, this downright insulting accusation, didn't get a rise out of Werktreu. He could think of nothing but the working capital he required for the evening's enterprise; he didn't care a damn about anything else.

"All right, then," he said. "I'll go and fetch another pack." He got up and left the room.

Gunner Vierbein came up to his friend in a great state of agitation.

"You can't go on like that," he said. "You simply can't treat an N.C.O. like that."

Asch looked him up and down.

"What a terrible old woman you are," he said.

"You must be careful," said Vierbein. And he added: "You simply can't do that."

"What's the matter with you?" The gunner leaned over him as if he were about to jump on him. "You're just not normal any more. First you show yourself to be utterly gutless and then you start preaching at me. Honestly, you know, I think you're a hopeless case."

Gunner Vierbein was really anxious about his friend.

209

"You saved me from doing something very stupid," he said. "And I'm grateful to you for that. I realize now that one's simply got to see this thing through. I understand exactly what you meant. I'm a changed man now. You'll see, I'll always do my duty now, however hard I find it and however much it may seem to me that I'm not being fairly treated. It's you who've made me see all that. I've adjusted myself to life on that basis now. And I can't bear it when I see you cheeking an N.C.O. like that. Don't you see? You're simply cutting the ground away from underneath my feet."

"All I see," said Asch slowly, "is that you're talking through the seat of your pants."

Gunner Asch found this conversation extremely unpleasant. He could hardly believe the evidence of his own ears. But at that moment they were interrupted by the arrival of Sergeant Werktreu with a new pack of cards.

Herbert Asch was quite amazed. He felt indignant at first and then furious. He wanted to kick Vierbein's bottom for him, to hit him in the face. And was it for an old woman like that that he was starting his revolt? No, he told himself, it was partly to put a stop to the mass production of old women like that that he was starting it. That too was one of his objectives.

"You've lost again, smart aleck!" said Werktreu, who had begun playing without more ado. "That means you owe me two marks now. Come on — next hand!"

But this happy little game, which looked as though it would end in a considerable implementation of Sergeant Werktreu's working capital, was soon rudely interrupted. Sergeant Platzek appeared with a cry of: "Ah! There you are, Asch. I need you badly."

Werktreu tried to put him off.

"Sorry, not a hope! I need him here."

210

"Sergeant major's orders," said Platzek without turning a hair. "Come on, Asch!"

The gunner had no objection. He wouldn't have to look at Vierbein's idiotic face any more. And he was glad too to get away from Werktreu. It seemed quite impossible to get any sort of rise out of him, and apart from that Asch's losses were by now considerable, amounting to something like ten marks. Platzek's appearance was a welcome one in the circumstances.

The sergeant treated Asch with marked politeness, which was altogether unusual for him. Anyone else would have felt that this heralded something very sinister. But Asch knew better. He sensed just such an opportunity as he was looking for.

Platzek took the gunner off to his room, which was stuffed full of every kind of barrack furniture. He offered him a chair. He asked him if he'd like a schnapps, or a cigarette, or a glass of beer. "No? Well, and how's everything with you, my dear fellow? I hear you've been put up for promotion. Many congratulations, my boy. I'm all in favor of it."

"What do you want from me, Sergeant?" asked Asch simply.

Platzek didn't like the way Asch addressed him by his rank. But he was prepared to overlook that. He was even prepared to overlook worse things than that. For he knew well enough what he wanted.

He took the score sheets out from under a cushion and laid them on the table.

"You were in charge of these yesterday, weren't you?"

"That's right," said Asch, and he knew at once what was coming. He, if anyone, knew the secret of the six missing rounds of ammunition. "Yes, I was responsible for the first entries."

"Well, the figures don't work out right. There are six rounds missing. What have you got to say to that?"

"Well, we'll have to put them back in, that's all. It's quite simple."

Platzek beamed with pleasure. "You're a bright lad, Asch," he said. "A born N.C.O. Will you make the alteration, then? It has to be entered in the same handwriting, you see. I'll sign my approval underneath."

"Why not?" said Asch, as if it were the most natural thing in the world. "Give them here!"

They both pored over the score sheets. Platzek was tremendously excited. That's more like it, he thought; much more like it. Things were going far better than he had expected. This man Asch was really a most excellent fellow.

The gunner carried out the sergeant's instructions to the letter. It was all done very calmly and with a good deal of concentration. Asch crossed out six scores and put six new scores in. Then he wrote: *Alteration made, as original entry incorrect. Rifleman fired in wrong sequence and ordered to carry out shoot again. Signed*................*Sergeant.*

Asch also struck out the total number of rounds fired and added six more. Here he wrote: *Alteration made to comply with rectification above. Signed* ....*Sergeant.*

"Perfect," said Platzek rubbing his hands. "And now my signature." He signed twice, carefully and very clearly, with a fine flourish at the end. Then he sat back and smiled. A great load had been taken off his mind.

"Well, that's that," he said.

Asch leaned right back in his chair. He took one look round the little room, which was clean but smelled of soapsuds, shoe polish and damp sheets. Then he said calmly: "Of course, that's a falsification of the record, you know."

Platzek laughed.

"Just a small alteration, shall we say?" he said. He grinned like a conspirator drinking to the success of the conspiracy.

"A falsification of the record," repeated Asch. "I mean a falsification of the record in the sense of the military code."

"Now don't try and be funny, Asch," said Platzek, slightly

212

put out. "And even if it is, you've had your share in it, my friend!"

"You're wrong there," said Asch, fixing the N.C.O. with a steady gaze. Platzek was beginning to feel a little nervous. "My entry means nothing by itself. It's your signature that makes the whole thing valid."

"Don't talk nonsense, Asch."

"Put it to the test, then," said Asch, quite unperturbed. "I'm ready any time."

Sergeant Platzek, the iron Platzek, Bully Platzek, the tyrant of the barrack square, was utterly bewildered. He felt rather as if he had been hit over the head with a bottle. Slowly it began to dawn on him that he had merely jumped out of the frying pan into the fire. His first reaction was one of outrage.

"Who the hell do you think you're talking to?" he shouted. "That's no way to talk to me."

"Just what I was going to say to you," declared Asch coolly. "You don't seem to realize the position you've put yourself into."

"You dirty swine!" roared Platzek. It seemed for a moment as if he were going to hurl himself at Asch. "You rotten miserable — "

He stopped short. His mouth stayed open, but no sound came out of it.

"Go on," said Asch.

Platzek was not a particularly intelligent sort of person. He regarded himself more as a man of action. But at the same time he was no fool. He had no small degree of cunning at his disposal. It took him a moment or two to appreciate the highly dangerous position into which he had been maneuvered, but once he had grasped it he had no more illusions. He was caught in a trap.

On this Thursday his whole world collapsed. His comrades, or rather those whom he had hitherto always supposed to be

213

his comrades, had left him shamefully in the lurch. He had been left to face the music alone. Now a stinking little gunner had made him put himself morally in the wrong, had cracked him open like a ripe walnut, had treated him with as much respect as if he had been a sheet of toilet paper. This was too much. It was more than any honest man could bear. But it was a fact all the same.

Sergeant Platzek drew in his chin, which normally jutted out very aggressively, and lowered his head. He collapsed on his camp bed. And there he sat like a great heap of misery.

"That's more how I like to see you," said Asch mercilessly.

Platzek shook with rage. His whole instinct told him to turn on Asch and tear him to pieces. But Asch was no weakling, and he had already proved that he was no coward either. Besides, if he were to beat him up, it would be a punishable offense — maltreatment of a subordinate. And if this business with the score sheets really got out it would mean a court-martial, reduction to the ranks, prison — the end of everything! Platzek gritted his teeth. They made a sort of champing noise like a horse.

"Well, so that's how it is," said Asch without any hint of triumph in his voice. "A man is prepared to do anything to keep his good position. He'll give no trouble, appear to behave perfectly. He'll do anything to try and get in the good books of his superiors. Anything! Bully, make false statements, drive people to suicide! That's one side of the picture. The other side of course is that he'll always carry out orders unquestioningly."

"What do you want from me?" asked Platzek numbly.

"Well, to start with," said Asch, "I want you at least to try and behave a little more like a civilized human being and a little less like a lunatic in a slaughterhouse. I'll let you know what else I want from you later."

☙ ☙ ☙

It was on this Thursday that the first shot was fired.

The sun had gone down. The sky was full of rain clouds and the light went quickly. It was just eighteen minutes past eight.

Shortly beforehand, Sergeant Major Schulz had been sitting quite happily at his desk in his office. He loved working late now and again. And he always saw to it that these bouts of work of his were brought to the attention of his men, for he worked by the open window with the lights full on. Anyone passing by could hardly fail to see him sitting there.

Of course Schulz could have got through his work much earlier if he had wanted to. But during normal working hours he spent his time strolling through the barracks, visiting the canteen, or paying calls on Lore, his wife, mainly for the purpose of showing her how much he despised her. But no sooner were normal working hours over than Schulz began to get down to it, or at least to give every appearance of doing so.

Sergeant Platzek handed him the score sheets. He turned the pages over and read through the correction. Then he looked at Platzek who stood there in gloomy silence.

"So far so good," said Schulz. "You've made a neat job of it."

"That's all right, then?" inquired Platzek sullenly.

"It looks like it," said the sergeant major. "The figures on the sheets are all right and that's what I care about. Let's just hope the six rounds stay lost."

"What do you mean by that?" asked Platzek without much interest, and clearly without any idea as to what the Chief was driving at.

The Chief spoke in an undertone so that even if there had been anyone listening outside, which he knew to be very unlikely, it would have been quite impossible to hear what was said.

"What do I mean by that? It's perfectly simple. Let's suppose that the six rounds, or some of them at any rate, turn up

215

again. Someone might blow his brains out, or murder a rival, or knock off some civilian he owes money to, or get his own back on some woman who's given him V.D. — or something like that! Such things happen, you know. Well then, there's an inquiry. And what if it transpires that the ammunition came from the range where a certain Platzek was in charge? What then?"

"Don't you start talking like that too!" muttered Platzek.

"Me too? Who else did it?"

Platzek didn't answer. He stared with an almost expressionless face at the sergeant major, who sat slumped at his desk.

"Can I go now, then?" said Platzek.

"So far as I'm concerned," said Schulz.

He watched Platzek go with a certain grim satisfaction. That's put him in his place all right, he thought. He suddenly looked quite weedy and contemptible. It would do him good to feel like that. He's a useful soldier, certainly, completely reliable for certain purposes, but it was just his success that had made him rather too full of himself. It had got to such a pitch that he had actually tried to play on his, the sergeant major's, comradely feelings and had seemed to forget that he was after all dealing with a man who was senior to him in rank. It would do him good to have a bit of a damper put on him.

Schulz just went on sitting there. He beamed with inward satisfaction. He had proved his mental superiority at every turn. Inevitably one or two people had fallen victim to him, but everything he touched seemed to prosper. He had that arrogant know-all Wedelmann where he wanted him now. Lore, his wife, was ready to eat out of his hand. Vierbein was hopping about like a cat on hot bricks. The N.C.O. in charge of the cookhouse had been sacked and was already packing his things; he would be replaced by an N.C.O. from No. 3 Troop, probably Schwitzke, who knew how to look after things all right.

216

Schulz fiddled with the telephone. Then he picked up the receiver and put a call through to the orderly N.C.O. He said: "Lieutenant Wedelmann's orderly is to be relieved at once. He'll be replaced by Gunner Wagner."

He listened to the voice at the other end and grinned broadly. "Do I think Wagner is capable of taking on the job? You can leave that to me, thank you. Which of the two of us do you imagine is the sergeant major? Right, then. Off you go and tell Lieutenant Wedelmann that those are my arrangements. Understand?"

The sergeant major replaced the receiver with a flourish. He rubbed the palms of his hands together and cracked the joints of his fingers.

He pulled out the right-hand drawer of his desk, took out a roll of toilet paper and tore off three sheets. He laid them carefully one on top of the other and then folded them over. He tucked them into the cuff of his left sleeve. Then he put the roll of toilet paper back in the drawer and shut it.

He got to his feet with a feeling of pleasurable anticipation, cast a quick glance out of the window into the gathering dusk and strode briskly out of the office. It was his habit to disappear twice a day behind the door marked *For N.C.O.s only* in the ground-floor latrine. But on this occasion he didn't go there right away. First he pushed his way through the swing doors on the staircase and went towards his own quarters.

He didn't go in. He merely stood in the corridor just outside and called through the open door: "A beer at half-past eight. And a newspaper and a cigar."

Lore received her orders quite unmoved. She didn't bother to reply.

"Understand?" he shouted.

"Yes, I understand," she drawled back in a distinctly disagreeable tone of voice.

Schulz nodded to himself and seemed quite satisfied. His

217

authority, as one might have expected, remained unquestioned. She showed respect for his orders, even if not exactly enthusiasm. But that would come. You couldn't expect it right away, particularly from a woman.

The sergeant major shut the door of his apartment behind him, went through the swing doors and down the brightly lit passage to the latrine. He looked at his watch for a moment: it was a quarter past eight! He could take his time, then, read the interesting information that was invariably to be found scribbled up on the walls, and listen to a few latrine rumors.

He walked in and hung about the main washroom for a bit. He opened the big window. The lower panes were made of frosted glass. He was always one for fresh air, at least when the temperature was anything over fifty. He stood silhouetted in the window for a minute looking out into the darkness, to the place where the dustbins were. This was the much-trodden area where washing was hung out to dry and carpets were beaten. This was where the gun sheds stood. The parade ground could just be seen in the distance.

Then he lit a cigarette and threw the used match out of the window in a wide arc. He made a mental note to look first thing tomorrow morning to see if it had been cleaned up properly.

He automatically began unbuttoning his tunic as he strode over to the last of the three doors, on which was written: *For N.C.O.s only. For key apply at office.* And since he had reserved the privilege of handing out this key himself and nobody naturally ever asked for it except for cleaning purposes, the cubicle had really come to be regarded as his private property.

He was just on the point of wondering whether to read the wall literature or continue pondering the subject of how he could further improve his already stable position, when he heard a sharp sound like the crack of a whip. Glass splintered on to the stone floor. Plaster trickled down from the wall.

He jumped up, pushed against the door, unbolted it and stood there staring. A pane of glass had been broken. There was a long rip in the ceiling. Schulz automatically pulled up his trousers.

Then the door of the latrine burst open. Corporal Schwitzke, Slacker Schwitzke, was standing there, peering curiously into the room.

"What's going on here?" he asked outright. Then he saw who it was pulling up his trousers. "Did the sergeant major fire a shot?" he asked.

"Someone fired a shot at me," said Schulz. And Schwitzke saw to his surprise that Schulz seemed considerably put out. "Through the window. Look out and see if there's anyone there."

Schwitzke looked out but couldn't seen anyone.

"There's no one there," he said.

"But there must be someone there!" shouted the Chief.

"If there was someone there and he shot at you," surmised Schwitzke, "he's not very likely to be there still."

Slacker Schwitzke felt furious with himself. He cursed the instinct that had made him go to see what had happened. He had been having a shower and was just in the corridor when the shot, or whatever it was, went off. He should simply have gone straight off and carried on as if he had heard nothing. Experience had taught him that this was always the best policy. At least it was a way of staying out of trouble. But no, some devil in him had made him go and turn straight into the Chief's arms. And it was high time for him to be off to the bowling alley too.

"We must stop everyone leaving barracks," said the sergeant major, taking good care not to go too near the open window.

"But why?" asked Schwitzke. "What good could it do?"

"That was an attempt to murder me!"

Slacker Schwitzke was very good at making light of things when there was any danger of extra work.

219

"But, Sergeant Major," he said ingenuously, "who could possibly want to murder you?"

"There's something in that," said Schulz doubtfully. "I expect it was something quite harmless. Probably just someone cleaning his rifle."

"Ass!" said Schulz, who was always one jump ahead of everyone else. "Cleaning his rifle! Out there in the dark? And where do you imagine he got the ammuntion from?"

"It might have been one of the sentries," said Schwitzke hurriedly. "It has happened, you know. The sentries have ammunition. It's not impossible for a rifle to go off accidentally. It happened once last year, in fact."

"Run off to the guardroom and see."

Schwitzke made no attempt to do so. This so-and-so had wasted at least fifteen minutes of his valuable time already.

"Or it could have been a shot from a pistol!" he cried. "The officers have their own ammunition. They're always firing their pistols off."

"I wouldn't put it past them," said Schulz. "Lieutenant Wedelmann particularly."

"Exactly," said Schwitzke. He was very clever at putting a show of enthusiasm into this sort of thing. "I bet it was something like that. It's quite unthinkable that anyone should have actually shot at you, Sergeant Major."

"I see that all right," said the sergeant major, and his nerve began to recover. But he wasn't absolutely convinced. He said to himself: It's not possible, though; it can't be that; it simply can't be.

"In any case," he said, "we'll be careful how we go. Go and fetch another corporal to help you and meet me down by the main gate."

"Very good, Sergeant Major," said Schwitzke, scarcely bothering to conceal his annoyance. He went off in search of

Lindenberg, for in the first place he was almost certain to be in barracks somewhere, and secondly he was always prepared to take on any extra duty.

Schwitzke found Lindenberg, as he had expected, hard at work studying army regulations. He was absorbed in the problem of the best way of storing gas masks.

"You're to come at once," said Schwitzke. "The sergeant major wants you."

Lindenberg nodded and got to his feet without a moment's hesitation. He thought it unsoldierly to waste time on unnecessary questions. He pulled on his boots, struggled into his tunic, seized cap and belt and hurried out of the room ahead of Schwitzke.

Sergeant Major Schulz was standing by the main gate. He was making a note of everyone who went in and out and asking a lot of very pertinent questions. By now he had worked out a way of bringing this extraordinary, potentially highly dangerous situation under control.

Schulz reasoned as follows: Someone out in the dark fired a shot. A rifle shot presumably. It wasn't altogether impossible to guess where the ammunition might have come from. The important point to establish now was whether this shot had been fired by a member of his own troop, No. 3 Troop. If so the man must have had a rifle. And that could easily be checked. Only the rank and file had rifles, and these were kept on open racks in the corridors.

Corporal Lindenberg reported to him. Schwitzke kept modestly in the background.

"Right," said the sergeant major. "You, Lindenberg, take over the second-floor corridor, and you, Schwitzke, the ground floor. Inspect every rifile to see if the barrel's clean. Make a note of any rifle with a dirty barrel. If you find anyone actually in the process of cleaning his rifle you're to report him to me at once. See? Schwitzke you — no, better Lindenberg — Lindenberg, go and tell the corporal in charge of the armory to report to me at once. All right, off you go!"

The two corporals moved off at the double. The sergeant major remained at his check point. There was a considerable amount of traffic. The Chief stood watching it thoughtfully. There can't be anything serious in this, he thought, to reassure himself. It would be quite unthinkable. Absurd! Ridiculous! For if . . .

Schwitzke reported that his orders had been carried out.

"Rifles in the lower corridor inspected. All barrels clean. Three rifles missing."

A moment later Lance Corporal Kowalski appeared.

"Corporal Wunderlich is out of barracks," he announced. "But I can give you any information you may want about the armory."

The sergeant major was thinking: None of the men in the troop were on guard today; those on leave have to hand their rifles into the store and remove their nameplates from the racks; those detailed for other duties take their rifles with them and also remove their nameplates. And yet there were three rifles missing.

"How many rifles are in the armory being repaired?" Schulz asked Kowalski.

"Three," he answered promptly.

Sergeant Major Schulz breathed again.

"It can't have been any of our people then," he said, with relief. "That really would have been the last straw!"

☙ ☙ ☙

Gunner Herbert Asch left the barracks at exactly twenty-one minutes past eight. He was wearing his dress uniform. There was a splendid crease in his trousers and his shoes shone

222

with a high polish. He had the air of a man who is particularly looking forward to something.

Purple shadows hung over the town. The moon looked down palely. Bright lights shone from one or two of the windows, making them stand out sharply in the gathering darkness. The barracks lay motionless, like some sullen animal. The evening breeze blew fitfully. It seemed as if there were going to be a storm.

Asch walked out through the main gate and went towards the workers' houses which were situated about eight hundred yards away. He looked neither to right nor left. He was going to Foreman Freitag's house, which was quite different from all the others, not because it was bigger, or any more imaginatively built, but because it was surrounded by young trees. These raised their heads curiously over the top of the fence, which was a high solid one and acted as a sort of wall round the house.

It was impossible to miss the Freitags' house even in the darkness. It filled up a far larger part of the sky than all the others. Father Freitag was leaning on the garden gate smoking a pipe and he opened the gate for Asch. It seemed to them that they had known each other for years.

"Come in," said Freitag. "The family's waiting for you."

"I really just wanted to say good evening to them and then take you off somewhere with me."

"Where to?"

"To my house, Herr Freitag."

"Aren't you muddling me up with my daughter?"

"Certainly not," said Asch. "I'm well aware of the difference. Later on, I hope she'll often come to my house. But it's you I want at the moment. There's something I've got to explain to my father."

"H'm," muttered Freitag thoughtfully. "Your father owns a café, doesn't he? He's a businessman, then. And I'm just a

223

factory worker. I can't really think he'll get much pleasure out of talking to me."

"In any case I've warned him you're coming," said Asch straightforwardly. "I've just rung him up. He's curious about you now and about what I've got to say to him."

"All right then," said Freitag with a nod. "But please don't think I'm being arrogant or difficult. I'm merely amazed by the speed at which you do things. We hardly know each other and already you're able to do what you like with me."

"Let's go and say hello to the family," suggested Asch.

They went in. Frau Freitag beamed at them. Elizabeth hardly looked up.

"You're late again," she said. "I suppose you've got to be back by lights-out?"

"No, I've got a late pass tonight," said Asch. "Until one o'clock."

"That's generous of them," said Elizabeth sarcastically.

"But I'm afraid I can't stay long. I've got to go and see my father."

"Oh!" said Elizabeth disappointedly.

"And I'm going with him," added old Freitag.

Elizabeth was very put out and she made no attempt to hide the fact. She wondered how on earth Herbert could have humiliated her so openly. She found a number of explanations for his behavior but none of them really satisfied her.

"Come on, Mother," said Freitag, "I must go and change."

"But you can do that by yourself."

"Of course I can, Mother. But you've got some business to do in the kitchen as a matter of fact."

Frau Freitag got the point at last. She wasn't wanted in the room. The two young people had to be left alone.

"Ah, I see!" she said. "Yes, of course."

Elizabeth felt ashamed of such an obvious maneuver.

"I don't in the least mind if you stay, Mother," she said firmly. "Please don't bother to move."

"But if you really have got something to do in the kitchen," said Asch agreeably, "then don't let me keep you from it."

The two older Freitags left the room. They could be heard laughing together after they had closed the door. They seemed to be greatly amused about something.

Elizabeth looked at Herbert reproachfully. Herbert got up and went over to her. She made it quite clear that she didn't like his being so close to her.

"Don't touch me!" she said.

Asch put his arm round her. She made a show of resistance but it wasn't very determined, and didn't prevent him from doing exactly what he had intended. He kissed her.

She said: "But what's the matter with you? Do you know what you want or not?"

"Perfectly well," said Asch, "but I'm saving it up for later; I'll come back to it in good time."

"It shouldn't be like this," said Elizabeth. "After — after what's happened, everything ought to be quite different."

Asch rested his hand gently on her shoulder.

"You're quite right," he said. "I think exactly the same. But I can't do just as I want at the moment. I'm not master of my own time. Strictly speaking, I'm not even supposed to have any will of my own."

"I don't understand," she said.

"You don't need to. I can't even explain it by saying it's a man's business. Because it isn't. It's worse than that. It just isn't normal. It's unnatural. Yes, that's it, the whole thing's against nature — it's inhuman!"

"I still don't understand," said Elizabeth.

"Elizabeth," he said painfully, "I'm no good at making love. You know that. At least I'm no good at talking about these

225

things. All I can say is: I love you, I really do, though, and can't stop thinking about it. High-sounding phrases seem quite absurd to me. I can't say things like 'Till death do us part' or 'To the end of time'! I can't talk about love as if it were so many yards of liver sausage, or about faithfulness as if it were so much bread and butter."

"What are you trying to say, Herbert?"

"Listen, Elizabeth, I want to marry you."

"Herbert!"

"Not at once; not even this week. A little later, when everything's been straightened out."

"When what's been straightened out, Herbert?"

"You'll soon see. And I'll see to it that you take it in all right. But what I've just said — I didn't want to keep that to myself. Whatever happens in the future nothing can change my feelings for you. And if you feel the same about me then I'm delighted. But if not, then just let me go on feeling as I do and I'll be quite happy."

"Herbert, you frighten me."

"I must go now," said Asch. "My father's expecting us."

He gave her arm a squeeze. Then he walked quickly out of the room.

Old Freitag was waiting for him. They walked through the town together, hardly speaking to each other, but keeping in step.

The Café Asch was brightly illuminated. It was full of customers. Sergeant Werktreu was sitting with a buxom girl in a corner. He waved to Asch.

"Your popularity with the senior ranks astonishes me," said Freitag good-humoredly.

"I don't get it for nothing," said Asch, "but I realize now that the capital outlay isn't worth it."

They walked the length of the room together. Asch nodded to the waiters.

226

"That's my sister at the back in the corner on the right," said Asch to Freitag.

"A very nice-looking girl," said Freitag.

"But unfortunately instead of a brain she's got a sort of Christmas tree growing inside her head: colored balls, blazing lights and a choir singing sentimentally in the background."

"And who's the soldier sitting next to her?"

"He's called Vierbein. He's the tree's Father Christmas."

Ingrid looked at her brother. Vierbein was about to get up to say hello to him. But Asch merely said:

"Carry on! You seem to have quite a lot of work to put in yet."

Asch didn't expect an answer. He showed Freitag the way. He opened the door at the back of the café. They went up some stairs and found themselves in a sort of large anteroom. And here they met the proprietor, Herr Asch himself.

Old Asch had put three bottles of wine on the ice, special bottles of Kitzinger Mainleite '37, and had brought out a box of cigars. He looked his visitor over as if he were thinking of buying him. He seemed to have some difficulty in fixing the price. He was polite in a vague sort of way.

The three of them sat down at the table, lit cigars and tasted the wine. Freitag and Asch Senior stole furtive glances at one another. Herbert gave them time to take each other in.

"I'm no expert on wines," said old Freitag finally. "So I can't tell what this is. It may be just a rather delicious sort of mouthwash. But delicious it certainly is."

"Mouthwash?" said Asch Senior, leaning forward a little. "Do you really mean that? Do you really think I might have given you something inferior?"

"Why not?" said old Freitag. "It's only the important guest who gets the good wine. Am I to assume I'm so welcome, then?"

"This is the finest wine I've got," said Asch Senior. "The

227

very finest, reserved for special occasions such as engagements, christenings, and the Führer's funeral."

The last remark slipped out quite unintentionally. He was very embarrassed. But he made no attempt to take it back. What's more, he was considerably interested to see how his guest would react to it.

"Then," said Freitag quietly, "I can only hope you will have an early opportunity of putting your excellent wine to good use on the third occasion which you mention."

"I hereby invite you to drink it with me on that day," said Asch Senior with a chuckle. "But I hope we don't have to wait until then before we drink it again, and that there'll be an engagement to celebrate before then. Here's to you, Herr Freitag."

They sipped at the wine and found it delicious. They rolled it round their mouths.

"It's full-bodied, clean, tangy, and has a bouquet that reminds one of well-stored apples," said old Freitag thoughtfully.

"Well done!" said Asch Senior in genuine admiration. "You're absolutely right. You should have been a landlord yourself."

"Impossible," answered Freitag. "I would have been my own best customer."

And so they talked on of this and that. Herbert left them to it for a time. They were getting on well with each other. They found that they had a lot more in common than they had originally supposed. Asch Senior admitted that he did all the repair jobs in the house himself because he enjoyed it so much. He had a bit of trouble with the big refrigerator sometimes, though. It leaked and he couldn't get it to a very low temperature.

Freitag said he'd repair the refrigerator for him there and then. Asch Senior was all for it. They were just about to take

228

off their coats, get out the tools and go down into the kitchen. Herbert Asch had quite a job to prevent them.

"You can do that another time," he said. "That isn't exactly what we're here for."

"We're here," said Asch Senior, "so that I can get to know your future father-in-law. Well, I've got to know him. I like him. Surely now we can have a little fun if we want to."

"Just a minute," said old Freitag in astonishment. "Who's whose father-in-law exactly? It's the first I've heard of anything like this."

"I must apologize," said Herbert Asch in embarrassment. "My father has misunderstood something I've said."

Asch Senior was also visibly embarrassed.

"Oh, what does it matter?" he said. "Father-in-law or not, we understand each other. And why are we here anyway?"

"I was just going to explain, Father."

"But I hope," said Freitag very firmly, "that this has nothing to do with my family. I'm not bought as easily as all that, you know, and certainly not behind my back."

"You're a clumsy fool," said Asch Senior crossly to his son. "You've put two grown men into an extremely embarrassing position. No offense I hope, Herr Freitag?"

"Of course not," said the other.

"Well, what do you want with us then?"

"You were a soldier once, weren't you, Father?"

"Of course."

"Did you like being in the army?"

Asch Senior hadn't the faintest idea what his son was driving at.

"Did I like it? What do you mean? I did my two years. They were two years."

"And what about you, Herr Freitag?"

"I'll subscribe to that too," he said without much interest.

"And were they good times, times to remember?"

The two older men looked at each other, then grinned in embarrassment and raised their glasses.

"There were times to remember all right," said Asch Senior, not without a certain bitterness.

"One of our lot was a cowhand," said Freitag. "It was his job to beat the captain's wife's carpets. He adored it. Another was a coachman. He became a sergeant and no longer had four horses, but thirty men to obey him. Another was so stupid he couldn't tell black from white, but he marched so well on parade that a real full-blown general asked for his name. He quite enjoyed himself."

"And then came the war," cried Asch Senior. "The local postman went for a tour of France and lived like a king. When he came back he could speak three words of French and he spoke them thirty times over when he got tight of an evening and started remembering the good old days. A man who worked in a coal merchant's and who had never been able to save enough money to buy himself a Sunday suit in his whole life destroyed three houses, two guns, four trucks, and several dozen human beings. An assistant schoolmaster from Lower Silesia became mess orderly to a regimental staff. When the colonel got tight he used to call him by his Christian name. He didn't mind it either."

"It's fundamentally the same today," said Herbert Asch. "War represents a glorious escape from everyday life, from the dreary rut of the office, the dull monotony of the factory. A man gets suddenly lifted right out of all this. He's given some ammunition and a license to kill. He's got men under him — he's allowed to bully them. He's helping to shape a nation's destiny. And he doesn't hesitate to play up to the role."

"But perhaps," said old Freitag thoughtfully, "men have some sort of primitive urge to be soldiers. I don't mean just an urge to kill and exercise power, but an urge to protect life and

230

limb, wife and child, the sick and the weak. Against wild beasts first of all, against robbers, lunatics, against the enemy. . . ."

"Yes, that may be," said Asch Senior, "but a perfectly justifiable primitive instinct like that often gets perverted for the worst of ends. Someone wants something the other man's got. So he simply declares him to be a wild beast, a lunatic, the enemy. It takes two sides to make a war, and each usually has the blessing of the Church. Each thinks it's in the right, each thinks its honor is at stake, each wants peace and only wishes to defend itself. But one or the other must be in the wrong. Or are both in the wrong?"

"One of the worst things about it," put in Freitag, "is that the ordinary soldier gets corrupted by the dirty work he's put to. Let's suppose for instance that this fellow Hitler starts a war, quite intentionally. The best of men will automatically become members of a murder gang. But there's nothing wrong with a soldier's career in itself, not in my view at any rate."

"And it's for that," cried Asch indignantly, "that a man has to let himself be dragged through the mud, obey every whim of some megalomaniac house painter as if his were the voice of God, abandon all moral standards, cease to think for himself so that his brain withers away entirely, shoot when he's told to, stand at attention when some halfwit talks to him, and stay at home when he wants to go out! He has to turn himself into an utter worm if he wants to survive at all."

"But who said that it need necessarily always be like this?" said Freitag with some feeling.

"We used to get up to all manner of tricks," admitted Asch Senior, smiling to himself. "Anyone who was at all bright or even just cheeky could always make a fool of an N.C.O. if he wanted to. Many people still feel a certain nostalgia for the way in which they used to get away with things. In fact when people talk about the fine times they used to have that's nearly always what they mean."

231

"The fault really lies in the whole structure of the military system," said Freitag. "The real trouble is that the army wants machines and not human beings at all. And the human beings resent being treated like machines. As the general standard of living improves, so do people's cultural aspirations. There are hardly any illiterates left. Your foreman, your taxi driver, your bookkeeper today is a hundred times more intelligent than your average professional N.C.O."

"Yes, but the methods employed in the Wehrmacht are exactly the same as those in use before the Great War or even worse. They just wear you down until you've got no more resistance left. They drill you and drill you until you just respond to every order automatically. Humiliation by numbers, so that every drop of individuality is squeezed out of you. The soldier only has any private life at all insofar as his superiors allow him to have one. The sort of life he leads depends entirely on the sort of mood they're in."

"Try and do something about it then," said Asch Senior with a gesture of resignation.

"That's just what I am doing, Father," said Herbert, looking straight at him.

His father didn't understand.

"What do you mean?" he said. "Are you determined to become a general and reform the Wehrmacht?"

"I'm going to say exactly what I think, and do only what I think is right. For as long as they'll let me."

Asch Senior leaned back in his chair.

"You must be mad," he said. "Do you want to start a mutiny?"

"I see what he means," said Freitag. "He wants to set an example."

"Completely mad," said Asch Senior with conviction. "Absolutely senseless. I would have believed you capable of a lot of things, Herbert, but never that."

"I can't help it," said Herbert Asch. "The sight of them just makes me sick."

"Then look the other way."

"It's time someone hit back at them."

"But why does it have to be you?"

"Someone must do it. Someone must make a start. Maybe it is idiotic, but I can't help it. I had a friend, Father. A nice, intelligent, straightforward sort of fellow, very lovable, a thoroughly decent chap. They've systematically broken his spirit. They've broken him as one breaks a stick over one's knee. They've made him into a spineless wreck. They drove him to the point of suicide."

"All right, then," said Asch Senior. "Do what you think best."

"I just wanted to let you know beforehand, Father," said Herbert Asch calmly. "I'll try and be a bit subtle about it. I'll try and take them on at their own game. They're astonishingly vulnerable really. I've already been sounding out their defenses a bit, and had a surprising amount of success. But of course there's always the chance that I'll end up in a military prison."

"It'd make me laugh," said old man Freitag with a grin, "if you ended up by being made an N.C.O. yourself. You never know. With God, and the Prussians, all things are possible!"

※ ※ ※

It goes without saying that in the worst hour of his whole life Corporal Lindenberg bore himself with his usual exemplary fortitude. He went out to meet it as heroes on the screen go out to meet death, fearless and true, blinded by superb stupidity. He was filled with an almost devout sense of dedication. He never wavered for an instant.

On this particular Friday his alarm clock went off just after

233

five. He was the only N.C.O. in the troop with an alarm clock. It was no ordinary alarm clock either, but a special one with a guarantee, which chimed and made a number of other remarkable noises. Lindenberg always used to shut it away in his locker before leaving the room, for otherwise the two other N.C.O.s with whom he shared the room would certainly have smashed the "infernal machine," as they called it, to smithereens.

The infernal machine, then, went off shortly after five. Lindenberg was wide awake at once. He sat up in bed, stretched up his arms, flung the blanket to one side and jumped onto the mat beside the bed. He danced about a bit, and did a few knee bends to get his circulation going properly.

The infernal machine, which had not yet been silenced, was now giving out a high shrill note. This was its second phase. The third was an appalling rattle with three notes on a bell at the end.

"You bastard!" shouted one of the other corporals, who had been waked up. "Turn that horrible box of tricks off at once or I'll finish it off forever."

He felt around for a slipper to hurl at the infernal machine. But the ammunition didn't come to hand at once.

Lindenberg turned his alarm clock off.

"I'm so sorry," he said politely.

Secretly he couldn't help regretting that his companions had so little understanding for his keenness. But he had sufficient self-control to hide the fact.

Once a week Lindenberg made a point of inspecting his section immediately after the sounding of reveille. One of his most important objects in doing this was to show them that he himself was always on the alert and that it would be as well for them to realize that there was no moment of the day or night in which he might not suddenly appear before them. "Even in the latrines!" he had once told his men very seriously.

234

In an entirely balanced way Lindenberg loved these first minutes of the day. They enabled him to breathe the air of the calm before the storm, of the silence before the first shell burst, of the peace that precedes chaos. He filled his lungs with the sweet morning air.

The new day crept stealthily up on the barracks. It waited close to the walls, pale and silent. Lindenberg stood by the open windows and reveled in it. It was as if he could hear the regular breathing of a thousand men. They would be on the move soon, and the sound of the artillery preparing itself for action would ring through the concrete halls like some powerful engine that had just been started up.

The corporal nodded contentedly. His mood just now was a strange mixture of humility and pride. In moments like this he always felt overwhelmed by the thought of how lucky he was to be a soldier. This was what he lived for. His life was its own reward.

He skipped off to the washroom, shaved himself carefully and stepped under the shower. Then he put on his uniform, gave a final check to his appearance in front of the looking glass and found it entirely in order.

Five minutes before reveille he was in the central corridor standing by the door of the barrack room in which the men of his section were still unwittingly asleep. It delighted him to think of the surprise which his appearance would cause.

The orderly corporal came hurrying past him. He was unshaven, as Lindenberg noticed with disapproval, and his mouth gaped in an enormous yawn.

"Well, well," he said, without showing the slightest surprise at the "eternal soldier's" presence. "The last man to leave his post is the first man back to it. Your section will be delighted to see you, I'm sure."

"I hope so," said Lindenberg with a certain diffidence.

The orderly corporal went into action. He threw open one

235

door after the other, and as he did so, blew a piercing blast on his whistle and called out: "Rise and shine!"

Lindenberg gave a final, quite unnecessary straightening to his belt, and cast a quick glance at the fit of his gray leather gloves, which were equally pointless, for they had been washed so often that they were now quite limp and shapeless. He stepped through the door and took up his stance just inside it.

He stood there watching carefully everything that went on but not saying a word. The men slowly turned themselves out of bed, their nightshirts flapping. One of them yawned, making a noise more suited to a cowshed than a barrack room.

Gunner Vierbein was the first to spot the corporal. "Room: attention!" he roared, jumping to attention himself. Regardless of their state of undress or whatever they might be doing, all the others stiffened to attention. It seemed, as they stood there, as if they were just continuing the sleep in which they had been interrupted.

Lance Corporal Kowalski could see no alternative but to get out of bed himself. Quickly he sized up the situation from his corner and yelled out: "Nothing to report, Corporal!"

Corporal Lindenberg himself came to attention correctly in the most disciplined fashion, and snapped his hand smartly up to his cap.

"Thank you, Lance Corporal," he said. "Stand easy, men! Carry on!"

The men knew Lindenberg's little peculiarities. They had experienced dozens of his early morning inspections in their time. They knew that what the corporal wanted to see was whether they started the day with that zip and zest, that brisk and cheerful readiness to face the future which, in the corporal's view, was so indispensable an attitude in a soldier.

Kowalski as room senior played his part to perfection.

"Anyone reporting sick?" he asked.

236

There was no answer as usual.

"No one reported sick," he called out smartly.

Lindenberg nodded.

Kowalski then called out: "Wagner and Volkmann detailed for billet-cleaning.

Wagner wanted to protest. He had been detailed for billet-cleaning the day before and had been barrack-room orderly the day before that. And now again today? It was a dirty trick. But he couldn't say anything with Lindenberg there. He threw his nightshirt onto the bed in a fury and turned his posterior towards Kowalski in a gesture of sullen obedience.

Before going to the washroom Kowalski completed the drill: "Barrack-room orderly for the day, Gunner Vierbein!" he called out.

"Very good, Lance Corporal," said Vierbein at once. "Barrack-room orderly."

A faint smile of approval appeared on Lindenberg's face. He was not altogether displeased by Gunner Vierbein's appearance. He watched every movement he made and saw that they were all carried out with a certain energy and zest. He liked that. It confirmed the theory he had always held, namely, that it was possible to turn Vierbein into a perfectly respectable soldier. Certainly he was still a bit dreamy sometimes, a little soft even; but there was no denying that he tried, and that was a start at least. Vierbein was on the right track at any rate. And entirely thanks to him, Lindenberg.

"Gunner Vierbein," said the corporal.

Vierbein shot forward. He had his fatigues on already.

"Yes, Corporal!"

"Show me your brush and comb.

Vierbein showed them to him. The corporal inspected them.

"Shaving equipment."

Vierbein showed him that too.

"Toothbrush and tooth glass."

237

Lindenberg inspected the lot.

Then he said: "Good, Vierbein. Carry on the good work!"

And he couldn't help feeling the tiniest bit flattered, in of course an entirely masculine way, by Vierbein's obvious pleasure at such praise.

The corporal stood where he was by the door, almost motionless, still taking in everything that went on in the room. And as everything in the room seemed to him to be going on in a tolerably disciplined way, he felt thoroughly satisfied. Once more he felt overcome with happiness at the thought of his good fortune in being privileged to be a soldier.

"Where's Gunner Asch, by the way?" asked Lindenberg suddenly. He hadn't seen Asch at all yet. He quickly tried to remember all the people he had noted so far that morning. He had a splendid memory for details, but he had no recollection of seeing Gunner Asch.

The men seemed in a hurry to leave the room. There was nothing out of the ordinary about that. They picked up towels, soap, shaving things, toothpaste, toothbrushes and tooth glasses — the latter only because Lindenberg was watching — and went into the washroom. It would have been utter stupidity to expose themselves to the corporal's gaze any longer than necessary.

"Where's Gunner Asch?" asked Lindenberg again.

There was no answer. Even Kowalski, who was standing quite close to him, preferred to remain silent. The room was practically empty.

A thought now entered Lindenberg's head, but he could hardly allow himself to entertain it for a moment. He walked farther into the room and looked into the corner where Gunner Asch's bed was situated behind a couple of cupboards. He stood there staring for several seconds.

Gunner Asch was lying in bed with his hands behind his head, steadily eying the corporal. He looked perfectly happy.

238

He had got himself into a comfortable position with his right foot crossed over his left knee. There was a smile on his face.

Corporal Lindenberg was quite unable to hide his astonishment. He found it impossible to accept the evidence of his own eyes. For nearly a whole quarter of an hour Gunner Asch had had the audacity simply to ignore the presence of his section corporal. It was absolutely unheard-of. Such a thing had never happened to Lindenberg before in his whole life. And to be honest, it had never occurred to him; it had never, even in his wildest dreams, crossed his mind that such a thing could happen to anyone.

Lindenberg forced himself to keep calm. He said: "Aren't you going to get up, then, Asch?"

"My rank is gunner," replied Asch quietly.

It took the corporal several seconds to swallow this reply, but he eventually did so. His magnificent sense of correctness immediately told him that he had in fact been guilty of a mistake here. It was one of the Führer's orders that all subordinates were to be addressed by their name and rank. It was of course a breach of tact on Asch's part, almost one might say a breach of discipline, to have called attention to his mistake, but he had a right to do so.

The corporal amended his remark.

"Aren't you going to get up, Gunner Asch?"

"That's a difficult question to answer, Corporal."

Lance Corporal Kowalski, who was the sole witness of this conversation, felt the blood mounting to his cheeks. It wasn't easy to say whether this was a sign of joy or anger. He debated with himself for a moment whether to stay where he was in the line of fire or join the others in the washroom. Finally he decided to stay put.

Lindenberg had gone rather red in the face too. He pulled himself together and said in his gruffest voice: "Get up at once, Gunner Asch!"

239

"Ah!" said Asch, taking his time about sitting up. "Now that's a different matter altogether. That's a clear order. I never refuse to obey a clear authoritative order. But your first remark was simply a question, a challenging question at the very most. Improperly formulated, Corporal."

Lindenberg managed to swallow even this reproach. His overdeveloped sense of what was or was not correct, from the point of view of Wehrmacht regulations, compelled him to do this. But he felt it was high time the situation was brought under control. And while Asch got out of bed, and pulled his night-shirt over his head, the corporal said: "According to the regulations every man is to rise from his bed immediately on the sounding of reveille. You didn't do that, Gunner Asch. You are guilty therefore of an offense against regulations."

Asch stood there quite naked. He did not stand at attention, and indeed in the condition in which he found himself that seemed reasonable enough. He said: "Corporal, there are certain concepts which lay themselves open to different interpretations. 'Immediately,' for instance — that's a debatable concept, now. What does it mean exactly, 'immediately' — One second? Three minutes? A quarter of an hour? Regulations do not enlighten us. One can't do more than interpret it as one thinks fit, and that is what I've done."

The corporal gave his interpretation: " 'Immediately?' " he said. "That means ten seconds, or at the most a minute."

"Anybody can say that afterwards," maintained Asch stanchly.

Lindenberg clenched his teeth. He already regretted having let Asch draw him into this conversation. But now he realized he had to see it through. His whole soldierly way of looking at things was on trial.

"I am not just 'anybody,' " he sharply. "I am your senior in rank. I hold that you have been guilty of an offense against regulations. A punishable offense."

240

"But, Corporal," said Asch, "how can something which you expressly allow be termed punishable?"

"What?"

Asch showed himself quite prepared to go into details.

"I lay in bed in the presence of the corporal in charge of my section. For you've been here, Corporal, ever since reveille. And all that time no reprimand or word of censure or order came my way. I therefore naturally supposed, Corporal, that my behavior had your approval."

Lindenberg shuddered as if he had just been hit a great blow over the back of the head. He shook himself a little. Then with an effort he succeeded in pulling himself together.

"I'm not going to continue this conversation, Gunner Asch."

"That's a great pity, Corporal."

"I shall report you for insubordination."

"It's rather disturbing to see how whenever there's trouble it always seems to be in your section, Corporal," said Asch. And it sounded as if he was really very concerned about the matter.

Nothing seemed to make sense to Corporal Lindenberg any more. He simply couldn't believe his ears. He searched around for some convincing explanation of all this but could find none.

"Listen, Gunner Asch," he said, "are you all right? I mean, are you feeling ill? Or is anything else the matter with you?"

"I'm in full possession of my senses, if that's what you mean. I merely feel rather annoyed, and what's more, Corporal, it's you who have annoyed me."

"Take care what you say!" cried Lindenberg excitedly.

Meanwhile, Lance Corporal Kowalski had seen to it that the two of them were left alone. The men who had finished washing were standing around outside the barrack room, stripped to the waist, exchanging opinions about how all this would end. They were hoping for the worst.

"Everything I'm saying," declared Asch, "has been very care-

241

fully thought out. You annoy me, Corporal. That's all there is to it. Why don't you let us get up and get ready for duty in peace? We're not robots. It's not only when we're asleep that we want to be allowed to have a little life of our own. But we're treated here as if we were serfs. You're not an N.C.O. — you're an overseer."

Lindenberg started scribbling in his notebook and said in a shaking voice: "I'm putting all that down!"

"I should hope so," said Asch. "And if you're not satisfied with the word 'overseer,' you can put down 'slavedriver' instead."

"Slavedriver!" yelled Lindenberg, beside himself with rage. He felt wounded to the bottom of his soul. He was bleeding to death. "Enough of this!" he cried with his last gasp. "This is going to stop!"

"If you've had enough," said Asch obligingly, "then let's stop by all means."

Lindenberg was as pale as a freshly laundered sheet. It was all he could do to stop himself from hitting Asch. The strain had been too much for him. And yet the rules against striking a subordinate were particularly strict. And Lindenberg obeyed all rules as if they were sacred.

With what he imagined to be icy bitterness, but in a voice which unfortunately rose to a quivering shriek and threatened to give way altogether under the strain, Lindenberg turned to Asch and said:

"You'll pay for this, Gunner Asch!"

Then he turned abruptly on his heel. He went over to Lance Corporal Kowalski and said:

"You're a witness!"

"What am I a witness of?" asked Kowalski, feigning stupidity with his usual success.

But Lindenberg paid no attention to him. Holding himself as stiff as a ramrod, he strode magnificently from the room. There

was only one thought in his mind: the appalling scene to which
he had just been subjected must be expiated in full. If not, it
was the end of everything!

᪥ ᪥ ᪥

Elizabeth Freitag, dressed in nothing but her pink under-
wear, stopped for a moment thoughtfully in the middle of the
room. With one hand she brushed the hair sideways off her
face. Then she seemed to take a decision of some sort. She went
over to the cupboard and carefully chose from it a green silk
dress which she knew suited her very well.

As she dressed she looked at her watch. Twenty minutes to
eight. In five minutes at the latest Father Freitag would have to
set off on his bicycle if he were to be at the factory on time. He
usually went there on foot in the mornings, but when he was
late — either because he had been doing a job of work or because breakfast was late, or because, like this morning, he had
overslept — then he would make up for lost time by sailing off
to the factory on his bicycle.

Five more minutes then! She took a lipstick from her handbag and carefully made up her lips. This was unusual for her,
and was in fact quite pointless. Her lips were quite red enough
and full enough and prettily enough shaped as it was. Then she
gave her hair one last comb, trying to get it to lie tidily to one
side. And she looked at her watch again. Ten minutes had gone
by and her father had still not left the house.

She couldn't wait any longer. She gave herself one last
anxious glance in the mirror, got to her feet and started to
make her way out of the house. In the hall she met her father.

"Where are you off to?" he asked.

"To the barracks," said Elizabeth.

"Are you on early this morning?"

"No," said Elizabeth, "not officially. But I want to go through the vouchers and do some stocktaking. There's always plenty of time for that sort of thing in the mornings."

"And what else are you going to do?"

"I'm not going to see Herbert Asch, if that's what you mean."

"Good," said old Freitag. Her answer seemed to have re-assured him. "If you say that, then I know you won't. I know that you'd never tell me a lie, not a real one."

"Why do you say that, Father?"

"Because I want things to stay as they are between us. And because I don't want you to try and influence Herbert Asch in anything connected with his duty. It would be quite useless if you did try, but it might also turn out to be a nuisance to him."

"You seem to have his interests very much at heart," said Elizabeth.

Old Freitag nodded. "That's because I've got your interests at heart. That's the only reason. But I won't keep you any longer. Look through your vouchers, do your stocktaking, but keep out of Herbert Asch's way."

"I'll keep my eyes open then. I'll be prepared for some surprise or other."

"You'll do nothing of the sort," said old Freitag firmly. "You will not keep your eyes open or be prepared for anything. You'll just keep out of his way."

"And do you think it's going to be so easy?"

"Elizabeth," said old Freitag severely, "you've already prom-ised me that you won't go and see Herbert Asch."

"And I shall keep my promise, Father."

Elizabeth left the house. She walked hurriedly off in the di-rection of the barracks and the nearer she got to them the faster she walked. She looked at her watch several times. It was just before eight. She was only just in time. For she couldn't afford to be late.

244

She pulled her pass out of her handbag as she went through the gate, but the sentry knew her and waved her on.

"Come in! Come in!" he called out. "We can't have enough of your sort!"

Without a moment's hesitation Elizabeth walked across to No. 3 Troop's block. She walked in through the open entrance, where she immediately became an object of interest to the soldiers standing about there, who either greeted her or stared at her in astonishment. She hurried up the stairs to the second floor. But once there she didn't turn in through the swing doors to the corridor. She stopped in front of a door which had a visiting card neatly pinned on to it bearing the words: *Wedelmann, Lieutenant*. She pressed the bell.

Shortly afterwards the door opened. Wedelmann's new orderly, Gunner Wagner, the man who had been surreptitiously allotted to the lieutenant by the sergeant major, stood in the doorway.

"Well," he said crossly, "what do you want?"

"Can I speak to Lieutenant Wedelmann, please?"

"What do you want with him?"

"I want to speak to him, please. About something private."

"Something private?" Wagner looked at her in astonishment. Then he said: "The lieutenant is only interested in service matters."

"Good. Then I want to speak to him about a service matter, please."

Wagner leaned against the doorpost. "You what? A service matter! And what sort of service matter have you got to discuss with him, pray?"

Elizabeth was desperate. This man was causing her considerable embarrassment. She couldn't stay here on the stairs much longer. The number of men who had gathered round her was growing every minute. They were passing comments on her and weren't bothering to keep their voices down. At any moment

245

Asch or Vierbein or Kowalski might appear. And she couldn't let herself be seen here by any of them. She would have to go back.

But before she could do this she heard Lieutenant Wedelmann's voice calling out: "What is it, Wagner? What do you think you're here for? To gossip, or to clean my boots?"

"There's someone here," said Wagner.

Wedelmann came forward crossly. When he saw Elizabeth he felt very embarrassed. He looked down at his riding breeches, which had been stuck clumsily into the tops of his green woollen stockings.

"Excuse my dress," he said. "What can I do for you, Fräulein Freitag?"

"May I speak to you?"

"To me? Here, in my quarters? At this hour?"

"Yes, please."

"Come in then," said Wedelmann hurriedly. He led the way and opened the door of his sitting room. "In here, please. Take a seat. I'll be back in a minute. I'll just go and finish dressing."

Elizabeth looked round the room. It wasn't a particularly large one and had nothing special in the way of furniture: a desk, a bookcase, three chairs, a little table, a lamp. On the walls: one or two diplomas, two watercolor prints, numerous photographs. A book was open on the desk: *Faith in Germany*, it was called, by Zöberlein. There were also a pile of newspapers, three blue copies of army regulations, some cigarette ends, a bottle of schnapps and a glass.

Wedelmann came back into the room fully dressed in his uniform. He gave her a friendly smile.

"And what brings you here at this hour of the morning?"

"I hope I'm not disturbing you."

"You could never disturb me," Wedelmann reassured her. He was delighted to be allowed just to look at her like this. She was a pretty girl, even in the harsh light of early morning.

246

She looked prettier even than she had looked in the dance hall or in the N.C.O.s' canteen.

"I'm not taking up too much of your time?"

"My time is entirely at your disposal," said Wedelmann, and he meant what he said. Besides, he could afford the gesture. Artillery drill didn't begin until eight-fifteen, and if he wasn't there on time it was agreed that it should begin without him. There was no need to expect any sort of inspection before nine.

"I wanted to ask your help," said Elizabeth.

"How can I help you?" said Wedelmann, who was prepared to do anything for her. He liked Elizabeth Freitag. He had always thought her a pretty girl. She wasn't nearly so difficult as Ingrid Asch and a good deal nicer and more reliable than Lore Schulz. And of course she was in a completely different class from all the little bourgeois girls on the lookout for husbands, and the good-time girls on the lookout for business, who were the only other girls he seemed to meet. This Elizabeth Freitag was a thoroughly decent girl. And she could be relied on to behave decently in any situation.

"I'll be absolutely honest with you," said Elizabeth. "And I think it's all right for me to be." She hesitated for a moment. Then she said quickly: "You know that Herbert Asch and I . . . that I and Herbert Asch . . . You sat with us at the same table last Saturday, remember?"

"But of course," said Wedelmann, "I remember very well." He found it hard to conceal his disappointment. He felt suddenly terribly depressed. He said to himself: That's always the way with me; it's always like that. They all slip through my fingers one after the other. A lieutenant's life is a wretched one, particularly in this way. And I'm one of the most wretched of them all, for I've got too strong a sense of propriety to make the best of even my most favorable opportunities.

"I got the impression then," said Elizabeth frankly, "that you thought highly of Herbert, and that, if I may put it like

247

this, that's to say if such a thing is possible between an officer and one of his men, that you had quite friendly feelings towards him."

"But certainly," said Wedelmann warmly. "Certainly I have." He felt rather touched and flattered.

"And Herbert Asch, that's to say Gunner Asch, likes you too, Lieutenant. He finds you sympathetic. He has a high regard for you, he admires you. He thinks you're a man of honor."

"I'm delighted to hear it," said Wedelmann cheerfully, with visible pride. That his men should treat him with respect was only natural, that they should have a high regard for him was his sincerest wish, but that there should be some who were actually fond of him and admired him, that filled him with the deepest joy and satisfaction.

"My dear Fräulein Freitag," said the lieutenant, "I also admire Gunner Asch, even as a soldier, although — and this is no criticism, I am just stating a fact — he is by no means a perfect one. But I find him extremely sympathetic as a human being, not least on your account. I have no idea of what you've come to see me about, but if by chance Gunner Asch should be refusing to accept the consequences of any situation that may have arisen between you, then you can rely on me implicitly. I'll be able to bring him to his senses and show him where his happiness lies, not least because I have such a high regard for him."

The lieutenant fell silent. And he noticed that Elizabeth was giving him a searching look, almost as if she didn't quite trust him. Had he been talking utter nonsense? It was always possible. He was a soldier, not a psychologist. He was always liable to make a blunder where people's private affairs were concerned. This fact no longer surprised him, though it always rather upset him.

"Lieutenant," said Elizabeth amiably, "it's nothing to do with my private life, nor with Herbert Asch's."

"Aha!" said Wedelmann, delighted. He felt himself on firmer ground at once. "A purely service matter then?"

"I think so."

"You only think so, Fräulein Freitag? You're not certain?"

"I presume so."

"And what is it you presume?"

Elizabeth started to tell her story. She was completely honest about it. She didn't know all there was to know, but she told him all she could. She gave him a very frank picture of the state of affairs as she imagined it.

Lieutenant Wedelmann listened attentively. His embarrassment had gone. His long youthful face looked calm and serious. His self-confidence could almost be felt as a physical presence in the room. He was on his own ground now. There was no need to feel confused here and to go blundering about over all sorts of psychological and sexual problems.

"What you maintain, or rather presume to be happening, sounds absurd, I admit," he said after a long pause. "But in my view it's perfectly possible."

"You think he'll do it then?"

"It's not altogether beyond the bounds of possibility — in certain circumstances. The motives too, which you put forward as his, or rather which you presume to be his — these also make sense. If I had a friend myself and saw him being driven to the point of suicide before my eyes, I think I'd . . . But I have no friend."

"I've added it all up, Lieutenant," said Elizabeth confidingly. "I'm not sure whether I've got it quite right, or whether I've only got somewhere near the answer. Perhaps I'm absolutely wrong, perhaps it's all quite different and nothing like so serious. But I had to come and see you, and it can only be you, because there's no one else I trust."

"I'll do my very best not to let you down," said Wedelmann honestly.

249

"You're a wonderful man," said Elizabeth. "I like you very much indeed."

Wedelmann blushed.

"No, no," he said modestly. "No, you mustn't say that. Please don't think of me as some sort of knight-errant or anything like that. I'm just a cold calculating person who has managed to strip himself of all individual emotions. Understand?"

"I understand," said Elizabeth, and she beamed at him. She had every confidence in him.

Wedelmann got to his feet. He tried not to catch her eye.

"If I take this matter on," he said, "I do so in the long run solely in the interests of duty. For me this is a question of discipline; the honor of the Wehrmacht is at stake. Or to put it in even simpler terms: I'm not going to have a tricky situation like this cropping up in the troop in which I serve. It would, after all, all come back on me in the long run."

"It's really awfully good of you, Herr Wedelmann."

"Oh, nonsense," cried Wedelmann, trying to suppress the powerful emotions which were again stirring within him. "It's just that I can't afford to let something like this develop when there's any risk of its reflecting on myself — much as I would love to see certain N.C.O.s get into trouble over it. But let's keep to the facts. For the time being we've got to reckon with the probability that Asch has, purely mentally of course, run amok. There's been no time for anything to have happened yet. It's only eight-thirty at the moment and artillery drill will have only just begun. Previous to that, between seven and eight there's been only a troop lecture on first aid given by a medical sergeant. There can't have been any friction there. The men usually use it to snatch a little morning nap. Nothing very much happens at the beginning of the day here. But artillery drill could be a danger point if Asch chose to make it one."

"But what will you do, my dear Herr Wedelmann?"

"It's quite simple," he replied. "I'll see that Asch is kept out of harm's way. For example, I can shut him up all day in the clothing store. He can spend his time there sleeping or playing cards with Sergeant Werktreu. That's all the two of them do most of the time anyway."

"I don't know how to thank you, Herr Wedelmann."

"I'll tell you how," said Wedelmann gaily. "You can invite me to the wedding."

"You're hereby invited, and you'll be heartily welcome!"

"And I'd also rather like to be godfather," said the lieutenant. He was delighted to see Elizabeth blush slightly. He found it a remarkable experience to be able to talk so frankly with another human being; he had to admit to himself that it was just this that he had always longed for.

"But first of all," he said forcefully, "we must see to it that no disaster occurs."

Elizabeth took his hand and squeezed it. She said:

"Let's hope you won't be too late."

☙ ☙ ☙

Even at this hour of the morning Sergeant Major Schulz had already started lecturing his wife about her behavior. He avoided addressing her directly, for there would have been something too personal about that. She had not deserved such warmth. He just wanted her to know what he thought of her and how he expected her to behave in future.

He sat at the kitchen table.

"A sergeant major's wife," he said, "has certain duties which she cannot disregard. It is damaging to her dignity if she lets herself become involved with her husband's subordinates, and it's a threat to discipline if she goes around with his superior officers."

"What ranks is she allowed, then?" asked Lore Schulz, without any particular friendliness.

251

Schulz sent his coffee cup crashing down onto the saucer. He was full of righteous indignation. He looked up resentfully at his wife, who was leaning against the kitchen cupboard, for he had taken the precaution of not yet telling her to sit down beside him at the table. "So," he said, "you're really still proud of what you've done?"

"What do you want me to do?" she asked angrily. She was in despair. "Get down on my knees, shed bitter tears and implore your forgiveness? Forgiveness for what? For the fact that you neglect me? For the fact that you're not a normal human being?"

Schulz looked at his wife reproachfully. She was crying. This made him feel a little more magnanimous towards her, for her tears were a sure proof of his own superiority. Morally speaking, she was now as good as finished. Which was as it should be. Guns existed to be put in position, horses to be mastered, and human beings to be bent to one's will. It was the way things were. It was just not everyone who was capable of living up to the demands of life. "I won't forgive you," he said, "until I feel quite certain that you're really back on the rails at last."

He drank up his coffee with relish, and looked once more at the kitchen clock to make sure that his wife had set it by barrack time. It was ten minutes past eight. He got to his feet and walked out of the apartment.

The sergeant major was in an excellent mood when he arrived at his office. The office corporal, the orderly corporal, Corporal Lindenberg and Gunner Wagner were already there waiting for him. They all sprang to attention at the sight of him, produced magnificent salutes, and didn't stand easy again until he had given them permission to do so.

"What do you want, my fine fellow?" he said to Gunner Wagner.

"Lieutenant Wedelmann wishes me to be replaced at once," replied the gunner.

252

The sergeant major beamed with pleasure. Things had moved faster than he had expected them to. The appointment must have made Wedelmann hopping mad. Excellent.

"And what reason did he give?" asked the sergeant major amicably.

"The lieutenant said I was an idiot," announced Wagner without the slightest embarrassment.

Schulz was delighted.

"Go and tell the lieutenant," he said, "that my entire troop is composed of idiots like you. It would be quite pointless to change you for anyone else. You will remain Lieutenant Wedelmann's orderly. Now be off with you, man! Go and take him the good tidings!"

After Gunner Wagner had left the office, the sergeant major received the mail and the daily orders from the hands of the office corporal. He looked over the daily orders, cast a hurried glance at the mail and then said: "Right. The usual stuff. Next?"

The orderly corporal felt that this was in some way addressed to him and put in his report: "All late passes in on time. Two men sick. Damage in the ground-floor latrine repaired. Otherwise nothing to report."

The sergeant major took the orderly book from the orderly corporal and cast his eye over the entries.

"Damage in the ground-floor latrine repaired," he said thoughtfully.

"As ordered," said the orderly corporal. "The troop carpenters have put in a new pane of glass and repaired the damage to the ceiling."

"Has the bullet been found?"

"Yes, Sergeant Major," said the orderly corporal. He pulled a rather unclean handkerchief out of his pocket, unrolled it carefully and took from it a squashed little lump of lead about the size of a cigarette end.

253

"A rifle bullet," he said.

The sergeant major suddenly sat up, and seemed very interested.

"You're sure this is a rifle bullet?" he asked.

"Absolutely," said the orderly corporal. "A typical 98k rifle bullet. Wunderlich, the armory corporal, agrees."

Schulz picked up the little lump of lead. He did so with a certain distaste, as if it repelled him in some way. He put it down on his desk. And he said to himself: What if . . . ? It was unthinkable! The consequences were quite unforeseeable. If that were so he should never have let the record be altered, or rather obliterated, like that. But it hadn't come to that yet.

"Good," he said, shaking himself free of his gloomy thoughts. "The two fellows who have gone sick are to report here right away. We'll look into their cases." He turned to Frost, his office corporal. "Frost," he said, "make out a troop order to the effect that in future anyone going sick is to report to me in person immediately after he's been examined; the only exceptions being if the man has already collapsed or if he has an infectious disease."

"Very good, Sergeant Major," said Frost. He didn't say it particularly smartly. His answer was almost slovenly in fact. He was a useless soldier but an invaluable clerk, particularly to Schulz.

In the meantime the sergeant major was busy inspecting his various pencils — colored, plain and indelible — to see if they had been properly sharpened and arranged as he had ordered. This had been done. The orderly corporal felt he was not wanted any more, so he saluted and disappeared. Corporal Lindenberg still stood there like a monument.

"Well?" said the Chief ungraciously. "And what do you want?" For he always found it provoking to have to face the Iron Corporal, this supersoldier, this sea-green incorruptible.

"What are you trying to draw attention to yourself about now?"

"I have a report to put in, Sergeant Major."

"Let's have a look at it."

Lindenberg laid the snow-white sheet of paper down on the sergeant major's desk. The large letters could be seen drawn up on it in neat array.

The sergeant major cast his eye over it, and then jumped, sat up straight, and looked hard at Lindenberg, who didn't bat an eyelid. Schulz read through the report again, slowly this time, word for word.

This is what he read:

REPORT

I hereby report Gunner Herbert Asch for a disciplinary offense, inasmuch as this morning after the sounding of reveille he lay in bed in a provocative manner for fifteen minutes and when reprimanded by me answered back in an undisciplined fashion, not only omitting the use of the third person in his address but also employing certain derogatory phrases with reference to myself such as "overseer" and "slavedriver," and all this in the presence of other men.

LINDENBERG, CORPORAL

It was a long time before Sergeant Major Schulz spoke.

Then he said: "You haven't left a large enough margin on the left-hand side of your report. I can't enter it in the files like this."

Corporal Lindenberg said nothing. He didn't betray the slightest sign that this remark of the sergeant major had severely shaken him. A formal rejection of this sort was the last thing he had expected and he had certainly not deserved it. Admittedly the left-hand margin was officially supposed to be five centimeters wide, but he was prepared to bet that this was at least four.

255

"And what," said the sergeant major, "do you mean exactly by 'lay in bed in a provocative manner'?"

"The top part of his body was bare and he looked at me provocatively."

Schulz shook his head angrily. He threw the report down on his desk and brought the palm of his hand down hard on top of it.

"Are you prepared to swear to all this?"

"By all means, Sergeant Major," answered the corporal at once. "And besides, I have a witness."

"Who is the witness?"

"Lance Corporal Kowalski, Sergeant Major."

"And who else?"

"Only Lance Corporal Kowalski, Sergeant Major."

"In that case," said Schulz very forcibly, "you have put in a false report. You say here: '. . . in the presence of other men.' Other men means more than one. And if in fact this had happened in front of more than one man, which has not yet been proved to be the case, then it would amount to mutiny. 'In the presence of other men.' But suddenly it turns out that there's only been one of them. What the hell do you think you're playing at, Lindenberg?"

Lindenberg felt himself completely at a loss. The sergeant major's technique was simply too much for him. And even if he had been equal to it, his delicate sense of discipline would presumably have prevented him from matching himself up to it. Making a great effort to maintain a correct attitude he said:

"But that doesn't alter the expressions which Gunner Asch used, Sergeant Major."

"Are you trying to teach me my job?" asked Schulz.

"No, Sergeant Major," said the corporal.

The sergeant major brought his hand down on top of the report again.

"A nasty business," he said, angrily. "And you're sure you didn't make a mistake?"

"No, Sergeant Major."

"You're not sure you didn't make a mistake?"

"I didn't make a mistake, Sergeant Major."

Schulz got to his feet and went and stood in front of the corporal.

"Lindenberg," he said, "this man Asch has always been a perfectly good soldier. Nothing like this has ever happened before. Are you sure you didn't provoke him in some way? Or do you think perhaps you misunderstood what he said? He probably didn't mean it like that at all."

"He meant it like that, Sergeant Major."

"Now listen to me, Lindenberg. I don't hold much with reports of this sort. Settle the matter in some other way. Put him through it good and proper, until he comes to you with his tongue hanging out simply begging for mercy. I'll gladly lend you a hand. Now then, what about it, Lindenberg? Do you still insist on putting in your report?"

"Yes, Sergeant Major."

"Even though you would be doing me a personal favor by withdrawing it?"

"I'm sorry, Sergeant Major," said Lindenberg, quite unshaken. "I must insist on it."

"Right, then," roared the Chief. "All right, then. If that's what you wan't we'll look into the matter. But may the Lord have mercy on you if your report doesn't turn out to be one hundred per cent correct in every respect. And now go off and bring Kowalski and Asch here at once. And double up, man!"

Lindenberg produced one of his most superb salutes and disappeared at the double.

Sergeant Major Schulz walked crossly over to the telephone. Frost, the office corporal, stole a glance at him. He knew quite well why the sergeant major didn't want this report to go in.

He couldn't afford to let it, for one particular reason. Frost felt convinced that Schulz was about to put a call through to someone on the battery staff.

"Battery staff, please," said Schulz into the telephone. "Sergeant Major Köhler, please. Hullo, Köhler, Schulz here. Listen, Köhler. A few days ago I sent the battery commander some recommendations for promotion to corporal. Yes, those are the ones. Can I have them back? . . . In the major's briefcase? Well, take them out. There's a slight alteration I want to make on one of them. . . . Impossible? The Major's already seen them? Already signed them? . . . My God, Köhler, this is a nice mess. And just at this moment too. Don't worry, I'll get it straightened out somehow."

Schulz slowly put back the receiver. That was a blow. He sank back into his wide comfortable chair and stared thoughtfully at the top of his desk. And there his attention was again caught by the little lump of lead that had once been a bullet, and which someone had fired from a 98k rifle. But who? And at whom? He seemed to be having trouble on all sides.

Corporal Lindenberg appeared again and announced that Lance Corporal Kowalski and Gunner Asch were waiting outside in the corridor.

"We'll see Kowalski first," cried the sergeant major. Kowalski entered the office with a good-natured grin on his face and Schulz asked him without further ado:

"Did you hear Gunner Asch describe Corporal Lindenberg as an overseer or a slavedriver?"

"No, Sergeant Major," said Kowalski meekly.

"But you were there, Lance Corporal Kowalski!" cried Lindenberg, losing control of himself for a second.

"Where was I?" asked Kowalski.

"In the barrack room this morning."

"You keep out of this, Lindenberg," rapped out the sergeant major sharply. He found the way the conversation was develop-

258

ing thoroughly satisfactory. It was just what he wanted. He was delighted to see the way in which Lindenberg was losing his self-control and changing color.

"Well, now, my dear Kowalski," said the Chief, "how was it exactly? You didn't hear anything of the sort?"

The lance corporal gave a charming grin.

"I heard nothing of the sort, Sergeant Major. At least I heard no details. The corporal seemed to be having some sort of excited conversation with Gunner Asch, certainly, but I don't know what it was about. I don't like to intervene in conversations when they're no business of mine."

"But you must have heard!" cried Lindenberg shrilly.

"Why must I have heard, Corporal?"

Lindenberg's voice got completely out of control. It gurgled and hissed. "You're an infamous liar!" he cried.

"Corporal Lindenberg!" cried the sergeant major sharply. "I forbid you to utter insults like that in my presence. You've completely lost your self-control, man! Are you ill?"

"Sergeant Major, I . . . I must ask . . . I beg you . . ."

"I'm conducting this investigation, Corporal Lindenberg. And I forbid you to interrupt. Where's your sense of discipline? I don't know what's come over you. You will go to your room at once, Corporal Lindenberg, and await my orders."

Lindenberg walked stiffly out of the room. The sergeant major watched him go with indescribable satisfaction. He felt he had won a great victory. He nodded contentedly.

"My dear Kowalski," he said to the lance corporal, who was standing in front of him listening attentively. "Your evidence is very valuable. You're prepared to swear to this of course if necessary?"

"Of course, Sergeant Major."

"Good, my dear fellow. Then I'll dismiss you for the present. But don't go too far away, I may be needing you later. I want to see Gunner Asch now."

259

Kowalski disappeared and Asch appeared in his place.

"Come closer, Asch," said the sergeant major, looking Asch up and down patronizingly. "I've got a report here from Corporal Lindenberg. You know what it's about? Well, now. In it Lindenberg maintains that you called him an overseer and even a slavedriver. What have you got to say to that?"

"It's quite true, Sergeant Major," said Asch tartly.

Schulz jumped.

"What's true?"

"I did call Corporal Lindenberg an overseer and a slavedriver. He is one."

"Did I hear you aright?" asked Schulz in amazement. "You can't mean that seriously?"

"Oh yes I do," said Asch. "Perfectly seriously. It's the truth."

"Now, I'm warning you, Asch!"

"What against? No one's going to take a pot shot at me."

"What did you say?"

"But the next time someone takes one at you, and presumably you won't have to wait long for that, it's quite possible that he'll take better aim. You can't be such a difficult target after all. There's quite a lot of you. What's the matter? Is something wrong with you? If I were in your shoes I shouldn't feel so good either. In fact I'd feel pretty bad."

Sergeant Major Schulz had risen to his feet. He stretched his arm out towards Asch as if he were putting a curse on him.

"You're under arrest," he said.

And there was something almost solemn about the way he said it.

※ ※ ※

Captain Derna, who was sitting at home having what he called "a drop of coffee," by which he meant at least five cups, looked anxiously at his watch.

"Isn't my car there yet?"

Frau Behrends, the widow with whom he lodged and who, though of a certain age, was well enough preserved, tried to calm him down.

"There's another four minutes until a quarter to nine," she said.

"Five minutes before the other goes, is the only time the soldier knows," said Captain Derna. He had just picked up this bit of North German, not to say Prussian doggerel, and had appropriated it to himself. He liked it. His musical ear was particularly pleased by the simple rhyme.

Captain Derna stood by the window staring impatiently out into the street. The widow Behrends, who looked after the charming Austrian with much care and devotion, disapproved strongly of the state he got himself into every morning.

But the truth was that to Derna every morning represented a new day fraught with potential difficulties — unpleasantnesses, misunderstandings, errors of judgment. He didn't find the Prussian life an easy one. He found he had to "watch how he went," as the people round here said, if he was to keep out of trouble. The ship with which he had been entrusted had somehow to be steered between the most treacherous rocks. The surest method of bringing it to safety was to go as carefully as possible and hope for good weather; and above all keep a sharp lookout for Major Lumpface!

"The car's here," said Frau Behrends. She hurried forward with the clothesbrush, searching for little hairs and bits of dust and fluff. Lovingly she brushed him down; first his well-padded shoulders and then all the way down his back to his large behind.

Derna was no longer a young man, but the spring in his step as he bounded down the stairs to his car and gave the driver a smart salute was really remarkable. He thought for a moment of ticking the driver off but changed his mind when he recollected that in fact the man hadn't been late at all. Besides, it

261

would have been most unwise to reprimand the fellow in any case, for it would have made him unsure of himself, he would have lost his self-confidence, become a prey to anxiety, and might easily have got involved in a serious accident.

"To the barracks," said Captain Derna, "but stop at Major Sämig's on the way."

"Very good, sir," said the driver. He found this order superfluous, for he got exactly the same one every morning. The wording never varied. He let in the clutch and drove off. Frau Behrends could be seen at an upper window. The curtain moved backwards and forwards as if someone were trying to wave with it.

Derna sat upright in the back of the car. He looked as if he were part of the fittings. The M.O. was already waiting for him in the "Street of the S.A."

"Good morning, my dear doctor," called out the captain heartily as he did every morning.

"Good morning, Captain," called out the doctor no less heartily. Then he climbed nimbly into the car and sat down on Derna's left. The car immediately drove off again.

Captain Derna, who always felt rather lonely up here in the "frozen North," had taken considerable trouble to cultivate the M.O.'s friendship, and it seemed that he had been successful. Derna, being a Viennese, had had to acclimatize himself to the atmosphere, and this had not been easy. His brother officers never quite came to accept him as one of themselves. Nor did they accept Major Dr. Sämig, for he automatically ranked in their minds as an inferior type of officer. He was an outsider. It was an unfortunate fact; it wasn't the poor fellow's fault of course, but it was a fact nevertheless. The two of them therefore naturally found themselves drawn towards each other. They cheered one another up.

"Nice day," said Derna.

"There won't be many people reporting sick," said Sämig.

Their car had now left the center of the town and was spinning along the highway which led to the barracks. The captain and the doctor felt that they understood one another without having to say a word. The driver accelerated in order to be back at the barracks as quickly as possible. He wanted to be rid of his passengers and spend the rest of the day washing the car and tinkering with the engine — having a quiet nap, in other words.

The sentry flung open the gate and let the car drive in without stopping it to inspect passes. He called through the window of the guardroom: "No. 3 Troop Commander and the M.O." Whereupon the warning was immediately telephoned all over the barracks."

The car didn't stop until it got to the administration building, where Dr. Sämig got out. But before he could say good-by to Captain Derna, a window opened above him and Major Lumpface Luschke appeared at it.

"Good morning, gentlemen," cried Major Luschke immediately, and waited to see what would happen next.

Captain Derna, who realized at once that it was quite impossible to salute the C.O. from a sitting position inside the car, quickly got to his feet and climbed out. Not till then did he raise his eyes to the second-floor window above him and bring his hand up in a smart salute. Dr. Sämig did the same.

Major Lumpface Luschke grinned happily. He waited calmly by the window, doing absolutely nothing. He just stared down at them.

Captain Derna began to feel embarrassed. He didn't know what to do. Nor did Dr. Sämig. What were they to do? Should they salute and turn away again, since the C.O. was making no attempt to talk to them? Or ought they wait until the C.O., who had after all called to them in the first place, dismissed them?

Luschke, whose unpredictable behavior was a byword, was

263

obviously delighted by the state of indecision to which he had reduced his officers. He still said nothing but continued to look down at them with interest.

Then Captain Derna had an idea. An admirable, typically Prussian idea, he thought. He merely called out: "No. 3 Troop — nothing special to report, sir!"

A broad grin spread over Major Luschke's face.

"And how do you know that, Captain?" he asked in his mildest voice. "Have you a telephone at home? Have you seen the sergeant major yet this morning? Or have you perhaps been into barracks once already?"

"N-no, sir!" stammered the captain, trying hard to put a good face on the situation.

"Ah, I see!" cried the major, obviously enjoying himself. "Then perhaps you're a clairvoyant?"

Derna did not reply. He felt utterly crushed. He would have liked to sink through a hole in the ground. This Major Luschke was a perpetual affliction to him, a continual source of humiliation, the author of an endless chain of unpleasant surprises.

"Well, anyway," said Major Luschke at the upper window, "at least this time some sort of idea entered your head. That's a definite advance. The excellent doctor on the other hand seems to have lost the power of speech altogether. You'd better examine yourself, at once, Doctor."

And with that Lumpface moved away from the window, grinning prodigiously. His two attendants were left standing about below in embarrassment. The driver, who had heard everything, had a broad grin on his face.

Dr. Sämig mustered what was left of his self-respect and formally took his leave.

"Thank you very much indeed, Captain," he said.

"Not at all, Doctor," said Captain Derna, with an attempt at the inimitable bow of an Austrian cavalry officer of the old school. Unfortunately it didn't quite come off this time. He turned to his driver and said: "No 3 Troop."

The driver didn't bother to acknowledge the order. He didn't even nod his head. It seemed quite unnecessary. He merely continued to grin, and hardly waited for Captain Derna to get in before roaring away. He came to an abrupt halt in front of No. 3 block.

"Thank you, my dear fellow," said the captain, who in the meantime had recovered something of his self-respect. He cast a glance up at the bright blue sky, another at the bright green turf of the lawn and another at the freshly swept roadway. Everything seemed to be under control.

Still moving with a spring in his step, he went up the stairs, past the swing doors and along the empty corridor towards his office. Lieutenant Wedelmann was standing just outside it. He saluted smartly.

"Good morning to you, my dear Lieutenant Wedelmann," cried Derna in a particularly friendly tone. "I'm delighted to see you."

"Good morning, Captain," said Wedelmann stiffly. "May I speak to you, Captain, please?"

"But of course, my dear fellow. Come into my private office." And he added with just a trace of anxiety: "Nothing unpleasant, I hope?"

"Unfortunately, yes, Captain," said Wedelmann. "I regret to have to say so."

Derna, who was just beginning to recover from the painful effects of Lumpface's teasing, began to feel uncomfortable again. He looked disappointedly at the bright sunlight which was streaming in through the window in the corridor. "Come in," he said.

They went into the office. The sergeant major was waiting for them there. A number of other people were also standing about and they all came to attention at once. With a click of his heels Schulz yelled out: "Troop Commander!" He gabbled through the routine reports for the morning and, when he had finished, added: "Gunner Asch under arrest!"

"Aha, aha," said Derna, for something to say. He pulled a snow-white handkerchief out of his pocket but didn't use it. He looked round the room: the Chief was standing in front of him like some sort of Nemesis, the office corporal was hanging about attentively in the background, Corporal Lindenberg was standing there like a tombstone as usual, and in the far corner stood Gunner Asch.

"Aha, aha," repeated Captain Derna.

"That's what I wanted to see you about," announced Lieutenant Wedelmann.

The captain nervously crumpled up his handkerchief. He was more than worried, he was positively terrified, but he didn't want to let anyone see this. He refrained from making any comment for the time being, partly because experience had taught him that this was always the best policy, but chiefly because he couldn't think of any comment to make.

"Come with me," said Derna. He led the way into his private office. Wedelmann and Schulz followed him in. No one said a word.

The captain threw his gloves down on the desk. He took off his cap and gave it to the sergeant major, then unbuckled his belt and gave that to the sergeant major too. The sergeant major hung up everything on the hooks at the back of the other door in the room, a padded one which led out into the corridor.

Derna sat down and took out a cigarette, for which Schulz offered him a light. Lieutenant Wedelmann had taken up his position over by the window. There was an oppressive silence in the room.

Captain Derna saw that he would have to say something and that he simply couldn't avoid asking questions any longer. "Did

I hear you correctly?" he asked the sergeant major. "You said that Gunner Asch was under arrest?"

Before Schulz could answer, Lieutenant Wedelmann intervened.

"It's ludicrous to speak of an arrest in this case," he said. "Before an arrest can be made there have to be specific grounds for it, or else a categorical order. In this case there is neither. In my view the sergeant major has exceeded his authority. It might even be a case of unwarrantable detention."

The sergeant major opened his mouth to reply but Derna raised his hand. He hurriedly wiped his charming Viennese face with his handkerchief. It was shining with sweat.

"My dear Lieutenant Wedelman," he began very affably, "I have the utmost regard for your expert knowledge on such matters. But before I make use of it, permit me to approach this matter methodically. Now, Sergeant Major, will you kindly tell me what led you to make this arrest?"

"Of course, it isn't an arrest in the strict sense of the word, sir, I mean not an affair of handcuffs and cells and all that. In fact Gunner Asch is standing outside now, without an escort even; not a hair of his head has been touched."

"Here I'd just like to put in," said Wedelmann, "that from a purely legal point of view it's quite enough for the word 'arrest' to have been pronounced. From that moment onward the arrested man is subject to a quite different, far stricter disciplinary code. For example, should he attempt to escape it is permissible to open fire on him without warning. Locking a man up or putting him in handcuffs has got nothing to do with it."

Schulz desperately tried to fight back.

"I never said: 'You're under arrest.' I merely said: 'I'll have you arrested.' "

"You had no right to do that even!" said Wedelmann. "Besides, Gunner Asch says that what you said to him was: 'You're under arrest.' "

"Sir!" asked Schulz, turning to the captain and trembling with rage. "Whose word is going to be believed here: a sergeant major's or a mere gunner's?"

"The fact that you hold a higher rank," argued Wedelmann, "doesn't necessarily mean that you have the more truthful character."

"Gentlemen, gentlemen!" cried Derna. Once again he wiped his forehead, his cheeks and his neck with his handkerchief. He was sweating profusely. "Let's keep the theoretical part of the discussion until later. I hope you understand me. What I want to know is: What actually happened? Now then, please, Sergeant Major, on what grounds were you led to suppose that there might eventually be a case for Gunner Asch's arrest?"

"Sir!" said the sergeant major, only just managing to contain himself. "In the first place the N.C.O. in charge of the cookhouse yesterday put in a report about the undisciplined behavior of Gunner Asch. I regarded this report as of no consequence and rejected it."

"Which," said Wedelmann, "is clear enough proof in itself that even you don't believe in the charges you bring against him."

"Please, Lieutenant Wedelmann," said Derna beseechingly.

Sergeant Major Schulz managed to ignore Wedelmann's remarks altogether.

"I shall be presenting the report of the corporal in charge of the cookhouse in due course," he said. "There is also a report from Corporal Lindenberg. And here it is."

Derna seized the report, which the sergeant major had placed before him on the table. Reluctantly he read it through. "Aha!" he said.

"On this point," said Wedelmann, "it should be noted that the alleged witness for the prosecution, Lance Corporal Kowalski, says that he didn't hear a word of what Corporal Lindenberg's report says he heard."

268

"Lance Corporal Kowalski is a crook," said the sergeant major, "but Corporal Lindenberg is the best N.C.O. in the troop, if not in the whole regiment. I'd stake my life on him. He is absolutely reliable."

"He's a plodding sort of fellow," said Wedelmann. "He can't see further than from one paragraph of the regulations to the next. He panics at the slightest provocation. He's always tripping himself up over some obstacle or other."

"I daresay that's what the lieutenant thinks," said the sergeant major angrily. "It's always interesting for N.C.O.s to know what their officers think of them."

"Really, I must insist!" said Derna sharply, leaving open — very skillfully as he thought — the question of whom he was having to insist to.

"Excuse me, sir," put in the sergeant major at once. "The important thing is that Gunner Asch himself does not deny using the expressions 'overseer' and 'slavedriver' to the corporal."

"Excuse me, sir," said Lieutenant Wedelmann, "but Gunner Asch can in no way be held liable for what he did or did not say on this occasion. He was provoked, and in my submission provoked beyond endurance. He's a very quick-tempered man, and a certain sort of N.C.O. acts on him like a red rag to a bull. If you leave him alone, this business will clear itself up of its own accord. Simply ignore the whole thing. I might even go so far as to say that Asch is not really responsible for his actions in this case at all."

"Aha!" said Captain Derna, beginning to feel rather bewildered.

"Shall I bring him in, sir?" asked the sergeant major. "Then you can judge for yourself whether he's off his head or not."

"I strongly advise against it," said Wedelmann, remarkably seriously.

"I don't," said the sergeant major.

269

Derna was playing nervously with the ends of his fingers. He stubbed out a cigarette, pulled out another and lit it.

"What I don't understand," he said, "is why Gunner Asch was arrested at all on the strength of this report."

"Ah, there's more to it than that, sir. This fellow took a pot shot at me yesterday evening."

Wedelmann became very indignant.

"Really, Sergeant Major, you're talking absolute nonsense!"

Derna let the cigarette which he had just lit fall from his fingers in horror. It lay on the top of the dsk, where it began to burn its way into the varnish. The smell was appalling. But no one took any notice.

"What did you say?" asked the captain. "He took a pot shot at you? And this is the first I've heard about it? How is that possible? Where did he get the ammunition from?"

"I really don't think you can have slept very well," said Wedelmann contemptuously to Schulz.

"Better than the lieutenant, I think," replied Schulz impertinently. "No girl left *my* quarters at eight o'clock this morning."

"Really, you must have gone mad!" said Wedelmann.

"I know what I'm saying all right," cried Schulz, beginning to lose his self-control. "I haven't forgotten what happened on Wednesday night, Lieutenant."

"Silence!" Derna tried to roar it out at the top of his voice. But he overdid the effort and it ended in a high squeak. It was the first time this had ever happened to him. He was bewildered at first and then amazed at himself. He looked into the astonished faces opposite.

"Gentlemen," said Captain Derna, "I really must insist on a little moderation. I have every understanding for the state of excitement you are both in, but you must allow me to form my own judgment on this matter. So far I know absolutely nothing about it. Let me attack the thing methodically. Now what about fetching Gunner Asch in?"

Derna waited to be contradicted but no one said anything. Wedelmann had turned away in a fury and was staring out of the window. Schulz could only approve of the proposal. He went to the door, opened it and called out: "Gunner Asch to the troop commander!"

Gunner Asch entered his troop commander's office, and looked about him. Wedelmann wouldn't catch his eye. There was nothing wrong with that. Schulz looked at him as if he wanted to eat him alive. There was nothing wrong with that either. He took a look at Captain Derna.

"Gunner Asch," said the captain, "I've got a report from Corporal Lindenberg here. Do you know what it's about?"

"It's entirely correct," said Asch. "I'm ready to give further details if you require them."

"Only answer the question put," said the Chief sharply.

"And who's asking the questions, as a matter of interest," asked Asch, "you or the captain?"

"I ask the questions here," said Derna, not without a certain pride. "And what I'm asking you now is this: Do you admit firing a shot at the sergeant major?"

"The man who thought that one up ought to be shot himself."

"You're trying to deny it?" asked Schulz menacingly. "You have the impertinence to call me a liar in front of the troop commander?"

"Impertinence doesn't come into it."

"How did you know that someone had taken a shot at me, then?" Schulz now seemed to be taking the whole interrogation on himself. Derna made no protest. Wedelmann suspected that Schulz might be heading for trouble. He was delighted at the prospect.

271

"Well, how did you know that?"

"The whole troop knew it. Everyone's been talking about it."

"And how did you know that the shot was fired at me personally?"

"You were the only person in the line of fire. Besides, it seems to me quite a natural thing to do. Most of the other members of the troop seem to think so too. And not a few of them say they hope the marksman will take better aim next time."

"So you want to see me murdered?"

"Oh, no," said Asch. "That wouldn't be murder, it would be more like self-defense. And quite apart from that, we don't actually want to see you hit, we just want to see you scared out of your wits. And surely it must scare you to realize that you're hated so much that someone is actually prepared to try and do you in, and that a lot of people see nothing wrong in that, while some even are delighted."

"You hear him, sir!" cried Schulz to the captain. He was beside himself with rage. "They're a gang of murderers."

"We were trained by you," said Asch. "Just give that a moment's thought. There's a lesson to be learned from that. It would be worth your while to study it."

"Enough of this!" cried Captain Derna. "We've had more than enough already."

His hands were trembling. Sweat was pouring down his face and he made no attempt to wipe it off. The room swam before his eyes and he felt absolutely exhausted.

"Leave the room, Gunner Asch," said Wedelmann.

Asch looked at the lieutenant thoughtfully for a moment, and then left the room with apparent indifference. Once outside, he leaned against the wall. He was feeling terrible. But he smiled to himself.

"This is an impossible situation," said Derna weakly. "An absolutely impossible, intolerable situation."

272

"I recommend that we take a summary of evidence," said the sergeant major.

"Ridiculous," said Lieutenant Wedelmann. "There's not sufficient evidence to take."

"What he said about the shooting alone," maintained Schulz, "would be enough to court-martial him!"

"No it wouldn't," said Wedelmann. "I listened very carefully. He didn't make a single positive statement, let alone any sort of confession. Nothing but hypotheses, hearsay, wishes."

"It's an impossible situation," repeated Derna. He was in a desperate state, and no longer made any attempt to hide the fact.

"I think it would be worth the captain's while to consider who it was that thought this situation up."

"Who else but Asch?" cried Schulz accusingly.

"I don't agree with you," said Wedelmann sharply. "It isn't Asch's fault."

"Mine perhaps, then?"

"You'll hardly believe it, Sergeant Major, but for once you're right. Yes!"

Captain Derna shook his head and said: "A damned embarrassing situation. And we've put this fellow Asch up for promotion to corporal too."

This was a piece of news of the highest importance for Wedelmann.

"Well now," he said, "this is really splendid. And whose idea was that?"

"Mine," said the sergeant major simply.

Wedelmann burst into helpless laughter. His chest heaved and the sound of his laughter filled the little room. He laughed till he cried. Then he held his sides, groaning with pleasure. "Well really," he gasped, "that's the best joke I've ever heard in my life."

Derna and Schulz said nothing. Their faces were deadly

serious as they watched the lieutenant rocking with laughter. It was as if they were watching some fantastic monster, or a clown who had made his way onto the scene of a tragedy by mistake.

"Yes, we made a bad blunder there," said the sergeant major. "It's very embarrassing. But we can't worry about that now."

Wedelmann wiped the tears from his eyes.

"And what's going to happen if the battery commander has already signed and confirmed the promotion? What if it appears in battery orders this very day?"

"Then it'll have to be revoked."

"You don't seem to know the battery commander very well. Such a thing is just not possible with Major Luschke."

"But we're dealing here with a man who isn't right in the head," put in Schulz stubbornly. "You said so yourself, Lieutenant. You said he wasn't responsible for his actions."

"That's the answer," said Captain Derna, like someone waking out of a long sleep. "That's the solution to all our problems," he continued with growing enthusiasm.

"What do you mean by that exactly?" asked Wedelmann warily.

"The scene we've all just been taking part in is quite abnormal," said Derna cheerfully. "You'll admit that. It's right outside the whole framework of the disciplinary code. If such a thing were allowed to see the light of day there'd be a really gigantic scandal. If on the other hand we could show that Asch had been temporarily deranged in his mind . . ."

"But, sir," said Wedelmann in a warning tone.

". . . had been suffering from a purely temporary, isolated attack of mental derangement, a sort of nervous breakdown really — if we could somehow prove that, then we'd be all right."

"How do you mean, sir?"

"But it's perfectly simple." Derna was glowing with excite-

274

ment. He could see land at last. And he was delighted with his discovery.

"Now look here, gentlemen," he said with a sudden burst of cheerfulness, "I think I can claim to be on pretty good terms with the M.O., Dr. Sämig. I'll simply ask him to take a look at Asch, to give him a thorough examination and put him under medical care. I won't hear a word against it, gentlemen. This *is* the answer. And our own investigation will be adjourned until we've heard the result of Dr. Sämig's examination. Now, what do you say to that?"

The lieutenant and the sergeant major had nothing to say.

᙭ ᙭ ᙭

"My dear Captain," said Dr. Sämig over the telephone, "I can't possibly give you my diagnosis until I've *seen* the patient. But apart from that I'm particularly interested in the case you describe, from a purely professional point of view. I know I'm a surgeon, but the psychological aspect of illness has been gravely neglected so far and I attach particular importance to it."

The doctor smiled. It was a pleasant smile but a slightly superior one at the same time. He listened patiently to such details as the captain saw fit to disclose. He understood well enough what this was all about. He had seen a lot of cases of this sort. He was well equipped to deal with them.

"It's very important," said Dr. Sämig, "that the patient shouldn't be alarmed in any way. I recommend that he should be treated perfectly normally even though it may prove a little awkward to do so. There should be no hint of the nature of the illness, not even in the most roundabout popular terms. The patient must be led to think that this is a purely routine examination, for V.D. perhaps, or to see that he's fit to undergo close arrest."

275

The doctor smiled knowledgeably down the telephone. He made it clear that he considered it an honor to be able to put his professional services at Captain Derna's disposal. He didn't attempt to conceal the fact that it was a pleasure for him to bring the latest developments of medical science to bear on a case of this sort, and even though he could not necessarily effect a cure, to produce a complete and reliable diagnosis.

"So perhaps you'll send the patient — Asch is his name? — over to me at once?"

Sämig put down the receiver with almost tender reverence. He felt very pleased with himself. He had every reason to be too, he thought. At last he had a chance to break the monotony of his dreary routine and show what he was really capable of. The general himself might even get to hear of his work and become interested in it and post him somewhere where his talents would be put to better purpose.

Dr. Sämig was the station medical officer allotted to the battery. And he had hardly ever been anything but a station medical officer. He had had his first experience of surgery as a very young man during the last months of the Great War: he hacked through limbs with and without anesthetic (they were the days when bandages were made of paper and drugs were priceless) with varying success. When the war ended he completed his medical studies, but always had the bad luck to be appointed assistant to men who were unable to appreciate his talents. Then he volunteered for the Reichswehr and was accepted. He became a station medical officer. He had been one ever since.

Sämig put a call through to the sergeant in charge of sick quarters.

"Is the isolation ward vacant?"

"Yes," said the sergeant, "the ward is vacant."

"It will be occupied shortly, Sergeant," announced the M.O. "Please have everything ready. The usual examination: height,

276

weight, temperature, pulse, urine. The patient's name is Asch, a gunner in No. 3 Troop."

"Very good," said the sergeant, and retired to pass on the orders to his medical orderly.

Sämig got up and went over to his bookcase. He looked rather sadly at the surgical textbooks which stood in the extreme left-hand corner. He knew them all inside out. But he had no further use for them, for, in spite of numerous applications, he had never been appointed to a military hospital. He was and had always been an ordinary station M.O.

This rankled with him and he made no attempt to hide the fact. He was still very conscious of his capabilities. And the daily sick parades drove him mad — a little first aid here, some pills there, staring at endless pairs of buttocks, supervising treatment for V.D. in the wards — all unutterably boring!

Then, spurred on by conversations he had listened to in the mess, he had tried running his sick quarters in as disciplined and militaristic way as possible: urine bottles had to be kept neatly in ranks, patients in bed had to have their hair properly cut, daily routine orders were hung up in wards, corridors and lavatories. Finally he even instituted a special one-man isolation ward, with bars on the windows and a double lock on the door. All this was very fine and splendid and looked well enough in the reports which he sent in to higher authority, but was in fact all utterly pointless and merely kept the sergeant in charge of sick quarters busy.

Sämig, standing in front of his bookcase and turning all this over in his mind with a patient smile, reached up and took down two large volumes which he carried over to his desk. There he sat looking at them for a time with something almost amounting to tenderness in his expression. On the cover of the first book stood the words: *Applied Psychoanalysis*. And on the second: *An Outline of Human Psychology*.

Ah! That was the stuff. They wouldn't let him be a surgeon;

277

but he had no wish to spend the rest of his life inspecting cases of male venereal disease. So now he had taken up psychoanalysis. It was a relatively new science, largely neglected in Germany — it was supposed to have been discovered or rather developed by a Jew — what was the fellow's name? Freud! But there couldn't be any truth in that of course.

Sämig opened his books. He wasn't so interested in theories about the id and the superego. He belonged more to what he called the complex school, with certain racial modifications. He had even, in an attempt to prove his theories, gone so far as to develop a Sämig Complex Test which he carefully tried out on all his patients in sick quarters. And these tests had been remarkably successful, inasmuch as nearly all the subjects submitted to them had stated that in obeying orders they were motivated more by wariness than instinct.

But experiments such as these had been mere preliminary spadework. What he had always lacked up till now had been some case which could be solved exclusively through the medium of psychoanalysis. Now at last with this fellow Asch he seemed to have got one. He looked forward to his interview with the man eagerly and with a certain feeling of excitement.

Sämig had got himself quite worked up about it all. He rose to his feet, walked out of his office and crossed the corridor to the isolation ward. The patient was already there, sitting on the bed with a corporal who was taking his pulse.

"So you're Gunner Asch," said the M.O., looking at his patient with obvious interest.

"Why am I here?" asked Asch. "There's nothing wrong with me."

Dr. Sämig gave him a charming smile. Aha! he said to himself, aggressive tendencies; so far impossible to tell if overdeveloped or not. To Asch he said:

"Well, you know, no one is a hundred per cent healthy. It never does any harm to have a checkup."

"Why don't you give the N.C.O.s a checkup?" asked Asch. "They could do with it."

Aha! said Dr. Sämig to himself, strong hate feelings, little attempt at concealment. To Asch he said amiably:

"All in good time. It's your turn first."

And he turned to the corporal.

"Taken his pulse? Normal? Good. Enter that. And then leave us alone together, will you"

The corporal entered Asch's pulse on the chart and handed it over to the M.O. Then he left the room.

Dr. Sämig studied the entries on the chart. He did this very thoroughly. For anyone else such things might be just routine facts. But to him they represented invaluable data. He was able to draw conclusions as to the patient's mental state from his physical condition. Dwarfs often suffered from inferiority complexes, giants from megalomania, thin people were tough, fat people lazy. Admittedly this was all very obvious stuff, but it was unmistakably something to be going on.

"Just lie down a moment, will you?" said the M.O. encouragingly. "Make yourself quite comfortable. Relax. Empty your mind."

"My dear Doctor," said Gunner Asch, "if you really want me to go to sleep, of course I don't mind at all. But I'm not sure I particularly want you to be looking on."

Sämig smiled resolutely. He was really extremely excited about such a case falling into his hands at last. He was a different man already.

"First of all we'll just have a little talk," he said. "We can sleep afterwards."

"We?" asked Asch mistrustfully. "Are you going to sleep with me?"

Dr. Sämig's smile froze on his face for a moment. It cost him quite an effort to keep it there at all. His mind worked quickly: extraordinary resilient patient; imagination dominated by obscene fantasies; impossible to say whether this is a permanent condition or not; no evidence as yet of compensatory guilt feelings. The diagnosis made him feel much better. It seemed an even more interesting case than he had supposed at first sight.

"You're a witty fellow, Asch," he said, thinking that he was leading the man on rather cunningly. "I must say you surprise me."

"And I must say you surprise me, Doctor," said Asch; and as with everything he said, it was impossible to tell for certain what he was really thinking. But his tone sounded bitterly ironic. "You have the reputation of being the sort of doctor who insists on passing people fit, however ill they are. You're supposed to be a match for any shammer. Your nickname, I believe, is Old Sawbones."

"Really," said Sämig, without enthusiasm.

"Some people call you Sawbrains. I can't think why. You seem harmless enough to me so far."

Dr. Sämig said nothing. He was rather taken aback. His patient was talking to him in a manner which was almost insulting. This was a provocative attack which in normal circumstances he would have had no hesitation in answering by throwing the man out. But he remembered in time that it was in just this sort of remark that he must try to find the cause of the man's illness.

"My dear friend," he asked, "have you a headache by any chance?"

"No," said Asch, "have you?"

The M.O. just managed to overlook this. He was determined not to let himself be held up by pointless skirmishing, but to try to get straight to the heart of the matter. Once more he recapitulated the symptoms which he had been able to establish so far: strong aggressive tendencies towards higher ranks expressed in the form of completely undisciplined behavior; need

280

to tear down all barriers — destruction mania here? Insane desire for superficial success? Some so far undetermined complex somewhere, root of the trouble psychological, obsessionally unbalanced.

"You probably had an unhappy childhood," said the M.O. helpfully. "I expect you didn't have much to eat, the home you lived in was very bleak and overcrowded. You can still feel the cold of the stone floor beneath your feet and the gnawing hunger pains in your stomach. You can still see in your mind's eye the next-door child eating a fresh slice of bread, butter and honey, and giving none to you. You lay awake through the long winter nights while the wind howled round the house and you curled yourself up into a ball because the blanket wasn't big enough to cover you. Your mother cried a great deal and your father beat you."

"But nothing of the sort!" cried Asch. "I had everything I wanted as a child. We weren't rich but we were perfectly comfortable. I overate at Christmas once but those are the only pains in my stomach I ever remember having. I never saw my mother cry, and my father never beat me. What utter nonsense you talk!"

"Now keep calm, keep calm, just a minute," said Dr. Sämig. He himself was not all calm. "I didn't just fire my questions off at random, you know. What sometimes seems like a quite harmless illness as a child often provides the foundation for some serious unexpected illness in an otherwise perfectly healthy adult."

"As a child," said Asch, "I never had any illness of any importance. I twisted my ankle once, when I was eleven, getting out of the bath, but that was all."

"It's not that sort of illness I'm interested in," said Sämig. "Something purely external like the twisting of an ankle is of no significance. Now just stay lying down. Tell me about other things. Did you perhaps have a friend who disappointed you

281

very much, who betrayed you in some way, and caused you a good deal of suffering? No? Have you ever found yourself in a situation where you were absolutely terrified of something? Were you ever alone in a dark room, or out at night in a wood, or in danger on the sea? Did you ever see anything which horrified you very much, men fighting together for instance, or someone run over by a car and squashed to pulp, or two people whom you suddenly came upon — well, you know what I mean? Nothing like that? Have you ever felt an urge to hurl yourself at someone's throat, to torment them, murder them?"

"Yes," said Gunner Asch.

"Aha! Now tell me about that. You can be quite honest with me. I'm a doctor, you know. When have you felt the urge to attack someone like this?"

"Now," said Asch.

Dr. Sämig sat up and moved his chair a little farther away. His pale blue eyes had opened wide. He clenched his fists but it was only a token gesture.

"Don't talk nonsense, now," he said gently.

"And what about the nonsense I've got to sit here and listen to?" said Asch.

"I'm examining you."

"You have already examined me," said Asch. "My temperature is normal, my heartbeats are regular. I have neither V.D. nor flat feet. My urine is free of infection. I have no varicose veins. And my brain is functioning perfectly well. I have no complexes to speak of, and I am not in any way neurotic. In fact I'm perfectly normal. Kindly order my discharge at once."

Dr. Sämig rose awkwardly to his feet.

"I am the one who decides what is best for my patients," he said. "I am the one who decides whether they are ill or not."

"And why, pray," asked Asch, "am I lying here in this cell?"

"This is not a cell, it's an isolation ward. This is where cases

282

for special treatment are brought, or those suffering from infectious diseases."

"Are you trying to maintain, my dear Doctor, that I am suffering from an infectious disease?"

"Suspicion alone is sufficient justification."

"My dear Doctor," said Asch, now very serious, "I hereby inform you that I intend to lodge a complaint about your treatment. I request you to provide me with paper, pen and ink for that purpose. I intend to lodge a complaint against unwarrantable detention. Furthermore, I must request you to write down your first or preliminary diagnosis immediately, with full reasons for detaining me here in the isolation ward. And furthermore, I demand to be examined by another doctor immediately."

Dr. Sämig shrank back in horror.

"Now just a minute," he said carefully, "just a minute. You seem to have a bit of a fever. Let me give you some good advice: get yourself some sleep. Then I'll come back again. And we'll see about everything."

※ ※ ※

Gunner Asch lay on his bed in the isolation ward, staring at the ceiling. He couldn't sleep. His food stood untouched beside him on a stool. Beyond the wide-meshed bars over the window the afternoon sun shone down in silence.

The room in which Asch lay was primitively furnished. Its basic color was a dirty white, patterned with finger marks. Bed, stool, table, chair, walls — all had once been white and all were now dirty and covered with finger marks.

"Well — how's it going?" inquired a friendly voice through the window. It was Lance Corporal Kowalski, who had stuck his head in through the bars.

Asch sat up.

"Difficult to say at the moment. Have you come to commiserate with me or to cheer me up?"

"I've come to bring you something to eat," announced Kowalski.

Asch shook his head. "I'm on hunger strike," he said.

"I know! That's just why I've brought it. Officially you're on hunger strike; that's one more thing that's worrying people. It's a scandal, it'll weaken them a good deal more than it does you. Unofficially I'm keeping you going. What'll you have, blood sausage, ham or salami?"

"I don't mind," said Asch.

"Hey!" said Kowalski in astonishment. "I don't much like the sound of that."

"I'm fed up with this whole business," said Asch. "It's exactly the same here as everywhere else. The whole system's rotten to the core. It's absolutely hopeless."

"But you're not giving up?"

"It just makes me sick."

"It doesn't me," said Kowalski. "Do you know what I'm doing?" He grinned meaningly. "I'm cleaning my rifle in the armory. We've got five rounds left after all."

"Put them down the lavatory," recommended Asch. "They wouldn't get us anywhere. These people are too securely dug in. They simply ignore anything that doesn't fit into their ludicrous way of looking at things. But if things don't change soon, and change very radically too, we'll do a good deal more than merely lose confidence in them, we'll grow to hate them; and you can't build an army on hate."

"You get on with your nap," said Kowalski. "I've got a bit of work to do in the meantime." He disappeared from view. And in the place where his head had been there was nothing but the glaring afternoon sun.

Gunner Asch fell back on the bed again. He was fed up with the way things were going. He had looked for an entirely different reaction on the part of the authorities. He had hoped that his revolt would blow the whole place sky-high, but he had merely got himself more hopelessly bogged down than ever. He had expected to hear lions roaring, but all he had done was to set a flock of sheep on the move. No one would allow himself to be provoked, no one would get exasperated and lose control of himself. Werktreu was too apathetic, Platzek too lacking in character, Lindenberg too correct, Schulz too cunning, Derna too soft, and Wedelmann too decent to do anything about it. All of them had bad consciences. None knew how far he could afford to let things go.

A key turned in the lock; a bolt was drawn back and Lieutenant Wedelmann came into the room.

"It's all right, Gunner Asch, I don't expect you to salute me, and if you think you can annoy me by just lying around in a bored way like that you're mistaken. You're a patient here, and I shall adapt my attitude accordingly."

"Are you paying the patient a visit, then, Lieutenant?"

"I've taken up your case," said Wedelmann. "I've appointed myself a sort of prisoner's friend. Besides, the troop commander has given me orders to interrogate you. As you know interrogations have to be conducted by an officer. But there's plenty of time for that; we don't need to hurry; we can postpone it for the time being. And so long as you're in here, you're out of harm's way; in fact I strongly suspect that there's not even any danger of another shot being fired. Now first of all let's straighten out everything that possibly can be straightened out."

"My dear Lieutenant," said Asch, "why are you putting your nose into this? Why are you trying to act as a brake on my initiative? If it hadn't been for you I would probably have achieved my object by now. Tell me, how did you manage to realize what was going on so astonishingly soon?"

"Fortunately for you," said Wedelmann, "someone put me wise. Fräulein Freitag told me all about it."

285

Herbert Asch didn't answer. He looked up at the lieutenant for a moment and then lowered his head, and started at the grayish-white blanket which covered him.

"So that's it," he said in an exhausted voice. "How could I have known that?"

"Fräulein Freitag acted very sensibly," said Wedelmann warmly, "and above all in time. You'll soon realize that. It was thanks to her that we were able to avoid disaster. I simply can't think what would have happened if I hadn't intervened in time."

"You flatter yourself," snapped Asch.

"I know very well what you meant to do," said Wedelmann. "Of course I could never bring myself to approve of such a thing, but I can understand it. You've just been seeing how far you could go with people. But from a strictly legal point of view, you've hardly laid yourself open to disciplinary action at all. At any rate it would be extremely difficult to prove anything against you. At least that was how you planned it all. But it didn't quite come off. Things haven't turned out quite as you meant them to."

"The reports are piling up against me anyway. Nothing will pacify Lindenberg; Schulz is howling for blood. The captain can't do anything to stop them. He'll just have to grin and bear it. And whatever action they decide to take against me — and they'll have to do something — either award summary punishment or start court-martial proceedings, they're bound to put a foot wrong somewhere. They're bound to overstep the mark in some way. And that'll be my chance."

"But I shall see to it that it doesn't come to that," Wedelmann reassured him. "You see, your tricks simply don't work with me. I know quite well, my friend, that strictly speaking you have neither refused an order nor been guilty of incitement to mutiny. You haven't even struck a superior officer."

"Not yet," said Gunner Asch.

286

"Nor will you, for you're not an idiot. You'd never do any-think so stupid. You know it'd be playing straight into your opponents' hands. This demonstration you're trying to make would degenerate simply into a squalid brawl; and you're after something better than that."

"Leave me alone," said Asch, "I'm under observation. I'm not supposed to get excited."

"Listen to me, my dear Asch," said Lieutenant Wedelmann, drawing the stool on which he was sitting up to the bed. "I don't know whether you've noticed but I'm rather fond of you. I find you extraordinarily sympathetic. But even if that wasn't so I'd be able to understand your point of view. You're absolutely right — there's a great deal wrong, and this isn't the first time I've noticed it. A soldier isn't just a machine; and a barracks ought to be something more than a mere factory producing heroes for the defense of the Fatherland. The present situation is not only wrong but dangerous. But the point is that these bullying and shouting methods of theirs which date back to before the time of Frederick the Great happen to be the most practical and convenient. Anyone who has ever tried to prepare an army for war knows that. These methods of theirs grind slowly but they grind exceedingly small. In fact they crush the individuality and character out of a man altogether."

"You don't need to tell me that!" cried Asch. "I know that all right. And it's just because I know it that I've started what you're now trying to stop me from going through with."

"You haven't a hope against this slow-grinding machinery of theirs."

"Maybe not, but I'll be able to throw a little sand in the works. And perhaps then someone or other will ask why the machine isn't running as smoothly as it was."

"My dear Asch," said Wedelmann, "whatever you do you won't get very far. I'm all in favor of doing away with the old system myself, but you've got to have something else to put in

287

its place. Something fundamentally different — you've got to bring about a complete reformation."

"Bravo!" cried Asch ironically. "Then don't let me stop you. Go right ahead. And hurry up about it!"

"Do be reasonable," said the lieutenant with a certain impatience. "Call the whole thing off. And I'll try and see to it that you come to as little harm as possible."

"I'm staying here," said Asch.

Wedelmann seemed to be getting really anxious.

"If you won't listen to me," he said, "then perhaps you'll listen to Fräulein Freitag!"

"None of this has anything to do with Fräulein Freitag. Tell her that, please, next time she tries to get you to convert people from their way of thinking."

Wedelmann wasn't annoyed; he was just worried. He had expected his mission to be a good deal easier. This fellow Asch was terribly stubborn. He simply wouldn't see that no system is perfect and that the only intelligent reasonable attitude to adopt to the present one was to accept it with all its imperfections.

"Your father's very worried too."

"How do you know?"

"I spoke to him on the telephone."

"There seems to be no limit to your concern for my welfare. And what did he say?"

"He wanted me to tell you that he was hoping you wouldn't let him down."

"Good old Father," said Asch quietly.

"Unfortunately he couldn't come to try to persuade you himself, but your sister is here."

Asch looked up in surprise. Then he said quietly: "Send her away again."

Wedelmann made one last effort to bring his mission to a

successful conclusion. "Why not just have a word with her?" he said. "You wouldn't refuse to see her?"

"This is no place for her."

"She's waiting outside in the corridor." Wedelmann got up. "I'll ask her to come in." He went over to the door. "Fräulein Asch? Your brother would be delighted to see you."

Ingrid Asch came into the isolation ward. She looked curiously at her brother and was a little shocked because he neither smiled nor made any gesture of welcome towards her. She hadn't expected that.

"I'll leave you two together," said Wedelmann obligingly. "Strictly speaking, it's my duty to be in attendance during this conversation. What's more I will be too. But I'll have to go and fetch pen and paper first, and I think that'll probably take me about half an hour."

"Herbert," said Ingrid Asch after the lieutenant had gone, "you shouldn't have done this!"

"Kindly mind your own business," said Asch crossly. "I don't meddle in your affairs, although God knows I've got good enough reason to."

"I don't know what you mean," said Ingrid.

"That doesn't surprise me."

"You must think of us a little, Herbert. When Father heard from Lieutenant Wedelmann what was happening, he picked up a bottle of brandy and went and locked himself up in his room with it."

"Here's to him," said Herbert Asch. "And so your conscience wouldn't let you rest until you had set eyes on your poor misguided brother?"

"Please don't talk like that. If it were just a question of yourself you could do what you liked. But you mustn't forget that you are in a town where everybody knows you. Your father's business is here; my home is here. Everything you do comes back on us in the end. We'll have to put up with all the gossip. People will point at us and keep away from us."

"I become more and more aware of your sisterly love for me every minute."

"And when have you ever behaved like a brother towards me? I only need to think of Johannes Vierbein. Do you realize you very nearly had him on your conscience as well?"

"Oh, no!" said Asch coldly. "You don't mean to say he told you that?"

"I've got my eyes in my head," said his sister in a great state of agitation. "And I know you. You'd stop at nothing. Nothing is sacred to you. You completely upset Vierbein. He hardly knew what he was doing. You worked him up to try and do the same sort of thing as you're doing. Thank God he had the sense to stop in time. He knows where his duty lies."

"And I," said Asch vigorously, "I see at last what a stupid little parrot you are. I've always known that you were a bore, Ingrid, but I never realized before just what a ridiculous parrot you were. You've got heroes on the brain, dear child. Your little pinhead thinks that wherever people talk of honor there honor must necessarily be. You can't see the difference between a leader and a cheerleader. In your idiotic eyes anyone who's in power must automatically be one of the elect. Anyone in uniform is automatically a hero. Anyone in jail is automatically a swine. Anyone who sits in a Mercedes is automatically a man of character. Go away and bury your head in it all!"

"I'm really ashamed of you," said Ingrid anxiously.

"What a word to use!" cried Asch. "You're ashamed of me and you can be ashamed of Vierbein too. You've got every reason to be ashamed of us. For what we are? The man who is your brother and the man who perhaps will one day be your husband — these two, together with some hundreds of thousands of others, are prepared to throw themselves down in the mud, crawl about on their bellies and stick their heads down ·

290

the lavatory at any given moment. We let ourselves be bullied and insulted; we stand motionless while people call us swine, bastards, and far worse names than that. We roar out 'Very good, Corporal' or 'Very good, Sergeant' when people try to get us to break our backs. We maintain our dignity by crawling about on all fours, and display our character by licking other people's boots. That's your brother for you, and the man whom you love. Yes indeed, you should feel ashamed of us!"

"Herbert," said Ingrid desperately.

"Go away now," he said. "Get out of here. Go off to that little garden gnome of yours, Vierbein, and throw yourself on his manly breast! There you can cry your eyes out over this monster you've been left alone with."

Gunner Asch stood up, took hold of his sister by the shoulders, opened the door and pushed her out into the corridor. Dr. Sämig was standing outside.

"You've come just in time," said Asch. He went back to his bed and threw himself down on it.

"One more proof," said Sämig, shutting the door smugly behind him. "The way you treat your sister is just one more proof."

"Proof of what? What are you trying to prove?"

Dr. Sämig was now strengthened in his belief in the correctness of his diagnosis. Long talks with his excellent brother officer Captain Derna, with the sterling Sergeant Major Schulz, with the exemplary Corporal Lindenberg, had all convinced him that Asch's case was too tricky to be solved by psychoanalysis alone.

"Have you put your diagnosis down in writing?" asked Asch. "Have you got hold of another doctor? Have my complaints been forwarded?"

Dr. Sämig looked at him with an air of superiority.

"That's no way to talk to an officer," he said. "Kindly remember that in future."

Asch was astonished by this new attitude of the doctor's. He sat down wondering what was going to happen next. The state of excitement he had got himself into during his conversation with his sister had not yet died down. His eyes flashed coldly.

"Here," said Dr. Sämig, taking a sheet of paper out of his cuff. I've set down everything that needed to be set down. You can be thankful that it's very favorable to you. It absolves you completely."

"What do you mean by that?" asked Asch, watching him carefully.

"I mean that you're not responsible for your actions, that's to say not fully responsible. That's really the best solution. That way you're in the clear and there's an end of the business."

"What do you mean? Do you mean that I can't be blamed for what I do?"

"Exactly," said Dr. Sämig contentedly. "You're simply not responsible for your actions."

"And you've put that down in writing? You've put it down in writing that I'm not responsible for my actions? That's to say that the balance of my mind is disturbed?"

"That's it," said Dr. Sämig, nodding happily.

"Might I just see, please?" asked Asch. He held up the sheet of paper, read it through carefully and handed it back again.

"It must be a joke," he said. "You can't mean it!"

"Oh, can't I?" said Sämig. "If you had any sense, you'd realize what a boon this piece of paper is to you."

"You really stand by what is written down here?"

"Yes. For your sake."

"All right, then," said Asch. "Just as you like."

Slowly he rose to his feet. Then he suddenly hurled himself at the M.O., flung him down on the floor and began punching him as hard as he could. He pulled him up again and threw him from one corner of the room to the other like an old sack.

The M.O. was panting and gasping for breath. He let out the

292

most bloodcurdling yells. His eyes were wide with panic. He puffed his way over to the door.

"There you are, then," said Asch, wiping his hands. "You can't do anything about that. According to your diagnosis the balance of my mind is disturbed and I'm not responsible for my actions."

※ ※ ※

The second shot was fired on Friday evening. Once again the barrack clocks pointed to eighteen minutes past eight. Darkness was falling at the time.

The plaster trickled down from the ceiling onto Sergeant Major Schulz. He was sitting in his office and some of it fell on the report which he was in the process of making out against Gunner Asch. The ink bottle was upset, and the ink trickled all over the report.

Schulz had thrown himself flat on the floor. He crouched against the wall, cursing himself for his habit of working by the open window with the light on. In order to keep out of range of the marksman, who was obviously out for his life, he crept across the room on all fours to the light switch.

The lights went out. Schulz ran over to the windows and peered cautiously out. As far as he could see the barrack square was quite empty.

"Dirty coward," he muttered. He seemed to think that the marksman ought to wait for Schulz to come and identify him.

Schulz felt himself trembling with delayed fear and rage. He crossed the room in three strides, flung open the door and roared at the top of his voice into the corridor: "Alarm! All N.C.O.s to me! Other ranks fall in outside their barrack rooms at once!"

He roared out these orders quite automatically, almost without thinking about them. The very act of roaring made him feel better. But nothing very impressive happened. One or two soldiers put their heads curiously round their barrack-room doors, apparently very cheerful and excited.

Then the orderly corporal started putting the sergeant major's orders into effect. His whistle could be heard blowing down all three corridors.

"N.C.O.s to the sergeant major in the office! Other ranks — fall in outside their barrack rooms!"

In the meantime the first of the N.C.O.s had arrived. Schulz put them to work at once.

"You bar the entrance. Stop anyone trying to get in or out. — You take over the rear of the block to see that no one tries to get out by the windows. — You go over to the guardroom and hold any men of our troop trying to leave camp. — You and you search the immediate vicinity of the barrack block. — You ransack the area round the gun sheds. — You search the barrack square. — You'll be getting reinforcements as soon as more N.C.O.s arrive."

No. 3 Troop's barrack block was now like an agitated bee-hive, with all the entrances blocked. The men stood about in amazement outside their barrack rooms talking to each other in animated voices. They had fallen in according to sections in two ranks, and were waiting in considerable tension to see what would happen next.

The Chief made for the telephone and got onto the sick quarters. "Go at once and see if Gunner Asch is in the isolation ward!" he shouted. He waited impatiently for the answer, and kept an eye as he did so on the N.C.O. who had been stationed at the office window.

"Are you sure you haven't made a mistake?" asked the Chief down the telephone at the top of his voice. "Are you sure, absolutely sure, that Gunner Asch is there? . . . Could he possibly have left the isolation ward in the last quarter of an hour or so? . . . Yes, I know the door's got a double lock on it and that the windows are barred, you don't need to tell me all that. But after all he might have managed to get out some-how. What's he doing? . . . Playing *vingt-et-un* with the medical orderly, so he can't possibly have . . . Oh! Shut up!"

Schulz slammed the receiver down again. He clenched his fists so that no one should see how much his hands were shaking. He picked on one of the N.C.O.s who had just arrived. "Run across to sick quarters," he said, "and see if that oaf of an orderly is speaking the truth."

The Chief then stood for several seconds with his legs planted wide apart, apparently deep in thought. He turned to Sergeant Waber, the N.C.O. in charge of equipment, and said, "We must fetch the troop commander. Captain Derna must be told about this. The best thing would be for you to take a car and go and fetch him yourself. Then you can tell him what's happened on the way here."

"All right, I'll do that," said Sergeant Waber, and trotted off at once.

The Chief counted up the number of men left at his disposal.

"One sergeant and one corporal," he ordered, "to every three sections. What we've got to find out is what everyone's been doing for the last hour. Anyone who comes under the slightest suspicion of having left the block around eight o'clock, whether to empty the refuse bins or to go to the canteen, is to be brought to me at once. All rifles are to be inspected too, and more thoroughly than last time!"

The sergeants and corporals sorted themselves out in the corridor. The Chief was walking excitedly round and round his office like some huge hungry lion suffering from the heat in a tiny cage. The corporal who had been stationed at the window stood there motionless.

Lieutenant Wedelmann appeared on the scene. He was wearing a dressing gown.

"What's going on?" he asked.

"I've been shot at again," said the Chief.

"Another miss?"

"The bullet went very close to me. I was sitting at the desk. The shot passed just over my head."

Wedelmann examined the bullet mark. It was high up on the wall. Then he looked out of the window. On a much lower level than the office were the barrack square itself and part of the roadway.

"Very odd things seem to be going on," said the Lieutenant, grinning. "Either the man who fired the shot must have been floating a couple of yards above the ground, or he brought a stepladder with him, or the bullet must have described an arc to pass just over your head."

Schulz maintained a hostile silence. He was too agitated to take the lieutenant up on his theory. All he said was: "This is what comes of treating them too softly. They can't help getting wrong ideas into their heads."

"It seems to me," said the lieutenant, "that all this gives one some idea of just how popular you are."

"Of course," said Schulz unpleasantly, "people have been known to use methods like these to get rid of their rivals in love before now."

"You don't say." The lieutenant pretended he hadn't understood what the sergeant major meant. "Who are you accusing? That certainly simplifies matters. There can't be as many men as all that who come under suspicion. However, I'm afraid your theory that it was Gunner Asch who wanted to murder you rather falls to the ground now, doesn't it? I always said he'd never bother his head with anything so trivial."

Wedelmann left the room feeling rather pleased with himself. He could sense the sergeant major staring furiously after his retreating figure, and this delighted him. For a moment it even occurred to him to pay a quick visit to Lore Schulz, not with any serious intentions but merely as a means of annoying

Schulz still further. But he resisted the temptation and felt proud of having done so.

The lieutenant went instead to the second-floor corridor where Lindenberg's section had fallen in. The men made way for him, shouting: "Attention!" A sergeant came and put himself at the lieutenant's disposal.

"Carry on, Sergeant," said the lieutenant. "Don't let me disturb you." And he went up to Corporal Lindenberg, who was going through his section with a fine-tooth comb.

"If you've no objections, Lindenberg, I'll just watch you at work for a bit."

"Very good, Lieutenant!" cried the corporal proudly.

Corporal Lindenberg turned his whole section upside down. He was like a bloodhound hot on the scent. His ardor and persistence were quite unequaled. He searched the lockers, took the beds to bits, turned the tables over on their sides, crept along the window sill and fingered the curtain rail, searched each of his men personally and then disappeared for a longish time into the broom cupboard.

"What are you looking for actually?" asked the lieutenant amiably.

"Ammunition, Lieutenant," answered Lindenberg promptly.

"Do you expect to find ammunition hidden in your section, then?" asked Wedelmann, full of curiosity.

"Of course not, Lieutenant."

"But you look for it all the same?"

"Yes, Lieutenant," said Lindenberg with remarkable enthusiasm. "Those are the orders!"

"Don't let me disturb you," repeated the lieutenant, continuing to look about him. He counted up the number of men present. He knew that Lindenberg's section consisted of twelve men. There were seven present. That was quite normal. Friday wasn't a specially popular day for going out. He let Lindenberg go on searching and started talking with some of the men.

297

"Who's missing actually?" he asked.

Gunner Vierbein, the man he had addressed, answered smartly, "There are five men missing, sir. One of them is away on a course, two left the camp on passes at seven o'clock. Gunner Asch is in sick quarters, and Lance Corporal Kowalski isn't back from work yet."

"Where does he work, then?" asked Wedelmann.

"In the armory, sir."

Wedelmann appeared to show little interest in the answers and withdrew. "Carry on the good work, Lindenberg," he called out. Then he went to his own quarters and poured himself out a large glass of brandy. He drank it up, and grinned to himself.

In the meantime Sergeant Major Schulz had begun his examination of the men who had been detained at the entrance to the barrack block. They all seemed quite harmless. Two of them had been drinking beer in the canteen since half-past seven. They had paid for their drinks at twenty past eight, that is to say two minutes after the shot had been fired. The canteen contractor Bandurski was prepared to swear to this. Three others had been on their way out of camp when stopped; they hadn't left their barrack rooms until just before half-past eight — the occupants of their rooms could witness that they had been just sitting around or shaving before that. A sixth soldier had been sent out for some cigarettes for Sergeant Platzek. He too hadn't set out until after the shot had been fired.

Schulz cursed. The corporal who had been sent off to the guardroom came back without any concrete results. Schulz cursed again. The N.C.O.s who had been searching the vicinity of the barrack block, the area round the gun sheds and the parade ground also reported failures. Schulz cursed again.

Gradually the entire barracks started to become uneasy. The sergeant major's bloodhounds had apparently been behaving

298

with the utmost clumsiness. It wasn't long before all the other blocks knew that a shot had been fired in No. 3 Troop and that it had been meant for the sergeant major. In No. 5 Troop there was even talk of his being severely wounded, and in the canteen it was being said that there was a corpse lying about in No. 3 block.

First of all the guardroom rang up, then the sick quarters, then the orderly officer and finally the battery adjutant. Schulz cursed and swore down the telephone. The adjutant said he wasn't having any of that. Schulz, who realized he had made a bad mistake, apologized meekly. The adjutant demanded a full report at once. Schulz promised it and began to shake in his shoes.

It was in this mood that he happened to run into Sergeant Platzek.

"Platzek," said Schulz, "my patience is exhausted."

"I can understand that," said Platzek reassuringly.

"We must now establish once and for all where this ammunition that's being fired at me has come from, and above all who got hold of it."

"But . . ." stammered Platzek.

"There are no buts about it," said Schulz mercilessly. "It must be one of the people who shot with you on the range the other day. That's where the investigation must start."

"But if it does I'm ruined!"

"Better that you should be ruined than that I should be dead," said Schulz. "Or do you expect me to wait here quietly while this swine fires off all the rest of the ammunition?"

Schulz left Platzek standing there feeling utterly crushed, and went outside. He had just heard the troop commander's car approaching. He wanted to get his report in to Captain Derna as soon as possible.

Captain Derna looked pale even in the dark. Schulz felt that

299

he was in such a bad way that he ought to help him get out of the car, but his admirable sense of tact where superior officers were concerned told him that this would be going too far.

"But how can it have happened?" was Derna's first question.

Schulz spluttered out a long explanation.

"Let's go into my office," said Derna.

Once there, he turned and faced his sergeant major in desperation.

"What are we to do now?" he said.

🏴 🏴 🏴

It was not only Major Luschke's immediate subordinates who considered him unpredictable. Lumpface came and went whenever he wanted to and always seemed to act on the spur of the moment. But what appeared to be an entirely haphazard way of conducting things in fact had plenty of system behind it. It was Luschke's aim — one in which he was by no means unsuccessful and in which he took considerable delight — to keep his men in a state of perpetual anxiety. There was no moment of the day or night in which he might not suddenly appear from nowhere and drive them into action.

It went without saying therefore that Luschke attached the utmost importance to punctuality among his subordinates. The daily schedules which went out under his orders were all timed to the minute, and this timing was absolutely sacred. He himself always carried two watches about with him; he had one clock on his desk and another hung on the wall.

It so happened that Luschke had left the barracks early on Friday afternoon, wthout of course letting the adjutant know. The owner of a nearby sawmill had invited him to go shooting with him on Friday evening. This could mean one of two things: either that Luschke would be back in barracks at the

300

crack of dawn on Saturday morning, or that he would arrive fairly late. But of course even this was only supposition. It was just as likely that he would appear punctually on the stroke of eight, that is to say the time at which his staff was meant to be in the office. Lumpface was truly quite unpredictable.

The battery adjutant, who had soon learned to dissociate all calculations of probability or improbability from the appearance or disappearance of his commanding officer, turned up at eight o'clock as usual. Luschke wasn't there of course. But the adjutant was quite certain of one thing: namely, that if he had been only three minutes late he would have found the major sitting there before him with a nasty smile on his face.

While the adjutant sat there waiting as anxiously as ever for the appearance of his C.O., he looked through the various orders, instructions, reports and general dispositions for the day. There was nothing of any particular note among them. The adjutant was hardly surprised at that. Any man in his right mind would go to a good deal of trouble to prevent attracting the major's attention to himself. And as there was as yet no written report about the events of the previous evening in No. 3 Troop, he decided to act as if he knew nothing about them. The only trouble was that it was by no means certain that the major would not come in and ask about them at any moment.

At eight-fifteen Captain Derna came into the office. He looked as if he had been overworking. He greeted the adjutant with a feeble handshake. Then he pulled a whole sheaf of papers out of his briefcase and presented his report.

"What do you think the C.O. will have to say to this?" he asked.

The adjutant's anxiety had increased considerably. He shrugged his shoulders.

"I'm not a clairvoyant," he said.

They waited for the major's appearance and hardly said a word. The adjutant nervously went on with the morning's work.

Captain Derna stood by the window which looked out towards the main gate. He was keeping a sharp lookout for the major.

The door of the C.O.'s office was suddenly flung open from within. Major Luschke stuck his lumpy nose into the adjutant's office. It wasn't the first time he had arrived by a circuitous route.

"There's been a pane of glass broken in No. 2 Troop's washroom for three days now. The first door of No. 5 Troop's gun shed is heavily scratched and has a dent in it. The locks on the ammunition dumps haven't been oiled. Someone has forgotten to turn out the light over the entrance to sick quarters. Got all that? I want a written report as to who is responsible for all these things on my desk by twelve o'clock noon, understand?"

"Very good, sir. Written report on your desk by twelve o'clock noon, sir!"

Lumpface nodded. He was a small thickset man who moved neatly and unobtrusively. His voice was very soft and it was just this which made it terrifying. His sharp, cold little eyes sparkled with cunning.

"What brings you here, Captain Derna? Or did I ask you to come and see me? I don't seem to recall."

"An extremely painful business, sir!"

"Painful? Who for? A painful business means there's been some bungling somewhere. There's no bungling in my battery, I'd have you know, my dear Captain Derna."

Derna, who felt even more unsure of himself in the presence of his C.O. than usual, decided that it was best not to say too much at the moment but to let the facts speak for themselves. He laid report after report down in front of the battery commander.

Luschke slowly read them through without comment. He stood there apparently motionless beside his adjutant, his lumpy face bent low over the reports. It was very red, but this

302

had nothing to do with his state of mind; it was caused by the fact that in spite of the huge cap he always wore on his head, his face had been in contact with the rays of the sun on the previous day.

The major read through sheet after sheet of paper without flickering an eyelid. The adjutant watched him. He was prepared for the worst. Captain Derna kept an anxious lookout for the slightest sign of any reaction. But Luschke remained unmoved. There was a breathless hush in the room. There was no sound save the occasional rustle of paper as the major turned over one report after another.

Then he said quietly: "Idiots!"

He looked at Captain Derna with his cold glittering little eyes. Derna had gone purple in the face. He stood there very rigid, but there was something awkward and cramped about his stance at the same time.

Major Luschke threw the reports down on his adjutant's desk.

"This," he said, laying his hand flat on top of them, "is impossible. Do you understand that, Captain Derna? This sort of thing simply doesn't happen in my battery."

"Very good, sir," stammered Derna. "I quite agree with you, sir, but . . ."

"What's the 'but' about, Captain, if you agree with me?"

"The N.C.O.s, sir, particularly Sergeant Major Schulz . . ."

"Is it the N.C.O.s who decide what's what in your troop, then?"

The major raised the eyebrows which spanned his lumpy face in astonishment. His eyes flashed. His chin was jutting out and he had a nasty smile on his face. The adjutant who knew the signs well enough trembled for Captain Derna.

No. 3 Troop Commander was so put out he could think of no answer. He was a pitiable sight. He had a completely crumpled look about him. All his Viennese charm, his Imperial

303

Austrian manner, had been shattered on Major Luschke's heart of stone.

"If I understand you aright," said the major, "you are unable to keep your troop under proper control."

"I can assure the major that I do my very best to . . ."

"I don't doubt that, my dear Captain Derna," said Luschke with devastating mildness. "It all comes under the heading of incompetence. However, you have chosen to bring this insignificant little affair to my notice. Right. I'll show you how to deal with it."

Here the adjutant ventured to put in a remark:

"Lieutenant Wedelmann was saying to me on the telephone only yesterday evening that he too considered this a matter of no importance."

"Very interesting," said Major Luschke. "Perhaps a lieutenant has succeeded in grasping something which has eluded a captain. But then, Lieutenant Wedelmann was trained in the same school as myself; you, my dear Captain Derna, were merely seconded to me from elsewhere."

Luschke picked up the pile of reports, shooting a contemptuous look at Derna as he did so. "Right, then," he said. "We'll get on with it. I want to see the following: Corporal Lindenberg, Sergeant Platzek, Sergeant Major Schulz, and Major Sämig, the M.O. Lieutenant Wedelmann might as well come along too."

The adjutant rushed to the telephone at once and passed on the commanding officer's orders. Derna stood about like an unwanted piece of furniture. The major turned the reports over once more, stroking his chin with pleasure.

"Asch," he said, digging around in his prodigious memory. "Gunner Asch. I seem to have seen that name more than once in the last few days." Then his eyes suddenly lit up. "Didn't you put in a recommendation for his promotion to corporal, Captain Derna?"

"Y-yes, sir," stammered the captain.

Luschke turned away from him and muttered: "Nitwit."

Then he ordered Lieutenant Wedelmann to be brought in.

The lieutenant entered the room. Like everyone else who came into that office, he stopped by the door, saluted smartly and announced himself: "Lieutenant Wedelmann reporting, as ordered, sir."

"Come closer, my dear Wedelmann," murmured the major softly. "One day last week I was standing at this window looking out on the barrack square. It was a period of rifle drill and you were in charge. In one of the squads a man was driven to such a point that he lost control of himself and obviously had some sort of epileptic fit; he seemed to want to hurl himself at the corporal. And what did you do? Well?"

"I made off at once in the opposite direction, sir," said Wedelmann truthfully.

"And why did you do that?"

"There are certain things, sir, which, if one has any sense, one simply doesn't notice. They straighten themselves out in the end. If one starts meddling with them, on the other hand, then they assume gigantic proportions before one knows where one is."

"Yes, you're trained in my school all right!" said Luschke delightedly. Then he asked: "Tell me, my dear Wedelmann, have you heard about these reports that have been put in against Gunner Asch? What do you think of them?"

"Yes, I know about them, sir, and I don't think much of them. Why make such a fuss about things when there are other ways of settling them?"

Luschke looked crushingly in Derna's direction. Then he clapped the lieutenant on the back. The adjutant breathed a sigh of relief and put a comfortable distance between himself and the unfortunate commander of No. 3 Troop.

The major made a number of inquiries from Wedelmann

305

about the men he had just sent for. Wedelmann gave brief sketches of their characters.

The C.O. nodded with satisfaction. "Right! Corporal Lindenberg," he said.

Lindenberg presented himself and looked his commanding officer straight in the eye as the regulations laid down. He was convinced that one of the great moments in his life had arrived, and he had no doubt that he would come through it worthily.

"Corporal Lindenberg," said Major Luschke. "They tell me you're an extremely correct N.C.O. and a hundred per cent reliable. I am therefore all the more surprised to see that you let yourself become involved in long conversations, not to mention discussions, with your subordinates. You'll find nothing of that in the regulations. It is your duty to give clear, unambiguous orders. It is the duty of your subordinates to obey them. If they do not do so, then they have refused to obey an order. It is then your duty to report them. It's a test of personality to be able to get obedience from your men. Do you understand me, Corporal Lindenberg?"

"Yes, sir."

"If you really have understood me properly you will know that this report of yours is utter nonsense. It's fit only for the wastepaper basket. You can go now, Corporal Lindenberg."

Lindenberg clicked his heels and shot off like a comet. Major Luschke found that as it should be. He didn't even consider it necessary to look round the room in triumph. He picked up the next report. "Sergeant Platzek."

Platzek stood there like a lump of rock that has really been made out of cardboard. He thought his last hour had come. This, he thought, was his first step on the road to a military prison.

"I see here," said Luschke, "that some rounds of ammunition are missing. But that is obviously nonsense. Sergeants simply don't lose ammunition, especially not in my battery. And as for falsifications of the record — of course I've never heard anything so absurd. That too is utter nonsense. Or am I wrong?"

"No, sir," Sergeant Platzek hurriedly reassured him.

"So that there is no ammunition missing and the score sheets are entirely in order. Is that so?"

"Yes, sir."

"This report of yours is of no value then and goes straight into the wastepaper basket. You may go, Sergeant."

Sergeant Platzek couldn't believe his ears. He shot out through the door with an absolutely ridiculous but blissfully happy expression on his face.

"That man will be replaced at the next available opportunity," ordered Luschke. "Now I'll see Sergeant Major Schulz."

Schulz came in like an armored car. He stopped with a jerk, and stood there in the middle of the room taking up a great deal of space. He rattled through his report and waited. Luschke looked him over for a moment trying to decide what was the best way to deal with him. He decided to avoid anything complicated, and went straight to the heart of the matter at once.

"Do you intend to give up your post as sergeant major?" he inquired gently.

Schulz was visibly shaken. He first blushed and then turned pale. He stared at his commanding officer in silence.

"It would be a pity," said Luschke softly. "You've been a useful sergeant major, up till yesterday at any rate. I'd be sorry to lose you, but there are plenty of people to take your place. You'd just have to take off one of your stars, give up your quarters and become an ordinary sergeant again. It wouldn't be difficult."

Captain Derna was rash enough to try to intervene at this point. "Excuse me, sir, but . . ."

"Captain," said Luschke, "I do not recall having asked you for your opinion on this matter."

Derna shut up again and took a pace back. Schulz in the meanwhile had gone purple in the face. Wedelmann and the adjutant were grinning quietly to themselves. Luschke was in complete command of the situation.

"A sergeant major," continued Luschke, "must be a real personality. A personality is someone who gets his own way. But a report such as this one you've just put in is nothing less than an admission of helplessness."

"I respectfully beg to draw the major's attention to the fact that someone fired a shot at me," said Schulz with an effort.

Luschke gave a little toss of his head. This was the stumbling block, he knew that all right, but it had to be got over somehow.

"How can you prove that this someone was shooting specifically at you? The bullet had to end up somewhere. And you happened to be situated in the line of fire at the time. Such a thing has happened before, you know. If a man's got any guts he doesn't immediately go and panic about it. Besides, where do you imagine the ammunition came from? Certainly not from the range which Platzek was in charge of. He's assured me of that. Where from, then?"

"We were having a little shooting practice behind the mess yesterday evening, sir," said Lieutenant Wedelmann.

Luschke looked up at him in surprise. This entirely unexpected remark of the lieutenant's had suddenly got them over the stumbling block without any difficulty at all. The major's eyes twinkled with delight. His feelings towards Lieutenant Wedelmann were less those of gratitude (for he would have managed all right by himself somehow) than gratification. A man trained in the same school as himself! And a man after his own heart.

"Lieutenant Wedelmann," said Luschke with undisguised

pleasure, "I beg you and the other gentlemen in the mess to be more careful in future when you're practicing with live ammunition, and to do your very best to confine your activities to the range."

"Very good, sir," said Wedelmann.

Luschke turned towards Sergeant Major Schulz.

"So that clears that up. I'm all for keenness, Sergeant Major, as you know, but this time I must say I think you've rather overstepped the mark. Do you see that, or are you no longer interested in keeping your job as sergeant major?"

"Yes, sir."

"What do you mean — yes, sir?"

"I mean, I do see that, sir."

"Why couldn't you see it straight away?" He picked up the sergeant major's reports, held them poised over the wastepaper basket for a moment, and dropped them in. "Right, that's that. You may go."

The sergeant major obeyed at once and went spinning out of the room.

"God Almighty!" he said aloud to himself when he got outside. "That was a near thing." Ugh, he was heartily glad to see the back of the matter. His respect for Luschke had increased enormously.

In the meantime, Major Luschke was busying himself with Dr. Sämig. He behaved in a strictly formal manner towards him and refrained from shaking hands with him. Nor did he offer him a chair; though he rather gave the impression that he had merely forgotten to do this.

Luschke knew perfectly well that he couldn't deal with Sämig just as he liked. The M.O. was merely attached to his staff. He was his subordinate in his capacity as an officer but not in his capacity as a doctor. Sämig, however, had a natural feeling of respect for rank, and in particular for Major Luschke.

"What's this I hear?" asked Luschke in a perfectly friendly

manner. "You've been indulging in wrestling matches with your patients?"

"I was attacked," said Dr. Sämig bitterly.

"I think your choice of words is a little unfortunate," said the major, and his voice suddenly sounded very cold and ominously quiet. "An officer simply isn't attacked. Such a thing is impossible. Remember that. If matters really were to reach such a pitch, either the attacker would be a dead man or the officer so ineffectual and cowardly that he would have no right to wear uniform at all."

Dr. Sämig's blue eyes opened wide. He looked round for some support, but no one paid any attention to him.

"Sometimes," said Luschke, "I hear stories which simply make my hair stand on end, but of course I don't believe them. My reason tells me that I simply can't afford to. If, for instance, there were ever a case of a doctor who declared a perfectly sane man to be mentally sick — do you know what he would deserve? A hiding. A really good hiding. As for any soldier who might administer it, do you know what I would do with him? Offer him my hearty congratulations. But of course nothing like that ever happens. If it did, the entire officers' corps would laugh itself sick at the wretched doctor's expense. Did you say anything, Dr. Sämig?"

"No, Major."

"And this report I have here — I see it must be a joke. Good; well, we've had our laugh. It can go into the wastepaper basket."

And Major Luschke threw away his last remaining piece of paper. He rubbed his hands together and looked around him with eyes twinkling. But he still showed no signs of triumph.

"Lieutenant Wedelmann," said the C.O. "It's clear to me that No. 3 Troop needs a thorough reorganization. It needs a real man in charge of it, not just a figurehead. Army regulations are not enough in themselves; a certain amount of human

310

understanding is necessary as well. Do you think we can consider ourselves safe from further unpleasant surprises?"

"Certainly, Major."

"And what about Gunner Asch?"

"I'd stake my life on him."

"In spite of everything that's happened?"

"Just because of it, Major."

"Right, then," said the C.O. "Then you will take over command of the troop, Lieutenant Wedelmann. Captain Derna will go on leave; I'll see that that goes through at regimental level. And do you know all that's left for us to do now, Wedelmann?"

"No, Major."

"We must go to Gunner Asch and tell him of his promotion to corporal."